IF YOU BREAK

THE REDEEMED #1

JESSALYN THORN

WILTED ROSE PUBLISHING LTD

DEDICATION

For all the girls waiting for two drop-dead gorgeous, undead assholes to sweep them off their feet and raze the world to ash in their name. Let's face it... they do it better anyway.

TRIGGER WARNING

If You Break is an urban fantasy ménage romance, so the main character will have two love interests that she will not have to choose between.

This book is dark and contains scenes that may be triggering for some readers. This includes childhood sexual abuse, sexual assault, murder and PTSD.

If you are triggered by any of this content, please do not read this book.

"Memento mori, si vis vitam, para mortem."

- If you want to live, remember that you must die.

XV

THE DEVIL

PROLOGUE

CONTROL – HALSEY

*F*ear is my closest friend.
My one constant.
My saviour.

It spikes through me as Alex throws the half-empty vodka bottle straight at my head. It narrowly misses, shattering above me and raining down lethal spikes of glass that slice into my arms.

"Fuck you, Lex!" he screams.

He's drunk. High. Wasted.

"You're such an asshole!" I shout back.

Pressing a hand to the deeper slice he's inflicted in my left arm, I try to staunch the bleeding. It's warm and slick beneath my fingertips. This isn't the first time we've fought and drawn blood from each other.

"I know that you're cheating on me," he accuses in a drunken slur. "Just tell me who it is. Tell me."

A better person would walk away, but after years of these baseless accusations and pointless jealousy, I'm done. I stalk closer before slapping him across the face hard enough to ring his ears.

"We aren't together," I spit in his face. "If you weren't so

1

afraid to see what's right in front of you, you'd know the truth."

"What truth?" he lashes out.

My tongue freezes in my mouth, holding the words back. I've never uttered them out loud before, and I can't start now. It's a dirty secret. The darkest, filthiest kind. I swore that I'd never tell a soul.

Instead, I shove Alex so he hits his dirty, unmade bed. His apartment is gross, messy and unclean with the litter that evidences our regular alcohol and drug sessions together.

This isn't a relationship. Not really. We're just abusing each other to escape the pain of what others have done to us. What the cruel, uncaring world continues to do. Hurting each other helps manage that pain.

"Run away, then," he hisses. "That's what you do best, Lex."

"I have to get home for Eve. We're done here anyway."

"Yeah. We are."

"Good." I glower at him. "Lose my number. I mean it this time."

Still holding my bleeding arm, I limp from the room, leaving him slumped and breathing heavily. I'm outside into the frigid night air before he can chase after me and convince me to stick around again.

But I know, deep down... I'll be back.

I always come running back for more.

Without Alex, I have no other escapes. No way of coping with the darkness and turmoil in my life. No matter how toxic we are together, he gives me the freedom I so desperately crave.

Picking my way through the overgrown bushes that mark the council estate, I make a beeline for the quiet country road that will take me back home. Dad will still be out drinking at this time, so we should have some peace.

I left my younger sister, Eve, to do her homework and eat a

frozen dinner before heading to Alex's to drink. Leaving her is the last thing I wanted to do, but after what happened this afternoon at work, I needed a fix.

"Motherfucker," I curse as I continue walking.

That son of a bitch has hurt me for the last time. My arm has almost stopped bleeding, but the pain persists. I can add it to the array of scars we've left on each other, visible and not. This is what we do.

With rain beginning to fall, soaking into my skinny black jeans, I increase my speed, desperate to be back home with Eve. I stayed out for too long—she doesn't like it when she's alone in the dark.

The rumble of an approaching car engine breaks my solitude. It's a deep, throaty growl, old and sputtering. With a glance over my shoulder at the bright headlights, my blood freezes in my veins.

No.

Not him.

Speeding up into a half-run, I try to escape the incoming demon, but it's no use. He jolts ahead in his rusted red truck and cuts me off, slamming on the breaks before throwing open his door.

"Lexi girl," his sick voice rumbles.

I freeze on the spot like a timid child.

"Come here, sugar." His hulking frame lumbers out of the truck. "I didn't expect to see you out this late. What a nice surprise."

"Please," I gasp.

"That wasn't an invitation," he grunts, his lips curled with displeasure. "I said come here."

Forcing my numb legs to move, I inch closer, cowering in the glare of headlights that conceal his face. I don't need to see him to know what he looks like. His face is forever scarred onto my brain and has been since I was seven years old.

Yellow teeth. Fat lips. A crooked nose. Wide set eyes and a

3

sick, lascivious sneer that curls his mouth up at the corners when he studies me over the sticky bar at work. His flannel shirts and jeans always stink of beer.

"Ah, sugar. I missed you."

His meaty paw strokes over my wet hair, moving to cup my jaw before gently stroking it. A shudder rolls over me, and I bite my tongue, hoping to remain safe in silence instead.

"What are you doing all the way out here?" he slurs drunkenly.

"Walking home. You shouldn't be driving."

His grip on my chin tightens. "And who are you to tell me what I can and can't do, huh?"

"I'm s-sorry."

"You should be, Lexi girl."

His hand moves lower. Then lower still. When he squeezes my breast through my soaking wet, long-sleeved t-shirt, I have to blink aside tears and go to my numb, safe place. It's better when I feel nothing.

"Were you out with that waste of space boy again?" he accuses.

My knees wobble with fear, and I force myself not to cringe as his putrid breath hits me.

"N-No."

"Don't lie to me." He grips my chin even tighter. "You were. I thought we discussed this? You're not to see him anymore."

"I wasn't with Alex."

"Lies!" His spit hits me in the face.

Feeling it drip down my cheek, my numb sense of safety shatters. Implodes. Blown to pieces. I can't stand here and take a second more of others hurting me for their own pleasure.

"Fuck you," I snap at him.

His eyebrows lift. "Excuse me?"

"I said… Fuck. You. I'm allowed to see whoever I want to

see, and it's none of your business. Now take your hands off me."

Shoving him away, I take a big step back, the rain still slamming into me in painful bullets. Fire burns in his eyes, swallowing his irises in dark, dangerous flames that send prickles across my scalp.

Hand snapping out, he grabs hold of my wrist and yanks, sending me toppling into his arms. A fist connects with my stomach and knocks the wind out of me, pain flaring through my extremities.

"You belong to me," he snarls in my ear. "And I'll do whatever it takes to prove that to you."

Another fist smashes into my face. Abdomen. Chest. Throat. Over and over. He beats me into submission, not stopping when my blood flows thick and fast over his knuckles.

Attempting to shield myself from the onslaught, I don't see the flash of steel until it's too late. The penknife slips from his pocket, silent and deadly. Dragging the sharpened edge against my throat, he holds me at knife point.

"You will do as you're told, Lexi girl. Or Eve will pay the price."

"Leave my sister out of this, you sick bastard!"

"I promised not to touch her as long as you kept our little secret. Start disobeying me, and I'll have to go back on my word. You don't want me to do that, do you?"

Panic flares in my chest.

"No… Please. Leave her alone."

"Then do as you're fucking told and *obey*!"

The rainstorm swallows his scream of fury as his violence overcomes him. On the deserted road, my life forever changes. How fickle our existence is, turning on a dime, changing at the drop of a hat.

The knife slips into my belly first. Plunging. Parting flesh and muscle. Twisting. Oozing blood. Retracting. Slipping back in, deeper and deeper still. In. Out. Twist. Slash. Stab.

Lost to his bloodthirst, the monster of my childhood doesn't seem to realise what he's doing. It's like a red haze has descended over him. His eyes are so black, they resemble the deepest depths of the ocean.

Going limp in his arms, I spot the moment he realises what he's done. My slack body hits the rain-slick pavement with a thud as he takes a step back, the bloodstained knife clutched in his hand.

"Lexi," he whimpers.

I can't even summon a scream, the pain is so overwhelming. Already, my body is shutting down on me. I'm silent. Bleeding. Lifeless.

"Shit!"

Head lolling to the side, I stare up at the swollen clouds above me, ignoring his boot-covered feet slowly pacing away from me. His engine growls as it's fired up, cutting through a rumble of thunder from the heavens.

The truck peels away with a squeal of tyres. I watch the headlights fade, too weak to do anything more than silently sob into the darkness.

Oblivion approaches.

Merciful. Relief. Freedom.

But… *Eve.*

Her name turns into an internal, anguished scream that slices through my mind. It's the last thing I think as the world fades from existence, leaving me to float on a cloud of blissful nothingness.

WHEEL OF FORTUNE

CHAPTER 1

THOUSAND EYES – OF MONSTERS AND MEN

I was at peace in death.

It feels wrong to admit that. Unnatural even. Like I should pretend that my mortal life was anything more than a painful existence, ended too soon. But we're all friends here, right? I trust you to keep my secret.

Death was a blessing.

I'm not sure how it ended. One moment, the rolling, endless fields of lush verdure and blazing sunshine surrounded me. Nothing but peace and tranquillity as far as the eye could see.

I've been here since it happened. *It.*

That's the only word I can use.

When my life ended, blood and rain were swept away to reveal brilliant sunshine. I've been floating here ever since. Without body or form—a scattering of ash on the wind, the dust in a beam of sunlight.

Here.

But not really.

That's when it happened. The bolt of lightning. The thump of a heartbeat, pounding back into existence. Pain.

Awareness. Tingling. Electric bolts of defibrillation. Sunlight fading and darkness approaching.

"Please!" I scream.

But I have no voice. No form. No lungs to fill with air and expel on a desperate plea. The meadow around me is torn to shreds and pulled apart at the seams, allowing swirls of shadows to infect the landscape.

I'm dying again.

Over and over.

Something's dragging me back, kicking and screaming. Back through numbness. Safety. Relief and freedom. Back from the endless vegetation and peace into the cruel, cold reality of the real world.

Pain is the first thing I feel again. After floating for so long, it hits me like a tidal wave, battering me beneath its crushing weight. So much agony, I can't see past it barrelling straight towards me.

Pins and needles spread through me. I can feel my extremities again. Fingers. Toes. Legs. Arms. I'm stiff and aching for the first time since I laid on the side of that road, slowly bleeding out. My body... it's back.

"Holy shit, what is this?" a panicked voice asks.

Still, I'm bathed in darkness.

"She's s-supposed to be dead! She was in stage three rigor mortis."

"Someone get management on the line. Everyone step back!"

Their voices cut through the haze, but I can't escape my blacked-out prison of pain. I'm trapped here. Burning alive. On fire and crisping down to the bone, melting flesh and skin like candle wax.

Then... nothing.

Everything winks out of existence.

* * *

Buzz. Buzz. Buzz.

The hum of fluorescent lighting cuts through my haze. It's so bright, I can feel it burning my eyelids. Squinting into the bright light, I moan and writhe, unable to hide from the harshness.

"Reanimation now at 100 percent. She's ready."

The voice forces me to wake up further. As my mind restarts, shaking off the shackles of sleep, everything hits me all at once.

My eyes slam open, whiting out my vision. Blinking rapidly, I fight to clear the blurriness, desperate to catch sight of the luminous green meadow around me again.

When the haze clears, I'm met with a new reality. Instead of rolling grass hills and sunshine, white walls and a bare concrete ceiling welcomes me.

The smell of bleach hangs in the air, thick and heady. I'm lying on something hard, something that creaks as I fight to move, and pain lances through... *my body.* I have two legs, two arms and a whole-ass torso.

"Hello?" I sob frantically.

Trying to move again, I realise my wrists are bound by Velcro straps, securing me to the metal frame of a hospital bed. My body is partially covered by a crisp, white sheet, hiding most of the medical gown beneath it from sight.

A barrage of pain pummels me as memories resurface. The roadside. The knife. Being slashed and stabbed as blood poured out of me. The world disappeared from sight, replaced by a bright, green meadow.

Now... I'm in an empty, wood-lined room, dipped in shades of clinical white. Pain. Tingling. Hospital bed sheets covering my trembling body and a thick, white bandage on my left arm where Alex hit me with the bottle.

I'm back.

Alive.

Real.

"Lexi," a soft voice croons.

Through my tears, I search the room, finding an open doorway in the farthest corner. A tall, willowy woman stands inside, watching me beneath black-framed glasses and a neat headful of mousy-brown hair.

"Where a-a-am I?"

She steps into the room, a clipboard in hand. "Take some deep breaths for me, Lexi."

Her voice is nice. Soft. Calming. I watch her hand rise and fall as she blows out an exaggerated breath, encouraging me to follow along. My lungs stutter and protest with each drop of oxygen I inhale.

"That's it. Keep going."

In and out.

Breathe. Breathe. Breathe.

"You're safe," she assures me.

"S-Safe?" I whimper.

Her smile is calm, full of infinite patience, like she's explained this a million times.

"I know you've been through a lot, but no one is going to hurt you here. I promise you."

Eyes flicking up to the machines around me, she bustles about, checking needles and IV lines. I focus on my breathing, too overwhelmed to do anything but lay here and watch her work.

"My name is Ruth," she explains kindly. "I'm your physician."

"You're a doctor? Is this a hospital?"

"Of sorts, yes."

Sliding the needles out of my arm, she sets them on a metal trolley. I flex my fingers, straining against the Velcro restraints. They're so tight. I hate feeling trapped.

"Why am I restrained?"

"For your own protection."

"W-Why?"

"You've been through a great ordeal, Lexi. We wouldn't want you to hurt yourself in all the shock and confusion."

My throat catches. "What happened to me?"

"I know this must be very confusing for you. We're going to explain everything. You don't need to be afraid."

Fear. There it is again. Welcoming me back with open arms into the familiarity of its embrace. Shivering beneath her watchful eyes, I look around the room, searching for clues and coming up empty.

Adjusting the bed, she allows me to sit up, causing more pain to race through me. Ruth watches me wince and looks sympathetic, her neat brows pulled together.

"The pain should ease soon. Waking up is always a difficult experience."

"The meadow... sunshine... everything was so bright. Why did you wake me up?"

That's when her demeanour falters, and she looks uncertain. I stare up at her, tears welling in my eyes.

"I was happy there," I choke out. "I didn't want to wake up."

"What meadow, Lexi? What do you remember?"

"I was in this... this place. It was so beautiful."

Ruth leans closer, a frown etched across her face. "Tell me what you remember."

Looking down at my covered body, I feel the knife at my throat again, threatening to slice. Then it slammed into me, over and over again, determined to take my life from me.

"The knife... I was stabbed." My hands bunch in the sheets as I attempt to pull them off. "Oh my God. I thought... I thought I was dead."

Gently taking hold of the sheet, Ruth tugs it down then lifts the hem of my hospital gown. Thick swathes of bandages are unveiled, wound around my torso and secured tightly to hide the ruined skin beneath.

"It's true," she says softly. "You were dead. I'm so sorry."

The realisation hits me like a freight train, crushing my windpipe and leaving me gasping for air that seems forever out of reach.

It was all true.

All of my memories.

And that means the fragile sense of peace I found in the meadow was real. It happened. That quiet bubble of blissful existence was mine forever, yet Ruth ripped it away from me to bring me back here.

"You died, sweetheart. The police found your body on the side of the road with approximately thirteen stab wounds."

"I... died?"

Ruth nods solemnly. "I am so sorry. I know this is a lot to take in, but I need you to tell me about the meadow."

My voice raises, bordering on hysterical. "You woke me up. You did this to me!"

"Calm down. Let's talk about this."

"I will not calm down!"

Heat burns through me—boiling hot and unyielding. It sweeps over me like hot lava, and the curl of smoke in the air shocks me to my core. The Velcro restraints are on fire, the bite of heat searing my skin.

"Lexi!" Ruth exclaims.

Screaming at the top of my lungs, I watch the material burn to ash. With the flood of panic, the flames suddenly douse, vanishing from sight and leaving scorched ashes of Velcro behind.

"Christ," she curses in a panic. "Lexi, stop!"

Moving as fast as my injuries will allow, I leap upright, pulling my wrists free from the ruins. The sheets bunch around me as I fall from the bed and hit the smooth mahogany floor with a loud thud.

Getting my feet beneath me, I'm wobbling through the still-open door before Ruth can stop me from running away.

My legs are like strands of cooked spaghetti, barely obeying my orders.

When I stumble and trip over thin air, I fall to my knees in the corridor. My body fails me as I curl up in a tight ball, hugging my legs to my chest and battling for each breath.

"Lexi!" Ruth shouts again.

The sound of thudding footsteps echoes around me as people approach from all sides, but Ruth's shouting must cause them to halt. She falls down next to me, daring to reach out a single, shaking hand.

"Breathe," she implores. "Please believe me. You're safe. I want to explain everything, but I need you to calm down."

"Ruth," a man rumbles. "Need a hand with her?"

"That won't be necessary, Brunt."

"She looks like a hell of a handful." He cracks his knuckles menacingly. "Happy to help."

Whimpering under my breath, I cower away from him in fear. Ruth bands an arm around my shoulders, taking advantage of the distraction to pull me closer.

"We're fine," she snaps more firmly.

He takes a step back. "Suit yourself."

The click of shoes on the fine wooden floor approaches. Everyone immediately bows their heads, becoming subdued. Even Ruth swallows hard and ducks her chin in deference.

The corridor fills with a strange sense of tension. It feels like all of the air has been sucked out of the space and into a vacuum. When the owner of the shoes speaks, it's in a haughty, almost regal tone.

"What on earth is going on here?"

"Just a little trouble with the new intake, sir," Ruth rushes out.

Looking up, I meet the eyes of the newcomer, and everything else drops out of existence. He has the most radiant pair of eyes, a million different swirling hues all blurring into one maelstrom of colour.

But when he looks at me, it feels like I've been plunged into a lake of ice. My mind freezes, caught in a spider's web, and it feels like he's examining the deepest depths of my brain.

"I see," he hums.

Stooping down on one knee, he brings himself eye-level with me. "My name is Ravius."

His clearly expensive charcoal suit wrinkles over his thighs as he kneels down, and the waft of rich, aromatic aftershave slips over me. He's tall and slim, built like a graceful stick insect wrapped in designer finery.

Pearly-white, shoulder-length blonde hair is tied back at the nape of his neck, leaving his straight, narrow nose and thin face on clear display. But those eyes are the most disturbing thing about him, and they take me prisoner.

"What's your name, child?"

"L-Lexi," I stutter.

"You've been gifted a second chance, Lexi. Welcome to your afterlife."

Snapping his fingers, he gestures for the broad-shouldered man to step forward. I struggle as I'm lifted back onto my feet and shoved towards the hospital room I just fled from.

"Gently, Brunt," Ravius admonishes.

"Yes, Elder."

Back inside the room, I take a seat on the edge of the bed and begin to rock. Ravius and the others remain outside, pulling the door shut to talk without me, though it's cracked open enough for their voices to leak in.

"Why was I not notified immediately?" Ravius snaps. "Any potentially gifted are to be dealt with in a manner befitting their importance. I should have been summoned at once."

"I'm sorry, sir." Ruth sounds contrite. "We had no reason to believe that she was a unique case until now."

"What exactly happened?"

"She claimed to have memories of a meadow after the

point of death and all out accused me of waking her up. When she became upset, the restraints caught fire."

There's a long pause.

"Fire, you say?" Ravius asks.

"Yes, sir. She displayed no irregularities up until this happened. Her brain activity during reanimation was normal, so we believed her to be another regular admission."

The tears run thick and fast down my cheeks. Panic has truly taken hold, and all I can think about are Ruth's words. *You died. You died. You died.* He really did it this time—he took my life from me.

Worse still, I know what I've left behind... Eve. I was on my way home to her that fateful night, but I never made it. What happened to her? I have to get back, she needs me.

We only have each other in this world. Our father is a waste of space drunk who spends his days passed out in beer-stained sheets and nights drinking in the local bar with his disgusting friends.

Without me there to protect her, Eve will be vulnerable. I'm the one who keeps her safe. Fed. Clothed. Just thinking about her, terrified and all alone... it makes the tears fall even faster down my cheeks.

"Lexi."

A voice snaps me out of my rocking, semi-hysterical daze. It's Ruth, looming over me with a forced attempt at a smile. She rests a hand on my shoulder then lightly squeezes.

"I don't want to restrain you again, dear. Will you remain calm so we can explain everything?"

"Y-Yes," I stammer.

"If you're feeling overwhelmed again, we can stop."

Stepping into the room before clicking the door shut behind him, Ravius smooths a nimble hand down his suit. There's an ornate, gold ring on his pinkie finger, marked with an intricate crest and curling script.

But as soon as he nears, I'm trapped in his gaze again. It's

17

all I can see. Those incisive eyes, burrowing through my layers of skin to inspect my hollowed-out carcass.

As he stares at me, searing heat rises in my temples and spreads through my head. His gaze seems to be imbued with some kind of power, and it feels like my mind catches alight.

After several painful seconds of this sensation, he breaks eye contact, and the heat dissipates. I'm left shaken and feeling like I imagined the entire thing.

"Interesting," Ravius comments.

Taking a step back to allow him to move closer, Ruth retreats to the corner of the room where she can watch us. Ravius takes her place, his tall height stretching above me.

"Lexi, I apologise for how traumatic this all must have been for you. I understand this is a great shock, and I can only offer my sincerest condolences."

"I'm dead," I say flatly.

"Not quite, child." Waves of authority colour his words. "What if I told you that we live in a world where death is not the end of our lives but only the beginning?"

"That can't be possible."

He waves a hand over me. "And yet..."

Yet... here I am. A head full of impossible memories and a body littered with bandaged stab wounds. I can feel my heart pumping erratically in my chest. It's beating, and I'm undoubtedly alive.

"How?"

Ravius smiles widely. "The Vitae is a powerful supernatural force. It's the giver of life, and it brings all Redeemed beings back into their mortal flesh."

"Redeemed?"

"That is what we call ourselves. You are among The Redeemed. We are a society of beings all brought back after death."

Temples throbbing, I fight off a wave of dizziness. It's all too much. Too ridiculous. But that damned *yet* still refuses to let me dig myself into a hole of denial. I can't ignore that undeniable truth.

Ravius glances over at Ruth. "Please go and find Michael. She's in pain and it will take her too long to heal, even as one of us."

Scuttling out of the room, her head is lowered. They all seem to cower around Ravius, even the intimidating boulder of a man that seemed so keen to dive in and restrain me.

"Now." He clasps his hands behind his back. "You are in my facility. That means you're under my care and authority. So, when I ask you these next questions, bear that in mind. I will not tolerate lies."

Eyes ignited with burning curiosity, he looks over me, searching for answers. I nod and swallow hard.

"Who sent you?"

My mouth clicks open. "No one sent me. I don't know what happened."

"Where did you come from?"

"If this is your facility, shouldn't you be telling me this? How the hell should I know?"

He exhales sharply. "I need to know what you remember."

"I... I remember dying. I felt my body giving up and then... nothing. Until the meadow."

"Meadow?" he echoes with widened eyes.

"It was a never-ending field. I was happy there, and then this crazy feeling flowed through me, and it vanished. The darkness came back. I was sucked out of there like water down a drain."

Meeting my teary eyes, he studies me intensely. "We have over one hundred and thirty Redeemed beings in this facility, and hundreds more worldwide. None of them have ever remembered anything after death."

My heart beats even faster. "Then why me?"

"I don't know, Lexi. That's what I need to find out."

"There are so many of you."

Ravius begins to pace, agitation flowing off him in waves. "We are an international secret society, hidden from the real world. Our existence is the biggest kept secret in human history."

"And you're all… like me?"

"Everyone is different—backgrounds, ethnicities, walks of life. The Vitae is indiscriminate about who it brings back from death. It is the life force that binds all Redeemed beings."

"Is that what I felt?" I frown at the strange memory. "Flowing through me?"

Ravius halts his pacing and rounds on me. "No one remembers the moment of reanimation. They don't recall the life force that catalyses the process. I've spent years searching for answers into the nature of the Vitae."

He sounds awe-struck, the gleam in his eyes setting my teeth on edge. I want to crawl away from him and hide.

"And now… you," he finishes. "The key to the puzzle. As promised."

"Promised? What puzzle?"

He waves a hand again, dismissing me to resume his pacing. "Some Redeemed are gifted after death. They're bestowed with certain powers or affinities. Fire, for example."

The memory of the burning restraints comes flooding back to me. He cocks an eyebrow, as if watching the cogs turn in my mind.

"That wasn't me," I protest.

"Yes, Lexi. It was."

"I'm… not special! I don't have any p-powers… I didn't do anything."

"And I suppose restraints just spontaneously combust all the time, yes?"

Mouth hanging open on another protest, I can't say a word.

"I myself possess an affinity for the mind," Ravius continues. "It may be easier to show you."

Moving closer, he presses his forehead to mine before I can say a word, clamping down on my shoulders with a tight grip. The intrusive heat from before returns and spreads in a sizzling wildfire.

Images swim to the forefront. I'm sitting in a rich, plush office, drinking coffee in front of a lit fireplace. A newspaper is resting on my knee, the headlines viciously blazoned across the front.

Woman found dead by Cornish coast.
Local bartender, 24, killed in cold blood.
Search for roadside killer continues.

The scene changes as the office dissipates like melting clouds. Instead, the doors to a morgue fly open, revealing a pale, bloodied body laying on a slab, shaking and convulsing. A tortured scream explodes from their cracked and bloated lips.

Nausea rolls through me as I'm faced with the sight of my own corpse through the eyes of another. I'm watching that same moment—when the lightning hit and the meadow vanished—but from the outside.

Ravius abruptly lets go and removes his forehead from mine, severing the connection.

"How did you do that?" I struggle to get the question out.

"That is my gift," he replies with a light shrug. "I can harness and manipulate the mental world. That was graphic, but you needed to see the truth to fully understand."

Covering my face with my trembling hands, my chest rises and falls in sharp sobs. It's too much. None of this can possibly be true. But still, I've experienced death. Life beyond the grave. The afterlife.

I felt my body clawing its way back, desperate to reset its system and begin working again. The proof is irrefutable. I died. I came back. I'm... alive.

"Your murder remains unsolved." Ravius studies me. "So I have to ask... Standard procedure in cases like this."

Still sobbing, I want to scrub the memories of that night from my skin. The pain. A culmination of years of abuse as that monster tore his final strip off me.

"Do you have any information regarding your death that I should know?" Ravius presses. "A name, Lexi?"

I should tell him and get the bastard who stole my life locked up where he belongs. He deserves nothing more. But when I lower my hands to look up at Ravius, my courage dies a slow death as the monster's voice comes back to me.

You must never speak my name, Lexi girl.

This is our little secret.

"No," I force out.

"You didn't see who did this to you?"

I'm a fucking coward. His name is on the tip of my tongue, but I can't push the syllables out. I've never been able to. Not a single time in all the years of mindless degradation.

Ravius waits. Silent and patient.

"No. I don't know who killed me."

Liar.

VIII

STRENGTH

CHAPTER 2

FAITH – BELLEVUE DAYS

*W*ith Ravius gone and an instruction to rest, the hours pass in a numb blur. Darkness has fallen outside the barred window in the top corner of the room, leaking moonlight inside.

I doze in and out of unconsciousness, too tormented to properly sleep. All I can think about is what Eve must be doing right now and how long I've left her alone. Tears stain my pillow as the hours of anguish pass.

She's all alone in the world.

Just like me.

He'll hurt her. I know he will. Without me there, she has no one to protect her. My silence and complacency are the only things that have kept her safe for the eight years of her life. Nothing else.

Tossing and turning, pain still burns through me. I can feel the phantom path of the blade that ended my life more with each second that passes. The memories only deepen my confusion and panic.

Am I alive?

Is any of this real?

Against all the odds, I'm here. Breathing. Thinking.

Sobbing like a scared child in a strange, unknown room, lost and alone. How the hell did I end up here? None of this makes any sense.

When dawn breaks on the horizon, my solitude ends. There's a knock on the door before it clicks open, emitting Ruth in a fresh white coat and pressed black trousers. She gives me a little wave.

"Good morning, Lexi."

I struggle to sit upright. "Morning."

"I know it's early, but Michael is ready to see you, and I didn't want to leave you in pain any longer. He's going to help."

Holding the door open, she steps back to allow a short, curly-haired child to enter the room. He looks around seven or eight years old, his copper curls framing dimpled cheeks and a bright, welcoming smile.

"Lexi, right?" His voice is high and sweet.

I stare at him. "Um, yes."

"I'm Michael. I'll be taking care of you today."

Ruth flashes me a reassuring smile. "I'll go hunt down some clothes for you to wear and leave you in Michael's capable hands."

Once she's gone, he inches closer. "You don't need to be afraid. I'm one of the doctors here at the facility. I know what I'm doing."

"But… you're just a kid," I splutter.

"Ravius hasn't gotten to that part yet then," he surmises with a sigh. "Redeemed bodies don't age. We remain at the age we were when we died forever. I've been eight years old since 1914."

All I can do is gape at him.

"Now that that's blown your mind." He claps his hands together. "This will hopefully be a lot less shocking. Unlike the other doctors, I have the ability of healing, and Ravius has asked me to take a look at your injuries."

"You're... over one hundred years old?"

"More or less." Michael winks at me.

"Are you saying I'm going to remain like this forever?"

"Pretty much. Our bodies possess the ability of accelerated healing, so ageing is impossible. Dying cells are simply regenerated."

Instructing me to lay down, he moves to the edge of the bed, his head dipped in respect as he gestures for me to raise the hospital gown. I reluctantly do so, still feeling uncomfortable.

"What else do I need to know?" I grit out.

"Well, there will be no more sickness for you. Redeemed beings don't get sick or reproduce, so my job around here is pretty easy. I take care of new intakes and any serious injuries that don't automatically heal."

"Using your gift? Are there many like you?"

"Like us," he corrects.

"I'm not gifted."

"Come on, Lexi. Ravius has told me what happened. Trust me, denial gets old in this place... fast."

Gulping, I nod. "I might've burned something."

"Interesting. We haven't had a fire starter before."

He begins to peel off the bandages, unveiling deep, stitched wounds, oozing and raw. I immediately feel sick and have to look away from my mangled torso, torn to shreds by the path of the blade.

"Do you know what happened to me?" I ask to distract myself.

Michael inspects the wounds with pinched brows. "Your body was held in a morgue while an investigation took place. I believe a suspect was apprehended but later eliminated. Your death remains unsolved."

I have to bite down on my tongue to hold a scream in. Part of me wants to utter those handful of syllables aloud and name the monster hiding beneath the bed. A larger part of me is too afraid to even consider it.

"You returned to us before the funeral, thankfully," Michael adds. "Our team located you and transported you here. We silenced the undertakers, of course. They believe it was an elaborate prank."

"That's so messed up."

"Our world is, I'm afraid."

With all of the bandages removed, he holds his child-sized hands an inch above my torso. I gasp as a cool sensation washes over my burning skin, penetrating deep into my body until it feels like I'm submerged in frigid water.

Pins and needles spread, faster and faster still. The tiny pricks stab into me in rapid succession, slicing me into invisible ribbons.

"That hurts," I whimper.

"Sorry." Michael has the decency to look sympathetic. "I'll work as fast as I can."

Daring to glance down, I watch in astonishment as my raw skin knits itself back together. The deep slashes are replaced with swollen, pink scars, marring the curves of my body.

"This is your gift?"

"Yes."

"The uh… Vitae gave it to you, right?"

He nods. "That's the working theory. Not all Redeemed are gifted. We make up a small minority."

"So what can you do?"

Michael shrugs as he works. "I can sense your injuries, and I harness the body's natural healing ability to speed up the process. It's a little hard to explain."

Feeling nauseous at the sight of my body healing itself, I stare up at the ceiling. "This is all too much. I don't know what to believe anymore."

"It's overwhelming at first, but things will get easier. You'll see."

"And if I don't want this? What if I want to go home?"

Pausing, Michael glances at me. "This is your home now, Lexi."

Dread pools in my gut. "I'm a prisoner here?"

"The facility was built to house everyone in complete luxury. Trust me, it's far from a prison. But try to leave and you'll find yourself in a cell, not a swanky apartment in one of the residential wings."

With ice running through my veins, I breathe through the uncomfortable sensation while Michael works in silence. His warning still rings in my ears. I don't know these people, and I sure as hell don't trust them.

I have to get out of here and go home to Eve. She needs me. If I'm not there to protect her, there's no telling what will happen to her.

"Almost done," Michael hums.

"Did Ravius tell you about my... memories?"

His head tilts as he scans over me with interest. "He mentioned it. I've never seen him so excited."

"I'm not some lab experiment for him." I clench my teeth, on the verge of a breakdown. "Whatever answers he's looking for, I don't have them."

Obviously frustrated, he exhales sharply. "You don't understand. I've helped Ravius with his research for decades."

"And?"

"We've found that there's no brain activity or mental presence in the mind until full reanimation is complete. Wherever the mind goes... it can't be recollected when the subject awakens."

"Then how the fuck do I remember what happened to me?"

His eyes lock on me, burning with curiosity. "You're an impossibility, Lexi. And that's dangerous."

29

Staring at each other, I feel the unspoken threat. It shines in the depths of his pale green irises, imbued with power I can't begin to fathom. The need to run screams through me again.

"I don't want this," I choke out.

He drops a hand to my arm then gently squeezes. "I'm sorry, but the Vitae has chosen you for a reason. That isn't an accident. You're meant to be here."

Feeling tears spill over my cheeks, I blink them aside, hating the flash of weakness. "There's nothing special about me."

"That's where you're wrong. You were chosen for a second life. That's a blessing, whether you want this or not. You have to embrace it."

Tiny hands lifting from my skin, he rolls my hospital gown back down to cover my now heavily scarred, pink-streaked torso. The smile he offers me is sweet, even if I'm left shaken by his words.

"Listen," he begins. "I've healed the physical wounds. I don't want to speak out of turn, but you should know that I can see your broken spirit. And as much as I want to, I can't fix it."

"My s-spirit is broken?"

He nods solemnly. "Someone's broken it. I can tell."

A shiver rolls down my spine. I drop his gaze then lift myself upright, fiddling with the hospital gown. Michael bows his head and shuffles out of the room without uttering another word.

The tears are flowing thick and fast. I can't help it. Years of holding them back and it's all pouring out now. I always knew I was fucked up, but now I know... I'm broken. Perhaps irreparably so.

"Lexi?" Ruth's voice calls.

Scrubbing my face, I swipe the hot flow of tears aside. "Come in."

She takes Michael's place in the hospital room, placing a small pile of clothing down on the bed.

"Ravius is here to take you on a tour."

"I can go?"

She nods with a smile. "We have some more tests to run when you're done, but I'm happy to let you walk around for a little while."

Giving me some privacy again, she leaves me to change. I shakily pull on the black leggings and loose, oversized t-shirt left for me to wear, thankful to be out of the uncomfortable hospital gown.

After slipping the plain ballet flats on, I run a single finger over the raised scar on my arm where the bottle slashed into me, the memory almost dragging me back to that night. I wonder what Alex is thinking right now.

No.

Fuck him.

If I hadn't been forced to leave his place in that rainstorm, I never would've been walking along that damned road. My life wouldn't have ended how it did. I'm here because of people like him… And now Eve's all alone.

"I'm coming, Evie," I whisper to myself. "Just hold on."

Squaring my shoulders, I take a final glance around the room before stepping out into the corridor. I halt when I see Ravius and Ruth, sharing a conversation in low whispers. They stop as soon as they spot me.

"Lexi." The way he utters my name sends a shiver rolling down my spine.

Dressed in another spotless, charcoal suit that complements his sharp, poignant features, he looks as terrifying and aloof as ever. Ruth has shrivelled in his presence, now appearing meek and mouse-like.

"I'm here to show you around your new home." His smile is razor-sharp. "Are you ready to go?"

I wring my hands together. "As I'll ever be."

"Good. Let's go."

Turning on his heel, he marches down the corridor, leaving me to scuttle after him. Standing guard at the exit to the hospital ward is the tall, meaty beast who scared me so badly yesterday. His head bows as Ravius approaches.

"Elder."

"Lexi, this is Brunt. He presides over security for the facility."

The mountain of a man doesn't even spare me a glance. I linger back, keeping a safe distance between us in case he decides to launch himself at me again.

"Do you need me to accompany you, sir?"

"That won't be necessary." Ravius flicks his wrist, waving him off dismissively.

"Are you sure?" Brunt spares me a judgemental sneer. "She may be unstable."

"I'm not fucking unstable," I growl out.

"Enough!" Ravius booms. "Leave us, Brunt."

With a final flash of sparkling white teeth, he turns on his heel and strides away. I'm left staring after his wide-set shoulders, my entire body shaking with rage.

"What an asshole."

"He means well," Ravius supplies.

Somehow, I don't believe that.

Placing a hand on the exit door, Ravius looks down at me. "Ready to start your new life?"

No, I want to scream.

I swallow it and nod instead.

Breaking outside into sunshine so bright, it burns my retinas, the first thing that hits me is the scent of pine trees and fir. Squinting against the bright light, my vision clears, revealing a brand-new world.

"Welcome home, Lexi."

I take a tentative step out into the winter air. We're at the end of a cobbled stone path, leading towards a huge, round courtyard surrounded by towering trees that encapsulate us in a light-speckled canopy.

Paths snake off from the courtyard in all directions, forming a wheel and spoke pattern. Lanterns hang from carved wooden poles, swaying in the light breeze while clusters of fallen leaves dance across the grass.

"This is the main courtyard," Ravius explains as we walk. "The whole facility branches off from this central point. It's easy to navigate your way to the essential services such as the dining hall and hospital."

Studying the surrounding buildings, everything is old and antiquated, like we've stepped back in time through the thick cover of trees. I'm surrounded by lavish architecture straight off the pages of history books.

I follow Ravius's line of sight to the dining hall. It's a Victorian style, two-story building with criss-crossed bay windows that make it look like a cathedral. With intricately arched doorways, it's been carved from slabs of dark stone, adding to the gothic, otherworldly feel.

"How long have you been here?" I ask.

"As a race, we've existed for over a thousand years. Yet we were unorganised the majority of that time. Our global facilities were just built in recent decades, housing our people across four different nations."

My head spins with the rush of information.

"The Redeemed population are ruled over by the Council of Elders," he continues, walking slowly into the courtyard. "Each of the four countries have their own Elder like me."

His own miniature kingdom to rule. No wonder everyone looks at this guy like he's God on earth and carved from gold. I follow behind him, feeling dizzier with every footstep.

"What is an Elder, exactly?"

Ravius sighs. "We are the first Redeemed."

"The very first?"

"Yes. My siblings and I founded the society you are now a

part of after years spent running from persecution. We survived a millennium of war and turmoil to reach safety."

His voice is weary, weighed down by years of pain. We stop in the middle of the courtyard, where paths branch off in all directions and lead to the enclosed world beyond.

"Eventually, we were able to form a treaty with those who sought to persecute us. We now work with the governments of the outside world. After the accords were signed, the facilities were later constructed."

I shouldn't be letting myself get distracted, but hearing about this clandestine society hidden right beneath our noses is fascinating.

"So where are we now?"

"That's classified," he snips.

Frustrated with his evasiveness, I turn my back to him and look around. There are people milling around, looking completely ordinary as they go about their lives. It feels like the normal world but locked in a green cocoon.

"Lexi." Ravius stops at my side. "You have to trust me. Being here is for your own protection. The outside world isn't safe for people like us."

"I have a family," I croak.

"And they're safer far away from you now. Danger will follow you everywhere you go. The accords exist for a reason —these secret facilities keep us safe. You can't leave."

"What are you going to do? Lock me up?"

His gaze hardens. "If I have to."

We stare into each other's eyes as the wind picks up around us, stirring loose leaves. Danger radiates from him in palpable waves. I have no doubt that he has the means to do exactly that.

"Like I said, the real world poses a threat to people like us," he repeats firmly. "That's why we're hidden from the outside and live our lives under the cloak of secrecy. Do you want to keep your family safe?"

"Of course," I snap.

"Then staying far away from them is the only way to do that. Otherwise, you will be putting them at risk. Think about that."

Before I can argue back, the tinkle of laughter interrupts us. What appears to be several children on bicycles are riding down the path towards us, talking amongst themselves. I have no way of knowing how old they truly are though.

They halt upon spotting us, quickly throwing on the brakes and dipping their heads towards Ravius. I can't help but study them with fascination.

"Children." Ravius's demeanour softens as he smiles warmly at them. "What are you doing out of class?"

"Sorry, Elder," one answers guiltily.

"Run along now. Your teacher will be expecting you."

Heads bowed, they all take off on their bicycles, riding down the central spoke that bisects the courtyard towards another eerie, black-stone building in the distance. I watch them go, aghast.

"There are children here?"

Ravius clasps his hands behind his back. "Not everyone is fortunate enough to live a full life before meeting their demise. They're only a small proportion, but we do house children too."

"And there's a school?"

"Yes, we have a schooling system set up so they may continue their childhoods relatively undisturbed."

Watching the bicycles disappear, my eyes burn with tears. They appear to be the same age as Eve. The thought of her being put through this breaks my heart. Nobody that young should have to experience such pain.

"What about their parents? Their families?"

His mouth curves in a sad smile. "The children are placed in the care of other Redeemed families who volunteer to look after them until they reach a mental age of maturity."

35

"You mean they never see their families again."

"Their families cannot know the truth about our existence, Lexi. That's how it has to be."

"But... they'll never grow up. Not physically."

He gives me a side look. "I see Michael has informed you of our curse. It's true, the Vitae extracts a heavy toll for the gift of reanimation. Like the rest of us, the children will never physically age."

"So... we're immortal?"

"Close enough."

My brain hurts, overwhelmed with the impossibility of it all. I've lost everything. My entire life. My family. My freedom. I don't want the second chance he's offering me. Not if it means giving up Eve.

"I think that's enough for one day." Ravius gently touches my arm. "Let's get you back to the hospital."

Leaning on his arm as a wave of exhaustion crashes over me, I look down at my feet, the tears pouring.

"I'm never going to see her again, am I?"

"I'm sorry, Lexi."

And with those words, my world comes crashing down. I can't get to her. I can't ever save her again. All I can do is admit defeat because after all these years... I am finally too broken to go on.

II

THE HIGH PRIESTESS

CHAPTER 3

BURY ME FACE DOWN – GRANDSON

"*C*ome on, Lexi."
        Rolling over in the hospital bed, I turn my back on Ruth's pleading. She's been trying to drag me up for the last half an hour to little avail. I've given up on ever leaving this room.

"You've been cleared to leave," she tries again. "Your apartment is ready for you to move into. Don't you want to see it?"

"No."

"You need to—"

"I said no!"

With a sigh, she leaves me in peace. I squeeze my eyes shut and will myself back to the small, Cornish seaside town I've spent my entire life in. Eve's favourite place is by the sea, tasting the salty tang in the air.

When I saved up enough tips from working at the bar, we'd go to get ice cream and a loaf of stale bread from the local baker to feed to the seagulls. Eve loved to tear off chunks and feed them with her bare hands.

If she could see me now, she wouldn't recognise me. Beaten and broken. Unable to even lift a finger, let alone get out of bed. I'm the strong one. The reliable one. Eve would be ashamed of me now.

"Lexi?"

A sweet voice followed by a soft knock on the bedroom door interrupts my thoughts. I know it's Michael without turning over. His voice only reminds me of my sister even more.

"Go away, Michael."

"I'm coming in," he announces.

Groaning, I hide my face in my hands. "Great."

The door creaks as it opens. His footsteps approach but stop before reaching the bed.

"You need to get up," he says emphatically. "Laying here isn't going to help you."

"I have nowhere else to be," I manage through my tears. "Ravius has made it clear what will happen if I try to leave."

"This place doesn't have to be a prison, Lexi. You have a chance to make a life here."

"A life that I don't want. Not without her."

The bed dips as he takes a seat on the edge. "Your sister?"

Sniffling, I swipe tears from my face and look up to meet his eyes. "She's all alone out there, and she needs me. But I can't keep her safe anymore."

"I'm so sorry." His young face dips as he peers down at his hands. "I know this is unbelievably difficult."

"Do you? Really?"

"I had a family once too. You're not the only one who's lost someone."

Feeling like the worst person in the world, I stare into his moss-coloured eyes. "You had a family?"

"One that I can barely remember, but yes. I did. They're all dead now."

"How did you do this without them? Live?"

He reaches out a hand for me to take. "Not alone."

Biting my bottom lip, I contemplate his outstretched hand.

I want nothing more than to hide in this bed until this entire nightmare ends and I wake up back home, safe in the knowledge it was all a bad dream.

But that isn't going to happen, no matter how much I sob and plead. The world has taught me that begging God for mercy doesn't work. He doesn't care. The only person I can rely on is myself.

I have to find a way to survive. That's the only way out of this—by fighting to get back to her.

Cheeks wet, I tentatively put my hand in his. Michael squeezes as he offers me a kind, patient smile. I let him guide me up and I climb out of the bed I've spent what feels like days hiding in.

"I can show you to your new apartment." He drops my hand then smooths down his grey, button-down shirt. "Then we'll get dinner together, and I can introduce you to my friends."

"Friends?" I laugh weakly.

"We all need them. I have an opening, if you're interested." He winks humorously.

"I think I'd like that."

"Good. Then it's a deal."

Sliding on my shoes, I reluctantly follow him outside. Ruth waves us off, a huge smile on her lips at seeing me leave the hospital room.

Once out of the hospital, we head towards one of the tall, multiple-story apartment blocks in the distance, carved in the same excessive Victorian design. Every building we pass is lavish to the extreme and reminiscent of a time long gone.

If I wasn't sure about the wealth of The Redeemed before, I sure am now. No expense has been spared to make this place as comfortable as can be. We walk past countless grand buildings, all chiselled to perfection from slabs of stone and finished with twirling turrets that twist up into the heavens.

"All Redeemed are given accommodation and the means to establish new lives here in the facility," Michael explains. "You'll be granted a furnished apartment and expected to find a job."

"What kind of job?"

"There's plenty to do. We run all of our own public services. You'll see."

Stomping up to the apartment building surrounded by swaying willow trees, he holds open the lacquered red door for me. I gulp down my mistrust and step inside the plush space.

"This is the Nightingale building." Michael gestures around the well-lit entrance hall. "It's one of four residential quarters in the facility. You've been allocated a space here."

It's stifling hot inside and smells of bergamot and old books, the tantalising scents lacing the sweltering air. Fine art lines the royal-blue, wallpapered walls, locked in shining gold frames that drip with opulence.

My feet sink into the thick, luxurious carpet in the deepest shade of blood-red as I trail behind Michael's short strides. I'm almost shocked to see the shining elevator built into the wall amongst all the traditional decor.

"The residential quarters have been modernised overtime." He steps inside, waiting for me to follow. "Come on, you're on the top floor."

Following him, we lapse into silence as we ride the elevator to the top floor. The corridor matches the entrance in all its old-world charm, complete with lit sconces, more framed artwork and rich brocade wallpaper.

"You're next to me."

We stop outside a glossy black door where Michael flourishes a key card. I watch him unlock the door, my heartbeat thundering in my ears.

"That's convenient," I comment, unsure how to feel about his close proximity.

Michael shrugs. "Perks of the job. Ravius listens to me, and I didn't want you to be alone in here."

Despite everything, my chest warms. "Thank you."

"Don't mention it."

Holding open the door for me, he allows me to step into the apartment first. I stop in the doorway, my mouth hanging open, and my breath taken away by the grand space within.

"This is... for me?"

"Yes," Michael hums.

"Oh my God."

Stepping into the bright, open-plan unit, I spin in a circle, taking in all the details. Glinting crystal chandeliers hang from the high ceiling, lighting the speckled, black marble countertops of the kitchen nook.

The living room is rich and welcoming, complete with a velvet sofa sat atop a patterned rug. Little touches betray the expense of the space—more priceless artwork and sparkling crystal doorknobs that look straight out of a palace.

"The apartments were all updated a few years back to include modern amenities." Michael follows me in. "A lot has changed since the facility was first built."

"When was that?"

"The accords were ratified in 1870, and the global facilities were built shortly thereafter."

Jesus. These people are ancient. It's crazy to think this place has been strategically built and hidden from the world for so long. Whichever country Ravius's facility is in, I'm now part of the world's best kept secret.

Trailing my fingers over polished marble and butter-soft velvet, I feel completely out of place. Back home, Eve and I share a dank, messy bedroom and curl up together to sleep due to the lack of space.

"This is all too much." I shake my head. "I don't deserve any of this."

"Lexi," Michael scolds. "You've been chosen for this second life, and you deserve everything."

"How do you know?"

Stepping in front of me, his gaze softens. "Because I can tell things haven't been easy for you. I want to help change that. We all do."

"Even Ravius?"

Michael laughs. "Even Ravius."

Staring into his eyes, he seems sincere. Everything about him is genuine, even his small, hopeful smile. I want to trust him. I want to be his friend. I just don't know if I'm capable of it.

"Get cleaned up." He claps his hands together. "I'll come back and take you to dinner in the dining hall. It's time for you to meet some of the others."

Nerves shoot through me. "I'm not so sure."

He pins me with a stern look. "No arguments."

Leaving me alone, the front door clicks shut, and I'm enveloped in silence. I feel entirely out of place in the apartment, frozen on the spot. Forcing my feet to move, I eventually trail through the kitchen and into the bedroom.

It's another huge room, filled with a four-poster bed and crisp, white linens. I take a peek inside the massive, carved mahogany wardrobe in the corner, finding it full of clothing all in my exact size.

"What the fuck?" I mutter.

Designer tags are attached to everything, from the softest pairs of jeans to silky shirts and long, floral dresses. I've never seen such fine clothes before, let alone touched them. The contents of this wardrobe are worth more money than I've seen in my lifetime.

Slamming the door shut, I face the window instead. Glinting lights from nearby buildings penetrate the early evening shadows, the whole world concealed in a sarcophagus of towering trees. It feels like another planet.

I'm lost.

Far from home.

Far from... everything.

I have to mentally slap myself before I break down again.

Staring up at the night sky makes me wonder what Eve is doing right now, out there alone in the world. And whether she misses me as much as I miss her.

I'm so sorry, Evie.

I can't keep you safe anymore.

The tears come against my will—thick and fast. Abandoning the bedroom, I step into the shining, black and white bathroom and turn the walk-in shower on.

The water is scalding against my skin after I've stripped out of my borrowed clothes. I tilt my head up to face the spray and let myself fall apart, unable to hold my broken pieces together for a second longer.

It's all gone.

Everything I worked so hard for. My sanity. My relatively fragile sobriety. Eve's safety. I've lost everything that once mattered so much to me.

Yet I have a new life. A beautiful home. The freedom from abuse that I so desperately craved. Perhaps I have a chance to actually live here.

But it comes at a cost.

Whatever is wrong with me, the power that Ravius clearly thinks I have... it makes me valuable to him. I don't want to be another loyal subject for him to exploit. My life has to amount to more than that.

Once I'm all cried out and too tired to hold myself up anymore, I turn off the shower and wring out my long, lower-back length blonde hair. The mirror is steamed up as I face my reflection.

Swiping the moisture away, I stare into my weary, pale-blue eyes. Tormented ocean waves stare back at me beneath

45

thick lashes that dapple across my freckled cheeks, gaunt from years of fending for myself.

I always fed Eve first, even when I worked myself to the bone and was starving. She's the priority—above my own health. Who the hell is making sure she eats now?

My job as a bartender in the local pub didn't pay well, but after having to leave education early to provide for us, it was the best I could do. My father sure as hell wasn't going to look after us.

Turning my back on my reflection, I redress without looking down at the scarred mess of my body. One look was enough. The memories are still too fresh, bubbling away at the surface.

"Lexi?" Michael's voice calls out. "It's me. Are you ready to go?"

Smoothing down my new black jeans and t-shirt, I blow out a breath.

As I'll ever be.

XIII

DEATH

CHAPTER 4

WOLF – HIGHLY SUSPECT

he dining hall is a grandiose building, set amongst a backdrop of swaying trees that stir in the night time breeze. People walk towards it from all directions, whispering and not-so subtly staring at me.

"Why is everyone looking at me?"

Michael drops his voice. "You're new."

"Don't you get new people regularly?"

"Things have been slow for a long time. You're our first new arrival in almost two years. Pay no attention to them, though."

"Little hard not to."

"You're safe with me."

I feel a pang of warmth in my chest. I've never felt safe with someone before, let alone a stranger. I'm not sure how to deal with it.

"Michael!" someone yells.

We slow down then stop next to a black lamppost, casting light through the shadowed night. It was September when I was… *alive*. I have no idea what month it is now, but winter is well and truly here.

Racing across the courtyard, a blonde-haired man

approaches us through the rising mist. He stops short when he catches up to us, studying me intently.

The new guy's tall and gangly, but his slim frame is packed with wiry muscles that bulge against his jeans and t-shirt. Light, sandy-blonde hair flops over his eyes in a carefree way that betrays his young age.

His facial features are soft and boyish, from his round hazel eyes to his slightly upturned button nose. I'd say he's in his late teens, but with these people, I know looks can be deceiving.

"Sorry," he squeaks. "Didn't mean to interrupt."

Michael waves off his apology. "You're fine. Lexi, this is Felix."

A grin tugging at his full lips, Felix sticks out a hand for me to shake. "Hey."

I tentatively take it. "Hi."

"Welcome." He smiles broadly, flashing even, sparkling teeth. "Haven't seen a new face around here in a long time."

He's still holding my hand, enthusiastically shaking it like an over-excited puppy. I can't help but smile back. Something about his overflowing energy is infectious.

When he eventually lets my hand go, we resume walking to the dining hall. Felix walks with a skip in his step, falling in between us with casual ease as he slings an arm around my shoulders.

"So, Lexi. Tell me about yourself."

I gingerly extract myself from his embrace. "Um, there isn't much to tell."

"Now, I don't believe that. Everyone has a story to tell."

"Not me."

"I'll get it out of you eventually." He waggles his brows.

"Good luck trying."

Bursting into laughter, he skips ahead, turning to walk backwards so his warm eyes are lasered on me. I feel like I'm under a microscope. He's determined to pull all of my secrets out with a mere glance.

I cock an eyebrow. "Can I help you?"

"Nope." He pops the P. "Just enjoying the view."

"Alright." Michael shakes his head. "Knock it off, Felix. You'll scare her away."

"Hardly." Felix rolls his eyes. "She looks like she's made of tough stuff."

Brushing past him, Michael and I climb the wide-set steps into the building. It'll take more than some pop psychology to get through my barriers. I can hear Felix laughing behind us as he follows hot on our heels.

Inside the extravagant building, glinting chandeliers light the bustle of people, all taking their seats at long, dark-wood tables surrounded by high-backed chairs.

Silver platters fill every inch of space, boasting an unholy amount of food, with wine and all manner of drinks accompanying the feast. Clusters of flowers fill each table in gold-laced vases.

"Wow." I blink slowly, enraptured by the magnificent splendour. "This is some fancy shit."

"You're in the big leagues now." Felix playfully elbows me.

"Clearly."

All around us, people are staring and whispering. I can't help but stare back, fascinated by the wide spectrum of people. All ages, ethnicities and genders. No two Redeemed look alike.

Letting Michael guide me over to a table, we all take our seats. There's a low hum of chatter in the room from all directions. People fill all of the space while an empty head table presides over the packed room.

"That's where the Elder and his team sit," Michael answers my unspoken question. "There are several officials who work for Ravius."

"Ruling over us all?" I snort.

"Something like that."

"Why don't you sit up there?"

"Me?" His head jerks back in surprise.

"You're a big deal around here, aren't you?"

Michael laughs as he pulls out a seat for me to sit in. "Hardly. I keep to myself mostly. Only my friends matter to me."

Sitting down, I stifle another eye roll when Felix sits directly opposite. He steeples his fingers beneath his chin and resumes studying me with a smug grin.

"Jackass," I mutter.

"That's me, babe." He winks dramatically. "Better get used to it."

"How old are you? Sixteen?"

"Nineteen. Or I was when I... you know." He mimes dragging a finger over his throat. "That was six years ago. I've been here ever since. How old are you?"

"Twenty-four."

"What did you do out there in the real world?"

"I was a bartender." I sigh. "Nothing fancy."

"Sounds pretty cool to me. I was still in school. Hadn't even had my first drink." Sadness crosses his expression for a moment before it's replaced with his trademark grin. "I work with the security team now."

Michael takes the seat next to me, glowering at his friend. "Let the poor girl breathe, Felix."

"What? Just being friendly."

"Well, cut it out."

Felix sticks his tongue out at Michael, helping himself to a glass of wine from the jug on the table. When the chair next to him is pulled out, he startles, staring up at the newcomer with another big grin.

"Well, well, look who it is."

"Christ," the woman curses. "Is he on one today?"

"Yep." Michael grips the back of his neck.

"Good luck to us all."

With a short pixie cut dyed a lurid shade of bright pink, wide set, round blue eyes and full, kissable lips, she's stunning in a unique way. I can't help but stare.

Her clothes scream of attitude—leather jeans that hug her generous curves and a low-cut tank top showing off plenty of cleavage. Even her fingernails are painted neon pink to match her hair.

"Who's the newbie?" She tilts her head in my direction.

Michael places a hand on the back of my chair. "This is Lexi."

I wave awkwardly. "Hi."

"Hey, honey. Nice to meetcha. I'm Raven." She sits down next to Felix. "I've been dying for some female company in this place to break up all the testosterone."

"How much testosterone do you think this one has?" Felix waves at Michael.

Michael flips him off. "Not funny."

"Love you too."

"Like I was saying," Raven interrupts, her eyes narrowed. "Us girls have to stick together. Welcome to the family, Lexi."

"Thanks." I force a smile.

The chatter in the room dies down as the doors open, admitting a final group of people. Ravius strides ahead of the group, surveying the room with his lips pursed in a tight, tense line.

Everyone is hushed as he takes his seat at the head of the table, high above us all. All of the others sit around him, except for one gargantuan man who branches off and heads in our direction.

Michael waves a hand. "Over here."

"When did Daniel get back?" Felix whispers.

"They arrived yesterday afternoon."

"He sure doesn't look happy about that."

"When is Daniel happy?" Michael snorts.

53

The mysterious Daniel approaches, dressed in all-black cargo trousers that hug his long legs and a tight t-shirt, showing off all kinds of rippling muscle. From his brawny shoulders and strapping torso, he's built like a wrestler and drips with masculinity.

With a clenched jaw covered in a scruff of dark hair, his face is harsh and well-defined, cheekbones sharp enough to slice glass. I study his straight nose, generous lips and deep-set eyes coloured the brightest shade of aquamarine blue imaginable.

Even his hair is all business—a rigid, military buzz cut on the sides but with a stretch of long, tangled locks that sit haphazardly on top, reminiscent of molten milk chocolate.

"Friend of yours?" I murmur.

"Old friend," Michael replies.

Standing up, he clasps Daniel's hand, then the pair slap each other's backs. Felix and Raven offer greetings before those two jewels of arctic ice land on me, incisive and hardened with apprehension.

"Who's this?" he rumbles in a deep, whiskey-smooth voice.

"New arrival." Michael motions towards me. "This is Lexi."

Daniel studies me with a frown. "Leave."

"Excuse me?" I splutter.

"You heard me. Find another table to sit at."

His entire over-sized posture is carved from tension and mistrust. When his eyes flick over me, my heart does angry backflips inside my chest. He looks offended by my mere presence.

"She's with us, Daniel," Michael defends me. "Back off."

"You're always taking in strays."

"Hey," Felix snaps. "It's called being friendly. We all have to live together, after all. Sit down and play nice."

With a defeated sigh, Daniel takes his seat. He doesn't

spare me another glance. The man clearly has a huge chip on his shoulder and an extreme mistrust for strangers.

Michael clears his throat. "You here for long?"

Daniel shrugs casually. "Few days. Caine's here for negotiations."

Felix leans over the table to whisper to me. "Caine's the American Elder, sitting next to Ravius. They're brothers."

I peek up at the head table as subtly as possible. Sitting next to Ravius is a shorter man, his body stocky and well-built. With a shining bald head and three identical, vertical scars down his cheek, he looks even more terrifying than his brother.

The way he surveys the room is fucking clinical. From the cruel twist of his lips to the cold, dead look in his eyes, his disdain for everyone couldn't be clearer.

"The US signed the accords?" I ask carefully.

Michael pours himself a glass of wine. "Nice work, Felix. You're such a loudmouth."

"Sorry, sorry." Felix winces. "Uh, I shouldn't have said that. So keep your voice down."

I wrinkle my nose in frustration. This place and its goddamn secrets. I can't stand feeling so powerless.

"Ravius is a stickler for his secrets." Michael shrugs, as if that explanation will satisfy me.

Felix lowers his voice. "I hate secrets."

"Me too."

"You any good at keeping them?" he asks quietly, taking pity on my obvious annoyance.

I look up into Felix's gaze and smile. "The best."

"Felix," Michael warns.

"What?" He lifts a hand challengingly. "She deserves to know. Ravius shouldn't keep everyone in the dark."

"He has his reasons."

"That's bullshit," Felix replies curtly.

Michael sighs. "You can deal with his wrath when he finds out you've been gossiping with our new arrival."

Not at all perturbed by the notion of dealing with Ravius, Felix leans further across the table to continue our conversation.

"The other countries that signed are the United Kingdom, Sweden and Spain. Each has its own Elder, one of four siblings, who runs the facilities."

Excitement lights my chest. "So where are we?"

"Ravius runs the UK facility."

Shit! We're still in the same country as Eve. Maybe I'm not that far from home. This realisation is monumental after feeling so powerless for days.

Blood rushing in my ears, I take the glass of wine that Michael offers, gulping the rich liquid down to steady myself.

"Easy," Felix hums. "Don't go throwing up on us now, newbie."

"Let the girl drink," Raven scolds. "It's not every day you wake up in this hellhole. She can drink if she wants to."

I flash her an appreciative look. She gives me a thumb's up, encouraging me to refill my glass. Warmth is humming louder in my veins with each sip, emboldening me to look at the head table again.

Ravius is staring at me.

Right. Freaking. At. Me.

The corner of his mouth curls in a small smile, and he raises his glass in a toast just for me. Ice shoots through my veins. I quickly put the wine down and avert my gaze from his.

Too late.

"Attention!" his voice booms.

The room instantly falls silent.

I resolutely stare at the table, refusing to acknowledge him. It feels like the first day starting a new school, and I'm the awkward newcomer, facing petrifying introductions. But eventually my curiosity wins out and I risk a glance up.

"Good evening, all." Ravius looks around the room. "Tonight, it's my pleasure to introduce a new member of our family. Join me in wishing Lexi a warm welcome."

He raises his glass high again, and the entire room toasts, locking their eyes on me. I feel my cheeks flame. Even the acerbic stranger is watching me with a strange look on his face, though he glowers when I stare back.

"Let us also welcome Elder Caine and his associates from our extended family. We wish them a pleasant stay."

Ravius smiles coolly at the short man on his left, tension practically dripping from his narrow, suit-covered frame. Caine only offers him a head tilt, his mouth still pressed in a firm line, pulling his violent facial scars taut.

"And finally," Ravius continues. "I would like to offer a personal thank you to our security team for their continuous hard work. In these unprecedented times, our privacy is more important than ever."

Ravius retakes his seat then begins to dig in. Once he's started, everyone else follows suit. All around me, people of all shapes and sizes—including several children—are eating and chatting. Yet I can't bring myself to pick up my fork.

"Tuck in, Lexi," Michael urges.

Staring at the wide array of roasted meats, vegetables and fresh salads, I feel sick to my stomach. None of this is right. I shouldn't be here, sharing a meal with these people while Eve's all alone.

"I'm not hungry," I choke out.

A foot nudges mine beneath the table and Felix nods towards the food. "It's tasty. Rick and his team in the kitchen are talented."

Looking up, I notice that the sour-faced Daniel isn't eating either. His thick brows are pulled together in a frown instead. He's preoccupied with surveying the room, cataloguing every last person in it with narrowed eyes.

"Not hungry either?"

I'm not sure what drives me to ask. He's made it clear how he feels about newcomers, but the words just slip out. Dragging his caustic stare back to me, his lip curls.

"What makes you think that you can talk to me?"

I recoil like I've been slapped. He's deadly serious. Any hope of him cracking a smile and admitting that this entire encounter was a joke is extinguished by his raised eyebrow.

"Well?" he demands.

"I don't know. Must be your sparkling personality."

Choking on a mouthful, Felix sprays food across his plate. Raven has to hammer him on the back before he hacks up a lung. Even Michael is fighting to smother a smile.

Daniel's glare doesn't lift. "Cute."

"Did I kick your puppy in a past life or something?"

Teeth ground together, his chair scrapes back as he rises. "I have business to attend to."

I watch him go, storming from the room without another word. The door slams shut behind him with a resounding thunk. Michael sighs before taking a large gulp of wine.

"What charming friends you have," I huff bitterly.

"I'd apologise for him, but I doubt it will be the last time. Daniel's a complicated man. Don't take it personally."

"Little hard not to."

"Complicated is a code word for asshole," Raven informs me. "And a hot one at that."

"Hey!" Felix pouts.

"What?" She laughs.

"Thought you only had eyes for me?"

"Dream on, kid."

The sound of their playful back and forth melts into the background. I stare at my empty plate, willing my appetite to make an appearance, but all I feel is fucking sick.

I don't belong here.

This isn't my home.

If I'm not there to feed her, who will take care of Eve? My

father will be passed out in a puddle of his own vomit like usual. He's never shown any parental responsibility.

She's alone now.

I can't keep her safe.

Heartbeat roaring in my ears, I abruptly push my chair back and stand up. "Excuse me."

"Lexi?" Michael asks in concern.

"I… need some fresh air."

The room is a blur around me as I flee, leaving their surprised faces behind. I barely manage to break outside before I fall to my knees and a panic attack takes hold.

Fingers digging into the wet grass, I pant and heave, frantically trying to catch a single breath. Though I don't deserve to draw another breath while my sister is out there all alone.

My chest is on fire as my vision swims from a lack of oxygen. I know from experience that if I don't snap out of this soon, I'll pass out. It's happened enough times before.

I can't do this. All I want is to crawl back into the bed I woke up in and will myself to wake up from this awful nightmare. I want to go home. I'd take the horror of my past over this confusing reality any day.

When a hand meets my back and begins circling, I drag in an uneven breath, shocked by the light touch. I didn't hear Michael following me out of the dining hall.

"M-Michael," I hiccup.

He remains silent.

Managing to look up, I'm stunned at the brawny, muscled boulder that leans over me. His ice-blue eyes are locked on my tears with the same heavy frown as before.

"You should breathe," Daniel murmurs.

Fucking thanks, genius.

Hating the way his touch grants me a tether back to reality, I focus on the rise and fall of his chest. If he can do it, so can I. All I have to do is copy his movements.

Daniel watches me battle with myself, that frown painfully etched into his face like it's a permanent feature. I don't know how long we stay like that, glowering at each other.

When the iron-grip on my lungs finally releases, I suck in a stuttered breath, savouring the cool burst of relief. Air flows through me as the panic begins to recede.

It takes several minutes of deep breathing for my throat to open long enough for me to speak.

"What do you want?" I gasp.

He scoffs. "You're welcome."

"I didn't ask for your help."

"Seems like you needed it."

His hand is still on my back. I'm calm enough to feel the strange current of electricity passing between us, even through the thin material of my shirt.

Daniel looks at his hand like it's betrayed him. Does he feel it too? I have no idea what planet these people live on, but this doesn't feel normal—whatever normal is in this place.

"Who the hell are you?" he blurts.

"I'm nobody."

His head tilts to the side. "Somehow I doubt that."

Removing his hand severs the current passing between us. I suddenly feel cold and empty without it, like I've been kicked out of bed and banished into a rainstorm.

Striding away from me, Daniel disappears into the mist. He vanishes so fast, it's almost like I imagined the whole thing. I stare after him, my back still tingling.

THE WORLD

CHAPTER 5

BAD AS HELL – FRIDAY PILOTS CLUB

*S*taring up at the bottomless blue sky, cold winter air lashes my cheeks, leaving me frost-bitten. I shiver against the early morning chill, loving the sense of freshness. Winter's always been my favourite month.

After hiding out in the safety of my bed for a few days, I've decided to brave facing the world again. Ravius and Michael tried to coax me out during that time, but I ignored their knocks on the door.

In those lonely hours spent hidden under the duvet, my thoughts strayed from Eve to the electric buzz of Daniel's hand on my back, stroking in circles. His question has plagued me ever since.

Who the hell are you?

Forcing my cold feet to move, I crunch over frosty grass, parting the mist to walk away from the Nightingale building. There are a few people milling about, though most are hiding inside from the frigid temperature.

Everyone who spots me still stares at me with the same look of open curiosity. I'm the new girl on the block. It's painfully obvious that these people are bored to death and have nothing better to gawp at.

"Lexi!" a female voice calls. "Wait up."

Halting, I glance over my shoulder. "Hey."

Raven approaches from a building in the distance, her short hair a lurid kaleidoscope of pink against the white-dipped morning. I squeak in shock when she wastes no time pulling me into a tight hug.

"Sorry," she chirps. "I'm a hugger. How are you?"

"I'm doing okay. Just needed some air."

"We haven't seen you at dinner since the other night. What happened?"

I resume walking, and she falls into step beside me.

"I just got a bit overwhelmed," I admit. "This is all so new and crazy to me."

"I get it." She links her arm with mine. "I think I spent most of my first year here drunk in bed. You're not alone in feeling overwhelmed."

"You did?"

"Hell yeah. Come on, let's get coffee. I'll tell you all about what a hot fucking mess I was until you feel better."

Dragging me over slick cobblestones, she steers me past several more interested onlookers, paying them zero attention. I tune out their chatter, hating the feeling of eyes on me.

Even when I was younger and in school, I preferred to be invisible. No one wanted to be friends with the village drunk's daughter in her hole-filled uniform. Invisibility became my cloak of protection.

"I helped take care of you while you were out of it, you know." Raven's statement captures my attention. "Nasty wounds you had there. Someone butchered you up real nice."

I choke on a breath.

"Shit," she curses. "I'm so sorry. I need a bloody filter on my mouth."

"No, it's... fine. I didn't realise you'd helped to take care of me."

"I work as a medical assistant in the hospital alongside Michael and Ruth." She casts me a tight smile. "We hadn't had any admissions in a long time. Your arrival was big news."

"So I've been told."

"Normally, we just see patients with severe injuries, but even that's few and far between."

"How does it work? The advanced healing?"

"Ravius would give you some complicated lecture about the Vitae and our *divine purpose* in the world, but that's a load of bollocks. We have no purpose. Not anymore."

Her mouth snaps shut, cutting off her rant. She curses herself and tugs on my arm, making a beeline for a small, antiquated building nestled in a cluster of mist-soaked trees.

"This is the coffee shop. Martha runs the place. She's a caffeinated godsend."

An overhead bell tinkles as Raven pushes her way inside, pulling me along with her. The coffee shop is small and quaint, the walls lined with tightly packed bookshelves boasting an impressive collection of leather-bound tomes.

Clusters of armchairs line the roughened wood floor, dotted with brightly coloured pillows and throws. It's completely empty this early in the morning, apart from a short, grey-haired woman standing behind the espresso machine.

"Martha," Raven coos. "Please tell me you've got that thing fired up."

"Shouldn't you be at work?" She frowns at her.

Raven waves her off. "I'm showing our newest recruit around your fine establishment first. Michael can wait."

With a snort, Martha's eyes land on me and she smiles politely. She looks to be in her early sixties, and she's dressed in a tweed skirt and perfectly pressed blouse, matching the cluster of pearls around her wrinkled neck.

"Lexi, right?"

"That's me."

"Nice to meet you. What's your poison?"

Raven props herself against the coffee bar. "I'll take my usual."

"I was asking your guest," Martha snips, a twinkle in her eye. "Don't be shy now."

I bite my lip. "I'll take a black coffee please. Extra shot and hazelnut syrup."

"Strong and black. My kind of girl."

Raven mock-shudders. "You're both psychopaths."

While Martha tends her machine, I glance around the warm space. I like it. There's even a roaring fire in the corner of the room, breaking through the dreary, early morning shadows.

"How are you settling in, Lexi?" Martha asks.

"Fine," I reply, not having the desire or strength to answer honestly.

She places a steaming mug on the countertop. "No need to bullshit me, darling. I've been around long enough. I'm sure you're feeling all kinds of confused right now."

Taking the drink, I savour the warmth of it in my hands. "Something like that."

"Give it time. You'll find your place."

Raven nods as she takes her drink. "It's a big adjustment."

"Understatement of the century."

Both of them laugh, and I stifle a smile. I've barely begun to process my death, let alone all of the other impossibilities that have happened to lead me here. I feel like an alien in my own skin.

Pulling two strange gold coins from her pocket, Raven slides them over to Martha. She then tugs on my elbow to guide me to a set of armchairs in front of the open fireplace where we each take one.

"What were those? Money?"

"Chips." She slurps on her drink. "We all receive basic necessities like meals and accommodation. Everyone works but also gets a monthly payment of chips for luxuries like fresh coffee or things from the market."

"So you have your own currency?"

"Of sorts. It helps maintain a sense of normality and purpose. You work, you get paid. There's no crime or anything like that."

"You're just one big happy family, huh?"

Raven chuckles. "Not all of the time. We still drive each other mad. Can't live with the same people for centuries on end and not have a few fallings out."

Zoning out, she stares off into the fire. Her easy smile has fallen away, and she seems smaller somehow, reduced to a sad, young girl.

"Are you happy here?" I ask, genuinely interested.

She bites her lip, seeming reluctant to answer.

"You can be truthful," I add.

"Look, I've got my opinions about the way Ravius runs things. But we're stuck in this together. It's an adjustment, and one we've all been through. After the first few years, time begins to blur together."

Nothing about her answer gives me hope. I don't want the years to blur together. I have to get out of here before I become a zombie like everyone else. Eve needs me.

"What about you?" Her curious eyes slide over to me, a perfectly shaped brow raised. "Michael told me you didn't exactly have a regular... ah, experience."

"It's complicated." I shrug.

"What do you remember?"

"Everything. All the crazy shit that happened to my body during the reanimation and the place I was in before it happened."

Raven whistles under her breath. "That's insane.

Medically speaking, memories tend to need a living brain to be stored in. No wonder they're interested in you."

"I've been avoiding Ravius," I reply in a low voice. "His interest in me isn't something I want."

"I don't blame you. He can be intimidating."

"You see it too?"

"Sure." She places her now-empty mug down. "But you can't avoid him forever. If he wants answers, he'll do whatever it takes to get them."

"That's exactly what I'm afraid of."

We lapse back into silence as I finish off my coffee. I'm itching with the urge to run and hide again, before the elusive Elder himself tracks me down. It's only a matter of time before his patience expires.

"You said that you struggled with the adjustment too." I wring my hands together, eyes darting from side to side. "How did you figure this madness out?"

Raven gnaws on her bottom lip. "Before I ended up here, I was an addict. It was the '90s, so everyone partied. I quickly found myself in a sticky situation, owing money to all the wrong kinds of people. I was homeless, and nobody gave a shit about me."

I reach across to take her ring-laden hand in mine, feeling an instinctive need to protect her, even from the pain of the past.

"When the douchebag who killed me was beating the crap out of me, people just kept on walking. How messed up is that?"

"I'm so sorry, Raven."

"I spent a long time coming to terms with what happened to me." She sighs. "And then I started to rebuild... slowly, piece by piece. It took a long time, but I found myself again, and you will too."

She squeezes my hand, and I soak in the flash of reassurance. Finding myself feels like a luxury I can't afford.

I've spent years fighting to survive one day to the next. I didn't have the chance to be someone.

But here, I have that chance. It's been given to me. All that's holding me back is knowing that out there, my sister is all alone. If I just knew that she was going to be okay, I could try to find a way to move forward.

"That's the thing about scars, Lexi. They fade."

When she releases my hand, there are tears sparkling in her beryl-tinged eyes. My throat is thick with clogged-up emotion. I nod and blow out my breath, fighting to remain in control of my own tears.

"And you're not alone," she adds emphatically. "Even if you feel like it."

"I... do."

"That's why I'm here. We've got your back now."

Holding each other's gazes, we're trapped in our own private bubble until the bell above the door tinkles, breaking the moment. Raven clears her throat, and I quickly swipe beneath my eyes.

"Martha," a deep, baritone voice rumbles.

The hairs on the back of my neck stand on end. Risking a look out the corner of my eye, I catch sight of his wide-set shoulders first, the packed muscle accentuated by the tight fabric of his black t-shirt.

Daniel.

He leans against the coffee bar, an over-sized hand casually running through the wet, untidy mop of longish hair on top of his shaved head.

His luminous blue eyes search around the room, as if he's surveying enemy territory. When he finds us, his features harden into a familiar scowl. I don't miss the way he scans over me like he's looking for answers to all his burning questions.

Has the memory of that night haunted him too? Did his skin prickle for hours after he left like mine did? I've had to fight the urge to hunt him down and demand answers of my own.

Raven waves at him. "You're up early."

He glances at her. "Duty calls."

"Caine got you running all his errands?"

"Something like that," Daniel rumbles.

His eyes shift from Raven to fasten on me again. The entire coffee shop drops away until it's just the two of us, locked in a battle of wills, the air between us charged with the same strange, invisible tension.

His pouty lips are full, kissable. I'm startled to catch myself wondering how they'd feel locked on mine. Shaking myself out of it, I look away first.

My cheeks feel flushed with heat. I have no idea what it is about this son of a bitch that makes me so flustered. Maybe, it's the shadows I can see dancing in his azure eyes. Michael openly admitted he's a complicated man. That's the last thing I need.

"Thanks." Daniel accepts the takeout coffee.

"On the house," Martha replies with a genuine smile. "We missed your handsome face around here."

"You'll have to start charging me sometime. I haven't paid for coffee here since 1963."

"Not today, young man."

He scratches his lightly stubbled cheek. "Not sure I feel young these days."

Martha winks at him. "Age is but a number. Take this old lady's advice and find yourself some happiness before you spend another century alone."

Leaning over the counter to kiss Martha's cheek, Daniel manages a strange half-smile. So he does have a gentle side. Seeing them interact like old friends is another shock to the system.

The tilt to his lips is gone just as quickly. He whispers

goodbye then strides away without sparing us another glance. I can't stop myself from watching him leave.

When I turn to Raven, she rolls her eyes at me. "You have it bad, huh?"

"What? No I don't."

"Oh, please. Tell that to the big, puppy-dog eyes you were making all over him."

I wrinkle my nose. "Gross."

"Come on. I know you're dying to ask."

"Fine! What's his deal?"

Raven shrugs, inspecting her pink-painted nails. "He's a miserable bastard."

"Elaborate."

"Daniel doesn't care about anyone or anything but his precious Elder Caine. They visit every year or so. And he's been Michael's friend for decades."

Glancing out the window, I watch Daniel walk across the grounds with long, powerful strides, like he's trying to get as far away from us as possible.

I rub the ache in my chest. It feels like he's torn my already damaged heart out and taken the fractured pieces with him as a trophy. That only strengthens my resolve to avoid him for the rest of his visit.

"He'll be gone soon," she offers.

"Good. I hate that asshole."

"Uh-huh. I believe you."

Elbowing her in the ribs, I ignore the shit-eating grin on her face. "Don't you have somewhere to be?"

"Unfortunately, yes. Walk me to work?"

"Sure."

Leaving Martha's with a wave, we step back out into the morning mist. Raven resumes her mindless chatter for the entire walk over to the hospital.

I tune her out, my mind occupied by cruel blue irises and

that weird half-smile. The glimpse of something gentle and tender in the way he kissed Martha's cheek.

Is that the real Daniel?

Does anyone else see it?

Shaking myself, I crush the pointless thoughts. It doesn't matter. He'll be gone soon, taking this strange, empty feeling in my chest with him.

THE CHARIOT

CHAPTER 6

THE DAY I DIE – ISLAND

*S*harp banging on the door rouses me from the grip of sleep. I shoot upright on the sofa, my legs tangled in a soft, knitted blanket that covered me as I napped.

It comes again—harder this time.

"Dammit," I hiss, untangling myself.

By the time I've made it to the door, the banging has become constant and unrelenting. I throw the door open with a snarl and find an unwanted grimace on the other side waiting for me.

"You," Brunt snarls. "Come with me."

"Not a chance."

"That wasn't a damn request."

He grabs my arm in his iron-grip and drags me from the apartment. I shout and thrash against him, hating the feel of his skin on mine.

"Where are you taking me?"

Brunt remains silent.

"I have a right to know!"

"Shut up," he snaps.

He refuses to let go, holding me prisoner as we ride the

elevator downstairs. Still fighting against him, I'm dragged outside and towards the towering administration building at the centre of the facility.

It's marked with huge stone pillars and curved bay windows carved from dark, polished wood. Inside, the workers seated behind the various desks give us startled looks as we pass.

Brunt pays them no attention, and no one moves to challenge him on his rough handling. They all quickly avert their eyes.

Marched down a long, carpet-lined corridor, we stop outside a mahogany door. Brunt knocks once then waits, still holding me in his painfully tight grip.

"Enter."

Pushing the door open, he shoves me inside the stiflingly hot office. Sweat immediately beads on my brow from the heat pumping out of a wide, lit fireplace in the corner, surrounded by packed bookshelves.

The room is huge—intimidatingly so. The ceiling practically stretches up into the heavens, an impressive scene painted directly onto the domed material. I recognise Michelangelo's artwork from school. Two fingertips have been immortalised with paint, barely brushing each other in a tentative whisper.

Sat behind a gold-legged, black marble desk, Ravius looks up from the pile of paperwork he's studying and watches me stumble into the room. He dismisses Brunt with a flick of his fingers.

"Leave us."

When the door clicks shut behind me without an uttered word of protest, I gulp hard. I'm in the lion's den now, trapped with nowhere to run or hide. A shiver rolls down my spine.

"Lexi," Ravius greets stiffly. "Please take a seat."

"Was it really necessary to drag me here like that?"

"You've been avoiding me, and we need to talk."

I huff, taking a seat in one of the high-backed chairs opposite his desk. Fingers laced together, he props his pointed chin on top to stare directly at me.

"How are you settling in?"

"Peachy," I grumble.

"Is my facility not to your liking?"

"Not when I'm being held here against my will."

Ravius sighs, his thin nose wrinkled with obvious impatience. "I thought we already discussed this. You're not a prisoner. This is your home now."

A lump gathering in my throat, I stare right back. "What can I help you with, *Elder*?"

He blanches at my cold tone.

"We still have much to discuss, Lexi."

"I don't know anything that can help you."

"Now that's where we disagree." He leans forward in anticipation. "I want to see your memories. You're going to show them to me."

"Excuse me?"

"I may enter your mind to view your memories of the meadow. I want to see for myself what happened to you."

"Enter my mind?" I scoff. "Like hell."

"That wasn't a request, Lexi. This is important."

His voice carries an edge of desperation. Looking into his wild eyes, swirling with a kaleidoscope of colours, I can feel it. The urgency that's led me to this room, trapped opposite an Elder, on his knees and begging for answers.

"Why?" I ask him.

"Because before you, we hadn't had a new admission in over two years. The Vitae has never acted this sporadically before. I need to know what's going on for the sake of my people and our future."

"Are you religious?" I blurt, my eyes drifting back up to the expertly painted ceiling.

He shakes his head. "I am too old for blind faith. I have seen civilisations fall, wars waged, dynasties rise and land conquered. The boy who listened to Bible stories a millennia ago is a distant memory to me now."

Staring at him, I can't help wondering again exactly how old this unfathomable man is.

"For centuries, I fought to find a home in this world and to collect the lost souls cursed with this existence. All the while never knowing our true purpose on this earth and the why of it all. I never thought I would be able to answer those questions... until you."

Looking back up at the ceiling, I consider the fingertips again. God and man, connected through a single point of divinity. I may not like him, but I can't help but pity Ravius. Forever fumbling in the dark for the unknown.

"So no, I am not religious," he finishes. "I am, however, a pragmatist. There is a reason why we're here, and I've been searching for it for a very long time. Please help me, Lexi. Help me to understand."

Swallowing past the apprehension crawling up my throat, I gesture towards my head. "Look, then."

"You will allow me to?"

"Yes. Just... fuck, make it quick."

Ravius nods, his eyes lit with a gleam of excitement. "Thank you."

Unbuttoning his cuffs as he rounds the desk, Ravius rolls up his shirt sleeves. I wipe my sticky hands on my grey sweats. He takes the seat next to me then inches his chair closer.

"I need you to relax. Take some deep breaths and calm your mind."

"Calm my mind?" I quip back.

"You're tensing up, mentally preparing for an attack. I'm not going to hurt you, Lexi. You won't even feel me."

"How do you know that I'm tensing up?"

Ravius's smile is sly. "I told you that I have an affinity for the mind. I access the mental state of others, whether to peacefully examine what lay inside or show them the images that I choose."

Flinching, I make myself take a deep breath. All I can think about is the horrifying sight of my own body as seen through his eyes. I know full well just what images he's capable of inserting into my mind. I don't want to be faced with that again.

"Can you read my mind?"

A dry chuckle tumbles from his mouth. "No. It's not quite the same thing."

Breathing in and out, I roll my shoulders, letting my eyes slide shut. The fire crackles in the corner, soothing my anxiety. I focus on it, attempting to tune out everything else.

"That's it," Ravius praises.

After several silent seconds, I take another breath. "I'm ready."

Heat begins to rise in my temples almost immediately, the same as it did in the hospital. Warmth trickles through my extremities, pumping a thick, treacle-like sensation into my veins.

"Show me the meadow," his voice croons, sounding like it's echoing from inside my head. "Let the memory of it fill your mind. Take me back to the place you remember."

I let my mind wander, rewinding the confusing blur of time that's passed since I woke up here. Pushing aside the bleak memories that rushed back when I awoke in Ravius's care, I keep scrolling back, past the hospital and the blinding agony of my first moments in a stiff, semi-alive body.

And there it is.

With the endless verdure, rolling hills of luminous green stretching on for mile after mile and crystal-clear blue sky, it's as magnificent as I remember. There are no voices or shouting, nothing but a lightly whistling wind and chirping birdsong.

"How quaint."

Standing next to me, Ravius looks exactly the same with his crisp white shirt sleeves rolled up and hands clasped regally behind his back.

"How are you here?" I gasp.

He flashes me a brilliant smile. "I followed your mind here."

We begin to walk at a leisurely pace, padding through soft, vibrant, green grass and sprouting wildflowers. Everything looks the same as before, but I can truly appreciate the beauty now. I'm no longer a whisper on the breeze, floating without form.

"Is this it?" Ravius asks, disappointment lacing his tone. "This is all you remember?"

I can't help scoffing at him.

"What did you expect? Angels floating around, pearly gates and a shining fucking throne?"

Rather than answer, he spins in all directions, searching for something unknown.

"What more do you want? It's beautiful, peaceful, and there's no suffering or noise. I was happy here."

"I was hoping for a little more than this," he answers evenly.

Sinking down onto the grass, I stretch my legs out and dig my nails into the earth to feel the dampness of the soil. It feels real, even though I know this is all in my imagination. The soft blades of grass somehow stroke against my skin.

Ravius sits down next to me with a sigh, still studying his surroundings. I feel a momentary flash of sympathy. Years of waiting for answers… and this is all he got. Nothing but lost memories of a far-off land.

"I'm sorry you didn't find what you're looking for," I offer.

He waves me off. "It just doesn't make sense. If this is it, why don't we all remember? What's so special about this place that no one else recollects their time here? Why are you the exception?"

"Maybe there is more, and I just don't remember it?"

His head whips towards me, interest sparkling in his iridescent eyes.

"How so?" he replies.

"Well, if we are assuming that I have been gifted these memories, then whoever made that decision could have taken some away too. What if I only remember what I'm allowed to?"

"An interesting theory."

His angular features morph as excitement takes root, causing his lips to split in a wide, almost frantic smile.

"Show me what happened next," he orders.

I comply, throwing myself back into the traumatic memory of what led me back into the dark trenches of reality. The crippling pain. Scorching. Blinding. Energy rushing through me. Being forced back into my body, hot-wired by a powerful force.

Once the memories are complete, my eyes fling open, and I'm back in Ravius's warm office, safe and sound. He's breathing heavily while sat opposite, his own eyes wide after enduring the reawakening with me.

"That was rather unpleasant." He rubs his temples.

I snort in derision. "Yep."

He gets up from his chair and begins to pace. "It's fascinating that you were able to feel the Vitae at work. It's almost like the energy wanted to be acknowledged by you, like it was part of you somehow."

Prickles pierce my chest. "I… don't think so."

"In the hospital, I told you that I suspected you were gifted, that there's something unique about you. This has only confirmed my beliefs."

"I'm nobody. There's nothing special about me."

"That's the thing about the Vitae," he continues, ignoring

my comment. "Once reanimation is over, it leaves the body and returns to whatever source it flows from. But I can sense a spark of it still inside of you, humming away. That is the source of your power, Lexi."

Rubbing a hand over my tight chest, I try not to feel the full impact of his words, but it hits me regardless. *My power.* Something I've never had before, in any sense of the word. Instead, I've always been the victim. The punching bag. The nobody.

"This is… too much," I choke out.

"I know this is overwhelming, but you deserve to know the truth. You've been granted this ability for an important reason… even if we don't know what that is yet."

Ducking behind his desk, Ravius retrieves a slim, black key card from the drawer then slides it across to me. I gingerly accept it, running my thumb over the matte black surface.

"What's this?"

"You wanted answers, right? About our history? This will grant you access to the special collections section in the library. You'll find all of your answers there."

"You're kidding?" I gawp at him.

He smiles patiently. "You've earned my trust, Lexi. I admire your curiosity and strength. It is clear to me now that you will be very important to our society and future. It's only fair you know what world you're joining."

This is a huge act of trust, an extended olive branch across the chasm that's separated us. I tuck the key card into my pocket and muster up a smile.

"Thank you."

"You're welcome," he says genuinely. "I don't need to mention that what you will see is top-level classified, of course. I'm sure you can understand the importance of keeping these secrets."

Rising from my chair, I nod. "I understand."

"Then you're free to leave."

He's playing the good guy by offering me his secrets, but I'm not naïve. Ravius is playing his own game. This act of good faith is exactly that—an act.

I move to leave before he can change his mind. Wrapping a hand around the doorknob, I'm about to flee his office when the door swings open, and a firm barrel chest smacks straight into me.

"Rav—"

Cut off mid-sentence, Daniel steadies me before I'm knocked off my feet. Electric warmth from his hands burns through my t-shirt while the scents of evergreen and peppercorns assault me.

"Lexi," he growls out.

I plant my feet so I don't fall. "Daniel."

At the sound of his name, he abruptly releases me and takes a big step to the side. I immediately feel cold as the electricity fades, leaving a dull ache in my chest behind.

"Excuse me," I mutter.

Moving as fast as I can, I hear him mumble an excuse to Ravius before heavy, determined footsteps chase after me. His shoulders soon block my path down the corridor.

"I saw you getting dragged over here." His cold gaze sweeps over me. "You alright?"

"You care?"

He stares me down. "Answer the question."

"I'm fine."

"What are you doing talking to Ravius?"

I gape up at him. "He's my Elder, and frankly, that's really none of your business."

Daniel's defined jawline clenches tight. "The Elders have their own agendas. Trust me."

"What does that mean?"

"It means you should watch your back."

"Why do you care?" I challenge, an eyebrow cocked.

He studies me for an extended pause, a confusing

maelstrom of unidentifiable emotions swirling in his bright, oceanic eyes. I feel like I'm drowning in those deep blue depths with no land in sight.

"I don't care," he deadpans, shutting down the brief glimpse of buried feelings. "This conversation is over."

When he tries to leave, I automatically snap out a hand to snag his shirt sleeve. Daniel startles, yanked back on the balls of his feet.

I'm so sick of being dismissed. Determined to chew him out, I cling on tight to his wrist. My fingertips brush up against his pulse point, finding bare skin.

The effect is instantaneous.

Everything grinds to a halt.

My lungs seize. Heart stutters. Blood freezes. Vision blackens. It feels like I've been swept out to sea and dumped in a vat of burning-hot, fiery lava, the heat lashing at my tingling skin.

Teetering on legs that have turned into gelatine, I feel my knees give out. The floor rushes up to meet me until a strong pair of arms latches around my waist.

We fall together.

Irrevocably.

With the certainty of the universe binding us, I collapse in Daniel's arms, my entire body alight with sparks of racing electric. I'm on fire. Tingling. Burning. Being reborn all over again.

"What's happening?" he grunts in pain.

My head lolls, too heavy to hold up. "You f-feel it too?"

Gasping, his brows furrow together. "It burns."

Pain snaps between us like an elastic band, but it isn't unwelcome. Instead, it feels like having every last dead skin cell sloughed off all at once, ready to be born anew.

"Stop," Daniel snarls. "Whatever you're doing to me... stop!"

"It's not me," I grind out.

As quickly as it started, the feeling disappears. Flames are doused in icy pinpricks of dread, and the remaining vestiges of my vision white out, devoured whole by nothingness.

I'm thrown into the depths of darkness.

Powerless, but not alone.

XVII

THE STAR

CHAPTER 7

DANCE WITH MY DEMONS – BLAME MY YOUTH

lood.
Ash.

Fire.

Deathly scents lay thick on my tongue, lacing the air with the familiar tang of death. It's all around me. Mortality. Crumpled bodies and blood-slick grass.

I'm surrounded by corpses, shot and ripped apart. Crimson sprays every brick, wall and window. Splatters of death mark the scene of a horrific battle, fought until the very end.

I did this.

Deep down, the realisation fills my veins like liquid concrete. Spreading, seeping into my extremities, dragging me further down into the pits of hell with the weight of my guilt.

They died for me.

It's my fault.

"Lexi. Open your eyes."

Distantly, I feel the warmth of a hand shaking my shoulder. It doesn't cut through the cloying aroma of blood and death in the air, keeping me trapped in this awful nightmare.

I can't run.

Can't hide.

Can't escape what I've done.

"Come on, Lex. Time to wake up."

Light breaks on the horizon, slicing through ash clouds and darkness. It spreads, lighting the path from this disaster zone back into the warmth of reality. I follow the blossoming sunshine with open arms.

"Mmmm," I groan.

"That's it. You're okay."

But it isn't sunlight. I'm not trapped in a bloodstained field, surrounded by corpses. A light hangs above me, illuminating the bright-white, clinical space of the hospital room.

I'm back where I started. It was just a nightmare. The real world settles around me as I come back to life, leaving the vivid dream behind in the recesses of my mind.

It wasn't real.

I'm... still here.

"There she is." Michael sits in the chair next to me, his small hand resting on my arm. "Thought we'd lost you for a moment there."

"M-Michael?" I whimper, squinting into the light.

"Take a moment. You've been out for a few hours."

"Hours?" I squeak in panic, my chest constricting.

He looks around the hospital room before turning back to me. His sweet, freckle-spotted face is marred by a worried frown.

"Do you remember what happened?"

My mind stutters. I can remember Brunt dragging me across the courtyard to his master and suffering through the intrusion of Ravius searching through my memories.

Then I left... only to be halted.

Daniel.

"Shit!" I attempt to sit up, my head spinning with dizziness. "Where... where is he? Is Daniel okay? I hurt him!"

Michael offers me a wry grin. "You did a little more than that, sweetheart."

"What are you talking about? Where is he?"

"Daniel's fine." He pats my arm reassuringly. "He's in the room across the hall. Still out cold."

"What the fuck happened to us?"

"It's a little hard to explain." Michael blows out a leaden breath. "We haven't seen a bonded pair in decades. None of us expected this, let alone with someone like Daniel."

Blinking hard, all I can do is stare at him in bemusement. Whatever the hell he means, it sure sounds bad.

"Explain," I demand.

"You should rest."

"Explain, Michael!"

He sighs loudly. "Sometimes, when a Redeemed possesses a high level of power, the Vitae seeks to balance it out by binding them with another individual. We call this soul bound."

My mouth clicks open and shut. "Soul bound?"

Michael nods solemnly. "That's what happened to you both, Lex. Your gift chose Daniel. He's been bound to you."

Struggling to pull in a full breath, I feel like I'm freefalling into a pit of vipers. Panic is battling to rise up and consume me again. But something holds it back, a low humming of power that wasn't there before, warming my chest.

I can feel it.

There's a fire burning inside of me.

Pleased, fucking *satisfied* fire.

For the first time, I can actually sense the power they've all spoken of. It's living and breathing deep inside of me, louder than ever before, purring like an engine slowly warming up.

"Oh my God. What have I done?"

"You're both going to be fine," Michael rushes to assure

me. "Things will just be… a little different from now on. We can figure this all out."

"I don't understand. I didn't choose anyone, let alone him!"

Spitting the last word, I squeeze my eyes shut, willing the last few hours to vanish. I've barely come to terms with my new reality. Now... this? It cannot be happening.

"Being soul bound isn't a bad thing." Michael pats my knee. "It means you will have better control over your gift. Daniel will be able to help you control the Vitae by syphoning off excess energy."

"But… Daniel isn't gifted."

"No." He shrugs, lips twisting in a grimace. "Bindings only happen between gifted pairs. That's what makes this so unexpected. It should be impossible."

"I'm getting really fucking sick of that word."

"You're rewriting what we all thought was possible," a new voice interjects.

Standing in the doorway to my hospital room, Ravius leans against the frame, those incisive eyes lasered directly on me. I shrivel beneath the weight of his fascinated gaze.

"Michael." Ravius tilts his head, silently instructing Michael to leave.

But Michael doesn't budge, remaining protectively close at my side. Ravius's lip curls in a displeased sneer.

"You may leave us now."

"She needs to rest," Michael argues. "Whatever conversation you want to have can wait."

"Enough. You've been given an order."

"Ravius—"

"I said enough! Leave us."

Eyes downturned, Michael mutters a curse under his breath before standing up. I internally beg for him to stay, hating the way Ravius looks at me like he wants to pull apart my insides for closer examination.

Taking Michael's place, Ravius sits down at my bedside. I shift upright, my hands trembling from the current of electricity still pouring through me.

"Lexi." His voice is flat. "We've taken things slowly up until now, but this is a very serious situation. We haven't had a soul bound pair in over sixty years."

"I don't understand what's happening."

"It means that you're a great deal more powerful than we anticipated. Your gift is growing by the hour. It won't be long before it manifests fully."

Right on cue, the fire licking at my insides peaks in a blistering wave, as if reacting to his words. I have to take a deep breath to fill my scorched lungs.

"Manifests? You mean this isn't it?"

"Far from it," Ravius says. "The Vitae inside of you will only grow in strength until your manifestation when it will reach its full potential. You are far stronger than we initially thought."

"I don't want this. Any of it!"

"You don't want power, Lexi?" His gaze burns with anticipation. "Power beyond your wildest imagination? You could raze our entire empire to the ground with a mere glance."

Realisation dawns. I shift farther away from him and the excited, almost manic gleam in his eyes. I may not want power, but Ravius certainly does.

"You will begin a training regimen with me immediately," he continues. "I'm afraid we don't have time to waste."

"Do I have a choice?"

Flicking invisible lint off his pristine suit, he flashes me a warning look. "If you lose control of your gift, it could have devastating consequences. No. You have no choice."

Training with Ravius. That means spending more time with him poking around inside my head. Letting him see my vulnerabilities. My weaknesses. I can't think of anything worse.

"What about Daniel? He isn't even from here. What happens when it's time for him to leave?"

"We will come to an arrangement," Ravius answers vaguely. "Non-gifted Redeemed do not bond. This is an unprecedented situation."

That can't mean anything good. Not in this confusing world of secrets and subterfuge. Power doesn't protect you here. Now that I'm under the threat of Ravius's fascination, I feel even more exposed.

"I'll give you some time to process everything that's happened. We will begin tomorrow at first light. Come to my office."

Nodding stiffly, I remain cowered away from him. "Ravius… what's going to happen to me?"

He trails his eyes over me, eventually settling on the terrified look I'm sure is painted all over my face.

"I don't know," he admits.

Unnerved by his response, I watch him leave, his suit jacket flapping behind him. The door clicks shut, and I'm left with my racing thoughts, wishing Michael would return to comfort me.

Staring up at the ceiling, I'm still shaking all over. Lightning is coursing through me, invisible yet all-consuming. The feeling is indescribable. My entire body is itching with pent up energy.

I'm out of bed and moving fast before my mind can catch up. It isn't a conscious decision. The power within me is calling out, screaming for a release, leading me to the one thing it's craving.

Him.

Bare feet padding over smooth mahogany floors, I creep through the hospital. The sun has fallen while I was passed out, bathing the entire facility in darkness.

I don't know where I'm going. Hell, I don't even need to. The humming drags me onwards into the shadows, past countless doors and empty hospital rooms.

Across the hall and several doors down, I freeze. The intensity of the fire burning inside me has picked up. It feels like an inferno is blazing beneath my flushed skin.

Creaking the door open, I'm dragged into the room. Unwilling. Terrified. Afraid of exactly what, or rather who, I'll find inside. But I can't run from this.

His mammoth frame curled up on the bed's mattress, Daniel's back rises and falls with each breath. I stand for several seconds, watching him sleeping peacefully.

Just looking at him calms me down in a way that feels so natural, it's unnerving. His cold, miserable exterior has never set me at ease, but now, I'm itching to move even closer to his sleeping form.

My feet move. Closer. Closer still. Soon, I'm standing right next to him, fingertips skating over the soft material of his t-shirt. I'm terrified to touch his skin again, but I can't stop myself.

Gently stroking down the hardened lines of his thick bicep, I relish in the warmth of his body. Daniel stirs in his sleep, a deep, rumbling purr of contentment emanating from his throat.

A mere touch is enough to douse the slow embers crisping my insides. I take in my first real breath since waking up, my lungs savouring the much-needed influx of oxygen.

He's literally the air in my lungs.

And I don't even fucking know him.

"Pen," he whimpers, barely audible.

I never thought I'd see Daniel, king of the assholes and lover of stony silences, whispering so brokenly in his sleep. Let alone mewling another woman's name.

Removing my hand, I begin to back away, chest stinging

with rejection. I'm being ridiculous. We don't know each other. He didn't ask for this, and he owes me nothing.

But the moment our skin contact breaks, his eyes slam open, revealing glazed-over orbs reminiscent of a tropical ocean. It takes several blinks for his vision to clear.

"You," he rasps throatily.

"Hi."

"Where…?"

"The hospital," I supply quickly. "We've both been out of it for a bit. How do you feel?"

His thick brows draw together. "I'm not sure. Different. Strange. What happened?"

Hands squeezing into fists, I look everywhere but at him. "I'm so sorry, Daniel. I didn't mean to do this. Believe me."

He sits up, wincing a little. "Do what?"

I gesture between us. "This… thing. It was an accident. I touched you, and next thing I knew, it was already done."

"What was done, dammit?"

Meeting his eyes again, I summon a flicker of courage. "We're soul bound."

Silenced, Daniel just stares at me. Blinks. Stutters out a shocked breath. Everything but responding to the news I've permanently, fucking *magically* tied his miserable backside to me.

"That's impossible," he finally croaks. "Only gifted pairs can be soul bound. I'm not gifted."

"So I've heard."

"Then you must be mistaken. This… we… it can't be."

Sighing, I reach out a trembling hand then rest it flat on his burnished skin. With the full contact, heat sweeps over me again, rising in an excited swarm of bees to fill my palm.

It moves—expanding, reaching across the chasm, following the beat of its own silent rhythm. I can't control it even if I wanted to. The force flows from me and trickles into the man whose life I've ruined.

Daniel stiffens, his eyes blowing wide and pupils dilating. A groan of what sounds a lot like pleasure slips from his full lips.

"Michael said that you can syphon off my excess energy or something," I mutter. "Ravius wants to start training me immediately. Apparently, my gift will only grow stronger."

Eyes barely open now, Daniel manages a head shake. "I can feel it. That's what I've been feeling all along."

"What?"

"The Vitae is pouring out of you, there's so much of it."

"So you feel it too? The electricity?"

"Yeah. I feel it."

"You're such an asshole." I glower at him. "I thought I was going crazy and imagining this fucked up feeling between us."

"It's not like I knew this was even possible." He curses under his breath. "What the actual fuck is this?"

"My thoughts precisely. I'm so sorry, Daniel. I didn't do this on purpose. I'll find a way to fix this, I swear."

Staring down at his clenched hands, his expression filters through a myriad of emotions. Shock. Disbelief. Even denial. It hurts more than I'd care to admit to see his reaction.

He doesn't want me.

I don't blame him. Everything about this situation is messed up—even more than it already was. But somehow, in the most irrational parts of my mind, his obvious rejection still stings.

"You can't," he snaps wearily. "A soul binding is everlasting. It cannot be broken."

"You mean… this is forever?"

"Forever," he echoes.

Staring at each other, neither of us knows what to say. I'm caught between running as far away from him as possible and falling into his arms for a sliver of comfort.

"I'm sorry." I back away towards the door. "I can't do this."

"Lexi—"

"We're total strangers! You hate my guts."

Pain sinks into his features. "I don't hate you."

"Could've fooled me. You were an asshole from the moment we met."

"You scared me. That's why."

My feet freeze, locking me in place. "What?"

He shifts awkwardly in the hospital bed. "It's like I could sense there was something off about you. My reflex was to protect myself from what I considered to be a threat."

"I sat at the same fucking table as you and tried to make conversation. How on earth does that constitute a threat?"

"I'm sorry, alright?" He sighs wearily. "I didn't know you would end up being my mate."

There's that word again. *Mate.* Like we're some predestined, written in the stars shit instead of two ill-suited people trapped in a never-ending nightmare.

"I don't even know you. You're talking about being mates, and I can't... I can't fucking do this."

"We don't have much of a choice," he says flatly. "The pain we felt when our souls intertwined is only a fraction of what we'll feel if we're apart."

Horror invades every inch of my mind.

"I can't do this to you!"

"You didn't. The Vitae did."

Moving farther away, I try to leave the room, but Daniel gasps in pain. I move closer again, and each step lessens the wince that marks his strained expression.

"Oh my God." I stare at him. "This is horrific. I can't even walk away from you."

"It's not ideal," he grunts. "Just... fucking come closer, will you? My head hurts, and I can't move yet."

Each step back to his bedside eases the excruciating ache in my chest. It feels like a black hole has opened up inside me, expelling anguish and fear, and only he can plug that gap.

"Closer," he rasps.

"Daniel, please."

"Closer, Lexi."

Taking a tentative seat on the edge of his bed, I can feel the heat from his body curling around me, silently whispering for me to move nearer.

I want to.

Lord, I fucking need to.

This is the stony-faced man who's held me at arm's length since we met. Even the night he found me in the middle of a panic attack, he ran away as fast as he could.

Now he's staring at me like I'm his salvation and doom, all wrapped up into one. When he shifts on the bed to make room for me to snuggle in, defeat visibly seeps over him.

"Just climb in already."

"We're so not doing this," I protest.

"We don't have much of a choice."

Too exhausted to fight him, I let my body sag, curling up in the shell of heat where he was laying. Daniel drags the sheets up to cover me then moves closer until his body is lined up against mine.

A breath I didn't even know I was holding whooshes out of me. He's fitted perfectly to my back like our bodies were made to do exactly this. I can feel every solid inch of him.

"Breathe," he murmurs tiredly. "We can figure this mess out."

"How?"

His sigh tickles the back of my neck. "I don't know, but we will."

"You just said this is forever. If that's true, I've ruined your life. I can't take it back."

And I don't want to.

Silencing the traitorous whisper, I gulp hard, willing myself to keep that secret safely buried inside. It's just the Vitae speaking for me. I don't actually want this man. Not in a million years.

That doesn't change the fact that I've never felt as safe as I do right now, locked in his arms, feeling the gentle stir of his breath on my over-sensitised skin.

"I don't know you," I whisper brokenly.

Every survival instinct in my head is telling me to run. Hide. Cower from this terrifying, cold-hearted man and the pain I know he can so easily inflict. Even to a total stranger.

But I can't.

Not now, not ever.

"As much as I don't like this either, it happened for a reason. The Vitae has chosen us. Your soul knows mine now."

"What does that mean for us?"

His chest vibrates with a bitter laugh. "I have no clue. We're screwed, love. Completely and utterly screwed."

When his breathing evens out, I know he's dropped back off, his body slackening against mine. I'm left in a stranger's arms with no clue how I ended up here.

He's right.

We're screwed.

THE MOON

CHAPTER 8

WE ARE WHO WE ARE – MISSIO

*W*aking up is never fun.

The harshness of reality awaits.

Enveloped in warmth and the spicy scent of peppercorns, I shift against the solid surface that's spooning me. But it isn't a mattress. It's warm and smells fucking delicious.

Something is prodding into my lower belly, rock-hard and generous. It takes a moment for the penny to drop. My lids fling open with a rush of panic, and I'm staring into Daniel's eyes.

"Are you… watching me sleep?"

"Sorry," he rumbles. "Just thinking."

Wriggling away from him, the rigid press of his cock disappears. Pretty sure I'm blushing my ass off right now. That tiny half-smile is back, causing my pulse to spike.

"Shut up," I grumble.

"You uncomfortable, princess?"

"Not your fucking princess, jackass. You were the one all snuggled up into me like a snoring puppy."

His expression grows serious. "It's been a long time since I shared a bed with anyone."

"Well, don't get used to it."

"I used to…" He runs a hand across his darkened stubble. "Never mind. How are you feeling?"

Sitting up, I stretch my limbs, searching for the burning fire that lashed at my insides yesterday. It's quietened to a low hum, the embers curling in my gut and pumping heat into my veins.

"Better," I admit.

"From what I understand of soul bindings, prolonged physical contact helps with the transfer of energy."

"Does that mean you get my gift?"

"Not quite." He sits up, rolling his shoulders. "More like I can safely syphon it off so the Vitae doesn't overwhelm you."

"How do you do that?"

"Fuck if I know."

Covering my face with my hands, I let out a rattled breath. "We really need to talk to Ravius. He'll know what to do."

Daniel groans. "We can't trust him. Ravius wants power, just like his brother. You can't be the one to give it to him."

"What choice do I have?"

Cracking his neck, he pushes back the bed's covers. "I don't know, alright? This is all new for me too."

"Well, we need a plan. Fast. Ravius wants me in his office to begin training, and if I don't go, he'll just send Brunt after me."

"Shit," Daniel snaps.

I stand up and stretch, my body filled with pleasant warmth. Despite what happened to lead us here, that was the best night's sleep I've had in a long time. I won't tell him that though.

"You can't go alone, Lexi. Ravius is a better man than his brother, but he still has an agenda. It isn't safe."

"Caine's your boss. How can you say that?"

"Because I know him better than anyone." Stretching his

long legs out, Daniel climbs to his feet. "Caine's an egotistical son of a bitch. He thinks The Redeemed are God-chosen and above everyone else."

"God-chosen?" I repeat in disgust. "Nothing about this life makes us better than the rest of the world. We're prisoners here."

"Don't let Ravius catch you saying that," Daniel warns.

"I've said it to his damn face, and I'll say it again. I couldn't care less."

The tiny smile that graces his lips makes butterflies explode in my belly. I mentally crush them. This asshole cannot get under my skin with his confusing, whiplash-causing emotions and broken-hearted half-smiles.

"Regardless, we found peace by joining forces with the rest of the world when we signed the accords," he continues. "But Caine doesn't see it that way."

"Why?"

"He's driven by prejudice against humankind. That's what makes him so dangerous—his thirst for supreme power. To him, The Redeemed are the superior race."

"We're not better than anyone else."

"No, we're not. But power changes people."

His words are quietly spoken but strong, unequivocal. He sees something in Caine that we can't see—the man behind the scarred mask. Danger wrapped in a formidable shell.

Looking into his eyes, I see the fear there, buried beneath his careful persona. Deep down, he's terrified of the man he works for. Seeing Daniel look afraid shakes me to my core.

"What are you so afraid of?" I dare to ask.

"Being soul bound is a big deal in our world," Daniel explains, darkness infecting his expression. "It means you're powerful. But claiming someone who's not even gifted? We don't know what that means."

"So?"

"So, Caine can never find out about this. He would be fascinated by you, and trust me, you don't want that kind of attention. Not from him."

"What would he do to me?"

"Nothing good," he mutters grimly.

Tendrils of fear tighten around my throat. "Ravius and Michael already know about us. Can we trust them to keep our secret?"

"Ravius wants to be better than all of the Elders. Having you on his side will achieve exactly that. He'll keep quiet just to stop Caine from interfering with his new toy."

"I'm not a fucking toy!" I snap before his words begin to process. "Wait, you're saying I can manipulate him."

Daniel nods. "I know this is far from ideal, but we can use what happened to our advantage. If Ravius wants your power, he'll have to keep you safe."

"From what?"

"The entire world, Lexi. Gifts always come at a cost." He casts me a lingering look, full of unspoken concern. "You're not safe here anymore. Hell, you're not safe anywhere."

Chest aching with the rapid beat of my heart against my ribcage, I wrestle with his words. Ravius told me I couldn't leave because it's not safe in the outside world for a member of The Redeemed.

But what happens when the safe place itself becomes a threat? Not even the forest-lined grounds of the facility are safe for me now. Not after what happened. I've painted a target on our backs.

If my miraculous memories and so-called gift weren't enough to make me a target, creating a soul bond with an ungifted Redeemed has sealed my fate.

But it isn't just my fate, is it? Eve is still out there. Alone. Afraid. Unprotected. I can't find a way to get back to her if I can't even protect myself from circling predators.

"Shit." I begin to panic, my breath coming in short rasps. "I've doomed us both."

"Something like that."

"You're not helping, Daniel! Why aren't you freaking out?"

Circling the hospital bed, he approaches with his hands raised, as if trying not to startle a frightened animal. The look on his drawn face is resigned.

"Panicking isn't going to make this go away," he says gruffly. "We need to stay calm and figure out what we're going to do now."

"How much longer are you even here for?"

His face pales. "A few more days."

"And what happens then?"

"I… don't know."

"Then don't tell me not to freak out!" I snarl at him.

My temper snaps, and heat burns through me. I can feel my gift rising, hissing in fury. Daniel's eyes widen as the tiniest of flames dance across my palms, licking at my skin.

I hold out my hands, staring at the otherworldly fire. "How do I put it out?"

"You need to calm down. The Vitae is tied to your emotions. Your gift is reacting to your fear."

"Tell me to calm down one more time, and I'll be sticking this fire somewhere very bloody painful for you."

"Lexi, focus. Breathe."

Squeezing my eyes shut, I suck in a breath, willing my anger to abate. When I reopen my eyes a few seconds later, the fire has vanished from sight.

"There," he murmurs.

"How did I do that?"

"You can do it if you focus and believe in yourself. This gift is a part of you. It can be controlled."

I shake out my trembling hands. "It's only going to get worse. I don't know if I can do this."

"You aren't alone."

"You're gonna help me?" I snort sarcastically.

"According to you, it's my job now. You've bound me to you for life. There's no getting out of this, even if I want to."

Looking up at his face—lips parted on a ragged breath, thick lashes that are impossibly long and cast shadows across his stubble-strewn cheekbones—I can't stop myself from wanting the truth.

"Do you want to get out of this?"

We stare at each other, inches apart but caught on two sides of an impassable ocean. I don't know him. I don't even know if I want to. But something binds us now. The inevitability of fate.

There's no escaping it.

No running.

Whatever's coming in the future, we'll face it together. Whether we want to or not. It makes me sick to admit it, but a broken, needy part of me is glad.

All I've ever wanted is someone to keep me safe. To love me. Protect me. Cherish me. The tumultuous force inside me has claimed Daniel as its own, so now I have no choice.

We're stuck together.

Come hell or high water.

"No one's needed me for a long time," he admits, looking down at his scarred knuckles. "And the last person who did.... Well, it didn't end well for her."

"What happened?"

"She's gone. Has been for decades. No one's meant a damn to me since, and that's just the way I like it."

Until now, a treacherous voice whispers. He didn't coax me out of that panic attack for his own entertainment. Something pulled him to me in my moment of need. Perhaps, the Vitae was planning this all along.

Daniel moves towards the door. "We have to talk to Ravius. He can train you to control your gift."

But my feet are frozen, and I can't move an inch. Ravius may be the lesser of two evils if what Daniel says about his Elder is true, but that doesn't make me trust him.

Daniel must read the trepidation on my face as he studies me, unmoved and trembling. I hold his intense gaze, the shimmering cerulean hue of his eyes flecked with faint streaks of silver.

"You're afraid."

"Wouldn't you be in my position?" I return shakily.

He flashes me a half-smile, pulling the lines around his mouth taut. "I will keep you safe, Lexi. That I can promise."

"I don't need you."

His smile falls, like it never existed. The brief glimpse of softness disappears, instantly replaced by familiar coldness. Somehow, the return to status quo is comforting. I know where I stand with asshole Daniel, not soft, gentle Daniel, full of whispered promises.

"And I don't need you," he parrots back without emotion. "So we're on the same page."

"Good."

Nodding to himself, his nostrils flare, like he's attempting to control his temper. "Good."

Daniel gestures for me to walk. With the weight of his glare searing a hole into my back, I slip out of the hospital room, holding my head high even as my cheeks flush. Thankfully, they left us fully clothed, so there's no need to redress.

It's cold and crisp outside with snow threatening to fall. No one stops us from leaving. The place is eerily quiet, our feet crunching on falling leaves as we cross the courtyard to the administration building.

Ravius's office is a short walk from the hospital, made much more pleasant by not being dragged kicking and screaming this time around. Instead, I have Mr Happy following me closely.

Passing the reception desk, we halt outside Ravius's office door. I knock loudly, squaring my shoulders and steeling myself for whatever chaos awaits inside.

"Come in," his voice calls.

"Remember," Daniel whispers in a rush. "Be careful. Ravius wants to help, but he has his own motives too."

Chin raised in defiance, I ignore the brush of anxiety his words cause and step inside the office. It's the same as I left it —stiflingly hot and full of antique crap.

"Lexi, Daniel."

Ravius stands up from behind his desk, watching us closely. His usual tailored suit is midnight-black today, accentuating his alabaster skin. We step inside the room together, moving with slow, uncertain steps.

"How are you both feeling after what happened?" he asks.

Daniel subtly shoots me a warning look, moving to the open bar in the corner of the plush office, despite the morning's early hour. I wave off the offer of a drink and take one of the armchairs.

"Okay," I answer vaguely.

Ravius scans over me, his eyes attempting to bury beneath the shell of my skin. "Quite the surprise you gave us there, Lexi. Any more tricks up your sleeve we can be expecting?"

"This isn't funny," Daniel snaps.

"Quite." Ravius hums, his plastered-on smile fading. "We are facing a complete unknown here. We've never had a soul bound pair without both parties having gifts."

"It's impossible, Ravius."

"And yet..." He gestures between us. "Here we are."

Exhaling loudly, Daniel takes the seat next to me, a glass of liquor in hand. "How the hell did this happen?"

"Lexi's powers appear to be much stronger than we anticipated. And they will only continue to grow in strength."

"I'm right here," I growl in irritation. "Don't talk about me like I'm not. I didn't mean for this to happen."

"What happened, then?" Ravius drones.

"Our skin touched, and… it was too late. I couldn't stop it. This crazy feeling washed over me, just like it did in the meadow. We both passed out from the force of it."

Ravius taps his chin. "A soul bound pair in itself is a very rare phenomena, but your situation is unheard of."

"It's impossible," Daniel splutters.

"Precisely. Until now."

"So what do we do?" I interject.

"We will begin a strict training regimen." He absently smooths a hand down his suit. "As your powers begin to manifest, it will be crucial for you to learn discipline and control. Daniel can't control your gift for you."

"If he's even around," I reply pointedly.

Ravius glances over at the stony-faced man in question. "Your visit is coming to an end this week."

Daniel looks uneasy, his long fingers flexing around his glass. "Caine isn't willing to stick around for negotiations any longer."

"You understand the consequences of a soul bound pair being separated? It cannot happen."

"What do you expect me to do?" Daniel barks. "If Caine finds out about Lexi's powers, we'll both be as good as dead. You know it."

"What are you talking about?"

Both ignore my question, locked in a silent conversation of hard stares and raised brows. When Daniel shakes his head and looks away, Ravius sighs.

"My brother has a certain interest, shall we say, in gifted Redeemed. It is imperative that he remains in the dark about this development."

Dread blooms in my gut.

"But you're his right-hand man." I look at Daniel. "How can you expect to keep such a secret from him? Plus, in a few days… you'll be gone."

Silence reigns. No one has an answer. This is an almighty mess of my own making, I have no one but myself to blame, even if I didn't choose this. I still did it to us.

"I have to go," Daniel blurts. "He'll be wondering where I am, and I don't want to rouse any suspicion."

Ravius waves for him to leave. "Lexi and I will commence her training. Please see to it that my brother remains oblivious. For all of our sakes."

Shooting me a final lingering glance, Daniel necks the last of his drink before rushing towards the door. With each step he takes away from me, the chasm in my chest expands, filling with pain.

I rub my spasming sternum, swallowing an anguished cry. The feeling builds until it peaks, settling into a low, ever-present ache that refuses to be ignored.

"Physical distance will be your biggest challenge." Ravius watches me rub my chest. "Soul bound pairs syphon energy through intimacy. The pain of being apart will ease overtime though."

"Hard to be intimate with someone who hates your guts and lives halfway across the goddamn world."

"Daniel has his challenges." He nods thoughtfully. "But this has happened for a reason. You need to trust the Vitae."

"Trust it? I don't even understand it!"

"And that's what we're here to achieve. You will learn to understand your gift, control it... harness its full potential."

Too tired to beat around the bush any longer, I face him head on. "What do you want from me, Ravius?"

"Your cooperation."

"Is that all?" I challenge.

He doesn't bat an eye at my sharp tone. "You're under my care, Lexi. Your welfare is my top concern."

"But not your only concern, right?"

He looks over his shoulder, out the window at the facility

beyond. "We live in unprecedented times. I'm fighting to keep The Redeemed afloat in an increasingly dangerous world."

"And I'm fighting to survive."

"Perhaps we can help each other then." He manages a small smile. "Work with me. Train. Learn to harness your gift. We live in an unstable world. This is your best shot at protection."

"Protection from what? Who?"

"Those who would seek to exploit your potential. Despite what you may think, that isn't me. I only want to help."

Every word from his mouth could be a lie. Another deception. The last-ditch act of a dangerous man clinging to power. But no matter the risk, I'm still trapped here.

I have no choice.

No one else can help me.

"You'll help me in exchange for what?" I ask, not bothering to hide my suspicions from my tone.

Ravius tilts his head in an evaluating way, fiddling with the cuffs of his fitted shirt. I can't decide if he's impressed by my ability to see through his bullshit or feels threatened.

"The understanding that if the time comes, I may one day call upon you." His thin lips purse into a flat, unyielding line. "We're playing a dark and dangerous game to keep our existence a secret. I need allies, Lexi. Powerful ones."

"I know nothing of your world."

"But you can learn," he reasons, a hopeful smile blossoming. "You've been gifted a great power, and with it comes a responsibility to our people. You are a part of this world now."

My shoulders sag as I grip the armchair, fighting a wave of hopelessness. "I never wanted any of this."

"And that's exactly why it's been given to you."

With the phantom pain still bubbling away in my chest, I admit defeat. "Fine. Tell me what I need to do."

Ravius stands then begins to pace, his hands laced behind his back. "Controlling gifts is all about mental discipline. It took me years of practice to master my own ability."

"I don't have years. Not unless I want to keep spontaneously setting things on fire."

Ravius doesn't need to know that I have no intention of being trapped here for years while Eve is all alone in the outside world. But that thought burns brightly at the forefront of my mind.

"You need to be patient," he urges. "This process takes time. I will teach you how to harness the energy inside you and channel it."

"How do we do that?"

Moving to sit in Daniel's vacated seat, Ravius shifts the chair closer so our knees are almost touching. I fight the urge to recoil away from him. My trust is razor-thin right now.

"By controlling yourself," Ravius replies. "Close your eyes. Focus on the force buried within you. Feel it flowing through your veins, your mind, your body. It's one with you."

Blowing out a nervous breath, I let my eyes slide shut. Tapping into the constant hum of energy is easy enough when it's screaming through my extremities, getting louder with every passing second.

"You don't need to fear it," Ravius advises. "This power is a part of you. Let it fill you up, from head to toe."

Keeping my eyes squeezed tightly shut, I feel my body twitch, alight with fiery electricity. It zips through me— burning, expanding, spreading into a wildfire.

"Ravius," I whine.

"Breathe, Lexi. You're in control."

Dragging in another uneven breath, I concentrate on the steady flow of warmth pumping through me. My chest aches, the pain spiking and intensifying with the increased sensation of heat.

"You have to learn to tap into this force, night and day. It will need controlling at all times so it doesn't overwhelm you."

"What about D-Daniel?" I gasp.

"He can help to control the excess energy, but you can't rely on him. Only you can harness and use this gift."

When the pain peaks, my concentration snaps. I lose grip of the unruly current lashing at my insides, and my eyes snap open, the fragile sense of calm I momentarily clung to dissipating in an instant.

"Shit!"

Ravius smiles reassuringly. "This was your first try. Over time, it will become easier to tap into the Vitae and learn to communicate with it."

"What will I be able to do?"

"Harness it. Control it." His eyes sparkle with interest. "Weaponise it."

Bingo.

He wants me to be his weapon.

"Again, Lexi."

Wringing my shaking hands together, I force my eyes to close again. Ravius doesn't direct me this time, leaving me to find my own way back into the fire-laden darkness of my mind.

The Vitae is waiting for me.

Burning.

Sizzling.

Baying for blood.

"Come on," I whisper to myself.

Imagining myself inching down the dark, winding pathway leading into the depths of my subconscious, I follow the trail of heat. It welcomes me back with open arms.

"There you go," Ravius praises. "Follow the energy, Lexi. Let it be your guide."

This time, the pain doesn't break my focus. I latch on to

the sharp sensation that sears my chest, using it to focus my fear. I'm not afraid. This is my power—my gift to own.

Ravius swears, shocking me to the core. I've never heard him utter a single curse before. But I understand why he does; even I can feel what's happening. The waves of power are pulsating off me.

"Control," he urges. "Don't let it overwhelm you."

"How?" I grit out.

"The Vitae is a force of nature. It listens to no one. Your job is to force its hand, make it obey you instead."

The sense of power is building. Higher. Faster. Hotter. The sensations grow with each stuttered breath I take, causing fire to fill every corner of my psyche. It takes all of my courage not to scream.

"Hold it," he instructs.

My muscles burn fiercely, trembling from exertion. "I c-can't. It's too strong."

"But you are stronger."

Pain. Flashes of light. Dizziness. Fireworks explode behind my shut eyes as I sit in the darkness, allowing the heat to consume me.

"Be strong. You're in control now."

The pain increases until I feel tears stain my cheeks. It's too much. Too strong. I can hardly hold it, my entire body shaking like a leaf from the waves of power crashing over me.

Until… bliss.

Daylight dawns behind the lids of my closed eyes, bathing me in light. Distantly, I hear myself gasp, but I'm locked in the dream-like flashes that fill my vision.

Long, chestnut hair.

Bright, intelligent green eyes.

Lips parting on a shocked inhale.

Cloaked in shadows, the image of a man fills my head. Impossibly tall. Handsome. Muscular body, covered in dark swirls of ink on every tanned inch. He's staring right at me.

"Mi amor?" an accented voice whispers through my mind. "Is that you?"

I reach out. Yearning. Silently begging for the comfort of his touch. This foreign stranger seems so familiar, like I've known him my whole life. All I want is to run from this place and fling myself into his arms.

"I'm coming for you, mi amor," he promises in that whiskey-smooth voice. "I'll find you."

He vanishes from sight in the blink of an eye. The dream shatters, and I'm flung back to the sound of Ravius shouting my name.

"Lexi! Come back!"

Gasping, I let his frantic voice drag me back to the present, hauling me out of the pitch-black darkness. Pain pulsates through every part of me like I've been hit by a truck.

Crouched in front of me with palpable anxiety, Ravius is clutching my hands tight, his entire body stiff with tension.

"Who... Who was that?"

His frown deepens. "What did you see?"

Don't tell him.

I don't know where the voice comes from. Like the man's soft, shocked whisper, it permeates the fabric of my mind. I immediately clam up, my body drenched in sweat.

"Lexi?" he urges.

"Nothing. I saw... nothing."

"You zoned out. I was afraid we'd lost you."

Shaking out my hands, I sit back, needing space to breathe. Ravius moves back to his chair, appearing as shaken as I am.

"How can I control such a powerful force?" I ask shakily. "It's so strong."

"With time and practice." He scans over me. "We're never given more than we can handle, Lexi. You were born for this."

Swiping the beads of sweat from my forehead, I roll my

shoulders, trying to ease the pent-up tension. Ravius is still staring at me, but all I can think about is what I saw.

I'm coming for you, mi amor. I'll find you.

And the most baffling realisation of all?

I want to be found.

By him.

THE SUN

CHAPTER 9

SUPERBLUES – LITTLE HURRICANE

I'm haunted by whispers, infecting my every waking moment. His voice follows me. When I'm eating. Sleeping. Hiding from Daniel and his shitty attitude.

After several sleepless nights, tossing and turning in sweat-stained sheets, I give up. Playing into Ravius's hands is the last thing I should do, but I need answers to the countless burning questions I have about The Redeemed.

There's only one place to get them.

A desperate last resort.

The library is an impressive building, carved from giant slabs of shining limestone that glisten in the sunset's rays, stone pillars and wide, rain-slick steps marking the entrance.

It looms above me, towering and intimidating in all its grandiosity. I stand in the warmth of the winter's setting sun, wrestling with myself.

"Come on," I mutter.

Squaring my shoulders, I climb the stone steps, stepping into the high-ceilinged entrance hall. Golden chandeliers illuminate the opulence, casting dappled light across framed artwork and fine antique furniture.

"Can I help you?" a curly-haired girl asks from behind the reception desk.

Clearing my throat, I pull out the key card that Ravius gifted me. "I'd like to see the special collections please."

Her eyes widen momentarily as she recognises the card. "Oh, of course. Right this way."

Following her kitten heels down the thick red carpet, we pass several fire-lit reading rooms filled with books. The silence is comforting, seeping deep into my bones. I've always loved libraries.

When I was a lonely child, long before Eve came along, I'd hide out in the library after school. Anything to avoid going home and dealing with my father's drunken slurring or Mum's ceaseless rage.

This was before she left us in his care and disappeared. I was almost nine years old at the time. One moment she was there, and the next, she ran off with her latest exploit, leaving us high and dry.

"You're Lexi, right?"

"That's me."

The girl tosses me a shy smile over her shoulder. "I'm Kara. Are you working on a research project for Elder Ravius?"

"Something like that," I deflect.

"Not many people have access to these collections," she chatters conversationally. "You must be very important for him to give you access."

At the end of another carpet-lined corridor, past an entire room of dusty, vintage tomes that dominate the floor-to-ceiling shelves, a final door awaits. Kara nervously rocks on her feet.

"Here we are. Good luck with your research."

"Thanks."

"You know where to find me if you need anything."

With a curious look, she walks away, glancing back over

her shoulder at me. I wait for her to disappear around the corner before facing the door, the key card clasped in my hand.

There's a security pad built into the varnished wood. Scanning the card, the door beeps loudly before swinging open, ushering me into the awaiting darkness.

I close the door then fumble for a light switch. A truly magnificent space is revealed. The room is huge with tall ceilings, embossed floral wallpaper and a glinting diamond chandelier hanging above me.

"Shit."

I thought the rest of the facility was fancy, but this place takes the biscuit. Every single wall is lined with glossy, black shelves filled with all manner of leather-bound books.

Running my fingers along the spines, I marvel at the huge collection. There must be hundreds of books in here, all in perfect condition and preserved to perfection.

Fingers hesitating over a dark, indigo-blue book, slim and tightly bound with silvery writing on the spine, I read the title.

The Redeemed Accords, 1870.

A memory sparks of Ravius telling me about the accords when I first arrived. It's not what I came looking for, but I can't resist pulling the book free.

It's old and crumbling; the pages are like fragile sheets of tissue paper. Inside, the text is hand-written in curling ink that drips across the translucent pages.

My heart skips a beat as I absorb what I'm reading. The book holds a treasure trove of information. Ravius was telling the truth when he mentioned their lengthy struggle for peace.

This book details years' worth of discussions, debates and intense negotiations between the newly established Redeemed society and the wider world.

When the accords were formed to broker peace, Ravius and the other Elders were each given their own territory to build a community. The numerous facilities across the globe were born from there.

I trace my finger over the next paragraph, written in neatly transcribed script.

> 17th June, 1870.
>
> UK & US Redeemed Negotiations.
>
> Present governing parties include President Ulysses S. Grant, Prime Minister William Ewart Gladstone and Prime Minister William Ewart Gladstone's advisors.
>
> Opposition representation from The Redeemed council present include Elder Caine and Elder Ravius of US and UK sites respectively.
>
> Topics of debate as pre-agreed limited to Redeemed regional boundaries and enforcement, security measures as pertains to government involvement and collaboration.

My thundering heart races with anticipation. This occurred over 150 years ago. I'm reading living history.

> Elder Ravius has agreed with PM Gladstone to establish The Redeemed facility in the Scottish Highlands to maintain total secrecy from the rest of society.
>
> PM Gladstone has agreed to provide financial aid to assist in the construction of a self-sufficient compound with monitored borders, thus establishing

peace within warring factions and protection from public involvement.

This agreement also includes the establishment of a new division in the UK government to manage the alliance and collaborate with Elder Ravius to maintain secrecy and good faith as we work towards common goals.

The accord is agreed upon by the relevant parties with the knowledge that secrecy is paramount, and cease-fire will be halted in the event of attack from Redeemed forces or deliberate breaking of the conditions agreed upon in this treaty.

"Motherfuck," I gasp, rereading the paragraph.

We're in Scotland.

I'm so far from home—hundreds of miles from the coast of the UK where Cornwall is located. I've never been this far from Eve before. She's on the opposite end of the country.

As I continue reading, a familiar name catches my attention. *Daniel.* He's on the attendee list, so he was present for the negotiations with Ravius and Caine over a century ago.

Slamming the book shut, I return it to the shelf, trying and failing not to think about the man I've somehow claimed as my own.

Since I bonded with Daniel, I've spent all my time in Ravius's office, trapped for hours under his watchful eye while Daniel makes it his mission to avoid me.

No matter the agony it causes us both, he can't stand to be

around me, preferring to be in pain rather than be in the same room as me. I shouldn't be surprised. I'm damaged goods.

I've tied him to me forever, and he can't stand to even look at me. The man ran away at the earliest opportunity and has barely seen me since.

He hates me.

I've ruined his life.

Not only that, but my nights are also haunted by thoughts of another. I don't even know if he's real, but the mysterious stranger with a thick, exotic accent pops up every time I shut my eyes.

With a sob, I launch myself across the room, my fist sailing into the wall in an attempt to expel the energy eating away at me. The plaster cracks, smearing blood on the smooth surface.

"Fuck!"

Cradling my aching hand, I don't try to suppress the tears flowing from my eyes. I've never let myself cry like this. Weakness wasn't an option at home. Eve always needed me to be strong for her.

That determination to survive kept me alive.

But not anymore.

Now I've got no one left. I'm alone in this life. Abandoned in my own personal darkness. I thought for a moment that Daniel wanted to save me, but he can't even save himself.

Scanning the shelves, I search the titles for more information. There's nothing about gifted Redeemed or soul bonds. Just more useless books about long-lost history.

Curling up in a high-backed armchair next to the fireplace, I let my eyes slide shut. He comes to me instantly. The nameless man with eyes that resemble precious emeralds.

I don't know him.

But my soul does.

After what feels like hours of drifting in and out, the door handle rattles. Voices sound from the other side before the security system buzzes, and it clicks open.

"Lexi?"

Michael steps into the room, overshadowed by the tall, wide-set figure looming behind him. I recognise his all-black clothing and imposing shoulders immediately. Daniel.

I plaster on a weak smile. "Hey."

"What are you doing in here?" Michael asks suspiciously. "You know it's classified, right?"

"Just... reading. Ravius gave me a key card so I could do some research. How did you find me?"

Michael jabs a finger over his shoulder at Daniel, who flushes and has the decency to look away, rubbing the back of his neck.

"So he can track me now too?" I scoff.

"You didn't show up for dinner," Daniel grumbles. "Michael insisted on coming to look for you."

"That doesn't answer my question."

"Yes." He sighs loudly. "I can find you."

"Could've fooled me. I haven't seen you for days."

"Days?" Michael casts his friend a stunned glare. "What the fuck are you playing at?"

"She's fine." Daniel gestures towards me.

"It's your job to help her regulate her gift. You know that requires physical contact! You're putting us all in jeopardy by fighting this."

Staring down at his boot-covered feet, Daniel doesn't utter a word. I wish I didn't pity him. I wish... I could hate him too. But more than anything, I regret doing this to him.

"This only works if you're both committed." Michael motions to both of us. "There's no breaking a soul bond. You need to get your shit together and figure this out."

With a huff, he storms from the room, leaving me alone with Daniel. He's still lingering awkwardly in the doorway, trapped by uncertainty.

"So," I begin.

His eyes lift to meet mine. "So."

Brows furrowed, Daniel studies my face, his frosty orbs trailing a burning path over me. Gazes locked, I know he sees straight through to my broken core.

Maybe it's his asshole attitude. Or the way he holds himself, like he's stranded himself alone on a frozen mountain because it's simpler than facing the fear of getting hurt.

But I know he understands. He knows how it feels to be broken, to lose yourself, to splinter apart at the seams. I can see the same agony I feel staring back at me in his icy-blue eyes.

"You need to eat," he rumbles.

"I'm fine."

"No. You're not."

"How would you know? Where have you been?"

Pinching the bridge of his nose, he shakes his head. "I'm trying to protect you, Lexi. If Caine finds out about us—"

"That's a shitty excuse."

"It's not an excuse. It's the truth."

"Convenient for you! Just admit it."

Daniel's nose scrunches up in confusion. "Admit what?"

An invisible hand clenches around my throat. "Admit that you hate me and can't stand the sight of me. Admit that I've ruined your life with this soul bond."

He blinks, seemingly lost for words. "Hate you?"

"Yes. It's plain as fucking day. Look, I will find a way to break this bond. Just give me some time, and I'll set you free."

Chest tight with emotion, I slip past him, storming down the corridor to put as much space between us as possible. Each step feels like a bullet is piercing my skin.

The tears come without warning. Thick and fast. I feel so fucking stupid for believing, even for a split second, that he cared. No one ever has or ever will.

"Lexi! Wait!"

"Leave me the fuck alone, Daniel!"

Moving fast, I pass the reception desk and Kara's stunned

expression. Cold air meets my lungs as I break outside into the cloak of night.

"Lexi!"

I keep walking, ignoring his shouts. Heavy, thudding footsteps catch up to me fast. When Daniel wrenches my arm to drag me to a halt, my patience snaps.

"What do you want now? I need to be alone."

"Just stop for a second," he begs.

"Why? There's nothing left to say."

His fingertips dig into my arm, hard enough to bruise. "I have plenty left to say, and you're going to listen, Lexi."

"Like hell I am. Let go of me."

"No. I won't."

"I said let go!"

"I won't," he yells back, face pinched with emotion.

A flash of light blinds us both as white-hot anger overwhelms me. When crackling flames engulf a nearby tree, Daniel's eyes bug out.

The flames reach up high, spreading fast. My anger summits with the burst of untamed energy ripping its way out of me, past my flimsy layers of control.

"Oh my God!"

"Lexi," Daniel shouts. "Stand back."

Pulling me out of the path of the uncontrollable fire, his arms band around me from behind, pinning my back to his barrel chest.

The flames only grow in strength, hissing and spitting angrily. Daniel keeps me tightly pinned, refusing to let go.

"You need to calm down," he urges. "It's the only way to make it stop."

"I can't do this," I gasp.

With my surging panic, a second rush of heat blazes over me, sending fire racing through my veins. When another tree bursts into bright, brilliant flames, Daniel barks a curse.

"No one can see this," he hisses in my ear. "It isn't safe!"

Clutching my tight chest, I try to drag in a breath, but watching the fire burn so wildly has pushed me over the edge. Anger and rejection are blurring into a furious maelstrom within me.

"Come on, love. You can do this. There's nothing to be afraid of."

His voice turns soft and coaxing in low, dulcet tones. With his voice cutting through the haze, I focus on my breathing, but I still can't drag in a complete breath.

The flames only grow higher and more intense, the heat licking against my skin. Any moment now, someone could come out and discover this madness. But I can't make it stop.

"Please, Lexi," Daniel implores. "I can't protect you from him if he sees this. Caine can never know about your powers."

"Can't… s-stop it…"

"Yes. You can, love."

Turning me around in his arms, he stares deep into my eyes, his roughened hands cupping my cheeks. With his skin touching mine, electricity zips down my spine.

My soul calls out to his.

Begging. Pleading. Yearning for more.

Trapped in his frigid blue gaze, I can't move. Not under the weight of his stare. Everything else falls away. All I can feel is the almighty force within me demanding more.

It wants him.

Needs him.

And I do too.

"You can do this." His gaze darts down to my lips. "Forget everything else. The entire world. Focus only on me."

He moves closer. Then closer still. So fucking close, I can feel the warm stir of his breath, enticing me in. His forehead teases mine, our lips just an inch from touching.

The air between us is charged with the Vitae pouring off my skin in palpable waves of raw power. It's tying us together in an unbreakable knot, cinching ever tighter.

"Lex," he rasps.

"It's just the bond. Nothing more."

"Do you really believe that?"

My heart somersaults. "Yes."

He drags a single fingertip along my jawline, his thumb lifting to trace the slope of my parted lips.

Need rockets through me, the chaos around us paling into insignificance. Not even the heat lashing at my skin can distract me from this moment.

"You're a terrible liar, love."

The tip of his nose grazing mine, I'm powerless to stop the brush of his lips against my mouth. It's the briefest of kisses. Barely even a whisper before we separate.

Breath stuttering, I peer up at him through my lashes. His pupils have blown wide, leaking darkness into his crystalline irises.

"And… you're fucking trouble too."

Then his mouth is back on mine. Lips. Teeth. Tongue. All hard and demanding. Our teeth clang as we're drawn together by violently fraying threads of control.

He kisses me like the world is crumbling around us, and we're both running for our damn lives, on the verge of falling off that dangerous precipice.

I can't breathe, and I don't even want to. Not now. I'd rather drown in his arms. I'll go willingly. Gladly. If it means I can stay here with him.

His hands thread into my long blonde hair, holding the strands tight as his tongue strokes mine. He tastes like salvation. Freedom. Everything I've wanted since I drew my first breath in this confusing afterlife.

Hard body pressing into mine, he traps me against him. Every line of carved muscle adds to the sense of friction causing my core to tighten.

Our tongues tangle, battling for consumption of the other.

I want to be devoured by him. Swallowed whole and held close in the safety of his embrace.

This can't be just the bond.

It's something more.

Something irrevocable.

Another surge of energy races through me, but the relief it brings is acute. Like coming up for air after sinking to the depths of the ocean, unable to stay afloat.

When we break apart, the crackling flames fizzle out. Nothing but darkness surrounds us and the two smoking, charred trees with twisted branches, both barely upright.

Daniel's still cupping my face.

Refusing to let go.

I rest my hands on top of his, breathing in his scent. Evergreen and peppercorns, the earthy, spicy fragrance washing over me in a tantalising mist.

"Fire's out." His tongue darts out to lick his bottom lip. "Sorry. Didn't mean to get carried away."

"You don't have to apologise."

He releases me and takes a step back. "I shouldn't have done that. I'm not what you need right now, trust me."

"And what do I need?"

Sadness swirls in his gaze.

"Something good."

He tries to back farther away. Snatching his arm, I stretch up onto my tiptoes to crash my lips against his again. This kiss is softer, more tender, a silent whisper for more than this life is willing to give us.

"Fuck you," I murmur into his wet lips. "You don't get to decide that. I don't want something good. I want *you*."

"You've bonded with a monster. Do you realise that? Do you even care?"

Grabbing hold of his t-shirt, I fist the material tightly, my fists slamming against his chest.

"No. I couldn't care less."

"You should." His voice lowers into a pained rasp. "The things I've done... What Caine has made me do to survive... You wouldn't be here if you knew."

Realisation dawns.

He doesn't hate me.

No... he hates himself.

"Is that what this is?" I stare up at him. "You think you're not good enough for this soul bond? For... me?"

I watch his Adam's apple bob when he tips his head back, studying the sky. "You don't know me."

"You're not giving me the chance to."

Voices break out of the nearby dining hall, but neither of us moves. We're in our own world. Nothing can penetrate it. Not even the threat of discovery.

"We can't do this, Lex. Us."

I reach up and cup his cheek, revelling in the purr of energy that hums through my bones. "Yes. We can."

Our lips meet again. His mouth brands itself on mine, our breath and bodies intertwining. Not even Daniel can stop this.

We're soul bound.

THE DEVIL

CHAPTER 10

GUEST ROOM – ECHOS

"*L*exi girl."

Like individual fingertips of death, his voice sends a shiver of terror down my spine. Overcome by revulsion, I focus on pouring the pint, ignoring the way my hands tremble at the fact that he's now standing in front of me.

"*Sugar. We need to talk.*"

"*I'm working,*" *I whisper dejectedly.*

"*Now.*"

With a sigh, I place the pint down then meekly slip out back where the pub's customers can't overhear us. He follows with stumbling, drunken strides, slamming the door shut behind us as we enter the storeroom.

"*You look sexy tonight,*" *he slurs.*

I shudder in revulsion. "*I should go.*"

"*No.*" *His hand darts out to grab me by the wrist, ragged nails digging deep into my skin.* "*You're going to stand there and do exactly as I fucking tell you.*"

"*Please—*"

"*I love it when you beg, sugar.*"

Eyes sliding shut, I let his hands wander, my cheeks blistering with the lash of fresh tears spilling over. It's easier this way. Simpler. Shutting down and retreating to the safety of my mind is what's kept me alive through years of this abuse.

"What's this?" His fingertip travels over the dark mark I know stains my neck—a reminder of last night's drunken antics with Alex. When his hand clenches around my throat and begins to squeeze, my lungs seize up.

"I am the only man allowed to touch you." His grip tightens into a crushing vice. "I'm the only one, you hear me? I'll fucking kill him."

"Ple—"

"No! You're mine!"

Releasing my throat, he slams his fist into my gut instead. I double over, coughing and spluttering as my lungs struggle to drag in a breath. Nausea is tearing my insides up as he hits me again, harder this time.

"Mine!"

"Lexi? You okay in there?" a voice seeps through the pain suffocating me.

Fuck.

Hugging myself, I manage to suck in a stuttered breath, enough to whimper back, "Fine. B-Be out in a m-minute."

The footsteps move away from the door, leaving us alone again. He's furious. Chest pumping. Eyes wild. Lips pursed. With a final sneering look of malice, he turns and bangs out of the storeroom, leaving me to sob into the silence.

I can't live like this anymore.

One day… he'll succeed in killing me.

* * *

AFTER TIGHTENING the laces on a pair of running shoes that I found in the wardrobe, I take off into the morning mist, my skin itching with the desire to run until I can't anymore.

I'm sleep deprived after memories tormented me last night for hours on end. Flashes of the past continue to plague me, over and over, never once relenting.

Him.

His touch.

Breath.

Taste.

The nameless monster of my childhood still terrorises me even when he isn't here to mark my skin. I can't escape him, despite being safely hidden far from his disgusting clutches.

Taking off, I pump my legs, moving faster. Harder. Farther. With each lap, the facility around me blurs more, but I pay no attention to my surroundings. Nothing matters but satisfying my need to escape the clinging remnants of the past.

Run, Lexi.

Run from him.

I spent years doing the opposite of that—hiding, tolerating, begging for relief. None of it worked. He still took exactly what he wanted from me, regardless of my feelings, indifferent to my tears and pain.

When the sun begins to rise on the horizon, I realise that I'm not running alone. Daniel falls into step beside me, clad in workout shorts and another tight t-shirt that accentuates his generous, rippling muscles.

We run together—silent partners in the shadows, both running from our own demons and battling to keep them from dragging us back into the darkness.

When I feel like I'm going to throw up from exertion, I stop outside the Nightingale building, a hand propped on the red brick wall.

"Shit," I pant.

"You did good." Daniel breathes hard, just inches away from me. "Didn't think you could run that fast."

"I needed to work through some stuff."

"Want to talk about it?"

"Not really."

Head tilted, he considers me, his eyes gleaming with some unnamed emotion. I stare back without apology. The memory of our kiss still shines bright in my mind.

"Think we've proven that bottling stuff up isn't a good idea," he retorts softly. "Not with your situation."

"That won't happen again."

"Won't it?"

"No. Everything is under control."

He snorts, using his arm to wipe sweat from his forehead. "You're delusional."

"Say that again and my fist will be in your face."

Daniel chuckles, and the treacle-smooth sound is a soothing balm to my frayed nerves. He has a nice, deep laugh. Rasping and masculine. Offering me a hand, he tugs me upright, his skin rough against mine.

"I should go. Caine needs me."

Fear of being alone with my memories washes over me in a terrifying wave. I clutch his hand tighter to stop him from leaving.

"Do you want a coffee or something?" I bite my lip. "It's still early. I'm sure Caine can live without you for another hour."

His mouth quirks into that alluring half-smile I'm growing to crave. "You'd be surprised. That man isn't capable of tying his own shoelaces without me."

"Now that I am surprised by. Isn't he some big, scary Elder?"

"Looks can be deceiving, love."

Hooking a thumb over my shoulder, I gesture up at the Nightingale building, the gaudy Victorian architecture cast in early morning light.

"Coffee?"

Daniel nods. "Coffee sounds good."

Inside the building, we ride the elevator in silence. All I can think about is tasting him again. Memories of that night have consumed me ever since we locked lips.

Stepping out of the elevator, Daniel follows me over to the

apartment. I unlock the door then gesture for him to step inside.

"This is me."

He glances around, cataloguing my private space. His eyes scan over all the little touches, from the washed dishes next to the sink to the dishevelled nest of blankets on the sofa.

Shutting the door behind us, I lean against it, watching him move around the apartment with the grace of a tiger. He's lithe. Silent. Deadly. Everything I should run from.

But that doesn't stop the excited energy swirling in my chest from preening in his presence. Around him, I feel alive. Whole.

"You didn't want to decorate?" he asks.

"This isn't my home."

"It is now."

"Not if I have anything to do with it."

Turning on the spot, he faces me. "You got some grand escape plan that I don't know about?"

"Wouldn't you like to know."

Stepping around his intimidating height, I flick the coffee machine on then set to work making our drinks. Daniel takes a seat at the marble breakfast bar and watches me work.

"You have family out there? On the outside?"

My throat catches. "A sister."

"That's who you want to get back to."

I bite my lip, battling a fresh wave of mental guilt. Even thinking about Eve is excruciating, let alone admitting the truth. That she's out there, alone and afraid, while we sip our morning coffee.

Getting my emotions back under control, I finish making his drink and place it in front of him. Daniel studies my facial expression, and I feel like he can see every twisted, shame-filled thought swirling in my mind.

"I'm all she has. Eve needs me."

He releases a pent-up breath. "I'll save you the whole

speech about how she's better off without you. I'm sure Ravius has already exhausted that."

"A long time ago. You want milk?"

"Nope. Tell me more about your sister."

Grabbing my coffee, I move to sit down on his left side. I'm too afraid to look into his penetrating gaze, knowing all of my vulnerabilities will be on display. I examine my hands, clasped around the mug.

"She's a smart kid, top of her class. Gentle. Sweet. Hell, nothing like me. I don't know how someone so pure came from so much... trauma."

"Trauma?" he repeats, darkness crossing his face.

"We didn't have the best childhood," I hedge. "Our mum left when Eve was a baby. My father's a waste of space drunk. I raised Eve alone."

"That must've been hard."

I shrug, taking a sip of coffee. "We always had each other. That was enough for us. Now, she has no one."

His voice softens, taking a sympathetic edge that reveals a glimpse of his humanity. "I'm sorry, Lex."

My defences splinter, causing my hard-built shields to lower an inch. I'm powerless to stop myself from disintegrating as my spiralling thoughts catch up to me.

"I just can't imagine what she's going through, thinking that I'm dead." I swallow hard. "She must be so scared and alone right now."

"There's no one to take care of her?"

Shaking my head, I look up at him. "Nobody. That's why I have to find a way out of here, no matter what it takes."

Calloused fingers tightening around his coffee cup, he looks torn, like he's desperate to find any alternative to stating the obvious.

"Lexi... there is no way out."

"I refuse to believe that. I can't."

Wiping underneath my eyes, I ignore the concerned

weight of his gaze scraping over me. I don't need his pity. I just want him to understand. This will never be my home.

"I spent years trying to escape too," he admits in a low rumble. "All I wanted was to start again without Caine and his claim on my life."

"What claim?"

"You know much about the American civil war?" His arctic eyes duck down, locking on his cup of coffee. "Battle of Gettysburg."

"That's how you died?"

His Adam's apple bobs beneath a layer of dark-brown stubble, broadcasting the tumultuous emotions that recounting his history triggers.

"I woke up in the aftermath. I'd been shot. That's where Caine found me. He got me to safety and took care of me. I've been by his side ever since."

"Why do you hate the man who saved your life?"

"He didn't save me out of the goodness of his heart," Daniel answers bitterly. "He wanted allies. People he could control and order to do his dirty work. That's all I am to him."

Hatred is a fickle thing. We can despise the people who hurt us the most but still feel terrified of what our life would look like without them in it.

I don't know who I'd be without *him*. His evil. The pain he inflicted on me, day in and day out. Those years of abuse formed my identity and made me who I am.

Even if I hate his fucking guts.

Fiddling with the half-full mug, I remember the slim, bound volume that caught my attention in the library. Daniel's name was there, written in black and white.

"You helped to set up the Redeemed facilities."

"How do you know that?" Daniel visibly startles.

"The special collections have a lot of interesting secrets. You were there for negotiations in 1870."

"I still can't believe that Ravius gave you access to the special collections. That man trusts no one."

"Did you decide to establish this facility here in Scotland?" I change the subject.

"Fuck, Lexi." He cocks an eyebrow, seeming almost impressed. "You're going to get yourself into trouble with that mouth of yours one day."

"As we've established, I don't care. Someone has to ask questions around here."

"That person doesn't have to be you."

I snort, shaking my head. Trouble doesn't scare me. Spending the rest of my life locked away in this place with no control over my fate does.

Daniel leans closer, pinning me with an intense, unflinching stare that would terrify most people. But not me. I can see past it now to the truth he's failing to hide. He actually cares all too much. This cold, detached act is just that—an act.

"You can't go around telling people that you know where we are. Ravius may be affording you these privileges now, but the moment you become a problem, he will eliminate you."

"And lose his precious pet project?" I retort. "Doesn't seem likely. I'm his favourite fucking toy right now."

"You're only useful for as long as you serve him. He isn't the type to tolerate disobedience, and something tells me that following orders isn't your strong suit."

It's my turn to bark a laugh. Following Ravius's orders is the last thing on my mind. He can go fuck himself long before I do his bidding.

"I told you about me." Daniel shifts on the bar stool, leaning even further into my personal space. "Return the favour."

"What do you want to know?"

His full lips twist into a grimace. "Tell me about your death."

"It's not a pretty story." I shudder in revulsion.

"Do I look like I scare easily?"

"I don't know. You've hardly been forthcoming before now. What's changed?"

"Apart from you binding our souls together?" he challenges, holding back a smartass grin.

"Yeah... apart from that."

Placing his mug down, Daniel folds his muscled arms. "Maybe we understand each other better than we think."

Tension crackles between us. Hot. Heady. There's something shining in his ice-cold gaze—a challenge, levied between opponents on two sides of the same war. No matter what he preaches, he's still Caine's right-hand man.

I want to cross enemy territory to bridge the gap between us. This unfathomable man has stolen my attention and refuses to give it back.

"What happened to you?" he presses.

"Why do you want to know so badly?"

"Your eyes." His jaw clenches tight. "I want to know who put the shadows there so I can have the pleasure of killing them myself."

My thighs press together to relieve the ache building low in my belly. I know he can see my reaction, but I don't care. That kiss wasn't enough to satisfy me.

"You can't do that," I say sadly.

"Like hell I can't. The rules don't apply to us."

"We're trapped here, aren't we? That sure sounds like a rule to me."

Daniel smirks. He fucking *smirks*. With the corners of his mouth crinkling upwards, he's even more handsome, though I'm coming to love that miserable scowl on his face too.

"We all have a story, love. Maybe I want to know yours. You said it yourself... We're stuck together now."

Sipping coffee, I gift him a challenging stare. "Good luck trying."

"I won't need it."

Warmth is pulsating through my veins, a steady flow of desire that I haven't felt before him. Not even with Alex during our sleazy, single-minded hook ups late at night.

It's different with Daniel. My soul calls out to his, no matter how hard we're fighting against it. That siren's call is binding us together, and neither of us has the strength to break the spell.

"So what happens now?" I ask nervously.

"I have to leave with Caine. We're flying back to the States."

My heart plummets. "You're going?"

His expression is resigned. "I have no choice but to go with Caine. I can hardly tell him about us. Leaving will keep you safe."

"You can't…. can't leave."

He sighs and scrubs a hand over his stubbled chin, the corners of his mouth pulled taut with frustration.

"I'm sorry, Lex. I know it's bad timing."

"Bad timing? We're in a world of shit, and you want to skip off thousands of miles away. I can't do…"

I bite my tongue, holding back the last words.

I can't do this without you.

Daniel quickly closes the last remaining gap between us. I hold my breath as he brushes his lips against mine with a defeated sigh, like he can't stand to restrain himself for a second longer.

He's done fighting.

And fuck… so am I.

Letting my lips part to grant him access, he deepens the kiss, the warm swipe of his tongue tangling with mine. He tastes like fresh coffee and spearmint, his lips velvet soft and hot on mine.

"Daniel," I gasp.

Palm sliding against my flushed cheek, he grips my face

tight, holding me in place so his mouth can attack mine. I can't run. Can't escape. Even if I wanted to.

His other hand slips into my hair, parting the long strands, fingertips tracing the surface of my skull as if committing every inch of me to memory.

The hum in my chest simmers down to low, sizzling embers, sending delicious heat pulsating through my veins and nervous system. Every part of me is screaming out for him. His touch. His attention.

"I need you to be safe," he whispers into my lips. "War is coming, Lex. There's nothing any of us can do to stop it."

"War?" I repeat breathlessly.

His lips fervently peck mine. "Why do you think Ravius is so desperate for answers about the Vitae? His control is fading with each passing day."

"Control over who? The Redeemed?"

Daniel rests his forehead against mine. "Caine's ready to rip the accords to shreds. The world is changing around us. We're more exposed than ever, and that's why Ravius is desperate for answers."

Answers that I have.

I'm what he wants.

Ravius is going to tear me apart to get to the truth about our existence and the Vitae. He needs a weapon. A smoking gun. Someone powerful enough to hold this crumbling world together.

"You can't trust anyone," Daniel warns, stroking his scarred knuckles against my cheekbone.

"Not even you?"

"Lexi... I'm part of the problem. I've spent centuries protecting a monster who would rather see this world disintegrate than remain hidden any longer."

"Would it be so bad if it disintegrated?" I blurt out. "All these rules... secrets... families ripped apart... None of this is fair."

"Our secrets keep us safe."

"Do yours?" I study the shadows dancing in his eyes, taunting me with everything I don't yet know.

He draws back ever so slightly, lips hanging open on a sharp breath. His eyes are plagued with grief so strong, I can almost taste it on the tip of my tongue.

"I have no secrets," he replies carefully.

"We both know that's not true."

Head lowering, Daniel looks away. When he releases his grip on my cheek, I know I've lost him all over again. The distance between us is expanding, dissolving all the progress we've just made.

"It's time for me to leave." He stands up, avoiding eye contact. "Be safe, Lex. I mean it."

"Yeah," I reply flatly.

"I'll come back when I can."

He doesn't kiss me again. My entire body throbs with sharp pain as he stalks from the apartment. Keeping my gaze lowered, I stare at my clenched fists until the front door slams shut.

He's gone.

Taking my heart with him.

WHEEL OF FORTUNE

CHAPTER 11

BLACK AND RED – REIGNWOLF

"*A*gain! You're unfocused."

Gritting my teeth, I feel sweat dribble down my face. "I'm trying."

"Try harder," Ravius demands.

Keeping my eyes screwed shut, I try to mentally grab hold of the wild force writhing within me, but it refuses to cooperate.

I haven't been able to connect to it since Daniel left. He's been gone for over a week, and each day is more painful than the last. I've been itching with frustration and anger ever since.

The power that I woke up feeling throughout my body in that hospital bed is gone, replaced by an endless, steady ache. Daniel's left a chasm in my chest that grows wider with each passing day.

"Focus your mind, Lexi."

"Fuck your focus!"

"Excuse me?" His voice is deathly cold.

Giving up, I let my eyes open, landing on his aghast expression. We've been at it for hours and getting nowhere. I can't be what he wants me to be. Not alone. Not like this.

"Again," he snaps.

"No. We're done here."

"Lexi—"

"Enough! What the hell do you want from me? I'm not some trained monkey, performing on demand for you."

He cocks a single blonde eyebrow. "Bags under your eyes."

"What?"

"There are bags under your eyes." He points at me, his shimmering eyes narrowed. "You're not sleeping. Eating. Interacting. I can't do this for you, Lexi! You're not even trying!"

Uncrossing my legs, I stand up from my perch on the carpeted floor, looming above him. Ravius looks like nothing more than a petulant child on his knees below me.

"I will never be your weapon," I spit at him. "Find someone else to fight your damn war. It won't be me."

Mouth comically flopping open, he looks stunned. Obviously, Ravius wasn't banking on me knowing his ulterior motive. But he isn't the only one playing a game.

"Unless you give me what I want."

His lip curls in a sneer. "And that is?"

"I want to see my sister."

Gracefully rising to his feet in his usual slick suit, Ravius nears. It feels like each footstep he takes seals my fate. I back away, inch by inch until my back hits his office wall and there's nowhere left to run.

"Listen well. You belong to me. Your life. Your gift. Your soul. I saved you, and you're going to do as I say."

"Or what?" I challenge, keeping my chin raised. "You going to kill me? I've died once. I'll die again and lose nothing."

"You're worth more to me alive."

Heat pierces my skull. It spreads fast, aggressively searching, invading the recesses of my psyche. Ravius's eyes seem to glow as he braces a hand on either side of my head.

"My brother wants to see our entire world crumble to rubble so he can conquer what remains. I can't let that happen."

"Rav—"

"I need power, Lexi. You're going to give it to me."

Choking on the invisible force that seeps from his gaze, I try to force him from my mind, but it's too late. He's inside me. Searching. Ripping me apart at the seams in search of the truth.

"The Vitae has chosen you. Just like she said it would."

"Who?" I manage to choke out.

Ravius scoffs. "Why don't you ask your beloved *bonded*? He knows more about the prophecy than anyone. Or did he fail to mention her?"

The invisible force releases its grip on me, and the heat piercing my mind retreats. Suddenly exhausted, I slump against the wall, slick with cold sweat.

Her.

Deep down, I know who Ravius is talking about. I don't need a name. The dark shadows in Daniel's eyes are there for a reason. No matter what he thinks, his grief is clear as day to me.

There was someone else.

Someone... gone.

"What did the prophecy say?" I spit.

"So much potential," Ravius hums, ignoring my question. "You will obey me. The Redeemed saved your life. Now you have a debt to repay."

If he thinks I give a shit about his precious rules and regulations, he's in for a shock. The Redeemed mean nothing to me. Not when my sister is out there, alone and afraid.

With a deep breath, I straighten my spine, taking a step towards him. "I owe you nothing. You can't keep me here."

"Where are you going to go?" he shouts, throwing up his

hands. "Nowhere is safe for you, Lexi! Not home. Not here. Not anywhere."

"You're right. I'm not safe here. Not with you."

Power crackles through me. Untamed and uncontrollable. I can't connect to the Vitae in this state of mind, but that doesn't mean it isn't there. Waiting. Biding its time to attack.

It's now or never.

I won't be a victim again.

Reading my subconscious, it lashes out without command, rising through me in an almighty, crackling wave. I watch like a spectator as the energy floods my extremities all on its own.

It doesn't need me.

I'm just a vessel.

Ravius's eyes widen as fire crackles across my palms. The flames rise. Smoke curls. I step closer to him with each breath, prepared to do whatever it takes to get the hell out of here.

"You can't stop me from leaving. I'm done. It's clear to me now that I cannot trust you… or The Redeemed."

"Lexi," he pleads. "Think about what you're doing. Our entire civilisation is under threat. We need your help."

"But you didn't ask for it. Instead, you tried to scare me. Manipulate me! All in the name of some war I don't care about."

Ravius shifts on his feet, eyes darting from side to side in a nervous tic. "This war will affect you too."

"Not if I leave."

"Like it or not, the secrecy of our race keeps us safe. If Caine reveals The Redeemed to the world, your life will be at risk too. And those you care about."

But I'm too far gone to listen to him. Angrier than I've ever felt in my life. All this time, weeks of false smiles, empty promises, hours spent locked in this office… all for nothing. I was fooling myself if I ever thought I could work with this man.

"You're no better than Caine," I snarl at him, my vision tunnelling. "Maybe I want to see this world burn."

Nostrils flaring, he appraises me. "You don't mean that. People will die."

"If I don't protect Eve, she might as well be dead. He'll hurt her, Ravius. Just like he hurt me."

Ravius cocks his head. "Who?"

The flames engulfing my hands burn hotter at the mention of *him*. Fire crackles and spits as energy pounds through me. I can't stop it from building into a destructive torrent.

My patience has expired.

Eve needs me.

"I don't want to hurt you," I warn him. "But I will if you stand in my way."

"I can't let you leave."

"Then you've left me with no choice."

Latching on to the swarm of heat living beneath my skin, I pour my will into it, begging the force to obey. For the first time in hours of frustration, it bows in submission.

Fire spreads from my palms, racing through the air in a blur and setting the thick office carpet alight. A wall of flames builds in no time, growing ever higher.

Ravius is trapped behind it, shouting furiously and choking on a cloud of smoke. He has no choice but to back away from the flames before they consume him too.

"Lexi!" he screams.

"I'm sorry. I just can't let you stop me from doing what needs to be done."

Turning my back on his rage, I direct the flow of power to one hand, watching as flames engulf it. Somehow, I feel no pain. It's like the Vitae knows I'm not the target. My right hand is free to open his office door so I can escape into the corridor.

After several steps, the silence is ruptured by an ear-

151

shattering alarm blaring down the corridor. Emergency lights begin to flash and voices shout over the chaos.

I'm running out of time.

It's now or never.

Feet thumping against the thickly carpeted floor, I run as fast as my legs will carry me. The building passes in a blur until I break outside, panting for air.

"Lexi!"

Running across the courtyard, Felix is dressed in his usual plain black uniform, accompanied by several other members of the facility's security team. I look down at my hand to find the fire safely extinguished.

I quickly plaster on a panicked expression. "Fire! It's inside!"

Felix skids to a halt, tossing an arm around my shoulders. "Are you hurt?"

"Help... Ravius. He's inside."

Cursing, Felix barks at the others to advance. People are pouring out of the administration building, their yelling pierced by the blare of the alarm.

"Go." I push Felix's shoulder. "They need you."

"Will you be okay?"

"I'm fine. Go."

Quickly pressing a kiss to my cheek, he takes off after his men, making a beeline for the smoke pouring out of the building. I wait for his headful of shining blonde hair to disappear before moving.

I have no escape plan.

But I've got to try.

In the back of my mind, a gruff, rasping voice is warning me off this stupid idea. His crystal-blue eyes are accusatory in the depths of my imagination. But he isn't here.

Daniel left me. He took off with no indication of when he'd be back, and I won't sit here waiting for him to return.

Not when Ravius is willing to threaten my life to get what he wants.

Legs pumping and heart racing, I slip between the buildings, melting into the shadows. Trees envelope me as the shouting becomes distant. I keep sprinting until I'm alone with the silence.

I can't slow down. Not yet. The looming, barbed wire security fence that encases the facility is approaching. Summoning the fire back into my hands feels effortless.

It's ready.

So am I.

Spotting a sealed black box containing the electrical components attached to one of the fence's tall posts, I raise my hands, aiming the furious blast of fire in its direction.

Responding without complaint, fire races through the air in a blazing blur. It hits the electrical box with a bang, engulfing the metal in glorious flames.

The effect is instantaneous. Violent destruction reigns as a sizzle races over the electrified barbed wire, frying circuits and knocking out the power.

When I approach and tentatively touch the metal chain links, there's no pain. Not even a tiny current. The entire system is down as the components happily sizzle.

Climb, Lexi.

Fucking run.

My fingers ache as I scale the barbed wire, higher and higher into the thick coverage of mist. Not even the fast-approaching shouts slow me down.

Spotting the swarm of black-clad security officers on the horizon, I swing a leg over the top of the fence, shaking in the strong wind. I'm teetering on the verge of a long drop.

"Lexi! Hold it right there!"

Felix's voice briefly breaks my concentration. My foot slips, causing me to plummet several heart-stopping inches before I somehow find my balance again.

I hang in the cold air, watching them approach. There are dozens of them—panting and wild-eyed, led by my least favourite asshole, Brunt. His cold eyes lock on mine.

I can't go back.

He'll lock me up and throw away the key.

I move fast, my numb fingers fumbling over the rain-slick chain links. Halfway down to the ground, I feel my grip slip.

No!

I'm falling.

Tumbling through the air, the ground rushes up to meet me. I squeeze my eyes shut before impact. Pain races up my spine as my body collides with the wet, hard ground.

Something cracks, and agony explodes in the back of my head when it makes contact with the ground. A rush of hot, sticky blood slides down my neck and throat.

It's like the force inside me has fled, the blow to my head expelling it from my body. The world flashes in and out, coming in heartbreaking snippets.

Eve.

Her face.

Her pigtails.

Her sweet, lilting voice.

Staring up at the weak morning light spreading across the sky, I blink hard, trying to clear my hazy vision. My surroundings are fading fast as mental flashes take over.

Flowing, light-brown hair.

Wide, green eyes.

Rosy lips open on a shout.

Where are you?

I'll find you, mi amor.

But I can't be found. Not here. Not like this. With the squeal of blades slicing through the metal fence to reach me, I force my trembling body to obey.

Blood pours faster from my head with each movement.

I'm woozy and weak, but that doesn't stop me from unsteadily finding my feet, begging my vision to clear.

Shouting.

Thudding footsteps.

Falling rain.

"Lexi!" Felix's voice filters through the haze. "You're hurt. Stop running, babe!"

"I'm so sorry," I slur.

"You don't have to do this."

"Stand down!" Brunt yells at him. "She's mine."

Drawing in a deep breath, I turn and run into the thicket of trees beyond the fence. I can barely stand, everything around me is so blurry. Reality begins to warp and morph, allowing the green-eyed stranger to slip back into my mind.

You're hurt, mi amor.

Please tell me where you are.

"Leave me alone," I whisper to the voice.

I can't do that.

You're mine.

Pushing onwards, darkness spreads as the tree coverage thickens. I realize I have no idea where I'm going. The sheer stupidity of my plan is hitting me in the face.

I have nothing.

No one.

Nowhere to go.

"Lexi! Hold it right there!"

I keep running, stumbling through the dense forest. It's no use though. The sound of footsteps grows louder, moving fast through the shadows to catch me.

With a loud buzz, something hits me square in the back. Pain snaps through my limbs, and I'm powerless to stop myself from smacking into the forest floor.

Sprawled out on my back, I'm twitching all over, flushed with cold sweat. Brunt's broad shoulders block the view above me, a taser clasped tight in his hand.

"Try anything and I'll hit you again." He leans down on one knee to inspect me. "You're done, little bitch."

"F-F-Felix," I somehow manage to call out. "Help."

Hanging behind Brunt, he stares at me with anguish in his eyes. "I'm sorry, Lexi. You shouldn't have run."

Climbing to his feet, Brunt looms over me, a steel-capped foot raised high. He offers no warning before bringing it down.

Impacting with my face and nose, bones shatter before numbness overcomes me. I choke on a mouthful of blood as the awaiting abyss approaches.

But I'm not alone. Eyes gliding shut, the stranger inevitably returns, sliding back into my mind while my defences are down.

He stares at me.

Wild-eyed and furious.

Only this time, I envisage Daniel standing next to him. Both men watch on in horror, standing shoulder to shoulder, like they belonged together all along.

I'm sorry, Eve.

I tried.

VIII

STRENGTH

CHAPTER 12

GODS – NOTHING BUT THIEVES

*F*rigid, biting cold.

Trickling water.

Unbearable hunger.

The scents of mould and rust permeate the damp air which soaks into my bones, causing my teeth to chatter violently. I've forgotten what it feels like to be warm.

My wrists are shackled behind my back, chaining me to a leaking water pipe. The limbs have long since gone numb, wiping away the searing pain in my shoulders.

I'm going to die here.

I know it.

The darkness is so heavy, it almost feels like it's alive. There's a single wall light outside of my small prison cell, but it does little to break the shadows inside.

This place is a frozen wasteland. Cold and empty. A prison of the mind and soul. I haven't felt the stirrings of my gift since I woke up in here, chained and alone.

It's like I've been completely abandoned. Not even the Vitae can help me now. The world has turned its back on me. Again.

"Evie," I whisper deliriously. "I miss you so much. Please tell me you're okay. Please be safe."

But she can't hear me. No one can. I'm as alone as I've ever been, with nothing but ghosts and memories to hold me close.

Time passes. I don't know how much. There are no meals, no break to my solitude. Nothing but the trickling water and my breath fogging in the icy air as the stone floor leaches the heat from my bones.

In my desperation, I mentally scream his name.

Daniel.

Please... I need you.

But like everyone else, he's left me too. I'm trapped in a prison of my own making. Dipping in and out of unconsciousness, I flit between reality and nightmares. I'm haunted by all that I've lost.

My whole life.

My sanity.

My freedom... all stripped away.

"Please," I sob into the darkness. "Enough. Just let me die."

Nobody answers me. Not even the careless God that doomed me to this afterlife. I'm truly on my own now.

When the clang of a door opening breaks my semi-lucid daze, I strain against the shackles, fighting to pull myself upright.

Footsteps descend into the darkness. Another light is illuminated outside of the rusted cell bars, revealing a displeased grimace framed by slick, pearly blonde hair.

"Lexi," Ravius murmurs stiffly.

I wrench on the tight grip of the shackles again, slicing deeper into my wrists. It's no use. I can't shift even an inch.

"Do you know why you're here?"

"Because I didn't run fast enough," I retort.

His eyes narrow on me. "You've proven yourself to be a liability. We cannot tolerate such a risk to our secrecy."

"So what? You're going to keep me locked up here forever?"

"Until such a time when you are no longer deemed a risk. I'm not asking for your cooperation, Lexi. I'm demanding it."

Struggling to gather saliva in my parched mouth, I spit it at him. "How about you go and fuck yourself instead?"

"Ever the charmer."

I thrash against the shackles again, longing to wrap my hands around his throat. I should've burned him to a crisp when I had the chance.

"All you've done since the moment I arrived is manipulate me. I'm done playing your games."

"This is not a game!" he hisses through the bars. "If Caine gets hold of you, he will use your power to destroy us all."

"Maybe you deserve it!"

Hands wrapping around the bars, his face is a mask of rage. "Watch your tongue."

"Or what? You won't kill me. Keep me locked up all you want, but it won't change a thing. I'll never fight for you."

Ravius shakes his head, expression carved with rage. "You were supposed to be the one. She promised me a weapon, not a disobedient child."

"Call me a child again. See what happens."

His lip curls in derision. "Go right ahead."

My chest pangs with emptiness. He knows I'm too injured to follow through with my threats. I'd gotten so used to the hum of power, I now feel cold and empty without it.

"You will stay here until you come to your senses." Ravius backs away from the bars. "Forever, if needed."

Panic coils around my lungs like a python. "You can't leave me here!"

"Watch me, child."

Screaming at the top of my lungs, I wail his name, begging for him to return. Even if it's just to hurl more abuse at him. But Ravius doesn't stop, slinking from this subterranean hell.

The sounds of the door slamming shut and locking follows his exit. Thrashing and writhing, I feel blood slip over my wrists from the shackles slicing into my skin.

Defeated, a trail of silent tears runs down my cheeks. I can't hold them back any longer. I came so close and lost everything all over again.

She's out there.

Going through only God knows what.

Ravius is wrong. Our secrecy doesn't protect us. Instead, it keeps the entire Redeemed population under his control and subjugation. Just the way he likes it.

Head slumping, I doze in and out, my throat aching from dehydration. My head is pounding. Every inch of my battered body throbs with pain.

"Lexi," a soft, gentle voice croons. "Open your eyes, Lex."

I groan as light pierces my closed lids.

"Lex. It's me."

"D-Daniel?"

The metal bars clatter with the force of someone shaking them. Managing to peel my eyes open, I find it isn't Daniel here to save me. Not this time.

Michael waits on the other side of the cell door, rumpled and pale in a long-sleeved sweater and tiny jeans. His face is drawn, marked with exhaustion.

"Hey," he whispers, his concerned eyes scanning over me.

"What are you doing here?"

"I heard about what happened. No one knows I'm here. Ravius would kill me if he knew."

"There's space for one more in here," I joke, but it falls flat.

Michael's face softens. "What the hell happened, Lex? Why did you attack Ravius?"

The reminder of what triggered me to escape causes white-hot anger to flood my body. Michael might be my friend, but he's still one of them. Part of the lie, the deception woven into this so-called safe haven.

"Did you know?" I choke out.

"Know what?"

"About the prophecy."

His mouth slackens. I don't need to ask again. I can see the truth tangled in his eyes. They all knew—every single one of them has lied to me. Even Daniel.

"Lex…"

"Who was she? What did the prophecy say?"

He fists a handful of his copper curls. "You weren't supposed to find out like this."

"Tell me the fucking truth, Michael! Why me? What did I do to deserve this? I just want to go home!"

Releasing his hair, he sinks to the stone floor, sitting cross-legged outside the cell.

"We've been waiting for you." His head slumps. "It was prophesied that a weapon would present itself during our time of need. Everyone knows that war is coming."

"Because of Caine?"

Michael nods solemnly. "Ravius invited him here to negotiate. They left because it was unsuccessful."

"Negotiate for what?"

He worries his bottom lip. "Our future. Caine wants to abandon the accords and reveal our existence to the world. Ravius is trying to stop him."

"Why would Caine do that? To what end?"

"Global domination. In his mind, we are the superior race. He wants to take his rightful place, ruling over the non-Redeemed."

Mind whirling, I lean back against the water pipe, awash with dizziness. "What does any of this have to do with me?"

"Because you're different." His malachite eyes pierce my

skin. "Your memories. Your gift. The Vitae pours from you in a way we've never seen before. That's the power Ravius is so desperate for."

"The power he was promised… by *her*."

His eyebrows raise. "You know about her?"

"I know enough. Who was she?"

Michael rubs the back of his neck. "I think Daniel would be best to answer that question."

"And where is he, huh?" Frustrated, tears continue to track down my cheeks. "He left me here so he could be with his precious Elder."

"There are things you don't know, Lex. Daniel isn't a bad person."

"I'm not sure he'd agree with you."

Forehead meeting the bars, Michael stares down at the dirt-streaked floor. "I'm going to get you out of here, but I need your help. You can't fight this."

"Like hell. I'm not a weapon. I'm a person!"

"Keep this up and you'll be nothing!"

"You think that scares me?" I scoff through my tears. "I've spent my entire life being nothing. Just walk away, Michael. Leave me here to rot."

Glancing at me, there's real, visceral pain in his gaze. "Is that what your sister would want? She needs you."

"I can't help her from this cell! I can't even help myself!"

"The only person keeping you in this cell is you. Ravius is angry, but he isn't a bad person. All he wants is to protect his people."

I jerk my head around the dank basement cell. "Is this what protection looks like?"

"You would've gotten yourself killed out there!" he replies angrily. "Believe it or not, this is protection. From yourself."

He stands up when the door to the prison clatters open again. Wearing a worried frown, Felix descends, carrying a food tray. When he spots Michael, he sighs.

"You want to be down here too?"

Michael shifts on his feet. "Someone needed to talk some sense into her."

"Ravius has forbidden any visitors. You know that."

"She's our friend, Felix!"

Felix places the tray down then pulls out a set of keys to unlock the door. I force myself to sit up, unable to move a single finger from the uncomfortable bind behind my back.

Carrying the tray in, he places it down at my side before kneeling to reach for the cuffs. I could sing in relief as he unlocks them and drops the metal circles onto the stone floor.

"Felix," I weep. "Please… get me out of here."

"You know I can't do that," he whispers back. "Here. You need to eat and drink. I'll leave the cuffs off."

Moving my stiff arms, I gasp at the flow of blood re-entering my limbs. "Thank you."

He scans over me. "You in pain?"

"Some."

Felix glances back over his shoulder at Michael, who is watching us both and wringing his small hands, visibly desperate to help.

Felix looks down at his ground, shaking his head. "I wasn't supposed to let anyone in here."

"Ravius really wants me to suffer, huh?"

Felix forces a small smile. "He's pissed, but he'll get over it. You're not the first person to be thrown in here."

Backing up, he waves for Michael to step into the cell. Michael rushes in, quickly kneeling down next to me and scanning my bloodied body from head to toe.

"You've got a fractured skull and a broken nose," he declares. "You're healing at our accelerated rate, but I can speed things along. No one will ever know."

"Hurry," Felix urges.

Hands moving to probe the painful slopes of my skull,

Michael works fast. I gasp as heat pours from his palms and into my head, knitting me back together.

"Daniel?" I breathe shakily.

Michael hesitates, his hands still gripping my head. "I'm trying to get hold of him."

"Where is he?"

"Still in the States."

After healing my stuffy nose, Michael releases me then sits back on his haunches. Too many conflicted emotions to count radiate from his green gaze as he pushes the food and bottled water closer to me.

"Don't let them win, Lex. You're more than a weapon. But this isn't the way to prove that."

Joining Felix outside of the cell, Michael watches me with sadness as the barred door slams shut. I quickly grab the bottle of water and gulp it down, my bloodstained hands shaking.

"I'll talk to Ravius," Felix promises as he locks my cell. "We're going to get you out, babe."

"Please… don't leave me alone in here."

"I'm sorry." Felix avoids my eyes again, his fist pressed to his mouth. "We'll come back when we can."

"Felix! Please!"

Grabbing Michael's arm, Felix tows him backwards. The slam of the door closing behind them throws me back into hopelessness.

Alone.

Not even the stranger's voice returns.

THE HIGH PRIESTESS

CHAPTER 13

AFTERLIFE – THE HARA

I'm running through long, soft, green grass. Carefree and light. Sunshine blazes down on me, warming my skin. Nothing but peaceful, empty meadows surround me.

I'm free.

Alive.

Skidding to a halt, the grass brushes my bare legs beneath the flowing white dress I wear. When someone's hand slips into mine, I startle, looking down to find my sister's familiar, innocent eyes peering up at me.

"Evie!"

She throws her arms around my legs. "I missed you, Lexi."

"You're here. I'm so sorry; I never meant to leave you."

"Where did you go?" Her bottom lip juts out.

Kneeling down, I stroke a hand over her braided hair. "It doesn't matter now. We're together again."

"Not forever." Eyes shining with tears, she grips my hand tight. "He's coming for you, Lexi. You have to stop him."

My heart flips behind my ribcage.

"Who's coming, Eve?"

Her fingernails dig into my palms.

"The devil."

I watch in horror as her entire body is consumed by burning flames.

169

Smoke and ash replace the space where my sister once stood, her bones crumbling to blackened dust at my feet. She's gone. Dead. And it's my fault.

"Evie!" Falling to my knees, I search through the still-hot ashes, begging for her to return. The meadow reverberates with my anguished screams, echoing endlessly into the abyss.

"No! Eve!"

It's too late.

She's gone.

Head falling, I sob into my ash-streaked hands, feeling my heart splinter into jagged pieces in my chest. I don't stop crying as a hand gently brushes my head, two fingers sliding beneath my chin to tilt my eyes back up.

"Mi amor."

The verdant meadow reflects back at me in the depths of his brilliant, green irises, framed by lashes so dark, the colour resembles the deepest pits of hell.

The stranger is so breathtaking, it's painful to look at his ethereal beauty. His features are sharp and defined, glowing with a warm, olive tan that complements his shoulder-length light brown hair.

"What happened?" He strokes my wet cheek.

"She's dead. My sister is gone."

Kneeling down in front of me, he pulls my hands into his, squeezing so tightly my bones grind together. The hum in my chest roars with the brush of contact, surging through me like rolling thunderclouds.

"Listen to me," he urges. "We don't have long until we both wake up. Where are you?"

I stare up at him through my coursing tears. "Who are you?"

"There's no time. Tell me your name."

"It's Lexi."

"Lexi," he repeats, tasting the word. "You don't know how long I've waited for you, Lexi."

"What do you mean?"

Leaning close, he presses his forehead to mine. "Feel that?"

Power sizzles between us, bolts of lightning crackling across the places where our skin touches. I'd forgotten what the bite of surging Vitae feels like. It's back with a vengeance, pulsating through my veins.

This is the same jittery feeling that consumes me in Daniel's presence, but now it feels different. Like identical snowflakes that are actually completely unique upon closer inspection.

"We were born for this," he purrs. "Born for each other."

"I don't understand what's happening."

"I'll explain everything, but I need to know where—"

Hands wrenched apart, I'm dragged backwards by a gust, tearing me away from the stranger. He shouts my name, desperately battling to chase after me, but he's held back by an invisible wall.

"Lexi!"

His voice changes. Hardening. Growing rougher, raspier, angrier... melting into an entirely different voice. The next shout of my name lances through my skull.

* * *

"Lexi! Lex!"

Slammed back into my aching body, I startle awake with a pained gasp. Instead of the shining, endless meadow, nothing but darkness and damp shadows surrounds me.

"You have crossed a fucking line this time, Ravius!"

"She attacked me—"

Their angry voices lash back and forth. Two looming shadows face off against each other outside my cell, barely visible through my swimming vision.

Shoulders hunched and fists raised, I recognise the giant that looms high above Ravius. The emptiness that has filled my chest since I woke up in here is gone, replaced with searing heat.

It expands and fills my extremities—crackling, sizzling, singeing my nerve-endings. The rush of power caused by his close proximity is overwhelming after so long spent alone in pain.

171

Daniel.

"I don't give a goddamn what she did! I'm out there fighting your battle for you, and you locked up my bonded!"

"Lexi is a threat to us all."

"The only threat you should be worried about right now is me. I've played your loyal soldier for long enough."

"I did not order you to abandon your bonded." Ravius's voice lashes with cold fury. "None of this would've happened if you did your job."

"My job? You're her Elder!"

"And she needed you here!" Ravius shouts back.

There's a long, pregnant pause. Daniel's barrel chest is heaving beneath his tight black t-shirt, hands braced on his hips as he battles to restrain his temper. He looks ready to physically attack Ravius.

"Unlock the cell," he instructs.

Ravius doesn't flinch beneath his furious stare. "It's not safe to reintroduce her to the general population."

"Unlock the cell, or I will tell your brother that you've spent the last century plotting against him. You can kiss your accords goodbye."

I watch Ravius freeze, stock-still.

"You wouldn't."

Daniel takes a menacing step closer to him. "This empire of yours means nothing to me. I have no qualms about destroying it and taking my chances out there in the outside world."

"Daniel—"

"Now! Or I'll be making that phone call to Caine."

Head bowing in defeat, Ravius reaches into his suit jacket then flourishes a set of keys. "You're a fool."

Daniel snatches them from his hands. "And you're a coward."

Quickly unlocking the cell door, he moves in a blur. Ravius

shakes his head and watches as Daniel crumples to his knees in front of me.

I want to scream at him. Shout. Spit. Beat and bruise him. He left me here alone then ran off after his Elder like an obedient puppy. But all I feel is overwhelming relief.

"Love," he breathes hoarsely, brushing matted hair behind my ear.

Mouth dry and throat sore, my voice comes out as a gravelly whisper. "You came back."

His hands hover over my bloodstained skin and dirty clothing, unsure of where to land. "I never should've left."

"Not gonna argue w-with that."

"You sure?" He summons a tiny half-smile.

"Maybe l-later."

"I'll hold you to it. Can you stand?"

Shaking all over from the frigid cold and days of starvation, I shake my head. "I don't think so."

"Hold on, love."

Spotting the raw skin on my wrists, his expression hardens into a visible mask of rage that contorts his chiselled features. I must look as bad as I feel.

I don't know how long I've been held here. It's been a while if I look terrifying enough to disturb the ice man himself. Michael and Felix never returned, leaving me to rot alone in the darkness.

Daniel grits out a breath before sliding his arms underneath my legs and easily lifting me into his arms. As soon as he touches me, the Vitae comes surging back to life, purring beneath his attention.

I curl up in his strong embrace, pooled against his firm chest and the unsteady pounding of his heart. He doesn't complain about the filthy state of me.

"This isn't over," Ravius warns as we pass him. "You can't protect her forever."

"Watch me," Daniel hisses at him. "Come near her again and we're through."

Winding my arms around his neck, I bury my face in Daniel's soft shirt, breathing in the comforting familiarity of his evergreen and peppercorn scent.

He moves fast, putting as much distance between us and that hellhole as possible.

"I've got you," he whispers.

With each step we take, rising from the darkness of the prison, heat prickles across my scalp. It burns hotter and hotter, thawing the ice frosted around my organs.

I need more.

He's bringing me back to life.

Hand snaking beneath the neckline of his t-shirt, I flatten my palm against his thudding pulse point. Daniel gasps as the invisible heat reaches a peak then spreads between us.

"Lexi…"

"P-Please."

Sliding my other hand downwards to dip beneath the hem of his shirt, I stroke across his defined, washboard abs, teasing the flushed expanse of skin.

"Fuck," he gasps.

My body is trembling all over with excess energy. After feeling disconnected and empty for so long, the return of the Vitae hits me hard. Even Daniel's walking unsteadily. He can feel it too through the bond.

"You l-left," I stutter out.

"I'm so sorry."

"My gift… I couldn't… Ravius…"

"What did he do to you?" he snarls.

My tears soak his skin, hot moisture slipping between us. "He told me the truth."

"What truth, Lex?"

Looking up, I ignore the swirling wind around us as we

cross the courtyard and stare deep into his widened, aqua eyes.

"Why didn't you tell me about her?"

He clears his throat, trying hard to conceal a visible flash of fear. "I don't know what you're talking about."

"I think you do."

His footsteps slow. Rain crashes down, soaking us to the bone and gluing our skin together. But we don't move. Not a single inch. Not while Daniel stares down at me in dismay.

I swipe dribbles of rain from his face. "Ravius believes in her prophecy, whether it's true or not. He thinks I'm some gift-wrapped miracle just for him."

"Lexi—"

"What do you believe?" I interrupt him.

Droplets cling to his thick lashes, mimicking the pearlescent gleam of tears. But he doesn't feel remorse. Not my cold, unfeeling Daniel, alone in his frozen wasteland.

Does he?

"I don't know anymore." His whisper is guttural.

"That makes two of us."

He tenderly swipes wet hair from my face. "You've been hurt. Please just let me take you home. I promise, I'll tell you everything. We can figure this out."

"I don't need you."

The corner of his mouth twitches. "And I don't need you. But that doesn't mean I don't want you."

Mistrust is screaming through me, but it isn't the only feeling making my brain glitch. I want to crawl inside the shell of his skin and curl around his heart so he can't leave me again.

This man infuriates me.

Confuses me.

Fucking terrifies me.

But that doesn't stop me from wanting him so badly it's

physically painful. Even though I tried to run without him... I guess that means we're even now.

"Come on." He starts walking again. "We're getting soaked."

Clinging to his shirt, I let him carry me through the steadily falling rain, towards the Nightingale building. It feels like years have passed since I left my apartment.

"How long were you gone?" I ask.

"Couple of weeks. Michael said that Ravius held you for over ten days. The son of a bitch didn't even call me."

"He knew you'd stop him."

"Or kill him," he mutters sinisterly.

Inside the elevator, exhaustion overcomes me. My lips tease the violent pounding of Daniel's jugular vein as I bury my face in his neck. I feel him inhale sharply.

"I fucking hate you," I murmur.

"I know."

"You left."

He sighs heavily, causing his chest to rumble. "I have a job to do. Appearances to maintain. This is bigger than the both of us."

"Caine?"

"He's on the verge of deposing Ravius. We came here to negotiate, but Caine had no intentions of abandoning his mission to rule the whole fucking world."

"How did you get away?"

The elevator doors open, and Daniel tightens his grip around me at the mention of his beloved, psychotic Elder. I doubt he even realises he's doing it.

"Caine thinks I'm visiting one of our other US facilities on business. Training security staff."

Fishing a key card from his pocket, Daniel scans it to unlock my apartment. I can't help but gape at him in shock.

"Who gave you a key?"

He has the audacity to wink at me.

"I have my ways."

"Talk about an invasion of privacy."

He barks an unimpressed laugh. "Did you see me complain about an invasion of privacy when you were busy binding our souls together?"

I thump my hand against his chest. "You're never going to let me live that down, are you?"

"Not a chance."

The apartment is dark and cold, filled with the sound of falling rain. Daniel ignores my feeble protests, flipping on lights as he carries me through to the bedroom where I'm placed back on my feet.

"You should get cleaned up."

But the moment he lets go, fierce pain lances through me, the ache in my chest expanding into a cavernous hole. Daniel freezes at the agonised moan that escapes my lips.

"Lex?"

"Hurts," I whimper.

"Fuck, love. What can I do?"

"The Vitae… it needs y-you… I need you."

Crouching down in front of me, he scans over my bloodstained clothing. "What happened to hating me?"

Taking his outstretched hand, I tangle our fingers together. "Not tonight. I'll be angry tomorrow."

Embers sizzling in the frosty depths of his eyes, he tugs on my hand, pulling me against him. Daniel's hand moves to press between my shoulder blades.

I'm pinned against the hard, unyielding slopes of his pectorals, our mouths an inch apart.

"Tell me what you need," he hums.

I can't help grinding against him, relishing in the firm press of his cock pushing into my core. His thick brows raise as I make my intentions clear.

"Touch me. Kiss me. Give me one good reason why I shouldn't try to climb that fence again."

"The fractured skull didn't put you off?"

I drag my lips along his stubbled jawline. "I'll break every bone in my body if that's what it takes to get back to Eve."

"If you think I'll let you put yourself at risk again, you've got another thing coming. I'm sticking by your side from now on."

Teasing his lips with mine, I gently peck his mouth. "Who says I want you here?"

His hand moves lower to squeeze the swell of my ass. "Your body tells a different story, love."

Lips latching on to mine, he kisses me with barely restrained fury. His mouth batters and bruises mine. Angry. Possessive. Staking his claim for the entire world to see.

I kiss him back with all the anger that led me to run in the first place. Daniel abandoned me. Left me to fend for myself with only half the truth. I can't trust this man—not when he didn't trust me enough to tell me about the prophecy.

Both hands moving to grip my backside, he lifts me up so my legs can circle his hips. I'm attached to his waist, writhing against him with each footstep.

Daniel walks me backwards into the attached ensuite bathroom. He places me down on the edge of the sink then moves to flick the walk-in shower on.

"Is that all your blood?"

I bite down on my lip. "Are you going to shout at me if I say yes?"

"Shouting is the last thing on my mind."

Pushing my legs open so he can step between them, he takes the hem of my filthy shirt then tears it over my head.

Dropping the soaking wet fabric to the bathroom floor, his hungry gaze roams over me. I know the moment he spots my scars, jagged and uneven, marring the expanse of my torso.

I'm littered with stab wounds, covering every inch of available skin. The shiny pink marks vary—some thin from the tip of the blade that carved me up, others deeper and longer.

Shame threatens to steal my courage, but I don't let my eyes drop from his. I won't hide my past. If he wants me… then he has to want all of me.

The tip of his calloused finger traces down my breastbone to meet a raised scar. "Who did this to you?"

"I told you my story."

Realisation dawns in his eyes.

"Just give me a name, Lex. I'll kill them myself."

Pushing his hands away, I hop down from the sink's edge and reach for my waistband. Daniel seethes as I unfasten my dirty jeans and push them over my hips, exposing my panties.

"Lexi."

I remain silent but hold eye contact. His throat bobs as I seize the flicker of bravery in my chest and stoke the flames, letting them steel my spine. My panties drop to the floor next.

My bra is the last thing to go, revealing my breasts. Standing in front of him, bare and trembling, I feel utterly exposed. I should be terrified. But instead, I feel liberated.

This is control.

Freedom.

He can't control me here. The monster. Every other man who's sought to control me since. Ravius. Caine. Unknown demons lurking in the shadows.

Turning my back, I step into the steam-filled shower. Hot water beats down on me, sending swirls of bright-red streaming down the drain. The relief is acute as my body starts to thaw beneath the steam.

Clothing rustles from outside the shower before there's a creak and a column of heat meets my back. I hold my breath as a single, teasing fingertip travels down the length of my spine.

"You're a dangerous creature," Daniel mutters.

Turning beneath the spray, I drag my hands down the wet

179

planes of his sculpted chest. He's completely bare and looks to be carved by the gods themselves.

The odd scar is dappled across his olive-toned torso, littered with dark patches of chest hair. Hardened ridges carve the lines of his muscles, sculpting him to perfection.

Each stroke of my fingertips across his skin fuels the electricity sparking between us. Daniel's hands move to grip my hips tight, drawing us even closer together.

"I've wanted to sink my cock inside you since the moment we met," he growls in my ear. "I just didn't want to admit it to myself."

I hook a leg up on his waist, feeling the nudge of his hardness against my pubic bone. "So do it."

"I want to take my time with you, love. By the time I'm done, you'll be fucking begging for me to give you relief."

"I'm not very patient."

"Learn to be."

Teeth sinking into my ear lobe, he bites down, sending delicious pain zipping up my spine. I moan, pushing my breasts into his chest as his mouth moves lower, down the slope of my neck.

Teeth nipping and mouth sucking, he marks his way across my skin, leaving a trail of destruction. By the time his mouth reaches my left nipple, I'm a wet, panting wreck.

He wraps his lips around my pebbled nipple. "Want me to make you feel good, baby?"

"God… yes."

"You don't answer to God." His hand crashes against my ass cheek, spanking me hard. "You answer to me."

More warmth floods my core, tightening and twisting. I grind up against the pressure of his cock, relishing in the friction.

I need him inside of me, regardless of the complications it will cause. He lied to me. Ran. Concealed the truth that everyone knew but me. My body doesn't give a fuck though.

Right now, neither do I.

We belong together.

"Up against the wall." He pushes my leg down his waist. "Now, Lexi."

"Daniel," I gasp.

"That was an order."

Chastised, I back up in the generous space of the shower. My back meets the warm tiles, and I pin myself against them.

Daniel slides a hand down his abdominals, reaching for the long, hard length of his vein-laced cock. He's huge. Intimidatingly so.

"Like what you see?" Wickedness gleams in his eyes.

I swallow hard. "Come and find out."

"Not yet. You've been hurt, so I want to take care of you first."

Prowling closer towards me, his lips capture mine in a hard, fast storm. Possessive and dominating, he steals my breath for his own, his tongue plundering my mouth.

Barely able to hold myself upright, I move to grip his shoulders as he begins kissing lower, working his way down. His lips trail between my breasts then down my scarred belly.

"I want to bury my face between your creamy thighs and taste what's mine," he says gruffly. "If you need me to stop, you're going to say so."

"Please," I whine.

"Please what, baby?"

Gripping my hips, he drops to his knees beneath the spray, peering up at me. His cerulean eyes are tainted by a carnal need I wouldn't mind drowning in.

"Words, Lexi. Tell me what you want me to do."

The Vitae surges through me again, burning a path through my core and throbbing pussy. I fist a hand in his mop of dark hair.

"Taste me," I beg shamelessly.

"Such a needy little thing, aren't you?"

Seizing a handful of hair, I tug sharply. "Your job is to look after me, isn't it? Go on and do it."

He licks his plump lips, quirking in a full-blown grin. "Yes, ma'am."

When his mouth descends on the heat twitching between my thighs, I throw my head back on a moan. His lips secure themselves to my pulsating clit, tongue flicking across the sensitised bud.

"Fuck!"

Alex never touched me like this. It would've been too personal for him. He was content to drink himself into a stupor and finish as quickly as possible when we fucked.

But Daniel isn't anything like him. He obviously has no qualms with dropping to his knees and lashing my aching core with his tongue. Each open-mouthed kiss blurs my vision with need.

Bringing his thumb to my clit, he circles the bud, spreading saliva across my sizzling nerve endings. His tongue parts my folds, licking and sucking a tantalising path to my slit.

"God, how I want to fuck this sweet pussy."

Fingertip replacing his thumb, he flicks my clit before sliding his digit lower to circle my tight hole. I grind myself against the heel of his palm, silently pleading for more.

I feel drunk with lust when his finger eases inside my slick opening, thrusting deep into my pussy. He stretches me wide, pushing in and out. Stars burst behind my eyes at the electric current humming between us.

"Can you take another finger?" he asks.

"Y-Yes."

After circling a second digit in my wetness, he pushes it inside me in one slick move. I cry out at the pressure. I never thought being touched like this could feel so good.

Moving both fingers in a pounding beat, he fucks me with his hand, pausing to secure his tongue to my clit every few thrusts. I undulate against his face, chasing the high.

The feeling of energy flowing from the pool in my chest into him only heightens the pleasure. We couldn't stop if we tried. The force that connects us wants this too much.

Tightening my grip on his hair, I feel my release begin to crest. Building ever higher, it approaches on the horizon. All I can do is let his mouth and tongue worship me into oblivion.

"Is my pretty little bonded going to come for me?" Daniel teases as he stops for a breath.

"Call me little again. I dare you."

"I'm going to silence that sharp tongue of yours with my cock in your throat. Try being a smart ass then."

Teeth grazing my nub, his fingers resume their angry pumping. I'm on the verge of letting go when a tower of heat crashes over me, flowing from the cradle in my chest.

Crying out, the Vitae fills me up as my orgasm hits. The two collide in a spectacular fashion like flames dancing in a snowstorm, both fighting for survival.

"Let go," Daniel commands.

I'm powerless to refuse. My vision dims as bliss fills every inch of me, rapidly expanding with the force of my gift playing right into its hands.

I swear, in those dark, hazy seconds, I can hear Daniel. His thoughts. His feelings. The anguish and despair that hardens the shell he wears for the world but turns him to putty around me.

We're connected.

Bound.

Fated… forever.

Slumping against the tiles, I fight to catch my breath. "Jesus."

Daniel's tongue darts out to clean the moisture scored across his mouth. "I love watching you fall apart for me."

"Did you feel that?" I pant.

"The Vitae?" he guesses, climbing to his feet. "Yeah. I felt it."

"What the hell is happening to us?"

He pushes wet hair away from my face. "I don't know, love. This is all uncharted territory."

Still soaked and trembling, I peer up at him through my lashes, pleading for more. Daniel snorts and shakes his head.

"Not tonight. You've just spent ten fucking days in a rotting cell. I'm not going to take advantage of you like that."

"You're cute for thinking I don't want this."

"Cute?" He wrinkles his nose.

Reaching onto my tiptoes, I brush my lips against the corner of his mouth. "Don't worry, I won't tell anyone."

Pecking his mouth again, I stroke the roughened stubble that covers his hard jawline. I can feel how turned on he is right now, and I'm aching with the desire to return the favour.

Hand sliding down his chest, I wrap it around the base of his shaft then gently squeeze. A low purr emanates from his throat.

"Lexi," he warns.

"Do you ever shut up?"

Stroking his hard length, I pump his cock, lightly twisting and squeezing with each rotation. Daniel's teeth sink into my bottom lip as he kisses me again.

Releasing his lips, I take his hand and hold it tight as I ease down onto my knees. He watches me sink to the shower floor, a look of wonderment filling his eyes.

Eye level with his long, hard cock, framed by a patch of dark hair, I glance up at him. Even from down here, I feel fucking powerful. There aren't many men I'd willingly get on my knees for.

Grasping his shaft, I drop a kiss on the tip of his dick, swirling my tongue over the velvet softness. He lifts the long, wet blonde hair from my shoulders to hold it in his fist.

My mouth wraps around his cock, then I take him deep into my throat. His grip on my hair tightens as his hips begin to move.

"How are you so perfect?" he growls.

Moving my hand lower, I take a handful of his balls, lightly squeezing the softness. Daniel groans, his head tipping back.

The energised feeling is still building between us. Ebbing and flowing, following the rhythm of our bodies. The hatred I should feel for him never comes. Not in this moment.

I doubt the Vitae would allow it.

We can't escape each other.

Popping off his dick, strands of saliva stretch from my mouth as I lick my lips. He peers down at me, his breathing ragged. I own his ass right now.

"I want you to tell me about her," I demand.

His brows disappear into his hair. "Who?"

"The one who made the prophecy."

"Right now?"

Kissing his cock, I carefully lick the length in a long, slow tease. "If you want to come, I get the truth."

His grip on my hair slackens. "Fuck, Lex. You know I can't talk about her."

"The same way you couldn't tell me the truth about the prophecy she made?"

Pulling away from his crotch, I refuse to lay another finger on him. Not until I get what I want. He reads the challenge in my gaze.

"She's gone," he says softly.

"No. She isn't." I gesture between us, licking my parted lips. "There is nothing *gone* about the way she makes you behave."

Bracing his hand against the wall, Daniel turns his face up into the shower spray, like drowning himself will allow him to escape. I wait on my knees, silent and demanding.

This is so wrong. I'm not a manipulative person. Not unless I have to be. But I need to know what I'm facing, and I don't mind playing dirty to finally get the truth out of him.

When his head falls in defeat, he shakes his head. "Her gift made her a target. I couldn't protect her."

"What gift?"

"The prophecy wasn't a one off. She could predict the future. Not always, but it came in flashes. She was always right."

Satisfied, I take his cock back into my mouth. Anguish and desire collide as he hisses out a curse. Bobbing on his shaft, I take him deep, loving the resultant burn in my throat.

"I loved her, Lex," he admits in a rasp. "She was my everything, and he took her from me."

I can feel him tensing up more, his muscles coiling tighter with each suck. His soul is bare and vulnerable for the first time. All it took was breaking him down into controllable pieces.

My pace picks up, determined to drag him all the way to the edge. I want all his secrets. He isn't allowed them anymore. Daniel curses gutturally as he nears his climax.

"I wonder if she knew that her death... her prophecy... would bring me you. The only woman who could ever replace her."

Teeth grazing against his tip, I rotate my head, sucking him back into my mouth at a different angle. He's close. His muscles are tense beneath my fingertips.

When his cock jerks in my mouth, I feel the energy inside me burgeon. Every second of his release flows through me, flooding my core all over again.

Daniel bellows as he pours his seed into my mouth, the salty fluid hitting the back of my throat. I release his length, making sure he's watching as I swallow every last drop of come.

"Fuck, Lex!"

I wipe off my mouth. "You think I could replace her?"

Averting his gaze, he doesn't answer me. Grabbing his

hand, I pull myself up then wrap my arms around his neck. He looks terrified of whatever he reads on my face.

"Who was she, Daniel?"

Stern lines bracket his mouth. "My wife. She was my wife."

Ignoring the confusing emotions his words bring, I cup his cheek, stroking a thumb over the defined bone.

"And who killed her?"

His eyes glimmer with unshed tears, illuminating the blue iris into a shining, almost oceanic hue. I've never seen him so emotional. I didn't even know it was possible.

He clears his throat.

"It was Caine."

XIII

DEATH

CHAPTER 14

DON'T TRUST THAT WOMAN – JAMES QUICK

"*T*wo americanos. One black, one with hazelnut syrup."

Daniel fires off our order, ignoring the playful smirk on Martha's face at seeing our hands entwined. She's barely managing to hold her laughter in.

"You know my coffee order?" I whisper to him.

Daniel shrugs, his lips sealed.

"Martha?" I level her with a stare. "Have you been gossiping about my coffee preferences?"

This time, she releases a chuckle. "I'd hardly call it gossiping. More like an interrogation for information."

"Daniel!" I exclaim. "You're creepy. You know that, right?"

His shoulder nudges mine as he smothers a laugh. "I'll take that as a compliment. I just wanted to see what she knew."

We move to the end of the coffee bar, trying to ignore the weight of people's gazes on us. After spending the night back in my bed, I'm feeling a hell of a lot more like myself.

Waking up to find Daniel fast asleep in the bed was a shock, his bare arms and legs wrapped around me. I assumed he would leave. Especially after I called him out and forced him to reveal the truth about his wife.

Wife.

It hurts to even think that word.

Working on our coffees, Martha offers me a sparkling smile. "How are you getting on, Lexi? All settled in?"

I rest against the bar. "Things have been a bit bumpy."

Her almond-shaped eyes soften with sympathy. "I heard you had a little… run in with Ravius."

"Does everyone know?" I sigh.

She pumps syrup into my steaming coffee. "He likes to make an example of punishing disobedience for others to see."

"That's just great."

"I wouldn't worry about it," she rushes to assure me. "I think you impressed a lot of people though."

Daniel snorts next to me. "Impressed isn't the word I'd use for almost getting herself killed."

"People need hope." Martha ignores his caustic tone. "Hope that there's more beyond this life. No one's ever tried to escape before."

"And no one will again," he snaps, looking pointedly at me.

I raise my hands in surrender. "Whatever you say."

"Lexi—"

"Coffee!" I interrupt, making grabby hands. "Gimme."

Martha passes the magical elixir over, and I greedily accept the steaming-hot drink. No amount of death-defying escape attempts will deter me from enjoying a good cup of coffee.

Sliding over a handful of chips to her, Daniel waves off Martha's attempts to shove them back. He slips an arm around my waist then guides me over to sit by the window.

We slump on the patterned, vintage sofa, our legs touching. Daniel sips his coffee before turning his attention to me. I can't help but blush as memories of last night resurface.

He brushes a finger over my heated cheek. "Cat got your tongue?"

"No."

"Then say what you're thinking."

"Trust me, this isn't the place."

His gaze is dark and smouldering beneath his thick lashes. "Looking for a repeat already?"

The warmth in my cheeks travels to my ears. Wishing that the ground would open up and swallow me whole, I slurp on my hot drink.

"Not a chance. I'm back to hating you today."

Placing a hand on my jean-clad thigh, he squeezes and drops his lips to my ear. "Tell your wet pussy that, love."

Excited shivers wrack my frame. God, what is wrong with me? I'm tempted to let him strip me bare, bend me over and fuck me raw in this coffee shop, audience be damned.

Sucking in an uneven breath, I focus on the pitch-black liquid in my cup, ignoring the way his presence makes my hands tremble. He's a fucking force to be reckoned with.

I turn my head when the bell above the door tinkles. Stepping into the cafe, Michael and Felix both spot us, their smiles instantly replaced with apprehension. I place my cup of coffee down before I throw it at them.

"Lexi, can we talk?" Michael asks pleadingly.

Standing up, Daniel steps in front of me. "Stay right there, the pair of you."

Felix tries for a placating smile. "We only want to apologise."

"You left her in there to rot!" Daniel roars.

"We had no choice." Felix's eyes remain downcast, his shoulders slumped. "You know what Ravius would've done to us if we opposed him."

"You think I give a fuck?"

"Guys," I interrupt. "Little loud? Just sit down, and let's talk about this without killing each other."

Reluctantly backing off, Daniel retakes his seat, allowing Michael and Felix to sit down opposite us. Silence reigns until I break it.

"You're both forgiven."

"What?" Daniel splutters. "You can't just—"

"I can, and I am."

"They left you in that cell, Lex!"

"And you left me here after failing to mention that your dead wife made a prophecy about me. You really want to go down that road?"

Daniel slumps on the sofa, his shoulders sagging as he grumbles a curse under his breath. The other two glance between us with matching stunned expressions.

"You told her then," Michael surmises.

"She... got it out of me."

I choke on a mouthful of hot coffee. The secret look Daniel shoots me is full of carnal promise. That asshole knows how to push my buttons in all the right places.

"The prophecy is a load of horse shit," Felix mutters. "No one actually believes in that crap. Only Ravius."

I look up at Michael. "What about you?"

He rubs his tired green eyes. "You're different, Lex. I'm not sure what that means yet."

"Lexi doesn't need this kind of pressure!" Felix leans towards Daniel, a muscle jumping in his cheek.

"Lexi can speak for herself," I interject. "And I've told Ravius where he can stick his precious prophecy. It doesn't interest me."

Both Michael and Felix seem to relax at that. Right now, none of us trust Ravius. He's spiralling and desperately grasping for any remaining threads of control.

Daniel steals my hand back. "What about your training with Ravius?"

"I'm not going back into that office."

"Maybe you could train her," Michael suggests.

Daniel stares at him. "I'm not gifted."

"No, but you are bonded. You can help Lexi control her gift. And after what happened, it wouldn't hurt if she could learn to defend herself."

Anticipation pierces my chest. "Wait, does this mean I get to beat up Daniel?"

The man in question snorts.

"I'd like to see you try. But maybe combat training isn't the worst idea. We can incorporate using your gift into it."

The idea of shooting fire at Daniel's annoying backside is both exhilarating and unnerving. Part of me wouldn't mind having the opportunity to punch him.

"It's better than nothing," Michael reasons.

"I can help too," Felix chimes in with a hopeful smile. "We train all the new security recruits in combat. In case you don't want to hit your new boyfriend."

This time, Daniel's the one to almost choke on his steaming drink. I have to hammer him on the back before he coughs up a lung.

"He isn't my boyfriend!"

Felix gestures to our entwined hands. "Then what is this?"

"Why is it any of your business?"

He shrugs with a knowing smirk. "I'm nosy."

"Well, butt out of it."

"Defensive, much?"

Laughing to himself, his expression is wiped clear of all amusement when Raven walks into the cafe. She looks terrible —exhausted, pale and wrung-out.

"She's left the hospital." Michael sounds shocked.

"Is that where she's been?" I follow his line of sight, frowning at my slouched-over friend.

"Raven's been caring for our newest arrival in the hospital. She's barely left his side since he woke up."

"The jumper you told me about?" Daniel asks.

Michael nods. "He's in a bad way."

"Wait, what jumper?" I look between them.

"The new arrival was a suicide." Michael winces at the thought. "Poor son of a bitch barely had a bone intact when he arrived. It took hours to heal him."

"Christ. That's horrific."

Abandoning my drink, I walk over to Raven, feeling equal parts pity and anger. She's been absent for weeks. I feel like a shitty friend for not realising sooner, but she hasn't been there for me either.

"Raven?"

Two weary eyes meet mine. "Oh, Lexi. You're here."

"Where have you been?"

"Work." She shrugs, reaching for her takeout coffee. "Sorry I haven't been around."

"That's it? You're sorry?"

"Yeah," she replies flatly. "I have to go."

"Raven, wait!"

She walks off, leaving me to chase after her. We step outside into the frigid air, the courtyard humming with people walking around, peacefully going about their afterlives.

I manage to dart in front of her, blocking her path. "Wait! What's going on with you?"

"I just have shit to do, Lexi."

"Like what? Is it to do with the new arrival?"

Her frame stiffens. "It has nothing to do with him."

"Who is he?"

"Lexi, back off."

"What's gotten into you?"

She dodges around me. "I just want to be alone! This place is suffocating, and you're not the only one who wants out!"

Her words strike a landing blow, and I let her pass,

stunned into silence. She stomps off towards the hospital, tossing her untouched coffee aside in her rage.

What the fuck?

Still gobsmacked, I walk back into the cafe, finding the boys unmoved as they talk in low whispers. Felix sits upright when he spots me returning.

"What did she say?"

I retake my seat at Daniel's side. "Not much. What's going on with her?"

Michael doesn't answer. He looks uneasy, his miniature fingers twisting together as he looks anywhere but at me.

"I'm worried about her." Felix scrapes a hand through his sandy hair.

"She's fine," Michael tells him.

I shake my head. "Clearly, she isn't."

"We have more important things to worry about." Daniel finishes his coffee then places the cup down. "Ravius won't take well to me threatening him."

"You threatened him?" Michael frowns. "With what?"

"I was going to ask about that too." I look up at Daniel, remembering hearing his words. "You said he's been plotting against Caine. What does that mean?"

"Yeah, Daniel." Michael leans back, his arms crossed. "Tell her what that means."

I glance between them. I'm missing something. Clearly, I don't yet own all of Daniel's secrets. He seems to be carrying around an endless supply.

Obviously uncomfortable, Daniel looks around the cafe, checking to see if anyone is listening. It's relatively empty in here. We're seated by the window in the quietest corner of the cosy, vintage space.

"It means that Ravius and I have a unique arrangement," he replies, unease colouring his words. "One that I could use against him."

"What does that mean in English?" I ask.

"Daniel's his spy," Michael answers for him.

Leaning forward, Felix braces his elbows on his knees. "Holy shit. How did I not know this?"

"It isn't exactly common knowledge." Daniel glances nervously at me. "I've been by Caine's side for over a century. Most assume that's where my loyalties lie."

"Wait, hold up." I raise a hand to silence him. "You're a double agent?"

He nods, the movement stirring the crop of dark-brown hair on top of his head. "You could call it that."

I stare, astounded. "All this time… you haven't been working for Caine at all, have you?"

"I played the loyal soldier, and I played it well," he explains in a clipped tone. "But my loyalties lie elsewhere. Every move Caine has ever made has been reported back to his brother."

Michael stares at his friend. "If it wasn't for Daniel, The Redeemed would have erupted into war decades ago."

"But then… why are you back here?" I ask in confusion. "Isn't it your job to watch Caine and stop him from doing anything without Ravius knowing?"

His eyes dip down to me and soften. "You needed me more."

Warmth pools in my chest, purring with contentment. He's spent a century fighting this war alone, yet he gave it up to come back when I needed him to save me.

"Alright, lovebirds." Felix snaps his fingers. "We're not in a romance movie. Stop staring at each other like that."

I pout at him. "Spoilsport."

Chuckling, Daniel lays a possessive hand on my thigh. Tingles erupt at his touch. I don't know what's gotten into him since last night, but something has changed.

"You shouldn't have come back." Michael's lips are pursed. "Now we have no way of knowing what Caine is planning next. Who's going to stop him from doing something rash?"

"You're the one who called me!" Daniel insists.

"For Lexi. Not to abandon your mission when we're on the precipice of war. Caine could be plotting anything."

"Then we need to be ready," I declare.

All of them look at me like I've gone insane. I squirm beneath their collective gaze.

"Thought you didn't give a shit about the prophecy or this war?" Felix laughs.

"I… don't." I stare down at where Daniel holds my thigh. "But the people here don't deserve to suffer."

"You owe them nothing," he reasons.

My hand moves to cover Daniel's firm grip. "Ravius's people are innocent. They don't deserve to suffer through whatever Caine is planning."

"What about Ravius?" Michael asks. "Like it or not, he's a part of this. You'll have to face him sometime."

"Face him or punch him?"

"Lex."

"What?" I scoff.

Michael pins me with a stern look. "He's made a lot of mistakes, but he cares about his people more than anything."

"Not all his people."

"He had no choice but to punish you."

"You're on his side? Seriously?"

Gaze filled with resignation, Michael stands. "It isn't a matter of taking sides. Look, I have to clock in for my shift. Be careful, alright?"

I shrug. "No promises."

Felix also rises to his feet. "I have to go too."

After giving me a final lingering look, they disappear, leaving me with the silent man on my left. He's twisted his hand to hold mine, staring at the place where our skin meets and energy races between us.

"What is it?"

A breath blows out his flared nostrils. "I just wish we could run away from all of this."

"And give up everything you've fought for?"

His eyes briefly close. "Maybe I'm tired of fighting."

"I thought you weren't so fond of my running plan."

"Not when it involves almost getting yourself killed." His fingers clench around mine. "But part of me wonders what life would look like beyond this place."

"Maybe one day we'll find out."

"Maybe," he echoes.

Reaching up to touch his stubbled face, I trace my thumb over his lips, memorising each carved angle. His lashes cast shadows across his cheekbones as his eyes squeeze shut.

"What do we do now?"

"We prepare." His eyes reopen to lock on mine with determination. "And hope to God that Caine doesn't try to kill us all before then."

XXXI

THE WORLD

CHAPTER 15

KOOL-AID – BRING ME THE HORIZON

*P*ulling on plain black workout leggings and a long-sleeved tee, I tie my damp hair up into a ponytail. Steam billows from the bathroom behind me.

Facing myself in the mirror, my feet freeze involuntarily, forcing me to look. I've avoided it until now, too afraid of facing my own reflection.

It's just a mirror.

You're still you.

Scanning over my reflection, I realise that something's changed. I'm not sure when. The dark, swirling shadows in my eyes have lifted. My shoulders are pulled back, no longer weighed down. I now have some meat on my bones.

I've spent my entire life afraid. Forced to endure pain and humiliation at every turn. *He* ruined my life and took pleasure in keeping the broken pieces.

Looking down at my outstretched hands, I watch the tiny flames dance across my palms. When I concentrate on the flickers of light, they grow brighter, curling with smoke.

I'm not afraid anymore.

Now I'm the one in control.

"Lexi? You done in the shower?"

I drop my hands. "Yeah, I'm done. You can come in."

Carrying a cup of coffee, Daniel steps into the bedroom in a fresh black t-shirt. His hair is strewn messily on his head, and he looks refreshed after a night spent sleeping soundly by my side.

He props himself against the doorframe then takes a slurp while eyeing me up. The intensity in his azure stare causes butterflies to explode in my lower belly.

"Can I help you?"

He doesn't look away. "Nope."

"You don't have to stick to me like glue, you know. I'm perfectly capable of living alone."

"You don't want me here?"

"I didn't say that."

Swallowing coffee, he shrugs. "I'm sure I can return to the guest quarters where Caine and I were staying. Feel free to warm your own bed."

Rolling my eyes, I pad over to him, stealing the mug from his hands. He watches me in exasperation as I take a sip.

"Then go," I deadpan. "You're the one who invited yourself in. I don't need a babysitter."

His teeth grind together. "You sure as hell need one."

Before I do something stupid like throw boiling hot coffee in his face, I breeze from the room. Living with that son of a bitch is not happening anytime soon.

"We need to start training," he calls after me.

"Let me eat my damn breakfast first!"

Walking into the open plan kitchen, I startle at the breakfast laid out on the table like he read my mind.

"What the hell is this?"

I hear him walk out of the bedroom, stopping just behind me.

"Problem, princess?"

Whirling on him, I want to wipe the infuriating half-smile from his face. "What game are you playing?"

"Just being a good bonded."

"I think I preferred it when you hated me."

Smirking, Daniel leans over me to steal his coffee back. "I just left my Elder for you. We're stuck together now."

"You're not going to go back to him?"

"I have no desire to leave you again."

Shocked by this revelation, I feel a pang of worry. "Caine will come for you eventually. He won't just let you walk away from him."

He takes one of the empty seats, pulling a plateful of eggs closer to him. I slide into the chair opposite.

"As far as Caine is aware, I'm doing his bidding. We have time before he realises that I'm not where I should be. By which time, we'll have this shit figured out."

I stab a piece of egg. "Great plan."

"Obviously. I thought of it."

"So what happens when he makes a move on Ravius, and you have to choose between them?"

"Then I'll finally get the chance to do what I've been wanting to for years."

His grip on his fork tightens, scar-laden knuckles turning white. I place my own fork down then lace my fingers together, holding his eye contact.

"You said Caine killed your wife."

Daniel cautiously nods, his lips sealed.

"Why would he do that to you?"

For a brief, hopeful moment, I think I'm actually going to get a straight answer from him. Then he pushes his plate back and stands up.

"Training. Let's go."

"Daniel…"

But his back is already turned as he carries his uneaten plateful into the kitchen. I stare after him, my heart aching.

* * *

WALKING AHEAD OF ME, Daniel strides into the huge, cavernous training room. It's a vast, concrete space with bare walls and wipe-clean linoleum floors. Felix follows closely behind us, slamming the door shut.

"This is the training facility for the security team," Felix explains.

Daniel drops his towel and water bottle on a corner bench. "We shouldn't be disturbed here."

Heading for a metal supply cupboard built into the wall, he leaves me with Felix. I drop my own gym towel then flex my tense shoulders. Felix must read my obvious anxiety.

"He'll go easy on you," he offers.

"No. He won't."

He leans casually against the concrete wall. "Well, no. But that isn't really the point of this, is it?"

There's a loud clattering from inside the cupboard before Daniel reappears, carrying two long, gilded silver swords in his hands. He offers one to me.

"Take it."

"I'm sorry, what century is this?"

His hardened eyes narrow. "You've had no prior combat training. We're starting from the beginning. Don't like it? Find another trainer."

I gingerly accept the sword. "Charming."

"We're wasting time."

Lifting his sword, he plants his feet. I take a step back and test the heavy, metallic weight. It feels natural in my hands. Perfectly balanced, the handle fitting snugly in my palm.

Daniel holds his sword with confidence, like it's an extension of himself. "We will train every day until you can defend yourself."

Adjusting my grip on the sword, I mirror his stance. He prowls around me, moving easily in the space. I'm itching with the urge to turn and run away. He looks fucking deadly.

"You're weak and unfocused. Caine won't hesitate to exploit that advantage. You need to learn to master your gift."

I take a menacing step closer. "I am not weak."

Advancing, Daniel strikes me with the sword, pulling his blow short of cutting me. I trip and fall flat on my ass, sending pain shooting up my lower spine.

"What were you saying?" he snarks.

"Ugh, asshole!"

"Name calling isn't going to protect you from the army that Caine has at his beck and call."

"Why are we so certain he wants me? I doubt he even knows that I'm gifted. We're assuming too much."

Daniel cocks his head, the sword poised. "Trust me, he knows by now. Caine makes it his business to keep track of all the gifted Redeemed across the globe."

"Why?"

"Get up. Again."

"Wait—"

"Again!"

Scrambling to my feet, I rub my aching tailbone and lift the sword back up. Daniel studies my form then barks off instructions to help me correct it.

Adjusting my body, I grip the handle, copying his posture. The sword's starting to feel heavy in my hands, making my muscles ache. I'm definitely not in the best of shapes.

"We'll start with defensive measures. You need to learn to block an attack and protect yourself before you can even think about advancing."

"We need to improve her physical fitness too." Felix studies us from his perch against the wall. "I can take her on training drills with the team twice a day."

"Twice?" I repeat.

He grins at me. "You're going to love it. Bright and early, baby. No more afterlife lie-ins for you."

"Great. Can't wait."

"Eyes up," Daniel snaps. "Get into position."

Spreading my feet, I square my shoulders and hold the sword in position, trying to find the correct stance. Daniel studies me intently before nodding once.

"Good."

Prowling closer, he moves fast and efficiently, weaving a path towards me. When he tries to strike me this time, I snap out of my daze long enough to side-step and dodge.

The blade swoops through the air, cutting through where I'd previously stood. Moving fast, I duck behind Daniel and raise my sword, preparing for him to spin around and face me.

He advances again, preparing to strike. This time, our blades connect with a metallic bang. I'm forced backwards, his overwhelming strength pushing me to the floor.

Landing on the workout mat, Daniel looms above me. He straddles my waist, and I can feel the solid pressure of his hard cock rocking into me.

"Checkmate," he murmurs.

"Pretty sure you're not supposed to fuck your enemies."

"Now, where's the fun in that?"

Pressing even more weight into me, the crisscrossed swords lower to my chest until his blade is pressing against my throat. He rocks into me, ensuring I feel how turned-on he is.

"Dead... Nasty way to go."

"I don't know." I lift my hips, pressing myself into him. "I could think of worse places for my deathbed."

"Um, guys?"

Felix's voice breaks the moment. He's standing awkwardly off to the side, trying to keep his gaze averted. I break out in laughter, and even Daniel cracks a smile.

Shoving him off me, I sit up then stretch my sore arms. "What does Caine want with the gifted Redeemed?"

Daniel hesitates, watching me a little too closely for comfort. Felix glances between the two of us.

"She's going to find out eventually."

"I know." Daniel sighs.

I stand then bend down to pick up the sword. "Talk about me like I'm not here and this sword is going to get rammed somewhere uncomfortable."

Daniel grabs his own sword then retakes his position. "Caine has been studying the gifted for over a century."

"Studying them how?"

"Illegal experimentation, mostly."

I almost drop the sword. "What the fuck? Does Ravius know about this?"

"Why do you think I was assigned to watch Caine in the first place?" he drawls.

"You're telling me that he's been testing on people for all these years? Against their will?"

He hesitates. "Something like that."

Raising the sword, I press the sharpened tip into his chest. "What else aren't you telling me?"

Daniel shakes his head. "Some stuff you don't need to know. Stuff that would change your opinion of me."

"Stuff that proves you're a miserable, arrogant asshole?"

His mouth quirks into a wide, full smile as he nudges the tip of the sword aside, removing it from his chest. I retake my position without being told, finding the stance easily.

"Caine needed someone to help run the program." Daniel advances, his smile quickly falling away like it never existed. "Someone... loyal."

The realisation is sickening. Shifting backwards to dodge his next strike, I meet his eyes and see the twisted truth waiting there.

"Someone?" I question him even though I know the answer.

He swallows hard. "It was the only way to monitor what he was doing with the gifted. I had to maintain cover by any means necessary."

"Jesus, Daniel."

Looking down at his feet, his face crumples. He looks so ashamed, it hurts to see. But for the life of me, I can't pity him.

"How many people did you give him?" I hiss.

"Too many."

"And what happened to those people?"

Taking advantage of his distraction, I step closer, the blade poised to meet his throat. Daniel doesn't even attempt to defend himself.

"What did you do?"

"Lex," he warns.

Sidestepping, I move to strike his side, pulling back at the last second so I don't cut him. My next blow connects with his chest, hard enough to bruise.

I move fast, advancing into his space, our blades banging together. Only this time, I have the advantage.

"I had no choice," he defends.

"So you sacrificed countless innocent people to protect your precious reputation?"

"This has nothing to do with my reputation!"

Temper flaring, I attack again, our swords clashing. Daniel feints to the left, but I see the move coming and step into his space. His eyebrows raise in surprise.

We both move fast. Swords smashing, feet advancing, bodies circling. Each jab is followed by another until we've moved all the way across the room, locked in a deadly dance.

"Let me explain," Daniel pleads.

"You've said enough."

"It's not what you think—"

"You've enabled a psychopath!"

He halts, his head dropping. "You're right. I stood by Caine's side for decades, knowing what he was doing to those people. Never saying a damn word. I didn't protect them."

"Who the hell even are you?"

"This is exactly why I didn't tell you."

"So what else are you hiding?" I jam the sword into his ribcage, relishing in his grunt. "Who else have you hurt?"

"I never claimed to be a saint!" he explodes in a torrent of emotion. "But someone has to do what's necessary."

"I bet your Elder has the exact same excuse."

"It isn't an excuse."

Advancing again, I back Daniel up against the wall. My blade presses into his throat, meeting the pulsing vulnerability of his jugular vein.

"That's it, Lex. You now know everything."

"How can I ever trust you?"

His clear eyes are steady on mine. "You can't. Neither of us asked for this, but we can't change it now."

"What about when he comes for me?" I press the sword in deeper, eliciting a thin stream of blood. "Will you get on your damn knees and surrender me yourself?"

An inferno blazes in his ice-cold irises, melding shame with fury. Daniel steps closer, into the path of the blade, causing more blood to spill down his throat.

"I'll stand between you and the devil until my last fucking breath, Lexi. Caine won't lay a finger on you."

"The same way you stood between him and your wife?"

Recoiling like I've slapped him, Daniel's face drains of all colour. He takes an unsteady step back, ignoring his bleeding wound. The real pain lies elsewhere.

"I tried to protect her," he says brokenly. "For years, I kept her gift a secret. If it wasn't for the prophecy, she'd still be alive."

I lower the sword, trembling all over. "And you'd be free of the curse I've put on us both."

He shakes his head. "Life doesn't work like that. We've been set upon this path for a reason."

"That may be true, but I have no intention of ending up like your dead wife. When I'm strong enough, I will get out of here and find my sister. You'll never have to see me again."

Daniel flinches. "You think I want that?"

"I think all you give a shit about is self-preservation. You care about nothing and no one but yourself."

I regret the harsh words as soon as they leave my mouth. Daniel's mouth twists into a hurt grimace, and he tosses his sword aside.

"Lesson's over."

Without another glance, he stalks from the room, leaving me gasping. Felix watches Daniel go then cups his hands around his mouth to shout at me.

"That went well!"

My forehead collides with the wall.

Real fucking well.

THE CHARIOT

CHAPTER 16

KAMIKAZEE - MISSIO

"*F*aster! I don't give a shit how cold it is!"

Barking off orders at the miserable group, Felix stands at the edge of the courtyard, his breath fogging in the air. I brace my hands on my knees, desperately puffing for oxygen.

"Lexi!" he shouts.

"Give me a minute."

"Shift your ass, or it's another ten laps."

I can't believe I actually thought he was a sweetheart when I met him. Turns out, Felix is an evil son of a bitch when it comes to training Brunt's recruits.

I've been on twice a day drills all week, and there isn't a single part of me that doesn't ache. Daniel's kept his distance since our blow up, sleeping elsewhere and avoiding me at mealtimes. We've regressed back into old patterns.

As much as it pisses me off to admit it, I miss him. His presence. His warmth. The buzz of energy being around him gives me. Instead, the pain that the lack of physical contact between us causes is a constant, aching presence in my chest.

Hands laced behind his back, Felix approaches me. "I can't give you any special treatment."

"I didn't ask for any."

"Then pick yourself up and keep moving. You wanted to get stronger, didn't you?"

Stretching to my full height, I gasp at the pain in my calves. "How is this torture making me stronger?"

"Discipline. You won't kick anyone's ass if you can't even run a mile without throwing your guts up."

"That was one time!"

He laughs at me. "Once was enough."

Stretching out a hand, I focus on my palm, watching with satisfaction as tiny flames spark from my fingertips. Felix takes a small step back when I wave my hand in his face.

"I may not be able to run, but I can sure crisp your ass for being a dick. You promised to take it easy on me."

Felix rolls his eyes. "I made no such promises. If you'd rather be training with Daniel, feel free to track him down instead."

A shudder rolls over me. "I'm good."

"You two will have to talk at some point. He looks fucking rough, Lex. Avoiding each other is bad for the bond."

"He should've thought of that before he kept another secret from me. I'm done with being treated like a fool."

"Don't take it personally." He shrugs, resting a hand on my shoulder. "He was only trying to protect you."

"From him?"

"From the truth."

Shaking out my hands, I shove away his touch then set off again. "I'm not a child. I don't need him or his protection."

I catch up to the rest of the recruits, a stitch digging into my side. Felix remains at the edge of the courtyard, watching us all run, but his concerned hazel gaze is locked on me.

Scalp tingling, I feel the weight of more eyes on me. When we complete another lap, taking a brief break to drain our water bottles, I spot him standing outside the administration building.

Bulging arms folded, Daniel makes no secret of watching me. He's dressed in his usual all-black ensemble. I gasp at the wave of mental anguish that crashes into me when our eyes meet.

I can feel him.

His grief.

His regret.

The pain steals my breath. It bites into me and lashes my skin like an invisible whip, striking without mercy. He stares for several seconds before turning and walking away.

With him gone, the relief I expected to feel never comes. Seeing him has just reminded me of how much his absence hurts.

It's another two hours before Felix relents, declaring our second drill of the day complete. The winter sun is swollen on the horizon, melting into shadows and darkness.

Everyone disperses. I limp back to my apartment, slick with cold sweat. My feet freeze into blocks of ice when I spot the hulking head of security standing outside my door.

"What do you want?"

Brunt lazily trails his gaze over me. "The Elder requests your immediate presence. You can walk or be dragged."

"Tell Ravius to fuck himself with a rusty knife. I have no interest in anything he has to say."

He snorts. "Did I say it was optional?"

"I couldn't care less."

Taking a threatening step towards me, he cracks his knuckles. "I'd take great pleasure in re-fracturing your skull. Just give me an excuse to."

Brushing past him, I unlock my apartment. "A pleasure as always, Brunt. Feel free to borrow that rusty knife for yourself."

Slamming the door in his face, I quickly twist the lock, though I doubt the flimsy metal will keep him out. I watch through the peephole as he stares for several seconds before storming off.

My back meets the door, and I slump, overcome with relief. As much as I hate that son of a bitch, I can't kid myself that I'd overpower him in a fight. He's already kicked my ass once.

Flopping onto the sofa in a boneless pile, I can't even bring myself to shower before my eyes fall shut. I'm exhausted after two training sessions and dealing with Felix all day.

Rolling over and snuggling into the butter-soft velvet sofa cushions, I quickly fall into the embrace of sleep. Shadows expand across my vision as the dream-world welcomes me.

"Lexi."

I should've known the stranger would be waiting. He always is. Every single night. Eyes opening, I find his rich green gaze on me, angled lips quirked in a smile.

"What is it, mi amor?"

Sighing, I glance around the familiar meadow. "Nothing."

"You don't usually sleep during the day."

"I'm tired. What are you doing here?"

"I have no control over it. When you dream, I'm pulled into this place."

"What were you doing?"

He shrugs a slender, shirt-covered shoulder. "Meetings. Nothing I wouldn't give up to see your face."

Beginning to pace, I ignore my serene surroundings. Usually, the meadow is a place of peace and tranquillity for me. But not today. I'm itching with energy and frustration.

None of this makes sense.

I spend my days tortured by the man who can't bring himself to be around me and my nights haunted by an imaginary stranger. The latter can't bleed into my waking hours too.

"Are you real?"

"As real as you."

"Where are you then?"

He makes a tsking noise. "I've been asking you the same thing every night for weeks. Why won't you tell me where you are?"

"Because I'm in enough trouble as it is without giving some crazy stranger my whereabouts."

"Are you in some kind of danger?" he growls, emerald eyes flashing with possessiveness. "Enough of these games. All I need is a location, and we can finally be together."

"Together?" I scoff. "Hold your horses, Romeo."

Snarling in impatience, he stalks towards me, crossing the luminous green grass. I can't help gasping as his tanned hands lift to cup my face, a single fingertip stroking over my lips.

"Why are you hiding from me?" he whispers. "As much as I enjoy these dreams, we could be together. In person."

"Because you're not real. This isn't real. My life... it's pretty complicated. I don't need everyone to think I'm losing my mind too."

His brows furrow. "You really don't believe that I'm real."

"You're a figment of my imagination." I look over his impressive, sculpted frame. "Albeit a gorgeous, mysterious figment. But imaginary nonetheless."

"Does this feel imaginary?"

Still clutching my face in his impossibly tight grip, I'm powerless to fend off his approach. The man brings his lips to mine in a crushing, passionate kiss, our mouths slanted together.

I can actually feel him.

His kiss

His touch.

His breath.

Tongue licking over my bottom lip, he kisses me with the gentleness of a lover and the ferocious anger of an enemy. Caught between the two extremes, my head is whirling with confusion.

This isn't real.

Not real.

Not... real.

217

Is it?

With the pressure of his lips devouring mine, I feel the first flickers of flames licking at my insides. Burning ever hotter, the fire grows, racing through my extremities faster with each passing second.

The harder he kisses me, our tongues meeting, the more my energy soars. Even in this fantasy world, the Vitae can't help but respond. It's surging through me like ozone building in the clouds.

Fuck it.

With fire biting at my heels, I run head-first into the abyss and kiss him back. A total stranger, but somehow... he isn't. I know this man. My soul recognises him on an intrinsic level.

Grunting low in his throat, his teeth sink into my lip, playfully nipping. I curl my arms around his neck and let my teeth scrape over his tongue. I want more. My thighs clench with need.

He tastes rich and exotic like tempting, forbidden fruit. When his hand trails lower, grasping my hip tight to bring our bodies flush together, I gasp into his mouth. The sense of untapped power erupts.

"Lexi," he grunts.

Separating, it's too late to stop the approaching storm. We're caught in its warpath now. His eyes bug wide as he looks around us, finding the bright, beautiful meadow engulfed in ravenous flames.

"Mierda! What is this?"

I stroke my thumb along his stubbled jawline. "I'm sorry. I can't control it."

His mouth falls open. "You did this?"

I take a step back from him. "Please leave me alone."

"You know I can't do that, mi amor. What's going on?" His eyes widen. "I see. This is your gift?"

My feet halt on the verge of running away into the smoke. "What did you just say to me?"

"This." He gestures around the burning meadow. "I should've known my mate would possess a strong affinity for the Vitae too."

"M-Mate?"

He takes a step closer, but I raise a hand to stop him. I thought I couldn't be surprised any more. Apparently, fate has crueller plans.

"*Oh my God. You're one of them.*"

"*Lexi—*"

"*You're Redeemed. You're... real?*"

He moves even closer. "I've scoured all of Spain's facilities looking for you. Where are you hiding, sweetheart?"

Shaking my head, I scan him up and down. His tight shirt and fitted, designer trousers. Dark ink begging to be touched as it spills through the thin material covering his muscled chest. His long, chestnut hair, and eyes so vibrant they glow with authority.

All this time... he was real.

This isn't a dream.

"We have to be together," he says urgently, eyeing the approaching flames. "It is dangerous for bonded to be apart."

Fuck.

Fuck.

Fuck!

"No. It can't be."

"Lexi?"

"You... We... It can't be. Not another one."

Understanding dawns on his face. "You have another mate?"

"Stop." I step back from him. "We're... soul bound?"

He nods slowly. "That's why you can see me. I live inside of you, Lexi. I'm real, and so is our connection."

Grabbing me again, his lips are back on mine. It feels like a piece of me has been missing, and it's just now slotting back into place. All I can hear is the crackle of fire encircling us as the Vitae grows wild.

Breaking the intense kiss, his lips hover just inches from mine. "I was searching in the wrong place all along. You're not in Spain, are you?"

Numb, I shake my head. "No one told me that... That I could have two. And Ravius..."

He abruptly straightens. "Ravius. So that's where you are."

Double fuck!

"You can't hide anymore." His tone is more sinister now, darker.

With panic surging through me, a burst of fire breaks free from the circle around us, lashing out in response. It connects with him, the flames engulfing his arm. He barks out a startled curse.

"No!" I scream.

But the fire isn't done. It's determined to protect me, even from him. Flames leap into the gap between us and build an impenetrable wall, stretching up into the smoke-hazed sunlight.

"Lexi!"

I hear my name., but his mouth isn't moving. The sound is coming from elsewhere, growing louder and closer, breaking through the dream.

"Lexi!"

My vision fades. The fire inches ever closer, licking at my skin before burning it to a crisp. I lock eyes on the stranger one last time.

"I'll find you," he shouts. "I. Will. Find. You!"

He vanishes, and so does the meadow.

Snapping back into the real world, pain barrels through me. It's everywhere. Spreading. Scorching. Eating away at my nerves until the pain gives way to numbness.

I begin to violently cough, my nose and throat full of acrid smoke. I'm still curled up on the sofa, but the apartment around me looks completely different.

All of the fancy furniture has vanished from sight. Nothing but fire remains. Brilliant, enraged fire, writhing and spitting in all directions.

I try to sit upright, but the flames are snaking over all of my exposed skin. My screams ricochet around me, absorbed by the thick, caustic smoke.

I'm going to die.

Rolling to the side, I hit the carpeted floor with a thud, swatting at the flames that have spread to my left arm. Fire rapidly consumes where I had just laid, quickly spreading and moving closer to me.

Everything is burning, from the plush carpets to the hanging curtains, engulfing me in glorious light. Even in my confusion, I can hear the banging of fists on the front door, attempting to breach the apartment.

I scream.

On and on and on.

"Help me!"

Wood splinters and explodes as the door eventually gives way. I drag myself into the corner of the room, running from the approaching wall of flames.

Through the smoke, I can make out two figures. One tall and muscled, one short and child-like. They can't get to me. Fire and destruction hold them back.

"Lexi!" Daniel yells.

Skin blistered and welted, I try to wave through the haze. "I'm... here!"

"Hold on!"

There's a crack above me as the curtain pole gives way. It comes flying down, bringing a sheet of fire swinging straight towards me. With a scream, I roll across the floor.

"Lexi!"

On my hands and knees, I can spy a path through the inferno. It's narrow and thick with black smoke. Flames chase after me as I begin to crawl, sobbing in horror the whole time.

"Daniel," I wail.

Sucking in hot air, my lungs burn in protest. I'm leaving a trail of bloody skin across the carpet, leaking from my crisped hands and arms.

"I'm here, Lex!" he bellows. "Follow the sound of my voice."

Eyes squeezed shut, I latch on to his frantic shouts, guiding my path through the unknown. His voice is getting closer. Louder. Clearer. When I hear a gasp, I know I've made it to the entrance.

"Lexi!"

Collapsing on the floor, I can't move another inch. There's a thud as Daniel falls to his knees in front of me, arms banding around my crumpled body until I'm pulled into his lap.

"I've got you, love."

"Fire," I whimper.

"Hold onto me. Don't let go."

Grasping the sweat-slick material of his t-shirt, I let myself doze, my body giving in to the blissful knowledge that I am now safe. Daniel lifts me then moves fast to break out of the apartment.

In the hallway, smoke is choking the air. People are running in all directions, screaming and shouting in a bid to escape. I've caused utter chaos.

"She's hurt," he barks.

"Outside." I hear Michael respond. "Elevator's out. Emergency stairwell."

Each footstep jolts me, sparking even more agony. A fire alarm is blaring loudly, interrupted by the panicked roar of voices as they escape the burning building.

When cold air kisses my blistered skin, I know we've made it outside. Wet grass meets my back as I'm laid down in front of the Nightingale building.

When Daniel tries to release me, I grip his t-shirt even tighter, and a moan falls loose from my lips.

"I'm here," he whispers.

"He… fire… Vitae…"

"Shh, love. Let Michael heal you."

Already I can feel the warmth of Michael's hands on my incinerated skin, patching me up. It's an uncomfortable, itching sensation as my body starts to knit itself back together.

I can't help crying out, causing Daniel to curse up a storm. He clutches me even tighter, his eyes frantic as he yells at Michael to hurry up.

"Sorry," Michael mutters. "I'm working as fast as I can."

When relief finally comes, I slump into Daniel's chest. He smells like smoke and ash. Blood and flames. Even in the madness, he refuses to let me go.

"W-What happened?"

Daniel's voice is grim.

"You manifested."

I can't summon a response before my mind pulls the plug, overwhelmed and in pain, leaving me to surrender to the darkness. Daniel calling my name is the last thing I hear.

THE STAR

CHAPTER 17

WHERE WE COME ALIVE – RUELLE

*D*rip. Drip. Drip.
    "She was badly hurt. Give her time to heal."
Drip. Drip. Drip.
"Why isn't she awake, dammit?"
Drip. Drip. Drip.
"She'll wake up when she's ready."

Their voices are a blur. Hell, life is a blur. I'm groggy and warm. So warm, I can't drag my eyes open. Not even to relieve my aching neck, resting at an odd angle on a fluffy pillow.

"This is all my fault. I've fucked this bond up so badly. I should've been there with her."

"You couldn't have known she'd manifest like that," a voice consoles.

"We knew how powerful she would become. It was never going to be subtle. I just didn't expect it to happen so soon."

"None of us did. Gifted Redeemed can take years to manifest fully, and we've barely begun training her."

"Because I ran away like a scared fucking child. She could've died. I'll never forgive myself."

Dragged back under, I dream of fire and smoke, green-eyed strangers and my sister's sweet, whispering voice, repeating the warning she gave in the meadow dream.

He's coming for you, Lexi.

With a gasp, I jolt awake, my lids finally daring to open. Bright lights slice into my foggy head, but I'm not surrounded by the white, clinical hospital. Not this time.

A plain bedroom surrounds me with cream walls and navy curtains drawn against the daylight. I'm curled up in a soft, queen-sized bed, an IV line hanging next to it.

The voices are gone, but I'm not alone. Not this time. Looking entirely uncomfortable, folded up in a navy, wing-backed armchair in the corner of the room, Daniel is fast asleep.

His head is propped on his hand, bee-stung lips parted, and brows furrowed as he frowns in his sleep. I look down at myself, finding my hands and arms swathed in bandages.

"I healed what I could."

Yelping, I look over at the doorway, finding Michael propped up in it. He watches me with a blank expression.

"You had second degree burns on your hands and arms," he continues in a hushed whisper. "There's only so much I can do. The rest will have to heal naturally."

I lick my dry, cracked lips. "W-Where?"

"My apartment."

"Hospital?"

He shakes his head. "Daniel doesn't want you anywhere near Ravius after what happened."

Managing to shift on the mattress, I stretch out my limbs, feeling the tight press of bandages and the tugging needle taped to my inner arm. My body is stiff and heavy.

"How l-long?"

"Only a few hours. The fire stopped as soon as you passed out—no one had to touch it—but your place is trashed."

Guilt ravages me. "Anyone... hurt?"

"Aside from you?"

I force a nod.

Michael's shoulders slump. "No, there were no casualties. I don't know that we could've stopped Ravius from locking you back up if there were."

"That's why I'm not in the hospital?"

"Let's just say he isn't feeling very forgiving right now."

My head hits the pillows with a huff. "When is he ever?"

Michael sits on the edge of the bed, running his little hand down the unbandaged part of my arm. The fear in his eyes is breathtakingly unnerving. I've never seen him look afraid.

"Your gift manifested," he reveals.

"Shit. I did this?"

"We found the place on fire and realised pretty quickly what was happening. I'm sorry we didn't get you out sooner."

"Not your fault."

"What happened, Lex?"

The memories trickle back like thick, gloopy molasses, coming in a slow realisation. Training. Laying down to sleep. The dream. Fire. The stranger kissing me.

My mate.

Another soul bond.

Gasping, I shoot upright, causing fierce pain to rip through me. Michael startles, trying to stop me from moving with a hand gently pushing my shoulder.

"Go slow."

"I... dreaming about... and the fire—"

"Lexi, slow down. You're not making any sense."

I search the unfamiliar room. "Is he here?"

"Who?"

But I don't even have a name to offer him. Not a single shred of evidence that I'm not losing my fucking shit, once and for all.

"Daniel's right there." Michael hooks a thumb over his shoulder. "He hasn't left your side."

Instead of pain, all I feel is guilt. Not for burning down the apartment and putting countless lives at risk. Nor for scaring them both half to death.

But for the mysterious, foreign stranger who claimed my lips and started this entire thing. His kiss set me on fire, and I manifested in the real world. We did this together.

"It was bound to happen eventually," Michael tries to placate. "Every manifestation is different. The good news is you'll have full access to your gift now."

Panic flares deep inside me. "What if I don't want it?"

"After what just happened, I wouldn't blame you," he consoles. "But it doesn't work like that. Control is more important now than ever. This can't happen again."

"Almost burning down the building and killing myself in the process?"

He flourishes a tiny smile. "Yeah."

Hands bunching in the sheets, I whoosh out a sigh. "On a scale of one to ten, how mad is Ravius right now?"

"That problem can wait. He won't get past us. Felix is stationed outside too. You're not going back into a cell."

"I don't know why you're protecting me." I feel tears well up then streak down my cheeks. "I'm not worth it."

"Don't say that," Michael chastises. "I can't speak for that lump of meat over there, but you're worth it to me."

Choking on a sob, I stare up into his rich green eyes, filled with wisdom beyond his physical age. Michael smiles softly, crinkling his freckled cheeks.

"I could've gotten you killed."

"What's friendship without a little near-death experience?" He laughs.

"I haven't had a friend for a long time."

"Well, you've got plenty now. None of us are going to let anything else happen to you. No matter how pissed Ravius is."

Blinking away the tears that hang heavy in my eyes, I rest a bandaged hand over his and squeeze. Michael's eyes shine with tears of his own, and we both laugh at our stupidness.

Daniel groans in his sleep, telling us the sound woke the third presence in the room. When his eyes flutter open and land on us, he shoots upright.

"You're awake."

I lift a white-swathed hand in a half-wave. "Hi."

Falling out of the chair, he stumbles over to the bed, stopping an inch away from me. Michael moves to slip from the room to give us some privacy.

The minute the door clicks shut, Daniel steps to the edge of the bed. He looks desperate to move even closer, but he can't bring himself to do it.

I pat the bedsheet. "Come and sit."

"You sure?"

"Just get over here."

Smiling thinly, he cautiously sits down on the bed, his muscled weight still causing the mattress to sink. He searches my face, looking for something, but I don't know what he finds.

"I thought I'd lost you for a moment there." His voice is a gruff rumble. "I was so fucking scared, Lex."

I lift my sore hand, resting it on his forearm. "I'm sorry for scaring you. Things just got out of control."

"That's one way to word it."

Cracking a sorry excuse for a smile, he stares down at me, emotional torment dancing in his eyes. I squeeze his arm, my thumb skating over his veins.

"I'm sorry about saying all that stuff to you."

"I'm sorry that I didn't tell you the truth." He clears his throat. "Again."

"I guess… we've both made mistakes."

Daniel nods. "No one prepares you for how hard this is. If I could go back, I would start fresh and tell you everything."

Shame lances through me as I see the stranger's green gaze in my mind again. He said he was coming for me. I'll have to face that sooner rather than later, but I can't bring myself to tell Daniel yet.

"No more secrets," he murmurs. "I want a clean slate. This has to work, Lex. If we can't trust each other, then who can we trust?"

Invisible thread wraps around my heart and squeezes. His voice is so soft, so hopeful, it kills me to swallow the truth.

"I want that too."

"So fresh start?" he asks.

"I'm willing to try if you are."

"Yes." Eyes scraping up and down me, his expression softens. "Can I hold you?"

At this moment, I don't care about the lie I'm keeping. Not a damn bit. I died already. I'll risk seeing hell again to feel Daniel's arms around me, if only for a second.

"Please," I consent.

"Shift over, then."

After gently helping me slide over in the bed, he pulls back the covers and shimmies in to join me. I curl up in his arms, burying my nose in the smoky material of his t-shirt.

"You didn't shower?"

His chest vibrates with a chuckle. "I didn't want to leave your side. Ravius is on the warpath."

"Good thing I have you here to defend my honour, then."

"Defend your honour?" he repeats with a laugh. "Let me just go find my shining armour."

"You'd look hot in armour."

He frowns at me. "I think the smoke inhalation has gotten to you."

"Probably."

Snuggled up to him, I stroke up and down his tightly packed abdominals, listening to his breathing as it evens out. It isn't long before he's out like a light.

"I'm so sorry," I whisper.

Waiting to make sure he's completely asleep, I disconnect

the IV and wriggle out of his arms. I'm terrified of closing my eyes again. Not after what just happened.

I'm clean, wearing a t-shirt and rolled up sweats that smell suspiciously like Daniel, my burned clothes nowhere in sight. My heart gallops at the realisation.

Stepping into Michael's low-lit living room, the moon shines through the windows. He's curled up in a ball on the sofa in front of a crackling fire and lightly snoring.

Pausing to grab the blanket off the back of the sofa, I drape it over him so he doesn't get cold then creep past. The door clicks shut behind me as I slink into the ash-streaked corridor.

"Lexi?"

I almost jump out of my skin. "Shit!"

Felix is leaning against the wall, dark and dangerous in his usual uniform. He straightens when he spots me, his pale brows knitted together in concern.

"Why are you up?"

"I… needed some air."

He folds his arms. "You're sneaking out. Why?"

"Jesus, Felix. I just need to breathe and think. Give a girl a break, will you?"

"It isn't safe for you to be alone right now. Your gift will be more volatile than ever, and Ravius won't hesitate to throw you back in a cell for everyone's protection."

My eyes creep over to the blackened shell of an apartment just down the corridor. "Alright. Come with me, then."

Shuffling away before he can protest, I approach my ruined apartment. I can hear Felix sighing behind me as he follows. The door is hanging off its hinges, revealing devastation inside.

It's destroyed.

Completely ruined.

Nothing but piles of ash and black-streaked bare walls remain. All of the furniture has been trashed, and the pristine kitchen is no more. All my meagre belongings are gone.

"I did this," I breathe out.

Felix stops at my side. "Well, kinda."

"What the fuck happened?"

He bumps my shoulder. "Don't blame yourself. Everyone manifests differently. It's not your fault it got out of control."

Looking around the apartment, my heart sinks. "No wonder Ravius wants to kill me right now."

"He'll get over it. Hell, the man should be thanking his lucky stars that he has someone as powerful as you on his side."

"But I'm not on his side, am I?"

"Whose fault is that?"

We both turn around at the regal voice that interrupts us. Lingering in the open doorway, Ravius glances around the gutted apartment, his expression severe.

"Lexi," he says stiffly.

I immediately back up. "Decided to come yourself this time instead of sending your guard dog?"

"Yes. I think it's time we talked."

Stepping in front of me, Felix blocks me from his view. "She isn't going anywhere with you, Elder. I won't watch you throw her in that prison again."

Ravius shakes his head. "You can stand down. I only want to talk. Nothing more."

Hesitating, Felix looks over his shoulder at me. I consider for a moment before nodding, giving him permission to back off. Felix glances between us indecisively.

"It's okay," I console. "I'm ready to hear him out."

He nods. "I'll wait outside. Shout if you need me."

Before leaving the apartment, Felix casts us both a final glance then heads down the corridor. I'm left with the stern-faced Elder himself.

"Quite the manifestation," he begins.

I back up, fiddling with the bandages on my arms. "Things got a little out of hand."

"This is precisely why I wanted to train you before your manifestation came."

"Like I could've trusted you after what you did to me." I snort sarcastically. "You locked me up and threw away the key."

Ravius grimaces. "You didn't give me much of a choice, Lexi. I told you not to run, and you disobeyed me."

I kick a pile of still-hot ashes. "What do you want? If it's just to rehash the past few weeks, I'm not interested."

"No. I wanted to make sure you're okay."

"You? Really?"

"I still care," he snaps angrily.

"Could've fooled me."

"Did it occur to you that I might have put you in a prison cell for your own protection?" He eyes me closely. "I want you to be safe."

"Safe... and controlled."

Ravius gestures around the apartment. "That control would've been helpful a few hours ago."

As much as I want to argue, my protests die in my throat. Nothing about this is controlled. Not a damn thing.

"Your gift is at its most volatile point now." He studies the destruction. "This is just the beginning."

"So what?"

"Train with me. Master your abilities and keep yourself safe. I will not force you to do anything that you don't want to."

"Like fight in your stupid war?"

Ravius lifts his shoulder in a shrug. "Refuse my offer and wait for Caine to come for you. Then we'll see how you feel about my *stupid war*."

"Caine knows nothing about me."

"You just manifested and almost burned down an entire

apartment block. Believe me, if he didn't already know… he does now."

"How?" I gasp.

"Daniel isn't his only spy in this facility, regardless of where his true loyalties lie. My brother is not a fool."

My heart slams behind my breastbone. "Does Caine know about me and Daniel? Is Daniel in danger?"

Ravius swipes a finger over a blackened countertop then frowns at the ash on his skin. "Probably."

"Christ! We have to warn him."

"Oh, he knows. The moment he chose to return here to be with you, Daniel sealed his fate. He can never go home."

Itching with agitation, I begin to pace, forcing myself to breathe. I don't want to start another fire. Ravius watches me closely, his eyes following my short steps.

"He's coming for you," I repeat my sister's words.

"What's that?"

I whirl on Ravius. "I've been having dreams."

He watches me apprehensively. "What kind of dreams?"

"About the meadow, my sister and… and…"

I can't bring myself to admit the truth out loud. Ravius watches me expectantly, but not a single word comes out.

"Lexi?"

"It's nothing." I rub my eyes. "Forget it."

"You know… dreams are often reflections of the soul. Oftentimes, there's more truth in fiction than reality."

Only, my dreams are becoming a reality. My fiction is bleeding into real life, and I can't run from it. Not anymore.

I stare at him. "Can I ask you a question?"

"Are we in the business of trusting each other now?"

"We could be."

Ravius gestures for me to continue. "I'll answer if I can."

"In confidence?"

Steeling his spine, he finally nods.

"Is it possible to have more than one soul bond?"

Licking his lips, he looks uncertain for a moment, glancing over his shoulder to ensure Felix is out of ear shot. When he looks back at me, suspicion marks his features.

"Theoretically? It's possible."

"But unheard of?" I press.

"It's not something I've seen in all my years." Ravius clears his throat. "Is there something you need to tell me, Lexi?"

Staring into his eyes, it's on the tip of my tongue. But then I remember the endless, agonising days I spent rotting in filth because of this man, and my need to spill dies.

"No. Just curious."

"Curious," he tests the word.

"That's all."

Ravius rests his hands on his narrow hips. "You have jeopardised the safety of this entire facility and caused irreparable damage. What are we going to do about that?"

I press a hand to my sternum, feeling my hammering heart. "I'd rather die than go back into that prison cell."

"I don't want to lock you up. We should be allies, not enemies. Agree to resume your training, and you may remain free."

"And if I don't agree?"

His iridescent eyes sparkle with danger. "I came here in peace. Let us not undo the progress we've made."

The threat hangs in the air. I find myself nodding, too exhausted to fight for a second longer. All I want is peace. Even if it means trusting the devil with my soul.

"Good. Then it's a deal."

"This changes nothing between us," I add. "Send your lackey after me again, and I'll be sending him back in ashes."

"Naturally." His smile actually looks a bit proud. "Get some rest, Lexi. Training resumes at first light."

With a final nod, he strides from the apartment, leaving me standing amongst the wreckage. I watch him go, stopping to speak to Felix in the corridor.

When the door to Michael's apartment opens, the tugging in my chest tells me who it is before he appears. Flames snake through my insides as Daniel scours the hall and spots me.

"Lex?"

"Go back to bed. I'm just looking around."

Running a hand over his rumpled brown hair, Daniel steps into the apartment, glancing around the ruined space. His mouth is tugged down in a scowl.

"What the hell are you doing talking to Ravius?"

I raise my palm, gesturing for him to take a breath. "Just talking. We've agreed to a truce. I'll resume training, and he won't lock me up again."

"You trust he'll keep his word?"

"I trust that he doesn't want to find out what happens if he doesn't keep it," I reply pointedly.

Daniel deflates. "One day, we'll stop living our lives lurching from one disaster to the other."

"Good luck waiting for that day to come."

Walking around the apartment, he checks each room, whistling at the sheer state of it.

"This place is trashed."

"I did a good job of wrecking it."

"You're gonna need somewhere else to stay."

"Doubt I can sleep in Michael's bed forever," I agree. "I'll figure something out."

He stops next to me, appearing thoughtful. "Maybe we should get somewhere together. I'm sure Ravius has a spare apartment."

"T-Together?"

Daniel smirks. "Don't look so terrified."

I step into his arms. "Thought we were taking things slow?"

"A fresh start doesn't mean slow. Besides, pretty sure you destroyed that possibility the day you claimed me."

Hiding my face in his chest, I breathe in smoke and ash.

Surrounded by destruction, I still manage to feel at home in his arms. Even if nothing else makes sense.

"I'm sorry I brought you into this shit," I whisper into his shirt.

Grasping my shoulders, Daniel pushes me back to search my face. "Fresh start, remember? We're in this together."

All I can do is nod.

Hand sliding along my jaw, he lowers his lips to mine. The kiss is gentle and sweet, in complete opposition to everything I know about Daniel.

When we break apart, his nose nudges mine. "Come back to bed. You're exhausted."

"I'm fine."

"For once, don't fight me. Just let me take care of you."

Too tired to protest, I let him lead me from the trashed apartment and back into Michael's empty bed. We curl up together without stopping to question it.

This time, I fall asleep, spooned in the safety of Daniel's warm cocoon wrapped around me. My dreams are devoid of rampant fire and green-eyed strangers.

He's gone.

But I know he'll be back.

XVIII

THE MOON

CHAPTER 18

BELLS – THE UNLIKELY CANDIDATES

"*P*erfect. Good work, Lexi."

With a triumphant smile tugging at my lips, I lower my bandaged hands, snuffing out the glowing fireballs floating in the air. It's taken hours of careful practice to get to this point.

Ravius cracks his neck. "Let's break for dinner. We've been sitting in this room for hours."

A wave of exhaustion crashes over me and I nod, shaking out my trembling hands. The energy racing through me has only picked up since my manifestation.

It feels unbalanced, volatile. Like it's missing a vital component to control the erratic flow of Vitae making my life a living hell. My mind isn't ready to comprehend what that could mean.

"Your control is improving." Ravius stands, offering me a hand up. "I am pleased with your progress."

"I wish I could say the same."

He frowns at me. "You're not satisfied?"

"No, I…" My voice catches.

I can't admit the truth—that I'm haunted by dreams of another man, another bond. My power rails against me at every opportunity, and no matter what Ravius says, I'll never have control on my own.

I need Daniel.

And I need… *him.*

"Dinner," Ravius states decisively. "Come along."

Sighing heavily, I stretch my aching limbs as I follow him out of the hot office. Pain pulls at my bandaged hands and arms even though I continue to heal at an accelerated rate.

We're halfway to the dining hall when Brunt jogs up to us without even breaking a sweat. He jerks to an immediate halt.

"Sir. We have an arrival at the gates."

Ravius spins toward Brunt. "We're not expecting anyone."

He remains silent, shifting on his feet. "It's urgent."

Ravius glances longingly towards the dining hall and the awaiting food. "I'm sorry, Lexi. You'll have to excuse me."

"Of course."

The pair disappear into the winter mist. Frowning to myself, I continue walking towards the imposing shadow of the dining hall until approaching voices stop me.

"Lex! Wait up!"

Michael and Felix are rushing to catch up to me, surrounded by other people heading for dinner. I don't miss the nervous looks that are shot my way.

Everyone's afraid of me.

I'm a freak, even among them.

Staring down at my feet, I'm engulfed into a tight hug by Felix. His soft blonde hair tickles my face as he clings to me, squeezing hard enough to elicit an exasperated giggle.

"Ignore them," he says in my ear. "They're just afraid of what a badass you are these days."

"I'd prefer to be invisible."

"Well… in the future, I'd avoid almost burning down their homes to achieve that. You've earned yourself a reputation."

Groaning, I hide my face in his uniformed chest. "Brilliant."

Patting my back, he releases me. Michael is watching us both with a small smile that brightens when I turn to him.

"How was training?"

I shrug and continue walking. "I'm improving, apparently."

"Did you manage to conjure the fireballs this time?"

"Michael!" I shoot him a glare.

He glances around then waves me off. "No one's listening. I doubt anyone will come near you ever again."

"You guys really aren't making me feel better."

Felix slings his arm around my shoulders. "You've got us! Who else do you need? Fuck the rest of these guys."

"I'd just prefer not to be hated by everyone."

"Well." He plants a big, sloppy kiss on my cheek. "I don't think anyone hates you. Besides, a bit of fear is healthy, right?"

Groaning again, I shrug off his arm and climb the wide stone steps leading to the dining hall. Our usual table already seats an occupant.

My heart skips a beat when I spot a familiar set of shoulders. Like he can sense my presence, Daniel's head turns on a swivel, easily spotting me across the room.

"You guys are so gross," Felix teases.

"Don't be jealous."

A look of pain flashes across his face. I reach out and squeeze his arm in a silent apology. I know more than anyone, he's missing Raven. She hasn't shown her face since the coffee shop.

Standing up from his seat, Daniel ignores the entire room watching us with trepidation and tugs me into his arms. I hardly have time to squeak in shock before his lips find mine.

His arms band around my waist to lift me onto my tiptoes. When his tongue strokes against mine, I can't help gasping in pleasure.

The Vitae is like a purring kitten in my chest. It reacts to him without any direction from me, picking up in intensity and spreading through my bandaged extremities.

"Daniel," I moan.

He carefully places me back on my feet. "Sorry, couldn't resist. Don't spark up on me."

"Trying not to."

When we separate, he casts a look around the room, radiating such intense, cold fury, everyone drops their gazes. He's had a century to perfect his terrifying death stare.

"Sit down," he grumbles.

"You started it."

Stealing his chair, I sit down then reach for the pitcher of wine on the table. After spending all day locked in an office with Ravius, I need a bloody drink.

Everyone else takes their places around me then begin to fill their wine glasses. Underneath the table, a warm hand moves to rest on my thigh.

"How did it go?" Daniel whispers.

"Better. We're making progress."

"Ravius wants to combine our training sessions next week. We can continue working on your combat skills and see if we can incorporate your gift into it."

"How would that work?"

He reaches for his glass before taking a sip. "You've proven that you can ignite inanimate objects. With practice, you could harness that ability and target it."

"Like setting things on fire on purpose?"

"Exactly. Weapons, buildings, people." He shrugs nonchalantly. "You'd be fucking deadly."

Trying not to hurl at the mention of burning people, I can imagine the glee that Ravius felt at suggesting this.

He's kept his war talk to a minimum, but we all know what he really wants from me. Our sessions are amicable for now. I have major doubts about how long that will last though.

"I hate this," I mutter.

Daniel squeezes my leg. "I know, love. But you have to be able to defend yourself, now more than ever."

"We both know that's not what Ravius is training me for."

"And we both know that you're under no obligation to do what he says. He's only being nice because he knows you could roast his arrogant backside with the flick of a finger."

Listening to our conversation, Michael snorts so loud, red wine shoots out of his nostrils. Felix has to smack him on the back several times to stop him from choking.

I hand Michael a napkin to clean his face. "No more crisping human beings talk. We're eating."

Tucking into the golden trays of food placed on the table, we all fill our plates with perfectly cooked slices of roasted meat, vegetables and the most heavenly, crispy potatoes.

One of The Redeemed's many talents? Food. These bastards sure as hell know how to cook. I've never eaten so well in my entire life.

"As long as we're changing the subject." Michael places the wine-stained napkin on his lap. "I've received word that your new apartment is ready."

"That fast?" I stab a potato.

"We pulled some strings to get an empty place furnished and cleaned up. It's in one of the older buildings though."

Daniel nods thoughtfully. "That's fine. Lex?"

"Works for me. You'll finally get your bed back."

Michael dramatically clicks his neck from side to side. "Good. I'm sick of sleeping on that bloody sofa."

"Look at the size of you." Felix points a fork in his indignant face. "The sofa is basically a king-sized bed for someone your size."

"Hey!" Michael splutters.

"He's not wrong." I laugh.

Narrowing his eyes at all of us, Michael mutters a curse and digs into his plateful of food. We lapse into comfortable conversation until Felix abruptly stops mid-sentence.

"Raven?"

Feet shuffle behind us. I crane my neck for a glimpse. She's standing several feet away, her hands wringing and bag-lined eyes darting from side to side beneath unbrushed, lurid pink hair.

"Can I sit with you guys?" she asks.

We all just stare at her—a little shell-shocked—until Felix breaks the heavy silence by yanking out an extra chair at his side.

"Get over here."

Breaking out in a meagre smile, Raven takes her place at the table and snags a wine glass. When her eyes meet mine, she frowns a little and bites her lip.

"Is everything okay?" I study her strange reaction.

She blows out a breath. "Yes, of course. I just… I feel like I've been a bit of a bitch recently. I'm sorry."

"Well, you're here now. That's what matters. We've missed you."

Her smile blooms at my acceptance of her apology. She reaches across the table to clasp my hand but pulls back at the last moment when she spots the bandages.

"I leave you with this bunch of idiots and look what happens."

"For that you owe me big time."

Raven chuckles. "I'll make it up to you."

"You better."

"Do you want to tell me what happened to your apartment? I've heard every rumour under the sun, including that you're a demon who crawled out of hell."

Choking on another mouthful of alcohol, Michael slams his wine glass down. "I give up."

All laughing, I watch as Felix loops his arm around the back of Raven's chair, unconsciously leaning closer to her. I doubt anyone else has noticed, but I've seen the way he lights up around her.

She's none the wiser, sipping her wine while listening to Daniel's whispered rundown of what happened the other night. I'm in no mood to rehash it.

"Fuck me, Lex." She whistles. "You seriously burned the place down?"

"Close enough," I mumble.

"You're lucky to be alive."

Daniel stiffens next to me, his hands curling into white-knuckled fists. I nudge my shoulder into his, encouraging him to take a breath.

Because of him, I'm here. Still alive.

"Now everyone is giving me a wide berth." I shove a piece of carrot into my mouth.

"You've got plenty of friends." Felix winks at me. "You don't need anymore, right?"

"Well, I won't make any new ones now."

Tucking back into my food, I let their conversation flow over me. It feels good to be surrounded by my friends, pretending our lives are normal, like the rest of the world.

I wonder what Eve is doing right now. Is she eating? Sleeping? Who's cooking her dinner? The mere thought tugs at my heartstrings, and I have to blink back tears.

With the meal wrapping up and plates being cleared, everyone is relaxed, full of food and wine. Michael and Daniel are reminiscing about a particularly hot summer in the '80s.

"I was on rotation in the States." Michael swirls his wine. "Caine needed help establishing the new medical facility. I'd never experienced Texan heat before."

My scalp prickles. "There's a facility in Texas?"

Michael grimaces. "Uh, I didn't say that."

"You totally did."

"Well, shit." He winces.

"Any more classified Redeemed secrets you'd like to spill over the dinner table?"

Daniel slaps him on the back. "Good job."

I turn a glower on him. "Don't get me started on your secrets. Not unless you want to find somewhere else to live."

He stares down at his empty plate. "I have no more secrets from you."

The sound of the doors to the dining hall slamming open punctuates his words. There's a low hum of surprised chatter around us, but I'm too focused on Daniel to give it my attention.

"Swear on it?"

"Lexi, I made a promise."

"Um, Daniel…" Michael begins.

Daniel's eyes are locked on mine, muddied with frustration. "When are you going to start trusting me?"

Michael's gaze is fixed behind us. "Uh, Daniel…"

"I've spent my entire life being manipulated," I point out. "Sorry if I'm having a hard time trusting you after you've done the exact same."

Michael curses when he fails to get Daniel's attention. Glancing at Michael, the momentary distraction breaks me free from the brewing argument.

I'm hit with a sudden wave of dizziness, causing me to slump against Daniel's shoulder. He immediately goes on high alert, gripping my neck and tilting my head so we're eye level.

"What is it?"

"I d-don't… I don't know."

My chest is searing, alight with fierce, almost out of control heat. The flow of Vitae picks up, preening beneath my attention like it's screaming for a release.

I rub my chest bone, gasping in discomfort. Daniel's eyes narrow as he shifts his face even closer, blocking everyone else's concerned expressions out.

"Are you having another panic attack?"

"N-No," I choke out.

The hum of chatter around us dies down, revealing two

raised, almost frantic voices elsewhere in the room. That's when Daniel looks up.

All I can see is his face, draining of colour, leaving nothing but ashen waxiness behind. Lips parting on a shocked intake of breath, his hand falls from my neck.

"Daniel?"

He doesn't even acknowledge me.

"Daniel? What is it?"

With bolts of electricity zipping up my spine, I slowly turn to look over my shoulder at the source of the commotion. Deep down, past my denial... I know what this is. His voice returns to me.

You can't hide anymore.

I'll find you.

The entire room is watching the drama unfold as Ravius and Brunt attempt to keep up with a gaggle of armed, suit-clad men, bursting into the full dining hall.

"Where is she?" someone yells.

They're dressed impeccably in dark suits with prominent gun holsters. Three olive-skinned men flank their leader, who strides with powerful, confident steps, taking him to his destiny.

My heart seizes.

Lungs squeeze.

Brain short-circuits.

The minute we lock eyes, the dizziness abates, replaced by cold certainty. His brilliant, forest-green orbs burn with the immense force of inevitability, and the world comes crashing down around me.

"Is that...?" Raven trails off.

"Yeah," Michael replies flatly.

"Fuck," I hear Felix curse. "What is the Spanish Elder doing here?"

But my heart knows.

He's here for me.

Footsteps briefly halting, the stranger I've spent countless nights dreaming about almost falters. *Almost.* Then his visible relief melts into a mask of determination that steals my breath.

My view is suddenly blocked when Daniel stands and moves in front of me, forming a protective stance. I fly to my feet and grab his shoulder.

"Daniel—"

He shrugs me off, moving in a blur to meet the stranger halfway across the room. I have no idea what's happening, and Daniel doesn't wait to explain his hostility.

Chasing after him, I ignore the stunned faces watching the scene. Ravius is rushing to catch up to the newcomers, but his attention is fixed on me, warning me off.

"Lexi" the stranger shouts.

Daniel's steps falter. He looks over his shoulder at me with a gut-wrenching look of disbelief. I feel a hot rush of panic and shame.

"You know him?" he spits.

"I... I..."

"Get away from her, Daniel," the stranger warns.

Grinding to a halt in his shining leather shoes, all of his attention is fixed on me. Unwavering and unafraid. His razor-sharp, symmetrical features look like they could slice glass with a mere glance.

Long, flowing hair the deepest shade of chestnut-brown is pulled back in a low man bun at the nape of his neck, highlighting the swell of his perfectly proportioned lips and golden, tanned skin.

His charcoal suit is fitted to perfection, accentuating his towering height and lithe, nimble limbs. Everything about him screams wealth and sophistication, but he walks with the threatening confidence of a seasoned predator.

A heavily tattooed hand lifting, the handsome stranger

looks like he wants to reach across the room to touch me. He never gets the chance.

"Valentine," Daniel deadpans.

Emerald eyes penetrating my skin, Valentine bristles. He finally looks up at Daniel, seeming to assess the threat he poses with an amused glance.

"Move," Valentine commands.

Daniel refuses to budge. "What are you doing here?"

"Final warning. Move."

I catch the almost imperceptible lifting of Daniel's mouth in a smirk. And that's when he strikes. A scream creeps up my throat as Daniel's fist swings, seeming to move in slow motion.

Valentine doesn't duck. He sees the incoming threat and lets Daniel pummel him like he was expecting the punishment all along.

The blow is brutal. I can hear the sharp crack it elicits from several feet away, followed by a spray of blood and Valentine's knees meeting the floor.

Rumbling a deep, rasping laugh, Valentine wipes blood from his nose. "Nice to see you too, comrade."

"What the fuck do you want?"

"I'm not here for you."

"Daniel!" Ravius booms as he catches up to them. "Stand down immediately."

Moving to defend their leader, Valentine's men form a well-muscled wall between him and Daniel. Valentine draws to his feet, brushing off his suit while ignoring the blood running down his face.

He's staring.

Triumphant and unapologetic.

Not at Daniel. Not at his men. Nor the entire shocked, gasping room watching things unravel. Nothing else exists beyond Valentine's gaze burrowing into me.

"Lexi," he says reverently.

Daniel looks between us. "What is this?"

Thick rivulets stream down my cheeks. I look down at my burned hands, overwhelmed by shame.

"I wanted to tell you."

"Lex?" His voice is a broken whisper. "Tell me what?"

"Please... I never meant for this to happen."

Valentine steps closer then claps his attacker on the arm. "Always a pleasure to see you, Daniel. But I'm here for my mate."

When Daniel turns to face him, he looks completely shattered, caught between all-consuming grief and the horror of betrayal.

"Mate?" he repeats.

Ravius intervenes, separating the two men with Brunt close in tow. He looks warily between the three of us, his disbelief evident as he clears his throat.

"Valentine and Lexi are soul bound."

THE SUN

CHAPTER 19

NEON OCEAN – NEW DIALOGUE

I'm not proud of it, but history has taught me to run. From relationships. Friendships. Welfare officers asking questions about bruises or visible ribs. My sister's questions. Debt collectors.

Run.

Run.

Run.

Internally screaming, my legs pump fast, carrying me into the murkiness. I don't care about the roar of voices behind me. I don't even feel ashamed for running like a scared child.

"Lexi!" someone bellows.

Ducking into the woodland between the residential buildings, I ignore the searing pain in my chest. Having my two bonds in close proximity then severing the connection so abruptly is excruciating.

"Lex!"

Weaving through thick, comforting gloom, I run until I can't feel the tingle of power in my chest anymore. My tears are freezing against my aching cheeks, and my lungs heave for breath.

I hit the perimeter fence then circle back, melting into the trees. When my legs are shaking too badly to carry me even an inch farther, I collapse against a tree trunk and sob.

All I wanted was to get back to my sister. I didn't ask for any of this, and I've tried my best to embrace the madness, even when my life was threatened by the very force living within me.

Silence envelopes me as I fall apart. There's nothing but the soft patter of rain beating against the waxy leaves hanging above me.

My tears eventually dry up, leaving me exhausted and trembling in the frigid cold. With my head resting against the roughened tree bark, I let my eyes slide shut.

Dozing in and out, I know I've left myself exposed, but I don't possess the mental or physical fortitude to do anything about it. Vivid green eyes flash through my awareness before I startle awake to the sound of crunching footsteps in the underbrush.

"Lexi," Valentine calls.

I hold my breath, hoping he doesn't come any closer. After what just happened, I don't want to face either of them. This whole mess is too much to handle.

"I know you're out here. I thought we were done running from each other, mi amor?"

As much as I should, I'm too tired to move. No matter where I run, he will still find me. He's already curled around my bones and tunnelled deep into my soul.

"I'm sorry for what happened back there, but I will not leave you out here alone. All I want is to talk."

Snap.

I lift my head when a tree branch cracks nearby, feeling the bite of wind and rain on my tear-stained cheeks. He's directly in front of me, shrouded by shadows.

"There you are."

"Go away," I croak.

"Not a chance," he clips out.

Approaching me, Valentine moves slow and steady, as if circling a startled deer on the verge of fleeing. When he drops down to his knees in front of me, his verdant eyes are wide and pleading.

"You're freezing. Why are you hiding?"

I wrap my arms around myself to suppress a shiver. "Because I want to be alone."

"Mind if I join you?"

"Yeah. I do."

Valentine studies me, from rain-mussed blonde hair to the thick swathes of bandages wrapped around my hands. His full, kissable lips are pressed into a tight line of displeasure.

"I've spent decades waiting for you," he whispers. "I'd started to think this moment would never come."

"What are you talking about? Decades?"

Lifting a tattooed hand, he reaches out but stops mid-air. "Please come inside. We need to face this together."

"I can't see Daniel. Not after what I've done."

Understanding flickers across his olive-toned features. "You feel like you've betrayed him."

"I kissed you!" I frantically gesture between us. "We're… we're… soul bound. But I'm already…"

"With him?" Valentine supplies.

"It's complicated."

"When is anything simple with Daniel?" He sighs.

As much as I want to defend Daniel, I can't disagree. That man redefines the word complicated. Apparently, Valentine has already had the pleasure of facing his wrath.

"Why did he attack you?"

Sitting back on his haunches, Valentine's head lowers. "It's a long and old story, but to summarise, I deserved that punch."

I blow out a breath. "It changes nothing. I've lied to him and broken his trust. He'll hate me again now."

"Lexi, this isn't a betrayal. You cannot control the bond no

255

more than you can stop breathing or blinking. Daniel knows that deep down."

"He does?"

Valentine slowly nods, a smile tugging at his mouth. "His anger was not with you."

"But... he does hate you?"

At that, he chuckles.

"More than life itself, I'd imagine."

Another wave of tears overcomes me, and I choke out a bitter laugh. "Then we're already doomed."

Valentine tentatively reaches out an inked hand. "I wouldn't be so sure. I'm asking you to trust me."

I don't know this man. He's exactly what I nicknamed him —a stranger. But that doesn't stop my heart from soaring in my chest, beating so hard, I fear it'll explode at any moment.

"When I touched Daniel, I bonded him to me," I blurt out. "Maybe if we don't touch... there's still a way out of this for you."

"Is that what you want?" Hurt swarms into his blazing green eyes, shuttering his easy smile and wiping it clean off his face.

"I don't... know."

Valentine curses in rich Spanish, his accent becoming more pronounced as his emotions rise. But he doesn't drop his outstretched hand. Not yet.

"It's too late. The bond was established the moment we kissed. That is when you manifested, yes?"

The memory of raging fire flicks through my mind.

"Yes."

"Because your bond was complete," he explains simply. "We did not have to physically touch to establish it. That's how powerful our connection is."

I feel myself flush beneath his rapt attention. "I've bound you to me for life. A complete stranger, no less! Why do you look so happy?"

He wriggles his outstretched fingers, encouraging me to take his hand. "Because we were made for each other."

Powerless to resist his dangerous siren's call, I slip a hand into his. The moment his fingers clench around mine, familiar electricity surges through me.

It's hot and heady, the feeling of supreme power that lashes between us. I have to fall back on my training with Ravius and lock down on it to stop the entire forest from exploding into an inferno.

But instead of battling against me, the Vitae calms, evening out into a still, undisturbed pool of power that resides in my chest. I rattle out a relieved sigh and look up at Valentine.

"Magnificent," he murmurs.

The look on his face is so contented, he looks utterly at peace with the world and all its inexplicable chaos. His eyes are at half-mast as his fingers gently caress mine.

"I see now why your gift has demanded two mates." He shakes his head. "It is so very strong. Unlike anything I've ever felt before. The Vitae is dripping off you."

"What do you mean?"

"Even in the Redeemed world, soul bonds are extremely rare and coveted. But two? That's unheard of. I didn't understand how it was possible until now."

The look of awe on his face makes me feel sick to my stomach. I've seen that look before. His brother looks the exact same way at me.

"So not only was I brutally murdered, resurrected, then thrown into this awful place with an out of control gift that makes everyone scared of me, the world decided to damn me with two men tied to my soul for an eternity too?"

His eyes widen, sparkling with amusement. "What a sharp tongue you have, sweetheart. You don't disappoint."

I shake off his hand. "Whatever."

"Fight against this all you want. I'm sure Daniel is trying

to convince himself of the same thing. It changes nothing between us."

Pushing up from my position on the ground, I put distance between us. Valentine looks disappointed at the way I flinch away from him, straightening to his full height. He's several feet taller than me.

"How long have you been watching me? Spying on me? Somehow worming your way into my dreams?"

He barks a whiskey-smooth laugh. "You're the one who pulled me into your dreams. I had no choice in the matter."

I feel my cheeks flush. "Well, I didn't mean to!"

"No more than I meant to invade your privacy," he points out. "It was the bond, drawing us together. There's no stopping this."

"We'll see about that," I grumble.

Stomping away, I hear him scrambling to stand up and chase after me.

"Lexi, wait!"

"Not for you."

He chuckles to himself, already hot on my tail. Even now, my body is tingling with a heightened awareness, fuelled by our close proximity.

In the distance, the excessive, old-world architecture of the administration building comes into view. The courtyard is quiet now the dinner crowd has dispersed, leaving us to traipse through the still falling rain.

"What's your plan here?" he calls after me.

Teeth chattering, I swipe drenched hair from my face. "Stop Daniel from freaking out, find a way to reverse this bond, and prevent your brother from tossing me in prison again."

Valentine grabs my arm. "Again?"

"You two have some catching up to do." I shrug him off. "How did I end up bonded to a damn Elder?"

Darting a step ahead, Valentine lifts a crooked tree branch out of my path. "Is that a problem?"

"I haven't exactly had the best experience of Elders so far. Ravius isn't my biggest fan."

"Has he harmed you?" Valentine's sharp tone threatens violence if he doesn't like my answer.

"I'll let him fill you in on the details."

He bars an arm across my chest. "And why on earth are you covered in bandages?"

"When your little kiss caused me to manifest, I woke up to find my apartment on fire. I almost burned myself to a crisp in the process."

Raising my arms, I push back my shirt sleeves to reveal more gauze and tightly wound bandages covering the healing burns. Valentine grits his teeth as he studies the cotton swathes.

"Daniel pulled me out. If he hadn't intervened, I'd be dead right now."

I push my sleeves back down then peel his arm from my chest to continue walking. Valentine quickly recovers and follows me.

"What else don't I know about?" he thunders.

"Where do I begin?"

Cursing again, his footsteps are heavy with rage as we enter the well-lit building and head for Ravius's office. I know Daniel's in there. The closer we get, the more my insides begin to itch.

He's probably furious.

Well, join the club.

Not bothering to knock, Valentine storms ahead of me and slams the office door open. I trail after him, sick with anxiety at what we'll find inside.

"What's this about a prison stay?" Valentine booms.

Sitting in one of the armchairs next to the bar, Ravius's head snaps up at his brother's harsh bark. Sitting opposite him, Daniel is gripping a half-empty glass, his head hanging low.

Wrestling my fear and sticking it in a mental lockbox, I enter the office then head for a safe corner. Nothing could convince me to move closer to any of these three men.

Ravius pins Valentine with a self-righteous glare. "Now, listen here—"

"You imprisoned my bonded?"

"We had no idea that Lexi was yours."

"But you knew she was his!" Valentine gestures at the silent man nursing his liquor. "What were you thinking?"

"She tried to escape and almost killed herself in the process!" Ravius defends.

Whirling on the spot, Valentine hits me with a disbelieving look. "You did what?"

I swallow hard. "It was nothing."

"Were you hurt?"

"I—"

"Answer me, Lexi!"

"She has been gifted with immense power," Ravius intervenes when I fail to summon a response. "It has led to some difficulties."

I scoff at his characterisation of recent chaos. Ravius narrows his eyes but chooses to ignore me. When Daniel snorts in derision, Valentine rounds on him with raised brows.

"Something to say, comrade?"

"Don't fucking call me that."

"This is *our* mate we're discussing." Acid drips from Valentine's words. "If you have something to add, don't be shy."

I watch the familiar cold mask drop over Daniel's features. He places his drink down then slowly stands.

"I will not lose to you again. You've taken enough from me already. You don't get her too."

"You think I would've chosen this?" Valentine flings out

his arms. "I'm no more thrilled by the idea of sharing her than you are!"

I step between them with a snarl. "I'm right here. And what makes you think I want to be shared by you two knuckleheads anyway?"

"Lexi—" Valentine begins.

"No! I've been kept in the dark and lied to since the moment I arrived here." I turn to Ravius. "Tell me how to break the bond."

Valentine seems to wither, his shoulders slumping beneath the weight of disappointment. Daniel just stares at the thick carpet, like he can't bring himself to believe this is happening.

"You can't break it," Ravius replies. "We've already discussed this. A soul bond is for eternity."

"There must be a way!"

"Death," Daniel cuts in. "Yours."

He flinches at his own clipped words. Valentine curls his tattoo-covered hands curled into fists at the mere thought.

"No." Dread is a sharp knife in my gut. "There must be another way. Look at this mess! We can't do this!"

"You have no choice." Ravius blows out a heavy breath. "The Vitae has made its choice. The soul bond is complete."

"I don't want this!"

"You think I do?" Daniel yells back.

Recoiling at the venom in his voice, I look up into his grief-stricken eyes. He looks ready to tear out of his own skin just to escape this room and its occupants.

"What did he do to you?" I whisper.

Daniel doesn't answer. It's the rich, accented voice of my stranger that intervenes.

"I betrayed him." Valentine looks straight at Daniel. "I took the one thing he loved more than anything in the world and ruined it."

"You killed her," Daniel utters menacingly.

"No, I protected her from you!"

"She was never under threat from me."

"And what about your Elder?" Valentine rages.

"You mean _your_ brother?"

"Enough, both of you." Ravius braces his hands on his hips. "You've been gifted a great honour. Where is your gratitude?"

"Gratitude?" Daniel scoffs.

"The Vitae has chosen you for this sacred bond. Not to mention that Lexi's life is in danger, and you're here squabbling over the past like children?"

"Caine." It takes Valentine a millisecond to catch on. "You think he'll try to come for her now."

Daniel folds his arms across his chest. "He poses a threat to all gifted Redeemed."

"And I have no doubt he is aware of Lexi's abilities after her manifestation," Ravius adds solemnly. "He'll stop at nothing to get his hands on her now."

All falling silent, they seem to contemplate that. But the threat Caine poses feels insignificant in the face of our current predicament.

"You keep saying that Caine is the enemy," I interject. "But I have no reason to trust anyone in this room."

"Lex," Daniel rasps.

The sheer pain in his baritone voice hits me like a tonne of bricks. He's staring straight at me, and despite our audience, his vulnerability is laid bare for the world to see.

"I'm sorry." I make myself meet his anguished gaze. "I didn't mean to keep this from you."

"How long have you known?"

"Since I manifested."

Brows shooting into his hair line, he gapes at me. "Dammit! We agreed on a clean slate."

"I didn't know what to think. I'd just gotten my head around having one soul bond. But two?"

I inch towards him, attempting to cross the chasm that's

ruptured between us. It feels like he's slipping further and further away with each second.

"Anyone in the entire world." He tilts his head back, eyes on the ceiling. "And you had to choose him."

"There wasn't much choice in the matter."

Daniel laughs coldly. "You have no idea what kind of person he is."

Stepping into the firing line, Valentine stops my approach. "There are two sides to every story. I'm not the villain he thinks I am."

"Then who are you?" I counter. "A stranger? My mate? The Spanish Elder? Ravius's brother?"

"How about just yours," he quips easily.

A threatening rumble emanates from Daniel's chest. I have no doubt he'd rather gouge Valentine's eyes out with his bare hands than listen to this.

"I didn't think you were real," I admit.

Valentine's head cocks, stirring loose strands of hair. "I know, mi amor. But I am. This... is."

Caught between the pair of them, I feel like I'm tied to the tracks and watching a high-speed train approach. I can't run from them. Not again. It's already too late.

"We can't do this," I mumble feebly.

To my complete shock, it's Daniel who speaks up. His voice is barely above a whisper, he's so defeated.

"We have no choice."

Valentine nods, visibly itching to move closer. "The three of us are bound together."

Hands curling into fists, I want nothing more than to run and hide. They're all watching me like I'm a ticking time bomb. I hate it.

"Perhaps we should call it a night," Ravius suggests as he studies me. "It's been a long day of training."

Daniel wastes no time standing up and booking it to the

door. Chancing a look at Valentine's face, he offers me a small, encouraging smile.

"Rest. I'm not going anywhere."

Ravius claps a hand on his shoulder. "I'll find suitable accommodation for you and your men."

"Near Lexi," Valentine specifies. "I'm not taking any more chances with her safety."

"I'm perfectly capable of keeping her safe," Daniel argues as he holds the door open for me.

Valentine gestures down at my bandaged hands on display. "Clearly."

I offer Ravius a terse nod. "I'm going to bed before I drown in testosterone."

Thankfully, no one dares to protest.

THE DEVIL

CHAPTER 20

HORNS – BRYCE FOX

$\mathcal{T}$he new apartment is clean and basic. Tucked away in a quiet corner of the facility behind the hospital, it's deathly quiet, surrounded by a copse of tall, swaying willow trees and manicured lawns.

Inside the isolated, red brick building, dust lays thick in the air. It clearly hasn't been used in a very long time. Beams of light emanate from the crystal chandeliers, highlighting the thick specks of dust marking its disuse.

Michael coughs as he shows us up the dark-wood staircase. "This place is mostly used for storage now. It's one of the original buildings."

Stepping into the second-floor apartment above rooms filled with stuffed boxes and old furniture, Daniel flicks on the lights. It's nowhere near as modern as my last apartment, but it works.

I glance around the space, noting the red velvet sofas and thick, patterned rugs on top of old carpet. It looks like it's been thoroughly cleaned for us. The attached kitchen is dated but functional, lit by bay windows that allow moonlight inside.

"Thanks for arranging this, Michael." I pull him into a quick hug. "And for letting us stay this past week."

He pats my back. "We only made this place liveable, you can do whatever you want to it now."

"Like bring in a wrecking ball?" Daniel moans.

Michael rolls his eyes. "Feel free to kick the ungrateful bastard out to sleep in the rain, Lex."

"Way ahead of you."

With twinkling eyes, Michael hands over the set of keys then hugs me again. He leaves us alone in the apartment, surrounded by antiques and awkward silence.

"I'm going to shower," Daniel declares.

Before I can say anything, he disappears through a set of doors into the back of the apartment. No matter what he said back there, I know I've hurt him.

Bouncing on the balls of my feet, I'm itching to turn and run out of this place. But hiding from him isn't going to make this mess go away. I owe Daniel more than that.

Creeping after him, I listen to the sound of the shower running in the ensuite and clothes rustling. I decide to give him some privacy and glance around the master bedroom instead.

There's a wide, king-sized bed fitted with fresh white sheets, a stocked wardrobe and a huge, floor-length mirror. With brushed gold fittings, cream wallpaper and tall ceilings, it's full of opulence.

Sitting down on the bed, I kick off my shoes then stretch out, listening to the shower running. It feels like hours pass before the water finally shuts off.

Here goes nothing.

Heart hammering in my chest, I sit up on the bed as Daniel steps out in a cloud of steam. He still refuses to look at me, swiping wet, chocolate-brown hair from his face instead.

"Daniel," I begin.

"I really don't want to talk," he mutters.

"Who said anything about talking?"

Hand braced on the doorframe, he looks every inch the

magazine-worth Greek god. He fills the doorway with muscle and dripping, burnished skin, covered only by the towel wrapped around his waist.

Feeling brave, I stand up from the bed and walk over, letting my hands traverse every ridged slope of his wet torso. He watches me explore his body with a predatory gleam in his eyes.

"Lex—"

"You're not the only one who doesn't want to talk."

"But I guess we should." He sighs.

"Why?" I press a kiss to his pectoral. "Everything is so messed up. I don't want to think about it right now."

"I've tried to keep my distance, but I won't control myself if you keep looking at me like that."

"Screw your control. I never asked for it."

His perfectly straight teeth are bared in a snarl. "Trust me, you don't know what you're starting. Back off."

"Why?"

"Lex."

"Tell me why, Daniel!"

His patience snaps. Chest rising and falling in rapid succession, he lets all his rage unfurl.

"Because you brought that backstabbing piece of shit into *our* bond!" he yells. "I know you didn't ask for this, but I hate you for it anyway."

Hurt pierces my chest at his admission. Rather than pushing me away, it fuels the supernatural fire raging inside my core.

"He's gifted, you know?" Daniel scoffs. "Valentine is everything that I'm not, and she knew it."

"Who knew it?" I breathe.

"He took her from me. Just like he'll take you from me too, bond be damned."

I stare at him for several seconds. The man who spent

269

weeks avoiding me and fighting our bond. Deep down, he's terrified of losing me.

"What makes you think I'd let him?"

"I'm sure she said the same thing," he retorts.

Sliding a hand up his toned forearm, I curl my arm around his neck to bring our chests flush together. I can feel each ragged breath he takes.

"Who was she?" I ask again.

"Pen."

I bury my fingers in the strands of wet hair on top of his shaved head. Daniel's eyes squeeze shut, like he's battling an onslaught of bad memories.

"Your wife?"

He inhales sharply and nods. "I've shared with Valentine before, even if I didn't know it at the time."

"He was with her too?"

"For years. I had no idea."

Releasing my tight grip on his hair, I step backwards, causing his eyes to slam open. He watches me with such raw desperation, I can almost taste it curling in the air.

"Now she's dead, and I can't lose you too," he adds raggedly. "You've given me something to fight for."

Maintaining eye contact, I lift my chin in hopeful defiance. "Then fight for it."

"What if I've already lost?"

"Shouldn't I be the decider of that?" My thighs clench together. "Valentine changes nothing between us."

"Then why lie about him?"

"Because… I guess I was afraid of losing you too."

His stare moves over me in a slow appraisal, from my legs tellingly pressed together to the rapid rise and fall of my chest. When he licks his lips, I know I've won.

Daniel loops a finger into the towel secured around his waist and tugs, letting it hit the floor. His bulging quads are revealed, but they're overshadowed by the hard promise of his cock.

I have no shame looking him over, taking in every muscle-carved inch. He just stands there and lets me drink my fill. When I've finished admiring him, I quickly pull my shirt off and toss it aside.

"Are you just going to stand there?"

His hand moves to fist his length, stroking it from base to tip. "Just enjoying the view."

Unzipping my jeans, I step out of them before crawling onto the bed in my black underwear. Daniel's attention doesn't waver as I take off my bra and remove my panties.

"You going to give me a show, princess?"

"You want to watch?" I tease back.

"Fuck yes, I do."

Spreading my legs, I dip a hand between my thighs, fingertips brushing over my pubic bone before moving to circle my heat. He continues stroking his cock, his hand slowly speeding up.

When I plunge a finger into my drenched slit, he moves closer to the bed. I throw my head back, sliding a finger deep into my pussy before pulling it out again.

With each swirl, I run a thumb over my clit, enjoying the delicious tingles it sends up my spine. Knowing he's watching every thrust of my finger makes this even hotter.

"Still enjoying the view?"

Jerking his length in long, frantic strokes, he looks me over under half-mast lids. "I could watch this all day long."

Nudging my legs farther open, I slide a second finger into my entrance. The pressure stretches me wider, and I gasp, letting my back arch off the bed.

His patience expiring, Daniel kneels on the mattress so he's braced above me for a better view. I shiver as he trails the tip of his finger between my breasts, barely touching me.

"Make yourself come," he commands.

"Now?" I whine.

"Yes. Now."

Speeding up my movements, I grind the heel of my palm against my clit as my two fingers pump in and out. He barely blinks, determined to capture every snapshot of my pleasure.

With my release building, I circle my thumb over my bundle of nerves, seconds from exploding. I can feel my orgasm on the horizon. Just as I resolve to let go, a hand grabs my wrist.

Daniel wrenches my arm upwards, dragging my fingers from my slit before I can make myself come. He pins my wrist to the bed so forcefully, my bones ache.

I cry out in frustration, feeling my orgasm ebbing away. His eyes gleam with satisfaction at watching me struggle.

"Poor Lexi," he taunts. "Bad timing, love?"

"You... I... Fuck!"

Lowering his lips to mine, he captures me in a heart-pounding kiss that scrambles my already fried brain. Our tongues meet as he kisses the very life from my soul.

Taking my other wrist, he pins that above my head, leaving me trapped and exposed. I writhe beneath him, attempting to rub my thighs together, but he settles between my legs to stop me.

"Frustrated?" he murmurs.

"Yes!"

"Good. That's how you make me feel."

Mouth travelling down my neck, he sinks his teeth in, over and over again until I'm mewling with need. I can practically feel the bruises blooming, and I fucking love it.

"Frustrated. Powerless. Vulnerable... I've spent years in enemy territory, but that didn't scare me like you do."

Lips finding my aching nipples, he takes one in his mouth, sucking and biting down. I arch off the bed again, pressing my throbbing pussy into his leg. His touch fills my extremities with the ever-present hum of electric caused by the Vitae surging between us.

"Daniel…"

"Yeah, princess?"

"Please."

"No. I warned you that you'd have to beg for it. You still chose to play this game with me."

Surrendering one nipple, he moves to the next, taking it between his lips. I push against his strong thigh again, hoping for relief yet finding more rejection.

Hands gripping my waist, he offers no warning before lifting me and pushing me up the mattress. I let him guide my outstretched hands to the bars of the bed frame.

"Hold them," he orders. "If even a single finger moves, I won't let you come. Understood?"

I grab hold of the cool metal and nod. "Yes."

"Good girl."

I'm soaked just hearing his praise. Unable to tear my eyes away, I watch him move down my body, kissing and licking a path over the violent map of scars covering every inch.

The pink-striped skin is extra sensitive, and his lips make me feel like I'm being tasered. Every kiss sends a silent command to the power pooling in my chest and makes me soar.

Energy is snapping between us, stoking the invisible flames eating me up inside. I can't stop my gift from reacting to him. It's in tune with each electrifying touch he dares to offer me.

"You're dripping wet," he hums. "I'd like that son of a bitch to see how your pussy reacts to me."

"You're twisted," I moan.

"Perhaps. But I couldn't care less."

When his mouth secures to my mound, I almost release my grip on the bed frame. His eyes dart up to make sure I'm still holding on before he dives back into his meal.

His lips travel down to my core, licking and sucking in a

perfect symphony. When his tongue glides through my folds and teases my tight hole, I see stars.

Lips worshipping me, he brings a finger to my slit then thrusts it inside, pushing me back to the edge of oblivion. Only this time, his patience is non-existent.

Thrusting his digit into me in hard, fast strokes, Daniel sneaks glances up at me as he fucks me with his hand. I'm gripping the bed frame so tight, the metal groans.

When he pushes a second finger inside, the need inside me peaks and I let go. Pleasure rolls over me as I cry out, bucking on the bed and pressing myself into his face for more.

Daniel grips my hips and holds my pussy against his mouth, refusing to surrender his claim over me. Each lash of his tongue stretches out my orgasm into punishing aftershocks.

Sprawled out on the bed, I gasp for air as I watch as his head lift. He slowly, deliberately licks his lips, cleaning the score of shining moisture from them.

"I will never get tired of hearing your moans." He smirks at me. "Or tasting this sweet pussy of mine."

Slumping onto the pillows, blood pounds in my ears. "I don't belong to you."

Grabbing my ankles, he drags me back down the bed until he's right above me, that damned infuriating half-smile looming in my face.

"Don't you?" he taunts.

Wrapping a hand around his stubble-covered throat, I drag him closer until our lips meet in a violent clash. Nipping his bottom lip, I lift my hips to grind against him.

When my free hand reaches down to wrap around his length, he releases my lips, pressing his forehead against mine. A rumbling, frustrated sound emanates from his chest.

"We should stop."

"Why?" I peck his mouth.

"Because neither of us are thinking straight."

Squeezing his throat again, I tease his thundering pulse

point. His eyes are full of temptation, swirling in the black, bottomless pits of his pupils.

"You want me to stop?" I stroke his cock with my other hand, lightly squeezing the pulsing length. "Right now?"

His face vanishes as he suddenly flips me over so my face is pressed into the bed sheets. I gasp loudly as his palm connects with my ass cheek, spreading exquisite tingles.

"You drive me insane." He spanks me again, daring to hit me even harder. "Every fucking day."

I grip the sheets, raising my ass in a silent plea for more. Each smack has heat flooding my pussy. He soothes the sore skin after each spank with a stroke before hitting me again.

Fingers digging into my hips, he raises me higher, then I feel the brush of his erection against my thigh. It's an inch from where I want it, and I'm on the verge of pleading for him to fill me up.

I've never been triggered by sex, no matter what happened to me over the years. It became a form of release for me, an escape from the constant onslaught of pain and humiliation.

That's what made my relationship with Alex so toxic—the more I endured, the more it sent me falling into his cold, unloving arms to numb the pain.

But I'm *choosing* this.

I'm *choosing* him.

"Daniel," I whine.

"What do you want, love?"

"Please... I need you to make it all go away."

"And how do you propose I do that?"

Growling in annoyance, I try to push back against his crotch so he'll finally enter me, but it's no use. My hips are trapped in his bruising grip. I can't move a muscle.

"Beg me," he demands. "Beg for me to fuck you, and maybe I'll think about giving you some relief."

"You're such an asshole!"

"I never disputed that."

He spanks me again, causing my teeth to rattle. The blistering waves of satisfaction are almost too much to bear. No matter what he says, my body continues to writhe beneath him.

"God, please." The desperate words slip from my mouth. "Please, Daniel. I want you."

That's all he needs to hear. The assurance that my body belongs to him, no matter the chaos threatening to come between us. With a guttural growl, he slams into me.

I scream out in equal parts pleasure and relief. Endless weeks of brewing tension explode as he draws back then pushes back into me again, his cock stretching my internal walls.

The most exquisite sense of pressure scrambles my mind. He's so big, I feel like I'm going to fall apart with his full length breaching me. It's intense beyond words.

"Fuck, Lex," he grunts.

Gripping the bed sheets tight, I hold on for dear life as he begins to move. Each pump of his hips is an individual knife stroke, slicing deeper and deeper into me.

"You take me so fucking well, princess."

All I can do is garble a non-intelligible response, the frantic slam of his cock worshipping me stealing all rational thought from my mind. He's melted me into a boneless puddle.

Fingertips bruising my hips with the ferocity of his grip, Daniel sheaths himself inside me with each thrust. His breathing is ragged, unsteady. We're both losing control.

When he abruptly pulls out, I almost cry out at the sense of loss. Then I'm roughly flipped over so my back meets the soft mattress, allowing his swirling blue orbs to cast over me.

"You're so beautiful," he mumbles in awe.

Hands circling his wrists, I guide them back to my hips, raised and ready for him to resume his torture. But he's far too preoccupied with staring at me like I hung the damn moon.

"I can't lose you, Lex."

"You're not going to."

"Don't make promises you can't keep."

Sitting up, I bring a hand to his cheek. "You promised to keep me safe, remember? I know you won't let anything happen to me."

Nostrils flaring, there's an unnamed emotion dancing in his irises. I can't decide if it's a swell of pride at my blatant show of trust or raw fear for the inevitable grief he seems to be expecting.

I decide to take matters into my own hands and grip his shoulders, lifting myself so I'm straddling his body. My legs wind around his waist, bringing us flush together.

With the heat from his silky smooth skin seeping into me, I reach down between my legs to find his hardness. Daniel's lips part on a sharp breath.

"All that matters is this," I purr, stroking him up and down. "The rest of the world's bullshit can wait until I'm done with you."

Lining him up to my entrance, I don't waste a second before sliding down on his cock. He slips deep inside, filling me to the brim at this new angle.

We both groan at the heady feeling flowing between us—powerful, overwhelming, our bodies alight with desire. The rush of Vitae tying us together only heightens each sensation.

Using his shoulders for leverage, I set a fast pace. I'm chasing a release, desperate to relieve the fiery ache within me.

Daniel ruts up into me, raising his hips to meet my strokes. We're a sweaty, breathless tangle, writhing in a tempo of gasps and moans.

My nails slice deeper into his skin with each movement, eliciting a thin stream of blood that coats my fingertips. I lean close to smack my mouth against his to chase the pain away.

His tongue pushes past my lips to capture me in a dangerous waltz. With his skilled mouth devouring mine and every inch of me filled to breaking point, another orgasm begins to build.

I pursue that elusive feeling, shoving out every distraction and shred of doubt. None of it matters. All I need is his skin on mine; the rest of the world can wait.

"Lex," he gasps.

But I'm too preoccupied with working myself on his cock, feeding my addiction and stealing every ounce of control away from him. He can't run from me again. Not this time.

"Lexi!"

"What?" I growl out.

"The fucking curtains!"

Snapping out of my lust-fuelled haze, I realise the scent of smoke lays heavy in the air. The world quickly filters back in.

My body is alight with invisible flames, crackling and writhing beneath my skin. Fire is battling to consume the drapes covering the bedroom window. They've combusted into a raging wildfire.

"Jesus Christ!"

Daniel snorts. "Put it out before you kill both of us."

"How do I do that?"

"Concentrate," he purrs.

"Little hard to do right now." I gesture between us as his hips raise, rutting up into me. "Fuck, Daniel!"

Hands gripping my waist, he retakes control despite being trapped beneath me. His cock slams upwards, filling every available inch of space I have to offer.

A guttural moan slips from my lips. My ears are ringing and limbs trembling with the force slamming through me. The flames grow brighter, stretching up to the ceiling and leaving dark scorch marks.

Each stroke of his cock only worsens the situation. We're connected at every available point, our skin touching, electricity zipping between us with the frenzied excitement of a puppy.

"Pour the energy into me," he commands without a hint of panic. "Let me take it from you, bonded."

Squeezing my eyes shut, I focus on the intensity of the storm whirling within me. Energy is spilling out of every pore, infecting the air around us and sparking off bright flames.

I mentally scream at the force to pull back, directing it to the place where our bodies are connected instead. Heat travels through my flushed body, straight down to the slick warmth between my thighs.

Every place our skin touches, the Vitae flows in a raging torrent, determined to seek out the life force of the man I've claimed as mine. Daniel's eyes widen as he barks out a curse.

The sensation is so intense, it shoves me into the awaiting arms of my building orgasm. I let myself fall apart, writhing on his lap and moaning his name in a desperate plea for mercy.

Each explosion wracks my frame, heightened by whatever fucked up transference of energy is happening between us. I scream out so loud, I doubt there's a single Redeemed who can't hear us.

Daniel's voice joins mine as he reaches his climax at the same time. Our orgasms collide in a spectacular riot of pleasure, leaving us both spent and breathless.

My head is too heavy to hold up as I slump against his sweat-slick shoulder, chancing a glance up at the window. The curtains hang blackened and damaged, but thankfully, the fire has stopped.

"Are you okay?" I pant out. "Did it hurt you?"

His breath is ragged in my ear. "No, not at all. It felt amazing. I could feel your gift syphoning into me."

"I had no idea it worked like that."

"I don't think we have to fuck every time you need to release excess energy, if that's what you're thinking."

"Damn." I wrestle for the strength to lift my head from his shoulder. "Now I'm disappointed."

A salacious grin curves his lips. "I wouldn't complain either way, but I'm sure we can find a more efficient way of controlling your gift."

"I don't know. That felt pretty efficient to me."

The smile falling from his mouth, Daniel brings a hand to my cheek, his thumb stroking over my skin. I can still feel the ghost of his earlier anger lingering in the air.

"I'm sorry for saying that I hate you. I don't."

I lean into his reverent touch. "I wouldn't blame you if you did. We hardly know each other, and I've utterly fucked your life up."

"I feel like I've known you forever." He frowns at his own words. "I don't know where the bond ends and my feelings begin, but I know that I can't walk away."

"Even after what happened?" I ask hesitantly. "With Valentine?"

"Believe me, I want to," he admits. "But this is bigger than my pride."

"For what it's worth, I'm sorry."

"Yeah." Daniel leans in to press his lips to mine again. "Me too."

We kiss lazily, taking our time to explore each other, our tongues tangling in a languid dance. When he draws back and rests his forehead against mine again, I breathe out an exhausted sigh.

"What happens now?"

Daniel's teeth dig into his plush bottom lip. "We train and prepare."

"For what?"

"Caine is going to come for us, one way or another. We need to be ready for when he does."

WHEEL OF FORTUNE

CHAPTER 21

I'M NOT MADE BY DESIGN – NOTHING BUT THIEVES

a wall of fire snaps across the training facility, hiding astonished faces from sight. I battle to control the unruly force, streaking up high to reach the ceiling and protect me from harm.

My teeth are gritted from exertion as sweat beads across my forehead. Since my manifestation, I can feel the sheer level of power now available to me in the endless cradle in my chest.

Ravius insisted that we ramp up our training after recent near-death events, combining Daniel's combat training with our Vitae-wielding sessions.

Focusing on the wall of flames, I'm distracted and miss the flash of black clothing approaching on my left. There's a roar before Daniel throws himself at me, and we collide hard.

I hit the training mat with a thud then cry out, rolling in an attempt to escape him. His weight is pressing into me as his hands attempt to latch around my throat.

"You should pay attention to your surroundings!" he thunders. "Enemies are everywhere, Lexi."

Pulling the shining silver dagger that's sheathed in his thigh holster, he brings it to my throat and lightly presses down, ending our short-lived battle. I let the fight drain out of me.

"You snuck up on me!"

Daniel pulls the blade back and relaxes. "You expect Caine and his army to fight fair?"

Releasing me, I'm free to suck in deep breaths. Every inch of me is aching from hours of this drill—facing off against him while Ravius helps me to master my mental control.

Blowing out the air held in my lungs, I focus on bringing down the wall of fire that's heating the cavernous room around us. It inches down until the flames disappear, unveiling Ravius's impressed grin.

"Excellent work, Lexi!"

Daniel rolls his eyes. "A twenty-foot fire wall is useless if she can't anticipate an oncoming attack. I'd have slit her throat while she was still fucking around with the Vitae."

"Hey." I glower at him. "Not all of us have been combat training for the last 150 years. Give a girl a break."

Scoffing, he easily leaps to his feet and offers me a hand. I smack it away and stand on my own, brushing myself off. I don't miss the way Daniel scans over me for any signs that he hurt me.

"He's right." Ravius approaches us. "That's why we've combined these sessions. You need to master both skills."

"I'm trying my best!" I throw my newly un-bandaged hands up. "This superhero, vigilante bullshit you're teaching me isn't exactly easy."

"Basic self-defence," Daniel mutters in correction.

Eyes narrowed, I gather a ball of heat in my palm then pour my will into it, watching as a swirling fireball forms. He's barely able to duck before it streaks over his head and smashes into the wall.

"Motherfuck," Daniel curses.

"You want to correct me again?"

He backs away from me. "Nope."

Laughing under his breath, Ravius returns to his side of the room so we can go again. I turn my back on Daniel's amused smile and shake out my limbs, trying to regain focus.

But no matter how many times we run through this, the tugging pain in my chest refuses to abate. It's more than the crippling fear that Daniel instilled in me with his warning.

It's an ache.

An absence.

I refuse to acknowledge why it feels like I'm missing a limb and trying to fight without it. Things with Daniel are still fragile, despite the night we spent together.

"Again!" Daniel barks.

Scowling at him, I crouch into position, my scarred hands raised at the ready. Ravius studies me closely as I watch Daniel approach, this time wielding one of the training swords we fought with before.

He hasn't furnished me with a weapon. I have to think on my feet and improvise each time we face off. Conjuring another fireball in my hands, I let it grow into a swirling, fire-fuelled bomb.

As Daniel nears, the sword raised in preparation, I let the ball of flames loose. It races across the room, headed straight for his head. But he's faster than the speed of light and soon whips to the side.

With a growl, Daniel rushes me. I pace backwards, ducking and dodging each swing of the sword attempting to decapitate me. I know he'd never really hurt me; he's still pulling his blows at the last second.

Throwing up another wall of fire, I separate us with the flames, building them brick by burning brick. It's painstaking work and gives him the time to leap over the barrier before I can build it high enough.

"You're too slow!"

"Fuck you," I snarl.

He flashes me a toothy smile. "Not until you manage to beat me."

We both move around each other in an elaborate game of cat and mouse, trading blows and ducking from the other's advances. As my patience expires, I summon another fireball into my palms.

Moving fast, I throw the handful of fire straight towards Daniel then watch in horror as he fails to duck in time to avoid it. My deadly energy is on a collision course with his chest.

"Daniel!"

Eyes widening, he's a second from being wiped out by fire when the bright ball of heat is swallowed whole. My horrified scream lodges in my throat as water is blasted across the training room.

Daniel emerges from the airborne wave, soaking wet but unharmed. He swipes dripping hair from his eyes and shoots a frigid death glare directly over my shoulder.

"You're welcome," an amused voice taunts.

I'm too shocked to move, but the warm, tingling sensation that rockets to life in my chest tells me who's standing behind me without looking.

"I didn't realise you were in the business of murdering your bonded, mi amor. Perhaps I should be on my guard."

Breaking free from my stunned trance, I whirl around to face Valentine and his easy, confident grin. He's standing next to his brother, arms casually folded as he studies me.

I hate myself for noticing how downright gorgeous he looks, from his charcoal, three-piece suit, clinging to his impossibly tall frame, to the shine of his loose man bun framing sparkling green irises.

Sauntering closer, Valentine lifts an inked hand, mimicking my last move by summoning a perfectly formed ball of water. It's a miniature ocean swelling in his palm, begging to be unleashed.

I want to reach out and take his hand in mine. I knew he was gifted but seeing it in action stirs something within me. An aching desire to explore exactly what he can do.

"This is a private training session," Daniel protests.

Valentine's smirk widens. "Perhaps I should have let her kill you to eliminate the competition."

"There is no competition." I step between the pair. "We're a little busy here, if you don't mind."

Valentine gestures for us to continue. "By all means."

Trying my best to ignore his gaze and the way it makes my insides quiver, I refocus on Daniel. He's looking even more pissed off than usual as he grits his teeth.

This time when he charges, I'm prepared. I feint to the left and toss blasts towards him, watching as he ducks and weaves past every last one. When he's close enough, I throw the first punch.

He easily captures my hand and twists, causing pain to flare in my wrist. I place a hand on top of his, watching as he yelps at my scalding touch.

Breaking free from his grasp before I burn him badly, I take advantage of his distraction and thrust my knee upwards to collide with his stomach.

Daniel releases a groan, attempting to regain control by seizing hold of my slicked-back ponytail. The sharp tug on my hair causes heat to pool in my lower belly.

Knowing Valentine has been watching us intently this entire time only encourages that delicious warmth to expand. I should be ashamed to admit it, but my body doesn't agree.

"Are we flirting or fighting?" I huff.

Tugging harder, he exposes my throat to him, bringing the tip of his sword to brush against my jugular vein. I gasp as he breaks skin, causing scintillating pain to sizzle through me.

"Can't we do both?" he counters slyly. "You're dead, princess."

That's when he notices his own pain and looks down.

While he was busy toying with me, I slipped the dagger from his thigh holster and brought it up to his kidney.

It's sliced through his t-shirt to elicit a thin stream of blood that soaks into the dark material. Daniel's brows raise in surprise.

"As are you. Who isn't paying attention now?"

"Nice work."

"Thanks, Obi Wan."

Lowering his sword, he scoffs. "How many *Star Wars* references are you going to make in these sessions?"

"Aren't you a little old to understand my pop-culture references anyway?"

Daniel shakes his head. "There are still movies in the afterlife."

"I don't see any cinemas around here."

"Take it up with the boss man." He jerks a head towards Ravius, still watching us both.

Flipping the dagger in my hand, I offer Daniel the handle. He accepts the weapon then re-sheaths it with a nod.

The slow round of applause coming from Valentine causes us both to halt. He's propped against the wall on one shoulder, looking like he doesn't have a single care in the world.

"Good show."

I shift on the balls of my feet. "Thanks."

Pushing off from the wall, Valentine saunters closer. I don't miss the way Daniel grips the sword a little tighter, looking like he wants to slice his enemy into ribbons.

"It's been a long time since I sparred." Valentine peels off his suit jacket then begins to roll up his shirt sleeves. "Care for a round, comrade?"

"This is Lexi's training session."

"Come now. Are you passing up the opportunity to run me through with that sword of yours? I'm sure you want to."

"Don't presume to know what I want," Daniel hisses.

"Guys," I try to intervene.

Stopping beside me, Valentine runs a single fingertip down the fresh burn scars on my arm, watching when I can't suppress a shiver. His grin is oh-so-smug.

"Worried that I'll hurt your mate?"

Or he'll hurt you, I want to fire back. But I swallow the traitorous words before they can escape my lips. I don't care about this tattooed slice of heaven next to me. Not one bit.

"I'll go easy on him," Valentine purrs.

His hand has curled around my wrist, sending swirls of delicious heat straight down south. He barely has to touch me, and I'm practically wavering on my feet.

"Take your hands off my bonded." Daniel's expression is apocalyptic. "Unless you'd prefer to live out your afterlife handless."

A flash of annoyance pulsates through me. It wasn't so long ago that Daniel wanted nothing to do with this bond and deserted me to chase his Elder across the Atlantic.

Prising Valentine's hand from my wrist, I step back to let the two men face each other. "Go ahead."

"What?" Daniel splutters.

"Like it or not, the three of us are connected. Even if you two hate each other. So fight or fuck it out, I don't care which."

"You offering for the latter?" Valentine winks at me.

Moving away from them with a glare, I stand next to Ravius. Two of Valentine's men have filtered into the room, eyeing their Elder.

"Lexi, right?" The salt and pepper haired bodyguard sticks out a hand. "I'm Alejandro, Valentine's second-in-command."

I take his extended hand. "Nice to meet you."

"I'll be honest, I didn't think you were real. He's been tearing his hair out while trying to track you down."

"And driving us insane," the other guard adds, casting me a decidedly cold look. "I'll wait outside."

I watch him go. "Something I said?"

Alejandro shrugs. "Valentine's been a little... highly strung of late."

"My fault, huh?"

"I wouldn't worry about it, chica. Where he goes, we go. The team knows that."

Refocusing on the two men currently squaring up to each other, I watch Valentine take the sword that Daniel begrudgingly gives him, opting for the spare he discarded earlier.

"This should be interesting," Ravius hums.

The way they're looking at each other is terrifying. Daniel's mouth is flattened into a furious line that betrays his rage, while Valentine looks ready to rip his head off purely for his own amusement.

"What happens if a member of a soul bond dies?"

Ravius's eyes are pinched with tension. "Picture the excruciating pain of a severed bond and scars that will last a lifetime."

"We don't die?"

"You'll wish you did."

"Shit. I really shouldn't have suggested this."

"Bit late now," Alejandro comments.

Swallowing a bubble of fear down, I watch Daniel assume his position, sword raised and feet spread apart. Valentine dances around him, moving lightly and grinning like a lunatic.

His forearms ripple with muscle beneath the thick coverage of what looks like tribal ink obscuring his skin. I didn't think anyone could rival Daniel, but the look on Valentine's face is downright predatory.

"It's been a long time since we fought," he taunts.

"Not long enough," Daniel sneers.

"You were never one to pass up the opportunity to exchange blows before, comrade. We spent many nights on the front-line sparring."

Daniel makes the first move, striking out and clattering

Valentine's sword with his own. The latter moves lightning fast, blocking the blow with the ease of a trained sword master.

"I told you not to call me that."

"There was a time when you considered yourself my brother in arms," Valentine muses, a wicked glint in his eye. "Don't care for a reminder of that, hmm?"

Snapping his sword out again, Daniel feints left, attempting to land another blow that's easily blocked. It's like Valentine knows where he's going to move before even Daniel does.

The two are completely in-tune with each other. Striking, ducking, weaving in an intricate dance. It's clear they've learned the innermost details of one another's skill set.

"Comrades don't betray their own." Daniel swings the sword high, managing to slash Valentine's tight black dress shirt. "You're nothing to me now."

"I think we both know that's not true." Valentine's gaze strays to me. "Our destinies have always been entwined."

Taking advantage of his momentary distraction, Daniel charges, stepping into the danger zone. His sword lowers as he thumps his fist into Valentine's face for the second time in twenty-four hours.

The Spanish Elder is completely unaffected. He shakes off the blow, then with a flick of the wrist, he slashes Daniel across the chest. I can't help calling out in panic as blood pours from the wound.

"I don't want to hurt you, but I will if I have to. You cannot keep her from me."

"She doesn't want you!" Daniel seethes.

"And what makes you think she wants you?"

"They're gonna take their dicks out and start comparing in a minute," I mutter in frustration.

Alejandro smothers a laugh by coughing while Ravius merely frowns at his laughing brother. Anyone would think that in Valentine's position, he'd at least feel remorse or act contrite.

Instead, he's having far too much fun pushing Daniel around and taunting him.

The difference between them is stark. For the ice that's frosted around Daniel's heart, Valentine offers an endless torrent of smouldering passion.

They're night and day. Sworn enemies and two sides of the same coin. Seriously, what the fuck is my gift thinking by claiming these two men as my own? I'm going to get us all killed.

"You don't even know her," Daniel spits, wiping blood on his black cargo trousers. "Now you think that you have some kind of claim on her?"

"Pretty sure she's the one who claimed me," he replies smoothly.

Daniel can't hide the flash of pain in his eyes. I can see it from afar. Guilt wraps around my insides and squeezes as Daniel advances into his space.

"Do you even feel remorse?"

"For what?" Valentine strikes out at him.

Daniel easily blocks the incoming attack. "For Pen, you egotistical son of a bitch. For my fucking wife."

His cool, collected mask of amusement cracking, Valentine strikes again. This time, Daniel moves too slow, and the sword slashes into his left arm.

It takes all of my control not to tear him away from Valentine for his own protection. All of my instincts are screaming out at me to intervene, but I know it would do no good.

"I protected her," Valentine utters in a deathly timbre. "You're the one who betrayed her trust. You think Caine would've gotten his hands on her if you didn't feed her to the wolves?"

"I did not betray her!"

"How else did Caine find out about her gift, Daniel? About the prophecy she created? He took her from us because you couldn't keep your damn mouth shut."

Shoulders slumping, anguish practically seeps from Daniel's pores. "I didn't know what he'd do to her. I thought I could trust him back then."

"Like she trusted both of us with her secret? Out of the two of us, who threw that away?"

"Enough!" Daniel roars.

Moving fast, he's a blur of violent wrath. Each blow is more brutal than the last, until Valentine's been forced across the training mat and pinned to a wall.

His smile doesn't falter as Daniel raises the blade to his exposed neck. No defence. Valentine lets Daniel trap him in the ultimate checkmate, with nowhere to run.

"I did betray you, brother," Valentine admits. "I fell for Pen, and nothing I can ever say will take that betrayal back. She wasn't mine to take, but I did it anyway."

Teeth bared, Daniel presses the edge of the blade deeper into Valentine's throat. Alejandro is growling next to me, resisting the urge to protect his Elder at all costs. I doubt his intervention would be appreciated.

"But don't for a second think that absolves you of your guilt," Valentine lashes out. "Pen is dead because of you. Caine took her from all of us because you were too blind to see he was manipulating you all along."

I watch the fight drain out of Daniel. One moment, he's a mere slip of the hand from slicing Valentine's damn throat open. The next, his sword has clattered loudly to the floor.

His head is lowered, eyes radiating pain and self-hatred. I watch with a lump growing in my throat as Valentine braces two hands on Daniel's shoulders to hold him upright.

"I tried to stop him from experimenting on her," Daniel rasps, his voice laced with grief. "But I couldn't save her. She's dead because I failed to keep her safe."

"We both failed. But don't you see we've been given a second chance? That we can make up for the past?"

"I can't do this. Not with you."

Shoving Valentine away, Daniel turns and leaves. I try to snatch his hand, but he brushes past me, an impenetrable mask shuttered over his face.

The door to the training room slams loudly behind him, cutting through the suffocating silence. Valentine sighs, any remaining traces of amusement long since wiped away.

"You." I stomp up to him, ignoring the static charge that snaps between us. "What the hell was that?"

"He has to face the past," Valentine states matter-of-factly. "We've spent decades avoiding each other and what happened back then. That's no longer an option."

"But did you really have to blame him for his wife's murder? Do you have any idea what that will do to him?"

"Trust me, he was already blaming himself. We can't move forward until he acknowledges his guilt and deals with it."

"That's exactly the problem." I glare at him. "I don't trust you. Soul bond or not, you're still a stranger to me."

Valentine opens his mouth to respond, but I don't give him a chance. I can't stand to look at him right now. No matter how much the force tying us together is begging for me to reach out and touch him once more.

Ravius and Alejandro step aside to let me chase after Daniel, but by the time I break outside into the frigid cold, he's long gone.

VIII

STRENGTH

CHAPTER 22

NATURAL VILLAIN – THE MAN WHO

"*W*ell, shit."

I slurp my strong black coffee, sweetened with the perfect amount of hazelnut syrup. Martha knows exactly how I like it and never fails to deliver, though she still refuses to charge me like she does everyone else.

"It's a cluster fuck, right?" I snort.

Raven shakes her head. "I still can't believe you bonded to the Spanish Elder. I mean, like one wasn't enough. You had to drag that lunatic into this mess too?"

"Thanks, Raven. You're really making me feel better about this. What would I do without you?"

Laughing, she sips on her coffee. "If you wanted sugar-coated comfort, you should've gone elsewhere."

Covering my face with my hands, I groan. She's right, I don't know what I'm looking for. At this point, I need a one-way ticket out of the hell I've created for myself.

"What do you know about him?"

"Valentine?" She raises a perfectly sculpted eyebrow beneath her pink hair. "You've heard Ravius banging on about the war before the accords, right?"

I nod, slurping more coffee.

"The Redeemed were being hunted and persecuted for centuries. Valentine led the resistance into every last slaughter. He was like the Grim fucking Reaper."

"How do you know all this?"

She shrugs. "Valentine has a reputation for being a ruthless son of a bitch. I hear there are five facilities in Spain under his control."

"That's a lot of power."

"And who do you think fought alongside Valentine before the accords were signed?" Raven grins. "Caine's precious second-in-command led the American forces into several large-scale battles."

"Fuck. Daniel?"

"The one and only."

"You're telling me they were... war heroes?"

"And best friends." She gestures with her coffee cup. "Until they fell for the same girl. You know the rest of the story."

"That's great. I'm bound to a pair of mortal enemies, and I've given them yet another reason to hate each other. They're already fighting over me."

"Not necessarily. I hear you don't have to be romantic within a soul bond." She shrugs. "Just tell them both it's platonic and steer clear of their bullshit."

"I can't exactly do that. The bond won't let me avoid either of them and... well, I don't want to either."

She stares at me for several thoughtful seconds before breaking out into a pleased smile.

"Who was it?"

"Hmm?" I hum innocently.

"Which one of them did you fuck, pink cheeks?"

Pressing a hand to my definitely flaming cheek, I groan again. "It just happened. I didn't exactly plan it."

"Both? Already?"

"No!" I screech. "Jesus, Raven."

Folding over with laughter, she swipes beneath her eyes. "Don't pretend like you haven't thought about it."

"I honestly haven't."

"So who was it?"

Finishing my coffee, I deposit my empty cup on the table and stand up. "I have to find Felix for training."

"Lexi! Don't leave me hanging!"

"Goodbye, weirdo!"

Leaving her still laughing like a hyena, I wave at Martha as I pass then slip out of the coffee shop. I was hoping to find Daniel here with Martha, but he's still nowhere to be found.

With people already gathering for our drill session, I jog towards Felix at the head of the group. My heart somersaults in my chest when a looming shadow steps in front of me to block my path.

"Lexi," Valentine greets, scanning over me with interest. "Would you be avoiding me?"

Yes.

"Believe it or not, I have better things to do than keep you entertained."

The corner of his mouth twitches as if my surliness entertains him. "If you're expecting an apology, you'd better get comfortable. You're in for a long wait."

"Somehow I figured that isn't your style."

"Then you catch on fast."

Attempting to duck around him, I'm stuck when he moves, blocking my way. The cocky asshole is grinning at me like this is all some entertaining game. I cross my arms over my chest.

"Can I help you?"

"Walk with me, mi amor."

"Felix has me on daily drills. I can't just bunk off."

"You have my permission." He waggles his eyebrows. "Believe me, I far outrank Felix and his little parade of toy soldiers."

Eyes dancing with mirth, he stretches out a hand to offer

me. That's when I spot the ornate gold ring on his pinkie finger, boasting the same delicate crest as the ring Ravius wears.

Unable to stop myself, I reach out and take his hand, drawing it closer to study the unique ring. A circular setting rests on the thick gold band, boasting a delicately engraved sand timer.

"*Memento mori.*" I trace the tiny, curved script. "What does it mean?"

Valentine's eyes have flicked shut as my fingers grip his. The place where our skin touches is a riot of pins and needles. His breath catches before he forces out a raspy answer.

"Roughly translated, it means remember you must die."

I feel my brows draw together. "Bit ironic for an ageless, immortal being, don't you think?"

"We're not immortal though, are we? Redeemed can still be killed with enough… brute force."

"But we're not exactly human anymore either."

Eyes slowly reopening, the bottomless depths seem to brim with intelligence only an ancient being can possess. I can't help but shiver beneath the intensity of that stare.

Valentine looks at me like the chase is over before it's begun—like he already knows all my secrets. I can run all I want, but it won't prevent the inevitable. He'll still be there to capture me at the finish line.

"That's precisely why we must fear death," he murmurs, his thumb stroking over my scar-twisted skin. "None of us would be here if human life wasn't such a fragile commodity."

"Would you prefer to be human still?"

"Walk the earth for a millennium, then tell me you wouldn't long for a normal, human life again."

Staring up at him, I'm shocked by his honesty. I don't know where the question came from, but he doesn't seem offended. I doubt there are many who dare to question him so freely.

Releasing his hand, I put space between us again, needing room to breathe. Just being near him scatters my thoughts. It's a mental battle to keep my gift from acting out in his presence.

Nostrils flaring, he scans me up and down. "I can practically smell the Vitae pouring from you. I've never seen such unadulterated power before."

"So I keep being told." I narrow my eyes on him. "What exactly are your intentions? Why are you here?"

"For you," he replies, like it's obvious.

"Well as you can see, I'm fine. Fucking great, in fact. I don't need another babysitter hanging around."

The corners of his eyes crinkle and his long, nimble fingers curl like he's longing to take my hand again.

"Are you really okay?"

My reflexive urge to lie clogs up my throat. "What do you think?"

Valentine takes another step closer. "I think you've been handed a terrible burden, and no one's stopped to consider the weight you must now carry for us all."

I should run. Hide. Put as much distance between myself and this unfathomable man as possible, before it's too late. He's seen inside my head, my dreams. His eyes slice me down to the quick with a mere glance.

Valentine plays a good game—grinning, winking, tormenting his opponents. Nothing and no one could challenge his authority. But I can see now that there's far more to him beneath the surface.

Those luminous eyes cloak a deadly darkness far more petrifying than any other threat levied against me. Others can imprison me, take my freedom away, make my life a living hell.

But Valentine could crush me with nothing more than a lingering glance into the depths of my soul. I don't know if it's the bond or the sheer force of his quiet perceptiveness, but I doubt I could ever lie to him.

"I wonder how long you've carried that burden alone." He stares at me with calculation. "And what other burdens put the shadows in your eyes. Tell me, how did you end up here?"

"It's a long story. Not a pleasant one."

"I have nothing but time, Lexi."

I glance around us. "Not here."

"Then perhaps it's time we left my brother's land. Would you accompany me back to Spain?"

Spluttering, I gape up at him. He's actually serious. Not even a hint of hesitation. This guy has too much fucking confidence for his own good, and I'm finding it entirely too attractive.

"I can't just leave."

"Why not?" He quirks an eyebrow.

"Did you miss the part where your brother threw my ass in prison for trying to escape?"

"My brother is no longer your concern." He lets out a laugh. "He wouldn't dare touch what's mine unless he wants another war on his hands. We can leave."

Fuck, I wish my core didn't flood with heat at the not-so-veiled threat in his words. I don't doubt him for a second. Valentine would drench this entire facility in blood to keep his word.

"I can't just leave the country. My sister is still here, and I have to get back to her."

Valentine offers me his arm. "Then perhaps some fresh air? I'd invite your other *bonded* along to be a good sport, but it seems he is avoiding us both."

"Tell me something I don't know."

Ignoring the pressure of Felix's disapproving stare burning a hole into me, I gingerly accept Valentine's arm. He tucks it into his firm, shirt-clad chest then steers me away from the courtyard.

I can't ignore the looks that others give us as we walk past. Curiosity. Shock. Awe. But above all, fear. Valentine's slick,

PR-perfect smile is firmly in place as he ignores every last one of them.

"They're all staring at you."

"Not me," he whispers back. "Us."

"Did everyone see that little show we put on in the dining hall the other night?"

"Those who didn't have undoubtedly heard about it by now."

"Like I didn't have enough unwanted attention."

"Are they bothering you?" He subtly lifts his suit jacket, giving me a flash of the holster wrapped around his torso.

"No! It's fine. Really."

"Just say the word." He grins at me indulgently. "I'll happily deal with the problem."

"Last I checked, it isn't illegal to stare and gossip."

"When they're staring at my bonded, it most certainly is."

I should not be savouring the rough note of possession in his voice. I've been owned by a man for long enough and died to escape his clutches. I won't be under anyone else's thumb.

Removing my arm from his, I walk ahead alone. "I'm more than capable of taking care of myself."

"Of that I have no doubt."

"Then you know that I don't need you to defend my honour or whatever you think this is."

Valentine chuckles. "In my day, any woman would've been overjoyed by such chivalry."

"It's a good thing we're not living in the dark ages anymore then, isn't it? I can fight my own battles, and I sure as hell don't need a man to do it for me."

His smile only broadens. "Loud and clear, mi amor."

Fighting the urge to wipe that smug grin from his face, I resume walking, letting him fall back into step beside me. We pass the hospital and administration building, lapsing into tense silence.

I can feel him studying me closely. Observing and

documenting every last clue he can puzzle out. I've never been the subject of such visceral infatuation before—not even from Daniel. He's a little too reserved for that.

When my surroundings become unfamiliar, I realise we've made it to the furthermost reaches of the facility, far past anywhere I've explored before.

Through the thick trees that hide us from the outside world, the perimeter fence ends at a tall, wrought iron gate. It's being manned by several patrolling security officers, their hard faces pinched in suspicion.

When they spot Valentine at my side, their postures immediately change, heads bowing in submission. Everyone knows exactly who he is and treats him just like they do Ravius.

There's a car parked off to the side, an armoured beast with tinted windows that hide the interior. Alejandro and his cold-eyed counterpart lounge against it, standing to attention when their Elder approaches.

"Sir." Alejandro tips his head in greeting.

Valentine spares the other man a glance. "Lexi, this is Pascal. Should you ever need assistance, my security team is at your disposal."

I don't miss the way Pascal's eyes briefly narrow on me, though he keeps his expression carefully blank. Mouth sealed, I simply nod.

"Very good. Let's go."

"Wait, what?" I dig my heels in.

Valentine gestures towards the SUV. "Fresh air? Promise I won't smuggle you onto any international flights."

"We're leaving the facility? Is it safe?"

"Don't you trust me?" he counters.

Lexi—*do not fucking answer that.*

My traitorous head seems to have a mind of its own, ignoring my inner voice and nodding. I'm desperate to get out of here, even if it's only for a brief glimpse of the outside world.

"Then climb in," he invites with an exaggerated wave. "You've been cooped up here for long enough."

Daniel is going to kill me, if Ravius doesn't beat him to it. That realisation doesn't stop me from blowing out a breath and climbing into the devil's car.

You can only die once, right?

 **THE HIGH PRIESTESS**

CHAPTER 23

MAYBE, I – DES ROCS

*T*he bleakness of the Scottish winter surrounds the car, offering glimpses of rolling fields and windswept cliffs. I drink it all in, hungry for every last desolate detail.

As I watch the world pass, Valentine watches me. I don't even mind. It's been so long since I saw the outside world, driving through the countryside leading away from Ravius's hidden facility is exhilarating.

"Where did you live before?" he asks.

"Cornwall. It's by the coast in England." The tinted glass fogs up with my breath. "You know it?"

"Only by reputation. I don't often visit the UK these days."

Turning away from the exquisite countryside, I focus on the man buckled in next to me. Valentine is his usual impeccable, elegant self in a tailored suit and matching pressed black shirt that's fitted to his muscular chest.

His glossy chestnut hair is slicked back in a low man bun that shows off the defined planes of his high cheekbones and straight nose. Everything about his picture perfect looks is beautiful in a masculine way.

"How often do you visit this facility?" I ask.

"Ravius hosts a yearly centenary celebration that my siblings and I usually attend. It's coming up in a couple of weeks."

A thick lump of terror gathers in my throat. "Will Caine be attending?"

"Not now that negotiations with Ravius have failed. He's been pushing for an end to the accords since they were ratified. More so in recent years."

"So what will happen next?"

Valentine shrugs. "My oldest brother is a fool and a hothead. He's returned to the States. If he makes a move against any of us, we will respond in kind."

"You don't sound worried."

"I'm not." He simpers. "Regardless of Caine's ambitions, the accords exist to protect us. If he intends to end the peace we fought so hard for, he will not make it very far."

"Then why is Ravius so concerned?"

"My brother does not want to see his people suffer anymore hardship. And he doesn't have the numbers to oppose Caine if it comes down to a fight."

"But you do?"

Valentine casts me an unreadable look. "Believe it or not, I don't want war any more than Ravius does. That doesn't mean I'm not prepared for it though."

A shiver rolls down my spine. The sporadic glimpses of Valentine's animalistic savagery are downright unnerving. His slick smile and sharp tongue hide a far more brutal truth.

"I hear you and Daniel fought together before."

"For several years," he confirms. "I met him shortly after he joined Caine. He became an invaluable asset in our offence against attacking human forces."

Thinking about Daniel increases the ache settling in my bones that being away from him causes. Valentine may be ready for war, but if he thinks a fight will bring his best friend back, he's setting himself up for failure.

"Will you stay until the centenary?"

"Why?" He tilts his head in interest. "Would you miss me if I left?"

"Don't flatter yourself."

Valentine snorts. "Ouch. Perhaps I should take the hint and leave my brother to his festivities if I'm not wanted here."

Panic lances across my chest, stirring the cradle of power that seems to pulsate with each word he utters. I grit my teeth and attempt to crush the feeling before Valentine can spot the fear in my eyes.

"Or you could stay," I try to sound nonchalant. "It's only a couple of weeks."

Closing the small gap between us, Valentine clasps my chin between his thumb and forefinger. I freeze still, trapped in his searching gaze. Any traces of humour have been wiped from his face.

"Do you want me to stay here with you, Lexi?"

I drag my hands down my face. "I don't know what I want. Not anymore."

"And yet your other mate has abandoned his post and Elder to remain by your side. I find that curious."

"It was Daniel's decision to return." I wince, remembering the pain of the bond stretched so thin. "I let him leave, no matter how much it hurt me."

"I have people depending on me. Responsibilities."

"Then you should go. I didn't ask you to come here to find me."

"And yet you called out to me every night," he purrs in satisfaction. "You pulled me into your dreams long before the soul bond was established."

Sweat prickles on my forehead as the waves of energy battering against my ribcage grow too intense to handle. My gift is screaming out for a release.

Valentine's fingertip coasts upwards from my chin to tease my bottom lip. He traces my mouth, his finger daring to touch

309

the tip of my tongue. I can't stop the whispered moan that escapes.

"Did you dream of me while he held you at night, mi amor?"

I'm trembling all over. Heart hammering. Skin flushed. Nipples pebbled. He caresses my jawline, content to wait for my answers, but I can't offer a single line of defence.

"What about when my comrade touched you?" His other hand moves to clasp my leg, tracing the seam of my leggings. "Whose name slipped off that tongue of yours?"

"I've never betrayed Daniel in our time together. Not in the way you're insinuating."

"But he has touched you. And you have thought of me."

Flustered, I press myself against the car door. "This… You're… We can't do this. Whatever *this* is."

"You tied my soul to yours from thousands of miles away," he points out. "Daniel should be begging me for the privilege of your touch, not the other way around."

Anger sizzles through my veins. "And what about what I want? Don't I get a say in this?"

Hand moving higher, he gently strokes my inner thigh, leaving a trail of heat even through my clothing. He barely has to touch me, and I can feel that I'm soaked through.

My body is rebelling against me. It's decided what it wants, and Valentine is at the top of that list. Rationality has left the building, and I can't bring myself to care.

"Tell me to stop," Valentine challenges. "Tell me that you don't want this, and I'll take the first flight out of the country. You have my word."

His fingernail scrapes against the seam covering my throbbing pussy, encased in layers of cotton. The tiniest touch makes me gasp, and I feel my hips move, seeking more friction.

Smirking at my eagerness, Valentine cups my mound above my clothing then squeezes. I blush hard at the realisation that he must be able to feel how wet I am right now.

"Answer me, mi amor. Words."

"Please," I mewl.

"Please what? Touch you? Leave?" He squeezes again, making my clit pulsate. "Tear these delightfully tight clothes from your body and take you in the back of this car?"

I'm thankful for the sealed screen hiding my pathetic, panting self from his men riding up front. Only Valentine can see me wrestling with the million reasons why this is a terrible idea.

When his hand vanishes and he leans away from me, I'm awash with disappointment. He clicks his tongue, returning to his side of the back seat.

"Perhaps you need some time to think about it. I'm a patient man, after all. I shall await your decision."

Every brain cell is begging me to rip off this seat belt, climb across the car and straddle his strong, powerful legs. I want to slip my hands in his long hair and claim those full lips as mine.

Memories of our last kiss fill my mind. Even if it was relegated to the shadows of the dreamworld, it was still real. His mouth devouring mine sparked a cataclysmic chain reaction.

Focusing on my breathing, I ignore him completely, returning to staring out the window. What feels like hours pass, and empty fields morph into rain-soaked, suburban streets as we re-enter civilisation.

It's no wonder Ravius is able to hide his facility from the outside world. We've been driving for forever and have hardly seen a single soul. The remote location was strategically chosen to maintain our secrecy.

"We're here." Valentine's declaration startles me out of my thoughts.

"Where?"

He winks at me. "You'll see."

Climbing out of the car, he dashes around it to open my door for me. I take his hand and step into the crisp winter air, far too excited to be out in the real world again.

Valentine frowns at me as he pulls the wool scarf from his neck. He's wearing a navy peacoat on top of his suit, the dark colour bringing out the rich, emerald hue of his eyes.

"You look cold."

"I'm fine."

"Lie to me again, and there will be consequences. I'll happily take you over my knee."

My mouth falls open on a surprised gasp. Is he saying what I think he is? Studying my reaction, the corner of his mouth twitches, almost breaking into a full smirk.

"Something tells me you'd like that."

Wrapping the scarf around my neck, he tightens it with a tug. I inhale his deep, spicy scent, reminiscent of cloves and cinnamon sticks seeped in mulled wine.

It's a complete contrast to Daniel's evergreen and peppercorn fragrance. Just thinking of him causes my heart to twinge painfully. I make myself step away from Valentine.

"Better." He nods.

"Where are we?"

"We're going shopping. This is your first centenary as part of The Redeemed. Whoever's arm you attend on, I think you should look the part."

Stepping aside, he unveils a quiet, cobblestone street. We're in an upper-class area, the shopfronts boasting fancy boutiques and designer clothing nestled amongst wine bars and jewellery stores.

"It's black tie," Valentine clarifies.

"I don't... uh, have any money."

He waves dismissively. "Let me worry about that."

"I don't need your charity."

"I'm sure you can find a way to make it up to me."

Offering me his arm, he lifts a brow. "Come along, little bonded."

Fighting the urge to smack that stupid nickname from his mouth, I reluctantly accept his arm. We begin to stroll down the street, his two armed guards boxing us in.

My scalp prickles as I avoid looking at the other people walking around, enjoying the weak winter sunshine. It feels entirely foreign to be outside, pretending like we're normal.

Even before my life was taken from me, I wasn't normal. I didn't have friendships or dates. We had no money to spend shopping or for getting our nails done. All I did was battle to survive.

He took that from me.

He took *everything*.

Valentine shoots me a questioning look when my grip involuntarily tightens on his arm. I make myself take a deep breath, forcing the depressing thoughts from my mind.

That monster can't control my life anymore. I may be trapped under Ravius's care, but at least I'm free from the horrors of my past after years of longing to escape.

"Tell me about your life," Valentine requests. "I, uh... have read your files. But I'd still like to hear about it from you."

He's done his research, huh? I'm not sure whether to be impressed or creeped out.

"There isn't much to tell. I worked. Looked after my sister. That's about it."

"How old is she?"

"Eve's eight-years-old."

"What about your parents?"

I stare straight ahead, pretending to survey the array of shopfronts while I decide how much I want to share.

"My dad is a deadbeat who doesn't acknowledge we exist. Eve was a baby when our mum left us."

"Do you know what happened to her?"

"No. One moment she was there, the next she wasn't. Dad was useless, so I had to take care of Eve and raise her myself."

"That must've been a great hardship." His voice is laced with sadness. "You were still young yourself."

"Old enough to get a job and fend for us both. I wouldn't let her starve. She's all I have left."

Spotting a boutique selling evening wear, Valentine tugs me to a halt. He gestures for his men to go ahead to sweep the store before we enter to make sure it's safe.

"Lexi."

Looking down at my feet, I avoid his hard, penetrating stare. He sees far too much for a relative stranger. I guess that's the benefit of the bond and weeks of living in each other's dreams.

"Look at me, mi amor."

"I don't need your pity," I choke out. "It was my life, and I was proud to live it, even in the toughest times."

"I don't pity you." His reply is surprisingly terse. "Quite the opposite. I admire your courage and strength. You survived."

In this moment, I want to tell him everything. About the years of humiliation and pain. Stolen looks. Unwanted touches. Threats against my sister if I refused to comply or keep my mouth shut.

I survived, but at what cost? Only scraps of me escaped that sordid life. The discarded pieces that he tossed aside for me to smuggle away when he was done abusing me.

"Surviving and living are two different things."

"Is that what you want?" Valentine asks. "To live?"

"The chance of a future was ripped away from me the day I woke up here. What chance do I have to live now? Stuck in this place?"

Gaze softening, he takes a strand of loose blonde hair then tucks it behind my ear. "You can still have a life."

"How?"

314

Opening his mouth to speak, he's interrupted by Pascal's harsh voice. "All clear, sir."

Valentine's mouth snaps shut. "Alright. Come on, Lexi. Let's get that dress sorted."

Taking the tight ball of emotion lodged in my chest and stuffing it down, I follow him into the boutique. Pascal and Alejandro have placed themselves in the corners at perfect vantage points.

The owner, Elaine, rushes over to shake our hands, smiling warmly as she flips the door's sign to *closed* to ensure we're not disturbed. She can clearly smell money on Valentine.

"What kind of dress are we looking for?"

My gaze bounces between them. "I... have no idea."

Valentine smothers a grin. "An evening gown would suffice. The event is formal, black tie."

"Any styles or colours in particular?" she asks me.

All I can do is stare at her, speechless. I don't belong here. I've never shopped for myself outside of cheap, second-hand stores, and even that was a laborious task.

"I'm easy." I shrug, acting nonchalant.

"A blank canvas! How exciting." She claps her hands together. "Come, let's browse through the selection."

Letting Elaine grab me by the elbow, Valentine saunters over to the small seating area then sits in an armchair. His eyes refuse to leave me as I'm guided over to stuffed racks.

Soon, she's gathered tons of bagged dresses next to the changing room for me to try on. I ignore the bored look on Pascal's face as he moves to guard the changing room at Valentine's request.

"Here, this one first I think." Elaine hands me a zipped bag. "The blue will compliment your skin tone."

Drawing the curtain shut, I strip out of my leggings and t-shirt, folding them to place aside. I'm painfully aware of Valentine's presence nearby as he chats to the shop owner.

Opening the dress bag, I stare at the garment inside. It's a flowing, blue chiffon dress that gathers at the waist then spills down in an oceanic curtain. The neckline is an elegant halter.

Biting my lip, I pull the barely-there dress on before peeking my head out of the curtain. Elaine rushes over to pull up the zipper for me then makes me do a twirl.

"Stunning. So elegant."

"Lexi," Valentine calls sharply.

Elaine smiles. "I think your gentleman wants a peek."

"I bet he does," I grind out.

Steeling myself, I step out into the store so Valentine can peruse me. His vibrant eyes widen, sliding over me to absorb every last detail as he motions in a circle with his index finger.

I hold my breath while slowly turning for him. The skirt swishes around me, the chiffon layers lifted by the air. When I stop, Valentine is shaking his head.

"Try the next dress."

"You don't like it?" Elaine asks.

"She looks too young and innocent." His brows furrow. "I want her to look… formidable."

Tingles spread across my skin everywhere his eyes touch. Valentine doesn't make me feel innocent. Far from it. The way he's drinking me in is far too sinful for that.

"Understood." Elaine schools her smile back into place. "That's fine, we have plenty more to try."

Moving back to the changing room, we try several more dresses, but they're all dismissed by Valentine. Too girly. Too tight. Too flouncy. He finds every excuse to reject each one.

"Fuck it," I snap in frustration. "I'll just go naked."

Elbows braced on his knees, Valentine's eyes languidly scan over me. "As much as I wouldn't mind seeing that, I'd have to pluck the eyeballs out of any man who dared to look at you."

I ignore Elaine's shiftiness beside me. She's looking between us with a slight frown, as if trying to fathom us out. It's clear that Valentine is no ordinary client.

"What do you want from me? I have no idea what I'm even shopping for, and your criteria is impossible. I'd rather not go at all at this rate."

Drawing to his feet, Valentine saunters over to the railings then begins combing through the remaining dresses. His nose is upturned as he dismisses the pickings.

"I received a new delivery this morning," Elaine offers. "I haven't had a chance to check the stock yet, but perhaps there is something more appropriate inside."

"Show me," Valentine commands before pinning me with an intense look. "Stay here, mi amor."

Huffing out a laugh, I mock salute him. "Yes, sir."

Before he can pass me to follow after Elaine, he leans down to press his lips to my ear. His teeth briefly nip the lobe, despite our audience, and my breath catches in my throat.

"You're to call me that when my head is between your thighs. Remember that."

Too stunned to formulate a response, I watch him disappear into the back of the store. I'm almost woozy from the lust filling me up and travelling straight to my quivering pussy.

It takes several breaths to get a hold of myself. The thought of what Daniel would say if he were here swiftly douses my desire. This is all such a mess. I need to keep a clear head.

"Watch her," Alejandro orders, his hand resting on his holster. "I'm going to survey the perimeter."

"You see something?" Pascal drones.

Without answering him, Alejandro slips out of the shop then disappears. His colleague seems nonplussed and goes straight back to ignoring me.

When Valentine reappears with Elaine and a final dress bag, Alejandro still hasn't returned. I dismiss my prickles of worry and watch as Valentine hangs the bag on the rack.

"This one," he deadpans.

"What makes you think I'll like it?"

"Trust me, you will. Put it on."

As much as I want to be a brat just to oppose him, I don't, sighing as I return to the dressing room. He knows far better than me what's appropriate for this event. I don't want to look foolish.

The dress is scarlet-red, the hue deep and sensual. With an intricate lace bodice that flows into a swishy A-line skirt, the soft, silky fabric is like blood in my hands, flowing and glimmering.

The thigh split will reveal the entire length of my leg, and as I study the fabric more, I realise there's a cape attached to the two straps. It looks far too regal for the likes of me.

But I force my judgements aside and step into it regardless. I don't want to analyse my desire to please Valentine too closely. It doesn't matter that this dress was his choice.

Does it?

Looking at myself in the mirror, I chew my lip until I taste copper on my tongue. I don't recognise the person staring back at me. She looks intimidating and fucking powerful.

The dress clings to my curves and hugs me in all the right places, showing a sexy hint of cleavage while maintaining my modesty. The thigh split is daring as hell, and I love it.

"My patience is wearing thin, Lexi," Valentine grumbles.

"Thought you were a patient man?"

"Not when it comes to you, apparently. Don't make me tear that curtain down and come in there."

Taking the tiny flicker of confidence that seeing my reflection gives me, I step out into the store. Elaine raises her hands over her mouth, and even Pascal does a double take.

All I can focus on is Valentine and the obvious lust that shimmers wildly in his eyes. He doesn't just look at me. His gaze *devours* me, consuming every last red-clad inch with reckless abandon.

Spreading my legs, I let the slit inch open, displaying my

bare leg. It rises all the way to my upper thigh, making me feel sexy and dangerous. I watch his throat bob.

"Yes," he says tightly. "That works."

Elaine claps her hands together. "Excellent."

His tongue darts out to wet his lips. "She will need the appropriate accessories."

"Of course."

As Elaine busies herself looking for heels, Valentine stalks over. He cups my cheek with one hand and drops his other to the split in my dress so he can caress my thigh.

"If you don't take that off, I'm going to tear it from your body and spread your legs open on the carpet."

My throat seizes. "To do what, exactly?"

"Whatever your heart desires."

My lungs have ceased to function, and I feel like the temperature in the store has rocketed. His hand drops from my leg, and he takes a step back.

"Get dressed. Now."

My head feels like it's full of cotton wool as I nod and return to the dressing room. I'm trembling all over, struggling to zip up the bag after placing the dress inside.

What is wrong with me?

Isn't one man enough?

With my clothes back on, I scrub my hands over my face and blow out a breath before returning to the shop floor. Elaine has located a pair of silver heels and a clutch bag that matches the dress.

She's smiling broadly as Valentine swipes his gold credit card after ringing up an eye-watering bill. I don't bother trying to protest. Even if I wanted to pay, I've never seen that much money in my life.

Handing the dress bag and shoe box off to Pascal, Valentine glances around the store. "Where is Alejandro?"

"He went to check the perimeter, sir." Pascal looks a little uneasy. "But he hasn't returned yet."

After saying goodbye to Elaine, we step back into the cool sunshine and look around, finding no sign of Alejandro. I can feel Valentine tensing up as he takes my hand.

"Let's go back to the car."

"Yes, sir." Pascal nods. "I'll lead the way."

Clutching Valentine's hand tight, we follow Pascal back to the car. He places my new dress in the back, glancing around apprehensively as he moves to open the door for us.

"Please wait inside, sir. I'll check around for Alejandro."

I don't miss the way Pascal's resting one hand over the bulge of a weapon beneath his suit jacket. Valentine nods once then gestures for me to climb in before him.

I'm halfway into the car when a loud bang rips through the air. It shatters the peace, causing all hell to break loose. A hand shoves me into the car, and I topple, sprawled across the back seat.

"Get down!"

Another loud bang follows, then another. It takes a second for realisation to dawn. It's gunshots. I twist in the seat, flipping over so I can see outside.

My heart stops.

No!

Slumped over the still-open car door, Valentine clutches his shoulder, blood pouring from between his fingers. His jaw is clenched tight as he covers the bullet wound.

Everything moves in slow snapshots of horror as another two bullets hit him from behind. He jerks with each impact, still refusing to show even a hint of pain.

"Valentine!" I screech.

"Stay down," he barks. "We've got this."

Glass suddenly shatters, sending sharp daggers spraying across me. I duck my head to protect my face. The back window has been shot out.

"On top of the building, nine o'clock!" Valentine yells.

Gun raised, Pascal pops off several shots. I can hear the

frightened screams of onlookers, hopefully fleeing the madness. We've turned this quiet town centre into a war zone.

"All clear!" Pascal shouts after I flinch from the sound of another gunshot. "Shooter is down."

Releasing his shoulder, Valentine retrieves the sleek black gun from his own chest holster. I gape as he clicks off the safety.

"We need to haul the bastard in for questioning," he snarls. "No one knows we're here, unless we're being monitored."

Nodding, Pascal keeps his gun cocked and sweeps his gaze over the street before taking off. I crawl over shattered glass to reach Valentine.

He keeps his gun raised and detached gaze trained on the chaos around us as I bring a hand to his blood-soaked shirt. I can't hope to cover all the bullet wounds and focus instead on the closest.

"Jesus Christ." I press down on his shoulder to stem the heavy bleeding. "We need to put pressure on this."

"It'll take more than a few bullets to kill me," he grunts.

"That doesn't mean I like seeing you bleed."

"Get in the car and keep your head down." His eyes rapidly survey our surroundings. "This wasn't a random attack."

"I'm trying to help you."

"Now, Lexi!"

Before he can snarl another order, the growl of a speeding engine shatters the momentary silence. Still ignoring his weeping wounds, Valentine jerks upright and turns to look down the street.

Another blacked-out SUV is hurtling towards us. Rolling down their window, a blonde-haired man leans out with what looks like a semi-automatic in his hands.

"Incoming," Valentine hisses.

Taking his outstretched hand, I let him yank me from the

car before there's a violent spray of bullets. The front window explodes a split-second later, and bullets hit the back seat.

We take off, running hard and fast to avoid being hit. Thanks to my daily drills with Felix, I can easily keep up with Valentine's long legs eating up the pavement.

Multiple car doors slam, and the thud of our pursuers accompanies more gunfire. I want to stop and help the sobbing woman cowering outside another shop, but Valentine won't surrender my hand.

"We can't run forever," I pant.

"Vantage point. Up ahead."

Spotting the black lacquered metal of the upcoming bus shelter, Valentine drags me behind it. I slam into the metal so hard, my teeth clack together.

Wasting no time, Valentine ducks around the obstacle to fire off several precise shots. I can hear the bellows of pain that accompany each round as he finds his targets.

"Enough!" a voice booms. "You're outnumbered, Valentine."

His grip on the gun tightens. "I've faced worse odds. What brings you to Scotland, Antonio?"

"Business."

"Rather bold of my brother to attack me in public. How long have you been waiting for an opportunity to strike?"

There's a scuffle of feet drawing to a halt nearby. I can only assume that our remaining attackers have stopped. Valentine's expression is steely as he keeps the gun cocked.

"Caine has no interest in a family reunion, Elder," Antonio responds coolly. "We're only here for the girl."

"He's declaring a civil war for this nobody?" Valentine snarks.

Although I know he's defending me, the cool bite of his words still stings. I focus on gulping down air and calming myself.

"You'd take a nobody out dress shopping?" Antonio

laughs. "Hand her over and we won't put another bullet in you."

Stepping out from behind the bus shelter, Valentine plants his feet. "Fire away. It won't stop me from peeling the skin from your bones for daring to threaten her."

There's a chorus of amused laughs. I tune the assholes out, focusing on tapping into the excited force that's swarming in my chest. I'll burn them all to a crisp if I have to.

Uncurling my fisted hands, I stare down at my palms and watch the swirling fireballs build. It's easier than ever to conjure my gift, like it can sense we're in danger.

"Time's up. Surrender the girl."

"Like hell," Valentine snaps.

"The authorities are undoubtedly on their way. Would you like to explain to them who we are? You care far more for the accords than we do."

Valentine spares me a glance. He looks down at my fire-lit hands, and his lips quirk. With a single eyebrow lifted, he conveys his message easily. I nod back, prepared to fight.

"Take her, then. She's all yours."

I watch with bated breath as Valentine raises his gun and spreads his hands in a mark of surrender.

"Good choice," Antonio says.

Before the approaching footsteps can surround us, I take a final breath and leap to the left to escape our hiding place. Four surprised faces lock onto me, and their guns shift to take aim.

"Now, Lexi!" Valentine shouts.

I don't hesitate before tossing the first fireball, watching it streak towards its target. The first dark-clothed man is hit straight in the chest, sending him flying backwards.

Flames engulf the attackers as my fireballs fly, one after another. Valentine's bullets find the two left standing, and I try not to flinch as their skulls implode, spraying blood and brain matter.

Pained screams echo around us from the men left burning to death. I extinguish the writhing flames in my hands then watch them eventually stop moving.

"Lexi. Come here, mi amor."

Seeing their bodies blacken and burn is the final straw. Darkness invades the edges of my vision as I feel myself falling, deeper and deeper into a spiral of panic.

We were shot at.

Almost killed.

Dying once wasn't enough to cure me of that all-too human fear. I still possess the survival instinct that drives our mammal brain to survive by any means necessary.

My lungs stutter and seize as air escapes me. The panic hits fast with a rallying war cry, taking over all my failing self-control.

"Lexi?"

I back away from Valentine. "Please… d-don't."

Hurt flashes across his face. "You're in shock."

"I just… I k-killed them!"

Slowly approaching me, he tucks his gun away, ignoring the steady stream of blood still soaking into his dress shirt. I clutch my tight chest, desperate to ignore the nearby crackle of flames.

The scent of charred flesh is heavy in the air. Thick. Pungent. Disgustingly strong. Each inhale further cements my panic until I can't breathe at all.

"We need to get out of here before the authorities arrive. You have to breathe, Lexi. I need you to be strong."

Valentine's poised in front of me, staring deep into my widened eyes. I flinch as his hands land on my shoulders and squeeze, encouraging me to calm down.

"Deep breaths. You're safe. They're dead."

Watching the rise and fall of his chest, I focus on the movement, putting all my energy into copying every move. I suffered with panic attacks through most of my teens, and they've made a reappearance since I arrived here.

They used to hit when I was backed into a corner with no means of escape. No choice but to open my legs and follow his commands, however disgusting and degrading. I indulged his every whim.

When I realised that he enjoyed my terror and got off on it, I learned to dissociate and lock my panic down. Becoming a numb, mute zombie kept me alive for years to come.

"Come on, brave girl," Valentine coaxes. "Be strong for me."

"Strong?" I wheeze. "I fucking killed them!"

He inches closer. "Trust me, they would've done the same to you in a heartbeat."

"You think that excuses what... what I've done?"

Still gripping my shoulders, he stares deep into my eyes, seeing every last fleck of despair threatening to consume me. I can't even hide it—my fear of becoming just another monster.

Lost in his gaze, I feel the tingles spread through my extremities. His fingers have slipped beneath my neckline to stroke my skin, allowing the Vitae to flow between us.

The familiar heat is like a defibrillator to the heart. It wraps around my spinal cord then rises, filling my lungs until they're forced to expand, and I can suck in painful breaths.

"That's my girl," he praises. "Breathe for me, baby."

"Valentine! Sir!" Shouts cut through the wail of sirens nearing.

Startling, Valentine looks across the street. Pascal has emerged from the building he made a beeline for to find our first attacker.

Alejandro limps beside him, a crimson curtain streaked down the side of his face. The pair carry an unconscious mass between them, dressed in the same clothing that Caine's men wore.

Valentine looks back at me. "You good?"

I force a nod.

"Then let's move."

Banding his good arm around me, Valentine directs me towards them, pulling me as fast as possible past the bodies we're leaving behind. I make a point not to look at the remains.

"*¿Qué ha pasado?*" Valentine nods to the man.

Alejandro replies in rapid, jerky Spanish. Together, the four of us hurry towards the SUV we abandoned. I climb in the back as Pascal takes the driver's seat, ignoring the smashed glass covering every surface.

Valentine has barely closed the door behind us before we take off with a squeal of tyres. I lean forward to gently touch Alejandro's shoulder.

"Are you okay?"

His eyes meet mine in the rearview mirror. "Fine, Lexi. I was jumped as I checked the perimeter and knocked unconscious."

"By the shooter?"

He nods. "He was watching us the whole time."

Valentine curses colourfully. "My brother has well and truly lost his mind. This is an act of war."

"How did he even know where we are? That we left the facility?" I watch the flash of blue lights fading behind us.

"Simple." Valentine grimaces as he peels off his bloodstained suit jacket. "Ravius has a mole."

XIII

DEATH

CHAPTER 24

BE MY QUEEN – SEAFRET

"*T*his is going to hurt."

Valentine stares straight ahead. "Begin."

Dousing the first ragged bullet wound with fluid, Michael lifts the surgical pliers to Valentine's shoulder. I clench my fists in the corner of the hospital room while watching him work.

Hours after the ambush, we made it back to the facility with no further incident. Neither Valentine nor Alejandro dared to re-holster their weapons until we were safely home.

Digging into Valentine's shoulder, Michael searches for the bullet still lodged deep in his tissue. The only sign of pain on Valentine's face is the slight tic of his clenched jaw. He's had centuries to conquer his reaction to pain.

I think this hurts me more than him.

Already, I care too much.

"Got it." Michael slides the pliers free, cinched around a bullet. "You're lucky it wasn't a few inches to the left. Chest wounds can be fatal."

"What about blood loss?" I dare to ask. "Or infections? Wouldn't that kill a Redeemed?"

"No." Michael shakes his head. "The body's cells

regenerate too fast for that. It takes lethal force that causes irreparable damage to end one of us."

Like a bullet to the skull or being burned alive, I think grimly. Those men we killed aren't coming back any time soon. I force back the panic that thought causes. I can't lose it again.

On the opposite bed, Alejandro sits on high alert as Ruth inspects the three-inch gash on his head. He took a nasty blow, but Michael will heal him in no time.

"Caine's lost his mind," Michael mutters as he works. "You were in broad daylight. Do the accords mean nothing to him?"

Valentine's eyes bore into mine from across the room. "He's forsaken our secret. All he wants is power."

"And me," I add.

"Well, he isn't getting you."

The note of finality in Valentine's voice may comfort him, but I can't be so easily coddled. Not after what we just went through. The threat suddenly feels very real.

"These four walls won't protect me if there really is a mole. Caine knows about my gift. He already knew about the prophecy. Why else would he be targeting me?"

"He's been experimenting with gifted Redeemed for decades," Michael replies. "None of them had the potential or access to power that you do."

I watch in awe as he begins to slowly heal Valentine, who doesn't even flinch as his skin knits back together. Those verdant eyes are far too busy attempting to burrow beneath my skin.

What's that look on his face?

Fear?

Is the almighty Spanish Elder afraid?

"Lexi?" Valentine gains my attention. "You're holding your breath. Stay with us."

Forcing my clenched teeth to unlock, I nod once and suck in a breath. That tempting pit of desolation wants to drag me under again to escape this horror. It's all I can do to stop it.

Watching me breathe, Valentine nods. "Good girl."

"What about the man we brought back?" I rasp.

"Pascal has him detained."

"Does he need medical attention?" Michael asks. "A dead prisoner isn't much use to us."

Valentine grimaces. "He certainly will be dead by the time I'm done with him."

Moving on to the next bullet wound that's shredded Valentine's back, Michael continues his healing. He's deep in concentration when the sound of shouting and doors banging open echoes down the corridor.

"Where is she? God-fucking-dammit!" a familiar voice howls.

"We survived a shootout only to be killed by Daniel and your other insane brother." I press my palms to my gritty eyes, feeling my pulse skyrocket.

Valentine musters a smirk. "Was worth it to see you in that red dress."

"Worth almost dying?"

"Most certainly."

Rolling my eyes, I push off from the white wall and prepare to be bombarded. The thud of boots precedes the door slamming open so hard, it cracks the wall's plaster.

"Where the fuck is she?" Daniel roars.

I fight to suppress a shudder. He sounds like a furious mountain lion that's had one of its cubs stolen. It's impossible not to feel intimidated by his rage.

"She's safe," Valentine drawls.

"I'm going to break every last bone in your body like I should have done a century ago."

I step into Daniel's line of sight. The moment his enraged blue eyes land on me, they widen, his fists raised to pummel the living daylights out of Valentine.

"I'd prefer it if you didn't beat each other to death. Clearly, I'm alive and… fine."

Searching me from head to toe, Daniel's frozen on the spot. The fury radiating off him is downright suffocating. But he isn't fooling me. Hidden in his gaze, spikes of terror darken his irises.

His fingers spasm, itching to reach out, but for some reason, he's not allowing himself to touch me. When he looks at me, I know he doesn't see love. Just the potential for even more loss.

"Hey." I step closer to him. "I'm here. No one hurt me. We're safe."

"Lex," he rasps.

Taking his hand, I lift it to my chest to rest above my heart. It's hammering away, battling to escape from behind my ribcage. His eyes close briefly as he sucks in a breath.

"You're in so much fucking trouble," he whispers.

"I know. It's okay."

"There is nothing remotely okay about this."

When someone clears their throat, Daniel opens his eyes, pulling his hand away from my chest. Ravius is standing in the doorway, looking flustered.

Eyes skirting around the room, he catalogues the chaos, from blood-soaked clothing to half-healed bullet wounds. When his eyes stop exploring, his expression has hardened into a clinical mask.

"Someone better start talking." His eyes land on his brother's state of undress. "You were shot?"

Gazing down at his tattooed chest, Valentine sighs. "Astute observation, brother."

Ravius storms farther into the room to approach him. For a moment, he silently watches Michael work, patching his brother back together. After setting down the gauze he was using, Michael inspects the newly healed skin, puckered and bright-pink.

"You're all done. No permanent damage. Your stupidity, however, isn't quite so easily fixable."

Valentine sits upright, rolling his shoulders. When he sees Ravius staring at him, he narrows his eyes.

"Relax. These aren't the first bullets I've taken."

I swear, I hear Daniel snort. When I look up at him, his impassive mask has smoothed back into place, and I wonder if I imagined it.

"You're a fool," Ravius spits at him. "Our entire existence is under threat, and your actions risk exposing us all. Do our rules mean nothing to you?"

"I'm allowed to do as I please," Valentine deflects.

"How's that working out for you?"

"Enough." I approach the pair of Elders. "Don't you think we have more pressing concerns right now?"

Ravius whirls on me. "Like the two men you burned alive in broad daylight for the entire world to see?"

Flinching, I duck my gaze. The shame is all-consuming. Even if those men deserved it, I still took their lives. Am I any better than Caine now? Or just another coldblooded killer?

"The RID has already been in touch," Ravius says angrily. "We can expect a visit from Elizabeth Pritchard."

"The RID?" I echo.

Michael washes his hands in the sink. "Redeemed Intelligence Department. Our branch of government."

"If they deem this to be a violation of the accords, I cannot protect anyone from what comes next." Ravius begins to pace. "It will be a bloodbath."

"We didn't hurt the humans," Valentine justifies. "Everyone had taken cover or fled when the real fight began."

"There were still witnesses! Bodies! The damn news is reporting it for the entire country to see."

Valentine raises his chin. "You think I don't know what's at stake? I couldn't just let them take her."

Everyone in the room focuses on me, trembling and barely

holding it together. Even Ravius summons the humanity to look concerned. His pinched eyes tell me as much.

I look down at my feet. "Caine shot up a town to get to me. It's all my fault."

Crossing the packed room, Daniel pulls me into his arms. I hide my face in his soft black t-shirt, breathing in his familiar scent as I struggle to hold a fresh burst of panic at bay.

His lips meet the top of my head, planting a gentle kiss. In his arms, I feel myself break. All the fear and shame that's been eating away at me spills out as a sob tears from my mouth.

Did *he* do this to me?

Am I a monster because he broke something in me that cannot be fixed?

Or was it there all along?

The thought drives me to the edge of despair, and I have to rely on Daniel to hold me upright. The weight of what just happened coupled with months of turmoil are catching up to me.

I hear Michael murmuring to Ravius and Alejandro about giving us some space before the hospital door clicks shut behind them. I can't even lift my head as I continue to quietly sob.

"I've got you, Lex." Daniel's breathing is shallow. "We won't let Caine lay a finger on you."

"I'm nothing! Why does he want me?"

Daniel forcibly lifts my head, guiding my eyes up to his. The pain reflected back at me is a burden too heavy to bear alone. I don't know how he's carried it for so long.

"You are everything," he says fiercely. "I've been alive for a long time, but I haven't lived. Not until you."

Lips lowering to mine, our mouths meet. Despite Valentine sitting mere inches away, Daniel kisses me like I'm the very air he breathes, intent on bruising my lips.

His tongue thrusts into my mouth, demanding and

possessive. I can taste his fear. Feel the claws of grief attempting to drag him back into the past with each reminder of all he could lose.

He kisses the life back into my soul, forcing the panic and despair to recede long enough for me to reciprocate. I don't care if the man he seems so desperate to hate is watching us.

Not even the shuffle of movement releases me from Daniel's orbit. For every inch the panic retreats, he fills the freed-up space with himself. His touch. His tongue. His love.

When a pair of hands moves to grip my hips from behind, it takes a second for my brain to catch up. Daniel's cradling my face in a tight, frantic grip. Not holding my hips.

"Now, now, comrade. You're stealing all of our mate's attention."

Valentine's silky-smooth voice is like a bucket of ice water dousing the pair of us. Breaking the kiss, Daniel doesn't release his hold on me as he tosses a scathing glare over my head.

"Some *mate* you are," he spits back. "You jeopardised her life. Got yourself shot. Put us all at risk."

"We got back in one piece, didn't we?" I can hear the smile in Valentine's voice.

"No thanks to your arrogance," Daniel argues. "It sounds like Lexi saved you, not the other way around."

"We're a team. That's how we survived."

"Your job is to protect her!"

"Guys," I say weakly.

But they're too busy arguing above me. Back and forth. Trading sharp barbs and acidic insults. When I try to slide out of their unlikely sandwich, neither man releases me.

I can't handle the current of electricity their touch is igniting. With both of them touching me, it feels like a circuit has been completed, and I'm lit up like a fucking Christmas tree.

"You think I wanted to put her at risk?" Valentine

combats. "She's as much mine as she is yours. I want to protect her."

"Then you should stay the fuck away from her. I can keep her safe far better than you can. Today has proven as much."

"Ha! Because your track record is so spotless."

Daniel's teeth grind together. "This again? When will you stop dredging up the past to punish me with?"

"When you stop doing the exact same thing to me!" Valentine squeezes my hips as anger screams from his tone. "We used to be brothers, or did you forget that?"

"Brothers don't betray each other."

"But they do forgive each other."

"That's what you want?" Daniel scoffs. "My forgiveness? Fuck off back to Spain and leave us to clean up your mess."

"I'll settle for you tolerating my existence! I'm here for Lexi, not us. I won't leave her. Not now that I've found her."

"She doesn't want you here!"

"Enough!" I scream. "Valentine stays. That's final."

Both of them quiet at the unhinged screech of my voice. I peel Daniel's fingers from my cheeks and elbow Valentine away, needing room to breathe.

With space between us, I can think more clearly. The tiny flames I could feel licking across my skin extinguish. Both look shocked as they finally notice the effect they're having on me.

Rather than syphoning my unruly gift, it seems their combined touch has quite the opposite effect. My entire body is vibrating with energy demanding to be released.

"This is less than ideal." I glower at them both. "But we can't afford to hate each other. Not anymore."

"Lex—" Daniel starts.

"No. I know Valentine did the unthinkable. In his mind, you did the same. But if we don't work together, none of us will survive this. Surely the past can wait?"

"You cannot trust him."

"Because you're so good at keeping secrets and protecting people?" Valentine quips.

Before Daniel can lunge for him and resume the fight, I raise a hand. "I said enough! No more!"

Eyes dropping to the floor, Daniel has the grace to look contrite. Valentine doesn't even react. I have no doubt that man would slaughter your whole family and still use his sharp tongue to talk you into defending him.

"I don't expect you to forgive each other." I look between them. "I don't even expect you to like each other. But I cannot battle wars on all sides. We need to work as a team."

"A team?" Daniel wrinkles his nose.

"We've been bonded for a reason. This feeling between us, the Vitae… it's telling us to stop fighting this connection."

"I can't just forget, Lex."

"I'm not asking you to," I say more softly. "But if Caine's coming for us, we won't survive by killing each other first."

Exhaling loudly through his nose, Valentine eventually nods. "She's right."

"I know she's fucking right," Daniel snarls in defeat. "That doesn't mean I have to like it. But if this is what it takes to keep her alive…"

He tosses his enemy a filthy look before finding the strength to nod once. Valentine watches Daniel then summons his own terse nod, an unspoken agreement passing between them.

"I guess I won't be returning to Spain." Valentine blows an escaped strand of hair off his forehead. "Not until this is done. Lexi takes priority above all else."

Daniel tilts his head in acknowledgment. The very tentative truce between them is a shock to the system after so much bickering and bad blood.

"I'll summon additional reinforcements," Valentine adds. "I can't leave my people unprotected, but if Caine escalating, we will need backup."

"When Josephine arrives for the centenary, this place will be crawling with security. It'll be a fortress."

"Josephine?" I question.

Valentine retrieves the stained remains of his black shirt then slides it on. "My sister. The fourth and final Elder."

Great. Another one.

"Please tell me she isn't a psychotic murderer intent on ruling the world like your brother?" I half-joke.

"Quite the opposite." He snickers before sobering. "But when she hears of Caine's actions, I have no doubt she'll offer her support to bring him to heel."

With Valentine dressed and Daniel clinging to some semblance of calm for the time being, we step out of the hospital room before the arguing starts back up.

Michael and Ruth have vanished with all the pressing injuries dealt with, leaving Ravius and Alejandro to wait just down the corridor. I notice the gash on Alejandro's head is gone.

"We need to question the prisoner," Valentine informs them.

"He's been moved to a prison cell." Ravius gestures for us to go ahead. "I need to deal with the RID before we're all slaughtered for this mess."

Separating from Ravius once we're inside the administration building, I follow Valentine, Daniel and Alejandro down into the subterranean hell that I called home for ten endless days.

The prison cells are all empty aside from one. Passing the cell I rotted in is less than pleasant, so I keep my eyes trained on Valentine's muscular back.

Guarding the barred cell at the very end, Pascal's scowl is firmly back in place. He looks mildly relieved when he sees his Elder approaching and stands at ease.

"Lexi!"

Stepping out of the ajar cell, Felix abandons the prisoner

to rush over to me. I don't hesitate before throwing myself into his open arms. He tugs me into a tight hug.

"Are you okay, babe?" He draws back to scan over me. "What the hell happened?"

"We were targeted." I try to put on a smile to ease his fear. "I probably should've stuck to the morning drill instead."

Scoffing, his usual boyish smile plumps his cheeks. "I'm going to assume you've already been chewed out, so I'll spare you the lecture. But miss a drill again and I won't be so forgiving."

"Got it."

"Ready for this?"

"As I'll ever be." I sigh.

"Stick with me. You'll be okay."

Giving me a final squeeze, he guides us over to the occupied cell. Our unconscious friend is chained to a metal chair in the centre, slumped over and bleeding profusely.

"He's still out?" Valentine frowns.

Daniel steps into the cell. "Not for much longer."

Cocking his fist, he slams it into the guy's stomach. A gasp of pain escapes his lips as he awakens, coughing up a mouthful of blood.

When his head finally lifts, he looks between us all, surveying the situation with hazy, confused eyes. Daniel crouches down to get a good look at his face.

"Arrow." He clicks his tongue. "You're far from home."

"Could say the same about you," Arrow struggles out. "Fucking traitor."

"I only see one traitor in this cell. Care to explain why the hell you're leading an armed attack against your own kind?"

More blood spilling from his mouth, Arrow grunts in pain. I can see where Pascal's bullet caught him when he took out his sniper on the rooftop. If he were still mortal, he'd be dead.

"Answer me!" Daniel demands.

"Just following orders. Like you should be doing."

"What does Caine want with her?"

"Come on, man." Arrow winces. "You've dragged in enough playthings for him to dissect. You know the drill."

His words are an unwelcome reminder of the price Daniel has paid to remain in Caine's good graces all these years. The pieces of his soul he sacrificed in order to report back to his true master.

"What does Caine want?" Daniel repeats.

Entering the cell, Valentine joins his comrade. "Answer the question."

"Hello, Elder. How's the shoulder?"

"Your aim is terrible. Couldn't even manage a kill shot," Valentine seethes. "Answer the question, and I'll stop."

"Stop what?" Arrow cackles.

Lifting his hand, I can see the swirling whirlpool that Valentine's conjured. The water builds into a river that he aims at our prisoner. Seeing his gift in action is mesmerising.

I watch the water force itself into Arrow's nostrils and down his throat. Valentine doesn't let up, creating more supernatural water and forcing it upon his victim until he's being waterboarded.

"You couldn't have done that to our friends earlier?" I point out. "Those assholes had semi-automatics."

Valentine casts me a look. "Your skill is far more offensive than mine, mi amor. I find a gun to be effective enough."

When dribbles of blood-tinged water drip from Arrow's chin as he slowly drowns, Valentine relents. His hand drops, and the flow of water ceases, granting Arrow a chance to splutter.

"Now." Valentine clears his throat. "Answer the question, and I'll grant you the mercy of a slit throat. Continue to play these games, and I'll ensure you drown on dry land. *Slowly.*"

Sucking in ragged breaths, Arrow fights to fill his lungs. "Caine's tired of failed experiments. But she's different."

"Why?" Daniel presses.

"Fuck you."

"Wrong answer," Valentine drones.

Waterboarding him again, the bored look on Valentine's face doesn't shift. He's far from the teasing, smirking man who made me twirl for him mere hours ago.

This creature is ruthless. Revelling in the pain he's inflicting and enjoying every second of it. I want to be disturbed, but the thought that he's doing all this for me stirs another feeling.

"If you kill him, we'll get nothing," Daniel warns.

"Are you protecting your colleague?"

"Hardly."

Valentine cocks his head. "My brother does have some knuckleheads on his payroll, doesn't he?"

I don't miss the veiled insult. Daniel's only response is the flexing of his stubble-covered jaw. When Valentine releases his gift again, it takes far longer for Arrow to recover.

He's choking, water and blood mingling as he spews mouthfuls of it over himself. I look up at Felix, and he gives me a tight smile, silently urging me to remain calm.

I've never seen someone be tortured before. But then again, I've never killed a man before, just fantasised about fighting back and somehow killing *him* in self-defence.

"She's... powerful," Arrow spits. "Caine wants her gift. Her m-memories. The access she has to the Vitae."

"How does he know about all that?" I wonder.

Valentine locks eyes with me, his head inclined. I catch on fast. My secrets aren't safe anymore. Not without Ravius's mysterious mole feeding information back to Caine.

But who knows about the meadow?

The dank cell suddenly feels too small. I can smell Arrow's blood. It's pooling on the filthy stone floor, joining the puddle of red-streaked water.

"He won't stop. Not until she's strapped to that lab table and ripped apart at the seams."

341

Arrow's warning is punctuated by the sharp ringing of a mobile phone. It startles us all. I can't remember the last time I even looked at a phone.

Reaching into Arrow's pocket, Daniel fishes out a black smartphone then hesitates. I watch him exchange a long, hard look with Valentine before he answers the call and puts it on loudspeaker.

"Is it done?" a clipped voice asks.

Daniel clenches the phone tight. "Perhaps you should check the news to see what a shoddy job your men did today."

There's a long pause.

"Daniel. Enjoying your little holiday? We've certainly missed you around here."

"Cut the shit, Caine. Your men are dead. Send more and they'll meet the same fate."

"Don't you mean your men?" He laughs coldly. "You trained them yourself, after all."

Head bowed, Daniel exhales. "How long have you known?"

"That you're a backstabbing turncoat? Come along, boy. I've lived enough lives to smell a traitor in my midst."

"So what? You just played along?"

"I wanted to see how long you could keep up the charade. You lasted several decades longer than I anticipated. It's been entertaining."

Defeat settles over Daniel like a cumulus cloud, his shoulders curved beneath the almighty weight of a cruel, indifferent world. He wordlessly hands the phone over to Valentine.

Valentine paces as he speaks. "You've made some mistakes since we fought over scraps of food by the firelight, but this time, you've truly outdone yourself."

"Two traitors for the price of one." Caine chuckles. "To what do I owe the pleasure, *Valentinus*?"

"I see you haven't heeded our last little chat. This road

only leads to one destination. We can still avoid an all-out war."

"There was a time when I admired you, little brother. Whole legions of mortal men fell beneath your sword during the conquests."

"I was defending our people from slaughter," Valentine replies smoothly. "Do not use the battles we fought together as justification for your hatred and prejudice. We were at war."

"We still are!" Caine spits venomously. "These humans… these animals… think they can hide us away, make us abide by their laws, like we are the inferior species."

I want Daniel to put his arms around me, but he's staring at his feet, seemingly numb to it all. Valentine casts me a look then offers his spare hand, fingers slightly curled in invitation.

Without a word, I tangle our hands together, anchoring myself in the increasingly familiar strength of his touch. We stand together, side-by-side, as Caine sighs.

"Your choice is simple, Valentinus. Hand over the girl, and I will endeavour to avoid further bloodshed. You have my word."

"Your word means nothing," I growl.

"Ah, Lexi. I don't believe we've been acquainted yet. How about we discuss this without such unpleasantries? I'm sure we can come to a mutually beneficial agreement."

"I won't surrender to you."

"Not even to protect the ones you love?" Caine asks slyly. "Tell me, child. Did you enjoy it?"

My chest tightens. "Enjoy… what?"

"When *he* touched you."

The edges of my vision blur until everything around me is staticky. I can't smell the blood anymore. My hand becomes limp in Valentine's, and it takes all of my mental strength to stop my knees from buckling.

I imagined it.

The day is just catching up to me.

"Nothing to say?" Caine hums. "I'm going to take your silence as a yes. All those years... you must have enjoyed it."

"Lexi?" Valentine murmurs.

Daniel has stiffened and inched closer to me, his head now raised. I can't bring myself to meet his wide, questioning eyes. They're all staring at me as the world crumbles around me.

Thought you could hide, Lexi girl?

I'll always live inside you.

"Ah," Caine sneers. "They don't know, hmm? How interesting. You didn't even tell your soul bonds about him."

"Stop," I plead.

"Not until you comply. Surrender yourself to me, and I'll let your mates live."

Palms slick with sweat, I search around the cell, my skin pulled so tight across my bones it feels like I'm going to explode. He isn't here. But that doesn't stop the terror from setting in.

"I've seen your file. Some nasty scars you've got there. He really didn't hold back, did he?"

"Enough!" Valentine booms.

"So quick to jump to her defence, little brother. Even when she's lied through her teeth about everything but her name."

"Whatever game you're playing, it won't work. Lexi is off the table. Now let's discuss the terms of your surrender instead."

"Will you still yearn for her when you know, I wonder?" Caine muses. "You always did want what you can't have."

"Caine—"

"Pen was a piece of work... But this one? Hell, brother. She's damaged goods."

Like a greedy black hole, the bottomless pit slowly caving in my chest is sucking in what fragile pieces are left of me. My hopes. My tentative dreams of finding a life here. The friendships I've forged. Any chance I had of ever seeing Eve again.

"You're right."

The harsh hiss of my voice silences them. I ignore Valentine and Daniel staring at me and lock eyes with Arrow. Does he know too? The slight curve of his lips answers me.

"You're right." I take a step closer to the prisoner. "I don't deserve this second chance. I don't deserve them. I am damaged goods."

"Lex," Daniel whispers.

I ignore him. He can never know. I've lost my life, my freedom, my family. I won't let Caine take them from me too.

"But that doesn't mean I will let you use me to destroy this world and everyone in it. I won't be your weapon. You'll have to kill me first."

Caine snorts. "Oh, I won't kill you. Not yet. But you can watch as I pluck the hearts from those you love and force them down your throat."

With an influx of rage steeling my spine, I snatch the phone from Valentine's grip and bring it closer to ensure there's no mistaking my words.

"Caine?"

"Yes, sugar?"

Flames erupt in my empty, raised hand. "You know where to find me. Send your best men. I'll return them in ashes."

The dank cell fills with blinding light as my flames engulf our prisoner. He's swallowed whole by supernatural fire.

Piercing wails surround us, bouncing off the stone walls and sending an unmistakable message back to Caine. When Arrow succumbs and falls silent, smoke billows from his charred remains.

"You hear that?" I snarl into the phone. "That's the sound of your reign ending."

XXI

THE WORLD

CHAPTER 25

I WAS JUST A KID – NOTHING BUT THIEVES

*P*eace envelopes me.

Lush, soft grass. Gently rolling hills. Bright, sparkling sunshine. The meadow stretches out around me, a sense of contentment slipping beneath my skin.

I'm not sure how an ethereal, otherworldly place can feel so much like home. But this meadow offered me a sanctuary when my entire life had been forcibly ripped away from me.

It lives inside me now.

A veritable well of power.

Spine tingling, I search around the familiar green space, unable to shake the feeling that I'm being watched. But there's no one here. I'm alone in my own personal purgatory.

Unable to shake the strange feeling pulling at my senses, I start to run. I don't care where. There's something here, hidden behind the veneer of tranquillity. Every night, I feel it stalking me.

"Leave me alone!" I scream.

Tripping and stumbling up a steep slope, I fight to escape, even though nothing is chasing me but thin air. It's a battle to reach the summit, but as I claw my nails through rough dirt, I finally reach the peak.

My feet freeze.

"Oh… my God."

All around me, the beautiful verdure has vanished. Where once there was a brilliant green meadow, a scorched wasteland now exists. The meadow is now blackened and dead, curling with remnants of smoke.

It's been razed.

Desecrated and destroyed.

Fire has spread like an infection. Poisoning everything around it, leaving no patch of earth untouched. The meadow is sick. We've opened this slice of divinity to the horrors of human touch.

I did this.

We're all doomed because of me.

"Lexi," a formless voice caresses my skin.

Whirling around, I search for the source and come up empty. I'm still alone. Surrounded by the consequences of my actions and nothing else.

"Lexi."

"Who are you?" I shout to the blue sky. "What do you want from me?"

Warmth slicks over my skin. It feels like I'm being wrapped in light, held steady in the face of such inevitable desolation. I'm not alone. It's in the air—whatever unknown force continues to bring me here.

"Remember, Lexi."

Trembling, I give myself to the invisible force.

"Remember what?"

"Death too must be earned."

* * *

My throat burns with the swig of liquor. I clutch the whiskey bottle tight, swirling the remaining amber liquid. It hasn't numbed the terrifying memory of my dream yet.

The forest is silent in front me. We're far enough from the rest of the facility to avoid the buzz of people. I'm growing to love the new apartment purely for the privacy it provides.

Taking another sip, I will my racing heart to slow. The same vision comes every night now. Valentine's vacant space in my dreams has been taken over, and I have no idea what that means.

"Lex?"

My head slumps. "Leave me alone, Daniel."

"So you can continue drinking yourself into oblivion?"

"Something like that."

He sits down on the wide stone entrance steps beside me. Without a word, I offer him the bottle, and Daniel accepts.

"How long have you been out here?"

I study the expanse of blackness above me, cold and crisp. "Couldn't sleep. I needed some air."

"You should've woken me up."

Taking the bottle back, I take another swig. Raven didn't ask any questions when I borrowed her chips to buy liquor from the market.

"We need to talk about this," he urges. "You can't keep shutting me out and expecting me not to ask questions."

"There's nothing to talk about."

Daniel looks up at the night sky. The stars are like gleaming jewels nestled in crushed velvet darkness this far from civilisation, with no air pollution to obscure the view.

"You don't owe me anything." He exhales sharply. "Not even the truth. But I thought we had agreed to trust each other."

Pulling the edges of the bottle's label, I'm a split-second from bolting into the trees to escape this conversation. I've closed myself off from everyone since we were attacked.

But Daniel's stuck by my side regardless, through sleepless nights, sweaty sheets and stony silences. He refuses to let me isolate myself from him like I have everyone else.

"The RID is investigating the attack," Daniel tells me. "Ravius is confident he can get them to rule in our favour."

"And if they don't?"

"Then Caine gets his wish. The accords will be null and

void. There will be nothing to stop an all-out war with the humans if they see us as a threat."

"We're human too, you know. If everyone saw it that way, we wouldn't be having this discussion at all."

"I know, Lex."

Before I can take another sip to drown my sorrows, Daniel intervenes and eases the bottle from my hands. I let him take it from me, fixing him with my tear-logged stare instead.

He looks pale and exhausted. Cocoa hair sticking up in all directions, his piercing blue eyes are swimming with concern. So much that it makes me sick.

Everything he fought for, all those years of turning over innocent lives to keep his cover intact for Ravius's benefit, and it was all for nothing. His life has been destroyed too.

But he's still here.

He refuses to let me drown.

"Please, love. You're the one who said we're a team. We need each other to survive now."

My throat swells with emotion. "I've spent my entire life isolating myself to survive. It's all I know."

"All you *knew*," he corrects. "That isn't your life now. You don't have to be that person."

"What if she's all I'll ever be? The scared little girl hiding from The Big Bad Wolf? Keeping his disgusting fucking secrets?"

Brushing my wet cheek with his knuckles, his touch is reverent. I want to pull away and keep my sky-high shields intact, but the shred of comfort obliterates my control.

Uncontrollable tears stream from my eyes in a violent outpour. I never allowed myself to feel. To hurt. To mourn. Crushing those feelings enabled me to keep going for Eve's sake.

But she isn't here now. I'm no closer to getting back to her than I was when I first woke up. That failure is getting harder and harder to tolerate.

"I didn't see a scared little girl in that prison cell," Daniel murmurs. "I saw a powerful, determined woman, putting her soul on the line to do what's right for her people."

"I didn't do it for them." I shake my head. "Caine didn't just threaten The Redeemed. He threatened you."

His hand slips into my loose mane of hair, exploring the topography of my skull. I can't let him into my head. No matter the days he's spent pleading for me to open up.

Once he knows my history, he'll go back to that angry, cold-eyed man I first had the misfortune to cross paths with. I'll lose him. The lives I've taken will be for nothing then.

"Tell me the truth, Lex," he begs.

"I c-can't do that."

"What are you afraid of?" He traps my head, holding me captive. "Nothing you can say will ever scare me away."

"You don't know that."

"I do," he clips out. "You know why?"

Trapped, all I can do is stare.

"Because you didn't run from me," he finishes. "Not when you learned the truth about the things I've done. You still stayed."

"Pen's death wasn't your fault. Hell, those people you handed over to Caine... that wasn't your fault either."

His mouth twists in a sad smile. "And whatever you're so petrified of me knowing, this secret I've seen hiding in your eyes for months... it isn't your fault either."

The night's blanket of solitude holding us close gives me the courage to reply.

"He told me it was my fault." My voice is nothing more than a whisper. "That I deserved what he was doing to me. And I could never tell a soul for that reason."

"He?" Daniel echoes.

"Stop pushing."

"I've been patient for days while watching you self-destruct. So has Valentine. But I won't watch you suffer anymore."

Little does he know how long my suffering has lasted. The years I've spent locked in that impenetrable level of hell. How many people abandoned me and willingly turned a blind eye.

"I… was never allowed to say his name. That was his number one rule."

The floodgates burst, and I'm speaking before I can sever my own tongue to keep his secret intact.

"Not even in my head. As the years passed and I grew up, I still never found the strength to name him."

Releasing his grip on my head, Daniel takes my hand instead. His thumb traces tiny circles on my skin, offering me silent support, his gaze never straying from mine.

"I can't remember how old I was when it started." My eyes clench shut. "Young enough to believe him when he said I was special, and he would never hurt me."

"But he did?" Daniel asks gently.

"Not at first. He gave me food when I was starving, too focused on keeping my baby sister alive after Mum abandoned us. I thought he was our knight in shining armour."

Throat closing up, I retake the discarded bottle and drink deeply. The alcohol does little to warm my cold, shaking frame.

"Eve needed things. Clothes. Nappies. Formula. I'd been stealing what I could, desperate to stop her being taken away from me by Child Protective Services."

Head shaking, I release a sob.

"I would've done anything to protect that tiny, innocent baby, but there was no one to protect me from him. Once he gained my trust, for every gift he bought there was a price."

Daniel's hand rapidly tightens around mine. It hurts, but I don't push him away. Not for what comes next.

"It was so painful," I choke out. "I was too young to

understand what was happening… What he'd taken from me. But I knew I had to keep my mouth shut. For her."

The tears are flowing so thick and fast, it's a wonder I haven't drowned. I'd take that easy escape right now.

"Years passed. The pain faded until I couldn't feel anything at all. That broken little girl inside me never grew up. She still believed his threats and lies and did as she was told."

"Fuck, Lex."

His voice is barely audible. With another chug of liquor, I let the darkness infringe upon my vision, taking me back to that stormy night when everything changed.

"I had this friend. Alex. He wasn't my boyfriend, but we weren't just friends either. More like partners in crime. We drank and smoked together, but the drugs were his thing."

Daniel's eyes tighten, wisely choosing to remain silent.

"He was a piece of shit, but I liked the pain that being with him caused. It was my choice to be there—being with him was pure escapism. I don't think he ever realised what I was running from."

"Did… he do this?"

I know what he's asking. Daniel's seen the scars that will forever tie me to my past. Shaking my head, I hand him the bottle. He's going to need it.

"I left Alex's apartment late that night. We'd fought like usual, and he threw a vodka bottle at me."

Rolling up the sleeve of my long-sleeved t-shirt, I motion to the jagged scar on my forearm. Daniel runs a single fingertip over it, his calloused touch making me shiver.

"I told him to lose my number. We couldn't afford a car, so I walked home. That's where *he* found me."

Flashbacks battle to take over. The slash of the knife. His frenzied panting as he lost control. Pain. My insides being stabbed to shreds. Bleeding out across the rain-soaked grass.

"You know the rest of the story. I guess all those years of

abuse were him showing great restraint. In the end, he couldn't help himself from taking that final piece from me."

After taking his own sip, Daniel deposits the bottle on the step below us. His eyes are fixed on the forest surrounding the old building. He can't even look at me. A lead weight settles in my stomach.

"Now you know. I lied to Ravius when I said that I didn't know who killed me. He could be locked up right now, but the truth is, I still can't say his name."

Releasing Daniel's hand, I unsteadily climb to my feet. Perhaps Raven or Michael will let me sleep on their sofa until I can make alternative arrangements.

"I'll pack my stuff."

That startles Daniel out of his reverie.

"What?"

I'm already heading inside the disused building, climbing the stairs as fast as possible. I don't need to be let down easily. He can spare me the long speech.

I'm disgusting.

Broken.

Damaged goods.

Back inside the apartment, I head for the bedroom to pack my clothes. At this rate, I'll take sleeping in the special collections room over being here. Anything to get away from Daniel's inevitable rejection.

"Lex!" his voice bellows.

Grabbing handfuls of t-shirts and clean underwear, I'm searching for a bag to stuff them in when the bedroom door slams open. He skids to a halt and captures my wrist.

"What the hell are you doing?"

"You don't have to say it. I knew the moment you found out that everything would change. Just let me grab my stuff, then I'll be gone, alright?"

"Are you fucking insane?" He gapes at me. "I'm not letting you leave. This is your home."

"I don't have a home. You know everything now. I'm not worthy of your protection or this bond. I never was."

Unable to wrench my arm from his grip, Daniel snatches the clothing then tosses it to the floor. I'm frozen in shock as he yanks me close, our chests smacking together.

Strong arms curl around me, and I'm pinned against him with such ferocity, I can feel my lungs struggling to expand. His breathing is ragged as it stirs my hair.

"Do you genuinely think that anything has changed? That I'd turn my back on you when I knew what happened to you?"

"Caine was right." A whimper erupts from me. "I am damaged goods. I just never wanted you to see that."

Fingers digging painfully into my arms, Daniel forces me to look up at him. There's anger in his gaze. Disbelief. But more than anything, his determination shines through.

"You are the most stubborn, infuriating creature I have ever met, Lex. The fact that you'd even think those things breaks my fucking heart. I told you nothing could ever change the way I see you."

"That was before."

"Before what? You sharing with me what a strong, downright formidable badass you are for surviving something no child should ever have to experience?"

I blink. Speechless.

"That's right. Keep your mouth shut, and listen for once." His lips quirk. "I need you to hear me and believe what I'm about to say."

Holding me close, I can feel the beat of his heart against my breastbone. It's wild. Out of control. Pounding hard.

"You did not deserve what happened to you. You are not disgusting. You are not damaged goods. *It was not your fault.*"

"Da—"

"No. Don't even think about arguing with me on this, or Caine will be the least of your worries. You need to hear me."

Hand lifting to grip my chin, Daniel leans close so our foreheads meet. I'm holding my breath, free-falling through too many emotions to fathom. He's the only thing I can see.

"That monster took something that wasn't his. Your life belongs to you, and if it's the last thing I do on this mortal plane, I will convince you that you deserve the fucking world."

My tears stream between us, soaking into his stubbled skin. I let him hold me close for several silent minutes, waiting for him to leave, but he never does.

"How does Caine know?" I break the silence.

"I don't know, love. You never told anyone? Or filed a police report? He could dig that kind of information up."

"Not a soul knew. My secret died with me."

He looks grim, eyes pinched and Adam's apple working overtime, like I've confirmed his worst fears.

"We will find out where Caine's getting his information from. But you can't let him get into your head like this. That's exactly what he wants."

I know he's right. I've been drowning in this despair for so long, I didn't realise the hole could get any deeper until that phone call. Caine knew exactly where to strike to land a killer blow.

"Valentine deserves to know, to decide what he wants. But I don't think I can talk about it again so soon. I need your help."

"You want me to talk to him?" Daniel asks uncertainly.

"Would you? It's a lot to ask."

"I'd do anything to make this better for you. If that means talking to the selfish son of a bitch, I suppose I will."

Laughter bubbles out of me, breaking the heavy tension. Daniel manages to crack a small smile before sobering.

"If you're telling him to push him away, you're in for a shock. Valentine is many things, but he would never turn his back on you like that."

"What makes you so sure? You hate the man."

He shrugs. "I've seen the way he looks at you. This connection between the three of us, it's more than a supernatural fluke."

Letting my hand trail down the bare, muscled length of his arm, I trace his protruding veins.

"Then what is it?" I ask.

"I have a feeling that will become clear."

My mind whispers to me. *There is someone who knows.* But that intangible whisper only exists in my dreams. I can't exactly demand to know the universe's secrets from a figment of my imagination.

"I'm scared of what Caine knows," I admit. "I'm scared of what he'll do to you. I'm scared of the way you make me feel."

"I guess that makes two of us, then." Daniel's lips thin. "I've been terrified since I found you having that panic attack. Seeing your pain felt like a dagger in the heart."

"You didn't exactly make me feel welcome."

"No one had called me out on being an asshole for a long time. I think I knew in that moment I was doomed, and I wanted you as far away from me as possible."

Sharing a laugh, we find our way back to the bed. Daniel fits his body to mine, and I'm spooned with my back to his chest, our legs entwined beneath the sheets.

"The only person I've ever shared a bed with is Eve."

"Not even with Alex?"

"It's not like I slept there."

His exhale tickles the back of my neck. "Am I a total bastard for being glad that was the case?"

"Jealous much?"

"I just don't like the thought of someone hurting you. I don't care if it was consensual. He should have known better."

I stare sightlessly into the black room. "Pain demands pain. My broken pieces fit with his. We both needed to hurt the other."

"That isn't love, Lex."

"I never said it was. Not all of us are lucky enough to experience that."

His hand shifts, sliding beneath my t-shirt to press against my stomach. Ever so gently, he strokes the gnarly scars there.

"Maybe you are that lucky."

"Daniel…"

"Don't pretend like this is just the bond. That might have brought us together, but my feelings for you are what's keeping me here."

"And what feelings would those be?"

Fingertips exploring the evidence of my death, I can almost feel him memorising each rigid lump and slash. My breathing speeds up as he teases me, setting off tiny explosions.

"The last time I loved someone, she was taken from me," he says so quietly, it's almost inaudible. "I won't say it until I know it's safe to have hope again."

"It's not like I'm going anywhere," I whisper back. "We have nothing but time."

A slow, treacle-like warmth filling my veins, I push backwards to grind into him. Each twirl of his fingertips is excruciating. I want more than a mere tease.

Hearing his breath catch, I undulate my hips. He's growing harder against my ass with each backwards rock. The power I hold over him is intoxicating.

"Lex," he warns.

"Yes?"

"We're not doing this. Not after what we just discussed. You need to rest and sober up."

"I'm not drunk." Losing patience, I shove his hand away and roll over. "I need to know that you don't see me any differently now."

"I don't."

"But you won't touch me?"

I can't see him in the darkness of the room, but I can feel his frustrated sigh caressing my skin. My hand twists in his t-shirt as I draw him closer, skating my lips against his.

Gently pecking the corner of his mouth, I plant soft kisses all the way around to his earlobe. Breath hisses out from between his teeth when I lightly bite down.

"Lexi, stop."

"You don't want me?"

"I didn't say that. I just don't want to use you to make myself feel better. I'm not like him."

I know who he's talking about. *Alex*. Does he not realise I need this too? The knowledge that he still desires me?

"You make the pain stop, even if it's just for a little while," I admit into the blackness. "I need that. I need you."

The silence grows suffocating until I can't bear it any longer. I shift to escape the bed and locate another bottle of liquor, but his hand captures my hip before I can get very far.

The bedside light flicks on, bathing the room in low light. Grabbing me hard, Daniel yanks me back into bed then flips me onto my back. I hit the mattress with a huff, his Herculean frame looming over me.

"Who am I to deny my mate what she needs?"

Enveloped in need, I feel his lips ghosting across mine before I feel him shift to straddle me. He holds most of his weight off me as our mouths collide.

Daniel has always been an intense kisser, but as his tongue thrusts into my mouth and shoves out every last twisted thought threatening to tear us apart, I discover a new level to his domination.

Teeth nipping at my bottom lip, he rolls his hips, pressing the hard bulge between his legs into my core. I moan against his mouth, my legs circling around his waist.

Each kiss is driven home with a thrust, sending bursts of ecstasy flooding between my thighs. His hands grab the hem of my shirt then tug as he breaks the kiss to pull it off.

My bare chest is exposed, and Daniel groans. "You were sitting out there drinking without a bra on?"

"Why would I wear a bra in the middle of the night?"

"I see nothing's changed. You're still trouble."

Head dipping, he takes my right nipple into his mouth, teeth nipping the hardened bud. I arch my back, luxuriating in the feel of his lips worshipping me as he squeezes my other breast.

Letting him mark a roadmap of flushed blossoms across my chest, I reach for the waistband of his sweatpants. My hand slips inside to find his steel sheath.

Pulling him free, I wrap my fingers around his shaft, working him up and down from base to tip. A guttural growl sounds in his throat as he releases my nipple.

Daniel straightens then swings his leg out to climb off me and stand at the bedside.

"Please," I whine.

"So impatient." A devilish smile blooms on his parted lips. "I'll touch you, but I want you on your hands and knees, love. Now."

Tingling with desire, I sit up to comply. My remaining clothing is tossed aside as I turn over on the mattress, coming to a kneel before resting my head on the pillow.

Daniel watches me follow his orders, exposing myself without a scrap of coverage. He kicks off his sweatpants, stroking his cock as he circles the bed to inspect me.

"Legs open."

Biting my lip, I spread my legs wider, arching my spine to give him a better view. His low groan is my kryptonite. Even while giving the commands, he's still wrapped around my finger.

"You are perfect, and I won't have you believing otherwise for a second longer. Do you understand me?"

When I don't answer, I feel the bed dip before the first

spank against my rear comes. My skin prickles and tightens, toes curling from the blow.

The inferno blazing inside me is growing hotter by the second. I'm not sure where the hum of supernatural power ends and my own desire begins, but it doesn't matter. Right now, they're one and the same.

"Answer me," Daniel orders. "I won't lay another finger on you until you do."

The next spank is harder, against my other ass cheek. Teeth grinding together, I lose myself to the collision of pleasure and pain. He soothes the sting with a silky caress.

"Yes," I gasp.

"Yes, what?"

Fingers sliding between my legs, he finds the slick warmth that belongs to him. I moan as he circles my clit, applying the perfect amount of pressure to drive me wild with need.

"Yes, I understand."

"That's my good girl. My perfect bonded."

Thumb bearing down on my bundle of nerves, he glides a single finger towards my entrance. I moan into the pillow as his digit pushes past my folds to enter me.

"So wet," he marvels.

Gliding his finger out, he thrusts it back in to repeat the movement, moving faster with each rotation. Spine curving, I raise my rear end higher to encourage him to finger-fuck me.

When he adds a second digit, my pussy stretches around him, accommodating the extra pressure. His touch is dizzying. It's not like I haven't been touched before, but not like this.

Instead of pain and humiliation or the single-minded need to retake my own sexuality that came with Alex, this feels like being worshipped. He wants me to feel good, to indulge. I've never felt so in control.

"Come on, love. Ride my fingers."

Fisting the bedsheets, I rock my hips, working myself on

his hand. Daniel's happy to let me dictate the pace and find my own rhythm as his thumb remains locked on my clit.

When his palm smacks into my ass cheek, it jostles his fingers buried inside me in the most delicious way. The vibrations set off a chain-reaction that has me gasping for air.

I'm on the precipice of surrendering to my release when his hand abruptly disappears, leaving me teetering on the brink. Head lifting, I cry out in frustration.

"Daniel!"

He chuckles. "Not yet, love. I want to look into your eyes as you fall apart for me."

Grasping my waist, he ignores my cursing and eases me onto my back. My legs fall open so he can settle between them, widening my thighs to give himself more room to work.

I raise my hips, impatient. "You left me hanging."

"So demanding," he scolds. "You don't trust me to finish the job?"

"More like I don't have the patience to play your games. I don't need loving and tender right now."

Fervour smouldering in his eyes, Daniel studies me, inch by naked inch. I writhe beneath him as his cock presses against my entrance.

Satisfied by whatever he sees, Daniel moves to capture my wrists. He pins them above my head with one hand, leaving me vulnerable, arms trapped in a vice and legs spread open.

Keeping his eyes fixed on me, he drives his hips forward, slamming his cock into me without another hint of hesitation. I barely have time to cry out before he retreats and surges forward again.

"Ah, fuck!" I shout.

His strokes are hard and fast, feeding his whole length into me before snatching it away again. With each pump, I hiss and eagerly take the harsh battering. It's everything I need.

"Don't set the curtains on fire this time," he grunts.

"No promises."

Pounding into me, I'm hammered into a gasping puddle of pure sensation. The fog that's engulfed me starts to lift with each stroke. He refuses to leave even a crack of doubt.

Returning his finger to my clit, Daniel rubs in slow circles, applying enough pressure to tease another moan free. My orgasm is back within reach, and I can't hold it off any longer.

"Oh, God!"

"Come for me, love."

Daniel doesn't let up even as my release takes hold. I scream through the exploding fireworks making me clench around his length. He drags it out by throwing me into a series of powerful aftershocks.

"That's it," he praises. "Squeeze my cock."

Arms still restrained above my head, all I can do is moan as he lowers his face to my breasts. His mouth secures to my nipple, rolling it between his lips and sucking deeply.

He's still rutting into me as I come down from my high, panting and seeing stars. But Daniel won't let me off so easily. His teeth scrape across my sensitive bud as he gives me exactly what I demanded.

"Would I dream about being buried in this tight cunt if I didn't want you?" he growls. "That's what you want, right? To know that you're still wanted?"

Garbling a response, I cry his name when he lightly pinches my clit. I can feel myself spasming around him, hugging his length tight as he plays me like an instrument.

"Is this proof enough for you, Lex? How many orgasms do I need to give you to make you believe me?"

I clench my legs around his waist. "Another would suffice."

He barks a laugh. "You're such a little brat."

Releasing my arms, he guides them around his neck. My shoulders ache from being pinned, but I savour the burn. Scooping me up, Daniel clambers to his feet then deposits me at the end of the bed.

Bent over with a faceful of bedsheets, I let him raise my

ass high to expose my drenched slit to him from behind. His hands engulf my hips before I feel his cock nudging back inside me.

The new position lets him fill me to the brim, until I'm overwhelmed by the pressure of his cock stretching my inner walls. It's only intensified as he starts to move.

"Goddammit, love. You're so wet and tight."

Gripping the sheets, I push back against him to meet his strokes. Each time he drives into me, I shift to take the full, brute force of his cock, loving the way he grunts in response.

We move like clockwork, both dragging the other to the finish line. My legs are like lead weights as I feel his length thicken and pulse inside me.

Pain burns across my scalp when he takes a handful of my hair and tugs to drag me upright. My back is pinned against his chest without breaking contact.

"I can feel your power flowing into me," he says, planting kisses on my neck. "It's everywhere our skin touches."

I can feel it too. The crackle of energy lies heavy in the dense air, like the metallic tang of ozone gathering before a storm breaks. I'm on the verge of losing control.

"Let go, Lex. Pour it all into me."

With a final punishing thrust, he sends me spiralling into the deep end without a tether to hold me afloat. My frenzied moans fill the room as I fall victim to my own climax.

Letting my last remaining shred of control rupture, I feel the tightly coiled spring inside me release. Fire lashes at my insides as the Vitae explodes out of me.

Daniel's forehead falls to my shoulder as he bellows through his own climax. I can feel the warmth of his seed as we exchange souls—my gift swarming into him, his release filling me up.

I know the Vitae would never hurt him. There's no chance of me burning him alive like I did those other men. The almost-sentient energy recognises what belongs to it.

We're one and the same.

Fated. Inevitable.

Soul bound.

After catching his breath, Daniel slides free and pulls me to slump on the bed with him. I'm cradled in his arms, exhausted but sated. It feels like I can breathe for the first time in days.

"What does it feel like when you syphon my gift?" I pant.

Face hidden in the crook of my neck, he mumbles tiredly. "Like being struck by lightning."

"Jesus! Did I hurt you?"

"I doubt you could if you tried."

Relaxing, I let my eyes flicker shut. "It feels different with Valentine. Like, instead of controlling my gift, he feeds it."

"You've... done this with him?"

"What? No!"

He doesn't lift his head. "I have no right to be mad if you did. He's your mate as much as I am."

"What happened to the Daniel who hates his guts?"

There's a beat of silence.

"He realised that if it's a choice between losing you or sharing you, he'd make peace with the latter."

Still wrapped up in his sweat-slick arms, I feel the last flickers of doubt fade. He's still here. No matter the carnage to come, I can count on one thing.

I won't be alone.

Not this time.

THE CHARIOT

CHAPTER 26

DIED IN MY TWENTIES – THE HARA

*R*acing through the woods, I duck and weave, ensuring that I conceal myself. The sword clenched in my hand is heavy, but I can't allow myself to slow down.

Snow swirls in the air, sticking to my slicked-back ponytail and frozen face. I'm in tight black thermals to protect against the cold while still giving me freedom of movement.

Hearing footsteps crunching through the forest, I flatten myself against a tall oak tree. I only had a few minutes head start to escape my pursuers.

"Come out, mi amor." Valentine emerges through the trees. "I'll go easy on you this time."

Shaking my head, I tighten my grip on the sword. To everyone's surprise, it was Daniel's idea to involve my other soul bond in our ongoing combat training.

He may hate the man, but Daniel begrudgingly respects his experience. Valentine's been wielding weapons and calculating battlefield strategies for longer than even he can remember.

I've channelled my rage and fear into our gruelling training sessions. We don't have time to waste. The centenary is mere days away, and I know not to take Caine's silence for defeat.

My breath fogging in the air, I crunch through frosty leaves and fallen branches as quietly as possible. I won't win this game by hiding. I have to formulate my own attack.

Spotting Alejandro and Pascal leaning against a tree while quietly talking, I raise a finger to my lips. Alejandro mimes zipping his mouth and tossing away the key.

We're in the safety of the facility, but everyone is on high alert, knowing there's a traitor in our midst. We can't be too careful. Valentine's men are our constant shadows.

"You're lucky we're not here to track each other." Daniel's voice sounds out. "I can hear you yelling from here."

"Stealth was always your thing," Valentine replies curtly.

"I hope she kicks your arrogant ass."

He chuckles. "I'd let her."

Rolling my eyes, I sheath my sword before locating a foothold to begin climbing the tree. I need a better vantage point to attack from. I'll never win against them head-on.

After ascending a few feet, I survey the woodland around me. Valentine and Daniel have emerged in a small clearing to my left. I was lucky they didn't spot me hiding.

Daniel offered me an array of weapons before we set off. Despite being schooled on the basics, I don't like the guns that Valentine seems to favour.

My lessons early-on with Daniel have instilled a preference for the sword. It's elegant but deadly. I like the feeling of power I have when my blade connects with flesh.

Steeling myself to work fast, I tap into the flowing energy in my chest then channel it outward. I don't have time to do this slowly or they'll come after me.

Throwing the fire outward, I envisage the wall I want to build, brick by flaming brick. Only this time, I pour all of my will into flinging it up in record time.

Daniel barks a curse at the barrier that encircles them

while Valentine watches the show with a look of amusement. Once they're trapped, I begin pelting them with fireballs.

None of the blows are deadly, but I make sure to strike the ground close to their feet to scare them. If I wanted to, I could engulf them in flames and end this right now.

"Do you yield?" I shout.

"Your enemies won't!" Daniel yells back.

Valentine simply kicks back and laughs.

Scaling the thick branch above me that brings me into their line of sight, I hold on tight then swing through the air to propel myself over the wall of fire.

My bones rattle with the impact of hitting the forest floor and rolling. I've pulled the sword from its sheath before Daniel has time to prepare himself.

"Move fast, strike first," Valentine orders.

He's drilled it into me enough times. Falling back on what I learned during the hours we've spent locked in the training facility, I position myself to strike.

Daniel brings his blade up to block, our swords clanging together. For each advance I make, he side-steps or pivots, preventing me from landing a blow.

"If you had a gun, he'd be dead already," Valentine drones.

I hiss through my teeth. "You have your preferred weapon, and I have mine."

"Stubborn as ever, Lexi."

Daniel feints to the left. "You have many guns in the Dark Ages, *Valentinus*?"

"It's been Valentine for the last six hundred years. Use my correct name, or lose your tongue."

"I'd like to see you try." Daniel snorts.

Watching us fight, Valentine analyses each move. "Only a fool refuses to adapt. Modern advancements like guns were made for a reason."

I try not to let the image of Valentine swinging a sword

and riding bareback on a horse distract me from kicking Daniel's ass. Now is not the time.

"Valentinus?" I ask.

"The original form of my name," he clarifies.

Hooking my foot around Daniel's ankle, I distract him with a jab to the side and trip him up. His legs bow as he topples, faceplanting on the forest floor. I stifle a laugh.

Valentine smirks. "I told you that fighting dirty is more fun. You going to finish the job?"

Twirling the sword, I bring the tip down on the centre of Daniel's back. He spits out a mouthful of dirt then mutters his reluctant defeat.

Before I can douse the hot lash of flames around us, Valentine rests a hand on my shoulder. "Allow me."

The wall of fire is extinguished by a tidal wave, conjured mid-air. When nothing but blackened leaves and the lingering smoke in the air remains, I glance up at Valentine.

His long, glossy chestnut hair is slicked back in a low ponytail that shows off his tanned skin and piercing eyes. He's staring at me intently, a single eyebrow raised.

"Do you think it's a coincidence that your gift is the exact opposite of mine?"

"Do you think I believe in coincidence?" he returns.

"I imagine you've seen enough of the world to believe otherwise."

"All things demand balance, mi amor." He pulls a stray leaf from my hair. "Even the elements themselves."

"These days, all I seem to do is question my place in this world. The why of it all. I'm not sure I believe in coincidence anymore either."

Shuffling to his feet, Daniel brushes himself off. "We should head back. I have to help Brunt with security procedures for the centenary."

"Take Alejandro," Valentine offers. "He can translate for the reinforcements from Spain."

Nodding, Daniel offers me his hand. I try not to feel awkward as I take it in front of Valentine. From the corner of my eye, I can see the smile curving his lips.

I'm not sure how Daniel's conversation with him went, but the pair have been on their best behaviour ever since. Valentine was there the next day to join our training session and didn't show any signs of being scared off.

Something tells me they discussed a hell of a lot more than the secret Caine's somehow stumbled upon. I'm still waiting for the penny to drop and for them to start fighting again.

Emerging from the forest with Alejandro and Pascal in tow, the snowy facility is humming with activity around us. Preparations for Ravius's grand celebration are in full swing.

"I'll deal with Brunt then find you." Daniel drops a kiss on my temple. "Don't get into trouble while I'm gone."

"Want me to take that?" I gesture to his sword. "I can get it back to the training facility."

"Yeah, thanks."

Taking Alejandro with him, he disappears into the hubbub of people. Valentine quickly plucks the two swords from my arms and passes them off to Pascal to be returned.

"I can deal with them," I protest.

He flashes me an innocent smile. "I've had to share your attention for too long. I'm taking advantage of some alone time."

With a grumble, Pascal sets off. Valentine offers me his hand, palm up in invitation. I roll my lips before hesitantly accepting the offer. It doesn't go unnoticed.

"You look afraid, mi amor. Still waiting for me to gather my men and leave?"

"No," I lie.

Valentine snickers. "Ravius has squared away the RID. Caine has been taught a much-needed lesson. You think this means I have no reason to stay?"

"You're here for the centenary. I know that."

"No, I'm not." He slides a finger beneath my chin to tilt my head up. "My purpose here is far greater than some ill-timed party."

"And what is your purpose, Elder?" I ask on a breath.

Thumb sliding over my bottom lip, he gently prises my mouth open, his viridescent gaze filled with longing.

"Have I not made my intentions clear enough?"

Unable to help myself, I lean closer, daring to drag a hand down his dress shirt. If he wanted to run away screaming, he's had plenty of opportunities to do so.

Still, he hasn't backed off. For the effort that Daniel's put into controlling his hatred, Valentine's returned in kind, keeping the antagonising to a minimum.

"That's debatable."

"Debatable?" He lifts an eyebrow.

"You're holding back."

Laughing, his fingers circle my wrist. "Oh, you have no idea. I wouldn't want to scare my precious little bonded."

"I don't scare easily."

"Well, we'll see about that."

Fingertips tracing across my cheekbone, he slides an escaped chunk of hair behind my ear. His gaze feels like a laser, melting bone and sloughing off skin to seek the truth buried deep inside.

"I miss you in my dreams," I blurt.

His mouth twitches. "You need only summon me."

"I didn't exactly do it on purpose before."

"Tell me, who do you dream about now?"

My line of sight narrows until it's just us, trapped in a whirling tornado with no hope of safe passage back to the ground. If he releases me, I know I'll fall.

"Whatever did this to us. I don't have a face or a name. Hell, I don't even know if it's real or all in my head. But something lives in that meadow."

Not seeming surprised, Valentine nods thoughtfully. "You

said it yourself. There's no such thing as coincidence in this world."

"So what? This was all part of some grand plan? What does it want with us?"

"If we knew that, we wouldn't be living. That's the joy of life, Lexi. The endless, infuriating mystery of the unknown."

The distance between us closes as if by some magnetic force, his nose teasing mine. I can feel the warm stir of his breath on my skin, setting my nerve endings alight. Still cradled in his grip, there's nothing stopping me from taking what's mine.

"I always knew you were coming," he admits roughly. "But I couldn't have imagined the way you would make me feel."

"How did you know? What does that even mean?"

"The last time I saw her alive, Pen told me that I would find my mate. I had no clue when, where or even how our paths would cross. She just warned me to be ready to forget everything I thought I knew."

"And you never told anyone?"

He shrugs. "Ravius received his own prophecy—a powerful weapon at his most dire time of need. I didn't know that our saviour would also be the mate I so desperately desired."

It's hard not to feel powerless. These people were discussing my life, my future, before I was even born. Does that mean it was predestined all along?

"Your life is yours to lead," Valentine says, reading my face. "You could still kill us all then run to a distant land where no one knows your name. May be simpler."

I laugh bitterly. "It's cute that you think I could ever walk away from either of you. I didn't ask for this, but that doesn't mean I don't care."

"And what if I said we could run together instead?" He quirks a brow. "You could even bring the American if it so pleased you."

"So you two can spend the rest of eternity threatening to kill the other on some uninhabited tropical island?"

"Could be fun."

Allowing myself to dream for just a moment, I can almost see it. Breathtaking, burnt-orange sunsets. The endless expanse of the ocean. No more games or politics or war. I can even imagine Eve there too.

It would just be us.

Growing old together.

But we'll never have that—a normal future. We can't grow old or have children. Our bodies will never wither and grant us the promise of a peaceful death, wrapped in each other's arms.

Instead, all we have is this life and the eternal struggle to survive as members of the world's best kept secret. For all The Redeemed's wealth and opulence, they lack what most take for granted.

Freedom.

Stroking his finger between my brows, Valentine smooths the crinkled skin. "You're thinking very hard about this tropical island of ours."

"Just thinking about what could but will never be. Do you miss your old life? Before this happened to you?"

"I hardly remember it."

"So what do you remember?"

His nostrils flare with a deep sigh. "Bleakness. Hunger. A straw-lined bed and the bleat of livestock. My mother's braids. My father's cruelty. My siblings."

"What made the first Redeemed? Will you tell me how this happened to you?"

"Yes, mi amor, but not today."

A shadow has slipped over him, stealing the bright gleam of confidence and assurance that first intrigued me. In this moment, he's that cold, hungry child again, a millennium ago.

"Come back," I whisper.

Shaking himself out of it, Valentine refocuses on me, the verdant green of the meadow bleeding back into his eyes. I tighten my grip on his dress shirt, twisting the material.

"Besides, I could never ask you to abandon your people and follow me to the ends of the earth. You have responsibilities."

"You think I wouldn't do that for you?" he replies easily.

"I don't know."

"You should by now. We haven't known each other for long, but that doesn't negate our connection. I've known you were mine since I first closed my eyes and saw you waiting for me."

"Maybe you're dreaming about a whole host of women on a nightly basis," I deadpan. "I'd keep looking if I were you."

Searching my face, he looks on the verge of panic when my resolve breaks, and I crack a grin. Valentine's eyes widen before he guffaws, realising it was a joke.

"Cruel, Lexi. Very cruel."

"Just keeping you on your toes."

"Thought that was my job."

A hand pressing into my lower back so our bodies fit together, he disregards the bustle of activity around us and seals his lips on mine. I'm too shocked to move.

Valentine kisses with the lazy pace of a marathon sprinter who knows they've already won the race. He doesn't need to mark me as his. That bond has already been sealed on a metaphysical level.

Lips moving against mine, his hand moves to grip the elastic holding my ponytail. I gasp into his mouth as he pulls it free and shakes my long hair out to wind his fingers into.

He tastes like rich, decadent mulled wine dancing across my palate. Tongue touching mine, it peruses my mouth in a slow, languorous exploration, deepening the kiss.

My chest tightens as the cradle of power responds,

pulsating with each stroke of his tongue. Icy coldness penetrates my skin as I feel his energy flow into me.

"Lexi," he murmurs.

"It's okay. I can feel you."

"Want me to stop?"

"No."

Dragging his lips back to mine, I take control of the kiss. My tongue licks the seam of his mouth before he grants access, allowing me to search for the answers I so desperately desire.

When I pour the Vitae into Daniel, it feels like the storm that lives inside me is being calmed. But with Valentine, his energy is like hot-wiring a dead engine and feeling it roar back to life.

He fuels me.

Feeds me.

Completes me.

Breaking the kiss, Valentine tilts his head to inspect his raised palm. I feel my eyes blow wide at the tiny flicker of flames that dances across his skin.

"Interesting," he hums.

"You're doing that?"

"I wanted to conjure a whirlpool to see if the transference had strengthened my ability. There was a soul bond many centuries ago who could do such a thing."

"Make each other stronger?"

He nods. "These bonds are rare enough. This… I have never seen before."

Releasing his shirt, I lift my hand and copy him. The tiny bonfire I had intended to create instead forms as a twirling whirlpool in the very centre of my palm.

Valentine glances between our hands with a grin blossoming. "How curious."

It doesn't last long. Soon, the water evaporates, and his

flames sputter out. When we try again, our gifts have returned, erasing any evidence of the transfer ever occurring.

"What does it mean?"

Valentine glances around, seeming to realise that we're exposed. Thankfully, no one is paying us any attention, far too busy rushing about and hiding from the snowfall.

"It means your abilities are not the only thing my brother will covet if he ever captures you."

"We can't tell anyone about this." I huff, folding my arms.

"Not until we know who we can trust. Everyone knowing that we're mates is bad enough."

"What about Daniel? Can I tell him?"

He casts me an inscrutable look. "You think I'd expect you to keep a secret from him?"

"Well, when you put it like that…"

Taking a step back, Valentine recaptures my hand. "I won't risk losing his trust again."

Fighting a smile, I snuggle into his side. "You seriously think he trusts you?"

He wraps an arm around my shoulders. "He hasn't tried to dismember me for at least forty-eight hours. I'm taking that as a sign of progress."

THE STAR

CHAPTER 27

I WANT YOU – REIGNWOLF

"*D*amn girl, those men are lucky fuckers."

"Does that mean we're done?" I ask hopefully.

"My legs have gone numb, I've been sitting here for so long."

"Hush. You can't rush a work of art."

"I'm not a bloody canvas. And we're late."

Raven steps back to look over her handiwork. I haven't looked in the mirror yet. I'm uncharacteristically excited. She knows what she's doing with this stuff.

I've been sitting here for nearly two hours under her expert care in a borrowed silk robe. My red dress hangs on her wardrobe door, still in its black velvet bag.

"Good thing I'm finished then." She chortles.

Twisting on the stool, I face the dressing table that she positioned me away from. My mouth falls open as she watches my reaction over my shoulder.

My tumbling blonde hair resembles a golden curtain, spilling down my back in perfectly curled waves. She's transformed my face with smoky eye shadow, perfect winged liner, thick lashes and blood-red lipstick.

"Hot, right?" she teases.

"Um. Can I say that about myself?"

"Sure." She waves dismissively. "If I were inclined that way, I'd jump your bones. I still might for the hell of it."

"Think I've got enough balls to juggle, but thanks."

"Literally?" She smirks.

"Raven!"

Laughing to herself, she retrieves my dress and unzips the bag. I shed the silk robe and let her help me into it. Raven whistles as she zips it up.

"You chose this?"

"Not exactly."

"Let me guess. Valentine?"

Nodding, I retrieve my silver heels to slide on. When the outfit is complete, I look every inch the formidable spectacle Valentine wanted to create.

Disappearing to find her own dress, Raven returns in a semi-sheer, black lace number. The material is skin-tight, showing off her generous curves and endless legs. I gape at her.

"You like?" She winks at me.

"Maybe I should ditch those two and consider you instead. You're looking incredible."

"I'm all yours, baby girl."

After adding a pair of black kitten heels, she ruffles her perfectly styled, pink pixie cut. With the dress and dramatic makeup, she looks like a '90s punk princess.

"Did we really have to get this glammed up to go to the dining hall?" I sigh.

"It's been transformed for tonight. You'll see. Besides, it isn't every day we go to a fancy party. This is the most fun I've had this decade. I'm going to wear what I want and drink as much as I can."

"You don't usually attend the centenary?"

Raven drops my eyes and shrugs. "No."

"So why the change of heart? Has it got something to do with your handsome date?"

Felix finally worked up the courage to make his feelings known after I gave him a firm pep talk during a morning drill session. He asked Raven to attend on his arm that afternoon.

"Sure," she replies evasively.

Following her out into the low-lit, carpeted living room, I grab my clutch bag. Without a phone or any need for money, I only have a tube of red lipstick to put inside.

"Which one of your hunks are we expecting at the door?" Raven asks. "Bet that was an interesting argument."

"Valentine has to be there with his siblings to represent the Elders, so it wasn't even discussed. Daniel's coming."

"You mean the pair didn't duel for the honour of your hand?" She snorts. "Disappointing."

"Trust me, they don't need even more of a reason to fight. It's just a stupid party."

The rap of fists on her front door interrupts us. I take a nervous breath as she moves to answer it.

"Well, hello gorgeous," Felix greets her with an enthusiastic wolf-whistle.

Raven laughs. "My eyes are up here, kid."

Stepping into the apartment, Felix can hardly tear his gaze from Raven. He looks good in a fitted, dark-grey suit, white shirt and blue bow tie that complements his tamed blonde locks.

"Lexi? Fuck me."

I roll my eyes. "I'll pass, Felix. You look handsome."

He puffs out his chest. "Anything for my best girls."

Smacking his arm, Raven tows him aside to let Daniel step into the apartment. All of the air in the room seems to dissipate. Our eyes lock, but neither of us speaks.

My pulse quickens at the sight of his elegant black tuxedo and slicked back hair. He's opted for a black shirt with an open collar, sans bow tie, refusing to break his monochromatic colour scheme.

The effect is breathtaking. He looks utterly menacing and entirely devilish. When I meet his eyes, raw heat and desire stare right back in a look reserved entirely for me.

No one else gets to see the emotion hidden in the depths of his soul. It feels like I've been given an all-access pass to the authentic side of Daniel, beyond the hard stares and frowns he reserves for everyone else.

And I fucking love it.

While I contemplate the planes of muscle emphasised by his tight shirt, he studies my dress with slightly widened eyes and that teasing half-smile.

I wait with bated breath as he purposefully strides over to me, ignoring the others to give me his undivided attention. When he stops a breath away, he reaches inside his jacket.

"For you."

Flourishing a delicate rose corsage, he beckons for my arm. His fingers caress my skin as he slides the simple arrangement onto my wrist, ensuring it's secured tightly.

"How did you know?" he breathes.

"Know what?"

"That my favourite colour is red."

My cheeks burn with the realisation. "You have your comrade to thank for that."

"That sneaky son of a bitch."

Ducking down to press a kiss to my knuckles, he blocks the other two from sight and opens his jacket. His usual chest holster is in place. He takes one of two guns from their hiding place.

"Put this in your bag."

"Daniel——"

"For me," he says simply. "The facility is crawling with security, no one is getting past them. But it will make me feel better."

"You know I don't like guns."

Pleading with his eyes, he holds it out to me. I reluctantly take the compact, black gun, testing its weight. Daniel picks up my clutch bag and hands it over.

With the weapon concealed, I slide my arm into his, then we turn to the others. Raven is looking around the apartment, her gaze faraway, until Felix touches her back.

"Raven? Ready?"

She plasters on a smile. "Yeah."

Felix bows and offers her his arm. "M'lady."

Rolling her eyes, she accepts then leads the way. We follow close behind, leaving the building to step out into the snow-lit night. It's been coming down steadily for days.

As we approach the festivities, lights blaze across the snow-covered lawns from the arched windows of the dining hall in the distance. A glamorous red carpet has been laid out on the steps, adding to the sense of occasion.

The sweet, melodic sound of violins playing floats out from inside. Guests swarm in from all directions in fancy gowns and evening wear, all hurrying inside to escape the snow.

While the outside hints at the opulence, the inside is positively extravagant. The long tables have been cleared away and replaced with circular event tables laden with thick tablecloths, silverware and flickering tea lights.

Waiters stand in crisp tuxedos, handing out flutes of champagne from silver trays. A huddle of musicians in the top corner of the hall play hauntingly beautiful music.

Like everything else here, the entire set up screams of excess and indulgence. I'm admittedly impressed by the grandiosity that Ravius has managed to create for the night.

"Fancy, huh?" Felix mutters.

Raven scoffs. "You know Ravius."

"I figured he'd tone it down, given all that's going on. If anything, he seems to have gone all out this year."

"When has Ravius ever toned anything down?" Daniel chimes in.

We all grab drinks then find a quieter corner to gather in. The hall is slowly filling up as the violins play. I sip my champagne, willing my nerves to calm. I hate not knowing where Valentine is.

"Lexi! Daniel!"

Squeezing through dolled-up guests, Michael makes his way to us. He looks adorable in his miniature tuxedo and green bow tie, his copper curls waxed back into a slick quiff.

"Look at you!" I grin. "Very… debonaire."

He flushes pink. "Thanks, Lex."

"Where've you been this week? I feel like I haven't seen you."

"There are some ongoing issues with our latest arrival." He exchanges a loaded look with Raven. "Nothing to be concerned about."

I look questioningly at my pink-haired friend. "That still hasn't been resolved?"

She clears her throat. "It's being taken care of."

"What exactly are you taking care of?"

Felix opens his mouth to speak, but he's interrupted by the hum of violins growing louder. The room stills, and everyone turns to look at the doorway where several armed guards have entered.

Standing aside, they make way for the three figures strolling in behind them. I spot Ravius first, dressed in a midnight-blue suit that contrasts with his slick blonde ponytail and iridescent eyes.

On his arm walks the most stunning woman I've ever seen. Her hair is a little lighter than his, almost white-blonde, and twisted into an intricate up-do on the crown of her head.

Dressed in a shimmering silver gown that clings to her willowy limbs and lithe frame, she walks with an air of superiority, her hips swaying from side to side.

"That's Elder Josephine?" I whisper.

Daniel nods cautiously. "In the flesh."

"I'm surprised she showed up despite Caine's threats," Michael comments.

"She hates him more than anyone," Daniel replies pointedly. "Consider this her *fuck you* to Caine for inconveniencing her."

Felix snickers. "Because threatening to bring our entire existence crashing down around us is an inconvenience?"

"To Josephine? Yes." Daniel eyes the newcomer with clear mistrust. "Not much fazes her. Even the threat of extinction."

Tuning them out, my entire focus is on the tingling warmth that penetrates me from across the room. I feel him before I see him. Valentine follows his siblings at a leisurely pace.

Dressed in a tailored, three-piece suit and crimson bow tie that perfectly matches my dress, his tumbling, caramel hair is loose for the first time, hanging in perfect waves around his face.

I'm used to seeing him dressed to the nines, but I doubt even the devil would stand firm in his presence tonight. He radiates power and sophistication with each step.

All I want is to close the distance stretching between us. Even with Daniel holding me close, I don't feel complete. Not with half of my soul trapped on the other side of the room.

The violins quiet to a normal level, and chatter resumes. When I finish my glass of champagne, Daniel plucks it from my hand to deposit on a table.

"You okay?" he asks.

"Just... hot."

"We can get some air."

"Please."

Clutching his arm, we're making our excuses to the others when a light, feminine voice causes Daniel to stop in his tracks.

385

"Daniel! I wasn't aware my brother's second-in-command would be in attendance tonight."

His eyes close briefly before he schools his expression and turns. "Josephine."

The modern-day princess has stopped in front of our small group, dragging Ravius with her. She doesn't even spare us a glance, her attention preoccupied with eyeing Daniel.

"Well?" Josephine prompts.

"I no longer work for your brother."

"Is that so?" She smiles wanly.

"There has been a change in my circumstances."

Her eyes finally dart to me and the tight grip I have on his sleeve. She looks me over, and I'm startled by the familiar green of her almond-shaped eyes, an identical match to Valentine's vibrant emerald hue.

"So I see." Josephine's smile possesses a shark-like quality. "Lexi, I presume? I've heard a great deal about you."

Bowing my head in what I hope is a respectful gesture, I hold her gaze. "Elder Josephine."

Ravius looks mildly startled by my obedience, blinking several times. I plaster on a sweet smile that only fuels his visible confusion. Little does he know, I can play nice.

"It sounds like you've entranced my brother," Josephine says slyly.

It takes a second for me to realise she's talking about Ravius and not Valentine. The latter is caught in conversation with another circle of people.

"Entranced?" I wrinkle my nose.

Ravius clears his throat. "Lexi has become a valued member of our society in the time she's been with us."

"Evidently." Josephine eyes Daniel's arm curled around my waist. "A soul bond is indeed a powerful thing."

"Two soul bonds," I interject.

"Two?" she repeats. "Impossible."

The back of my neck prickles with his arrival. Valentine

has escaped his audience and slunk over to join us. He takes one look at the situation and clasps my other hand.

"You wouldn't be interrogating my mate, would you, sister? She's here to have a nice time, after all."

Taking one look at Valentine, then me, before her eyes dart up to Daniel, Josephine appears flustered. It's more than a little entertaining to see her perfect façade falter.

"It seems all my brothers have been keeping secrets." She purses her lips.

"Josephine." Ravius clears his throat. "Let us take our seats. The food will be served shortly."

Still glancing between us, there's a calculating gleam in Josephine's eyes. I can't figure her out. Perhaps that's the point. She's as aloof as she is beautiful.

"Of course." Her plastered-on smile returns. "Lexi."

With that dismissal, she tows Ravius away to take their seats at the head table, surrounded by security. Daniel curses, and Valentine's shoulders visibly relax with her departure.

"She seems... nice?" I hedge.

"Josephine is a wolf in sheep's clothing." Daniel can't hide his disdain. "She won't appreciate being kept in the dark."

"Why didn't you tell her?" I look up at Valentine.

He doesn't even look remorseful. "The less of my siblings' attention on you, the better. My sister may prefer solitude to politics, but she's as dangerous as Caine when she feels threatened."

"Could've told me I was your dirty little secret before I outed us."

He peers down at me. "You are far from that. It's my job to protect you, even from my own family."

Looking me over, he takes in my dress and hair, his smile widening. I hold still, letting him drink his fill.

"Nice dress. Very... red."

"I wish I could take the credit."

"Did my comrade enjoy his present?"

Still holding Daniel tight, I flush between them. "Very much so."

"Then he'd better do a good job of keeping you entertained while I play politics." Valentine ducks down to kiss my hand. "Save me a dance."

With a cocky wink, he saunters away to find his seat. Daniel removes his arm from my waist and encircles my shoulders instead.

"Let's find our table."

Choosing a table on the left side of the room, he pulls a chair out for me to slide into. Michael takes my other side, leaving Raven and Felix to sit opposite.

When the final seat at the table is pulled out, we all look up to find Martha sitting down. She looks amazing in a floor-length, emerald-green gown and delicate gold jewellery.

"Well, doesn't everybody look smart." She peers at us all. "It's been many years since I attended one of these."

Daniel pours her a drink then softly kisses her cheek. "Never thought I'd see you drag yourself from that coffee machine."

"Not much demand for coffee with this grand affair unfolding," she retorts. "Where's your bow tie, boy?"

"I must've misplaced it."

Chuckling, she turns her critique on Felix, berating his table manners as the first round of food is served. I let myself relax, surrounded by friends and laughter.

Michael sinks in his chair. "Wake me up when it's over. I have to go and relieve Ruth."

"You should leave her to it and get some rest."

"She's been covering all day."

"Including watching your mystery patient?"

"Something like that," he mumbles.

I drink my way through the six-course meal, polishing off all the wine on the table. Daniel intervenes before I can locate another bottle, warning me to stay alert.

The entire room is lined with security staff, differentiated by their plain black clothing and visible weapons. I spot several of Valentine's newly arrived staff among them.

"Have you seen Alejandro? Or Pascal?"

Daniel takes a bite of dessert. "In the command centre with Brunt and Josephine's mate."

I almost drop my fork. "Josephine has a soul bond?"

"She's one of the few who do."

"How long have they been together?"

"A few decades. They run the Swedish facility together."

"Just the one, like Ravius?"

He nods. "Only Caine and Valentine have multiple facilities under their care."

"Why do they have more Redeemed?"

Michael leans closer to interject. "You know better than most that the Vitae has its own agenda. It dictates us all."

The clang of a fork striking glass silences the room. We all watch Ravius stand from between Valentine and Josephine. He looks over everyone, a genuine smile on his face.

"Thank you all for being here to celebrate with us. It's an honour to commemorate the 150th anniversary of the accords, our greatest achievement as a society."

Sipping his wine, Valentine looks bored. He's letting his brother take centre-stage and enjoy his moment.

"I look down on you tonight with great pride. I see all that we have accomplished and the fantastic future ahead of us. This is our lasting legacy, and for that I am truly thankful."

Ravius pauses, looking over the crowd and taking in his loyal subjects. When his gaze stops on me, he smiles broader.

"We must continue to strive for peace, just as we once did all those years ago. I look forward to the years to come and wish to raise a toast."

He lifts his glass, motioning for everyone to stand. Valentine rolls his eyes, and Josephine elbows him to drag him up.

"To the future!"

With the entire room on their feet, we toast glasses. The room roars with the clinking of glasses, but my attention is fixed on Valentine. He lifts his glass and holds my gaze. I watch his lips mouth the words just for me.

"To the future."

XVIII

THE MOON

CHAPTER 28

NEED TO KNOW – TROPIC GOLD

*W*hen the violins are joined by a miniature orchestra and the rich caress of music fills the room, Daniel peers down at me indulgently. He's been quiet, keeping a watchful eye while we drink and chat.

The night is drawing to a close. After consuming enough food to feed an army and plenty of alcohol, everyone's relaxed. Even Ravius is letting loose as he moves between tables, talking to people.

"What are you looking so pleased about?" I laugh.

Daniel tucks a blonde curl behind my ear. "It's been a long time since I've had company at something like this. Would you like to dance?"

I've never been asked to dance before. While other teenage girls obsessed over prom and dates, I was more concerned with working to keep food on the table.

"I don't know how to do fancy dancing," I admit quietly.

Unveiling a devilish smile, he leans close to whisper in my ear. The close proximity gives me an intoxicating hit of his peppercorn and evergreen scent.

"I'll lead. Don't worry, love. I won't let you fall over."

"Then how could I refuse?"

I let him pull me to my feet. Martha's deep in conversation with Felix. He's just returned from escorting Raven home when she couldn't stop yawning. Michael already left a while ago to relieve Ruth.

We leave them to it and melt into the crowd on the dance floor. The music is a slow, mournful harmony, filling the room with the sound of violins and flutes. Couples twirl and dance all around us.

Stopping in a clear space, Daniel lifts my hand to rest it on his shoulder. The other is tangled in his and held out to the right while he places a loose grip on my hip.

Beginning to sway, he keeps his attention on my face, indicating to me when he's going to move. I stumble a few steps before finding my rhythm and moving when he does.

"There." He smiles. "Not so hard, is it?"

"I feel like I'm going to trip over at any moment."

"I'd never let that happen."

Twirling us around, he moves with ease and confidence. My nerves fade as we waltz to the hum of music. I feel safe in his arms. Safer than I've ever felt in my life.

"When did you learn to dance?"

He thinks for a moment. "1860."

"That's weirdly specific."

"My mother was a socialite. I attended a debutante ball when I was twenty-one. She would've disowned me if I embarrassed her with improper ballroom skills."

"A debutante ball?" I laugh under my breath.

"It's an old tradition."

"Did you escort someone to this ball?"

Daniel smirks. "Might've."

"Lucky lady. Perhaps I should take my hands off her man."

"Given that she's been dead for at least a century, I think you can rest easy. Besides, I enlisted a year later and was shipped off to fight for the Union. No more dancing or balls."

He twirls me beneath his arm. Spinning out, I'm pulled back into him until my back meets his chest. Daniel leans close to trail his lips over my neck.

"Did you ever see your family again?"

"No," he answers. "When the battle was won, I woke up in Caine's care. Any hope I had of returning home to Pennsylvania was gone."

My heart aches for him. Nothing about this life is fair. Not for us, and not for the loved ones we leave behind.

"I'm sorry. You must miss them."

"Loss is inevitable in life. Once you accept that, I find it hurts a little less each time it comes around."

A hand on my lower back, he dips me low to the floor, wearing the infuriating half-smile that drives me insane. Swooped back upright, I wind my arms around his neck.

"What if we lived in a world where we didn't have to hide anymore?" I ask him. "Where loss isn't inevitable and loved ones could be together, Redeemed or not?"

"You didn't see the battles we waged when our existence was known. The Redeemed were hunted and enslaved for centuries. The world can't handle the truth about our existence."

"Do you really believe that, or is it just what Ravius has taught you to think?"

"I've seen first-hand what people are willing to do for power. Our freedom isn't worth the price of war."

Leaning in, I brush our lips together. "But it should be."

The clearing of a throat breaks us apart. Standing with a Cheshire Cat grin fixed in place, Valentine studies us. Daniel sighs and releases his hold on me.

"I should check in with command centre." He plants a kiss on my cheek. "Thanks for the dance, love."

I watch him walk away only to be replaced with Valentine's tall, slender height. He offers me a hand and even does a formal, little bow.

"Got another dance in you?"

"Depends who's asking."

Fingers wiggling, he cocks an eyebrow. "Would you do me the honour?"

"I suppose I could spare you five minutes."

"How generous."

Instead of guiding me into the standard position, Valentine places both hands on my waist and pulls me close. My hands are pressed against his chest as we gently sway.

"I've just spent the last two hours being chewed out by my baby sister," he complains. "All while watching you wine and dine."

"Should've sat with us instead."

"Believe me, I wanted to."

The ice queen herself is still seated at the head table, making no effort to hide the way she studies the room. Her eyes flick over to us every few seconds.

"Josephine's the youngest?"

"By several years," Valentine replies.

"Let me guess. Caine is the oldest, then you. Ravius is the middle child."

"Wrong." He grins. "Ravius is older than me."

"You're the middle child? Interesting. Josephine and Ravius look pretty alike. She has your eyes though."

"Technically, they're my mother's eyes. Caine takes after our father. I'm the mutt of the family."

"Did you all grow up together?" I prod.

"A lifetime ago. We used to be close, but war changes people. After the accords were signed, it was an easy decision to take control of the Spanish facilities and leave them to their own jurisdictions."

"Why did you take Spain?"

He shrugs. "Caine wanted the American territories, Ravius felt being in the UK would give him a political advantage, and Josephine simply wanted to be as far away from us as possible."

As he speaks, the bite of grief in his voice is clear. Valentine may play a good game, wearing his confidence and authority like a suit of armour, but he's lost just as much as the rest of us have.

In another life, he had a family. Two brothers and a sister. Parents. I don't know his full story yet, but something tells me The Redeemed's origin story promises to be a dark and bloody tale.

"You've lived in Spain since the accords were signed?" I guess. "That would explain the accent."

"Yes. A century spent living there and learning the language will do that to you. It's my home now."

Nose burying in my hair, he takes a deep inhale. The music has faded into the background along with the other swaying guests. I can't see anything but him.

When I'm with Valentine, he makes me feel like nothing else matters or even exists. The way he looks at me is like I'm the centre of his entire existence.

"I've wanted to get my hands on you all night," he murmurs.

"Thought you were playing politics?"

"It seems my tolerance for such nonsense cannot compete with my need to be with you."

Preening under his attention, I can feel the hard planes of his chest beneath my touch. I'm desperate to drag him back to my bedroom and trace the lines of his intricate tattoos with my tongue.

"As much as I love this dress, I'd take greater pleasure in tearing it off your body, little bonded."

"Is that all you want to do?" I whisper.

Valentine's eyes are hooded. "Far from it."

Trailing my hand lower, I splay it across his shirt-covered

abdomen. His touch dances from my hip to caress the swell of my ass. I'm too turned on to care that we're surrounded.

"I want to strip you bare and worship every perfect inch of what's mine," he purrs in my ear. "You'll be crying out my name as you come all over my tongue."

Throat spasming, I laugh. "Very presumptuous of you to assume I'd let you ruin this dress."

"My comrade is the gentler one. Perhaps I'll let him remove your dress while I ride this sexy, pouty mouth of yours."

His thumb pulls at my bottom lip as he grins. I dart my tongue out to lick the tip of his digit then watch his pupils expand, hunger leaking into his green orbs.

"Want to get out of here?"

He nods. "I'd like nothing more."

"Then let's get me out of this dress."

Clutching his lapel, I tow him off the dance floor. Martha shoots me a wink as we pass, but Felix only glares. He still hasn't forgiven Valentine for our little excursion.

Before we can escape the crowd, a strange rumble fills the hall. The sparkling crystal chandelier high above us tinkles with movement. We both freeze, looking up at the ceiling.

The ominous rattling intensifies. Tables begin to shake. Glasses fall and shatter on the floor. Panicked gasps sweep over the hall as everyone looks up in slow motion.

Spiderweb cracks appear in the ceiling, splintering outwards and causing thick plumes of dust to fall. Realisation seems to hit everyone when the first scream erupts.

"Move!" Valentine shouts.

Stuck behind a panicked gaggle of people, we're trapped in place. The whole room has exploded with shouting and screaming, adding to the confusion.

"Everyone out! Quickly!"

"We're stuck!"

"Move!"

Chunks of ceiling begin to fall in a destructive roar of noise. I watch numbly as a giant piece falls, curving through the air before hitting a couple grappling to escape nearby.

The sickening crunch can be heard through the screams. As the dust cloud clears, I can see a puddle of blood pouring out from beneath the fallen rubble.

"We need to get out of here!" I screech.

Valentine grips my hand tight. "Go left."

Pushing deeper into the crowd, we push and shove, dodging death at every turn. Everything is a blur. I can't see through the dust and smoke, using Valentine as an anchor.

With a blinding flash of light, an earth-shattering boom quickly follows. Heat sweeps through the hall, then twisted, burning bodies are flung back from the blast.

They land in the crowd, met with horrified screams. Another blast goes off on the opposite side of the hall. This inferno is bigger, engulfing nearby victims and shattering the building's structure.

"I've got you!" Valentine yells.

His strong arm wrapping around my waist, he drags me away from the nightmarish scene. Huge slabs of the ceiling are raining down, crushing anyone untouched by the blast.

When a piece falls and hits the floor mere inches from where we stood, I realise the screams I can hear are my own. We're trapped in a maelstrom with nowhere to run.

Valentine's ash-streaked face peers down at me. I can't make out what he's saying. The sound of another explosion reverberates around us, but this fire is far hotter than any before it.

The nearby blast sweeps us off our feet, and I feel Valentine's hand being ripped from mine. I fly through the hot air, twisting and tumbling in a tight spiral.

Pain flares in my temple as I collide with a solid surface. Blackness encroaches on my vision as my grasp on reality severs.

* * *

W HEN I GROGGILY COME TO, it takes all my strength to wrench my eyes open and blink away the coating of ash. The world has been turned upside down.

I raise my head for a moment after it bounces against someone's lower back. The carnage around us is clear, even through the smoky haze. Flames have engulfed the dining hall, casting light on rubble and countless unmoving bodies.

Death.

Destruction.

It's everywhere.

Fighting the urge to be sick, I push up from the muscular back I'm slung over. Whoever is carrying me is clambering over debris to escape into the night.

The distant sounds of shouting and sobbing grow louder. When cold, snowy air hits me, I gulp it down to escape the feeling of drowning. We've made it outside.

"You awake, mi amor?"

"V-Valentine?"

After escaping the fiery death trap, he pulls me over his shoulder and back into his arms. Haunted emerald eyes look down at me beneath blood-clumped hair and a thick coating of ash.

"You're bleeding," he worries.

"Hit my head. What h-happened?"

"We're under attack."

The far-off showering of gunfire accompanies his words. He tightens his grip on me and launches into a jog, heading towards the sound of yelling in the distance.

I squeeze my eyes shut, fighting waves of nausea while I'm jostled in his arms. With warm blood seeping down my neck, I have to swipe the sticky liquid from my face to see properly.

"Dammit, we need to put pressure on that," Valentine grinds out.

"I'm f-fine."

He releases one hand then presses it firmly to the side of my head. I grunt in pain and clench my teeth to stop from crying out. His strides lengthen, carrying us across the snow.

Muttering under his breath in rapid Spanish, Valentine's foot catches on a patch of ice, and he skids. Once he's righted himself, I tug on his shirt collar to gain his attention.

"Put me down."

"Not a chance," he rebukes.

"I'm not asking."

Shoving his shoulder, I escape his embrace to land unceremoniously on my feet. The world tilts on its axis for a heart-pounding second before I shove the nausea aside.

"We have to find Daniel."

Valentine steadies me. "Command centre's opposite Ravius's office. He should be there with Alejandro and the others."

Letting him guide me through the scream-filled night, we slip and slide over the snow, leaving a trail of blood. When the administration building comes into view, Valentine speeds up.

"Lex!"

My chest caves with relief. "Daniel."

Shoving past a gathering armada of security staff, Daniel races towards us. Valentine hands me over without a word so Daniel can run his hands all over my body.

"Where are you hurt?"

"Just a few scratches." I wince as my head pounds. "Lucky you left when you did."

Cupping my cheek, he inspects my bleeding head wound. "Our surveillance spotted the helicopters too late. Bombs were already dropping."

Looking up at Valentine, Daniel surveys him too, searching for injuries. If I didn't know better, I'd say he almost looks concerned.

"Thanks for getting her out."

Valentine nods. "We heard gunfire coming from the east. I don't think this is over yet."

"Felix and Martha," I gasp. "They were still in there."

"We'll get them out." Daniel watches the first wave of black-clad officers depart. "I have to get you somewhere safe."

"We need to find them! What about Raven and Michael? They both left earlier on."

"Wherever they are, they're safer than us right now," Valentine argues.

"Your sister and brother were in there too."

Shifting from one foot to the other, Valentine looks torn. "*Mierda*."

I flinch when another round of gunfire lances through the air. It sounds like it's getting closer. The dining hall is still a burning wreck, pumping out smoke and ash into the night sky.

"Anyone left alive in there will be dead soon," Daniel surmises. "Our teams will evacuate everyone they can."

"Valentine!" someone shouts. "Where is your sister?"

Surrounded by guards, a short, black-haired man skids to a halt next to us, his vivid amber eyes wild with rage. Valentine clasps his shoulder.

"Josephine was inside when the bombs went off, Tiernan. We've sent a team over to evacuate survivors."

Barking off orders in a distinct Scandinavian language, Tiernan pulls the gun from his hip holster then sets off in pursuit with his men.

"We have to go and help before those guns reach us," I insist. "They're going to kill anyone left alive."

"Lexi," Daniel warns. "This is Caine's doing. Those guns are here for you."

"That doesn't mean I can't help!"

"You need to get somewhere safe."

"I need to help my friends—"

"Enough," Valentine interrupts. "If you want to help, go find Michael. We'll need his healing skills."

Daniel shakes his head. "She's going nowhere alone. And Michael went to the hospital to relieve Ruth."

Joining their Elder, Alejandro and Pascal carry scarily large guns. Both are flanked by several more of the back-up security detail that arrived from Spain.

"Take Pascal with you to find Michael," Valentine instructs. "It isn't safe here. We'll deal with this."

"I can't leave you both."

Daniel pulls his own gun. "We won't let them get to you, love. Just get somewhere safe."

"We have to—"

"Get down!" Alejandro hollers.

The roar of gunfire has finally reached us. Flashes of light pierce the haze-filled air as company arrives. Daniel and Valentine turn to face the oncoming attack.

"Go!" Daniel yells.

Feeling like I'm being torn in half, I watch them lead the charge, taking my aching heart with them. Pascal stays by my side, his usual hard mask warped with rage. He clearly wishes he was running into battle with his Elder.

"Let's find the kid," he clips out.

"I have to go after them."

"I'm not above putting a bullet in your leg to get you to comply. I have my orders. Your call, *señorita*."

"Fuck! Fine. Lead the way."

Sticking behind him, I lift the hem of my dress so we can run through the snow. Gunfire echoes all around us as we race towards the hospital, bathed in flickering firelight.

Pascal clears the entrance with a sweep of his gun before I follow close behind him. My eyes catch on the two ornate, criss-crossed swords nailed to the wall in the formal waiting area.

Climbing on a chair, I grab the first one and tear it down. Never thought Ravius's love of antique crap would come in handy, but with my purse and gun lost in the blast, I need a weapon.

Holding it steady, I gesture for Pascal to head towards the medical wing where the offices and wards are located.

The heavy silence is broken by the sound of our footsteps. The deeper we head into the hospital, the more my scalp prickles with unease. This place is deserted. Each clinical room we check is empty, and there are no signs of life.

"Michael?" I call out.

"Shut up," Pascal hisses.

"He should be here."

Rounding a corner, I almost smack into Pascal's back. He's staring at the floor, and it takes a moment for me to process the bright-red stain streaked across it, evidence that someone's been dragged.

"We're leaving. Now."

"No!" I shove past him. "He could be hurt."

Sword raised, I follow the bloody trail into the ward where I first woke up. It's used exclusively for acclimatising new arrivals, so I haven't been back here since.

The drag-marks lead all the way into an ajar room. Pascal insists on entering first, leaving me to hang back. He searches the room for a moment before declaring it clear.

I step inside the room and gasp at the sight of a crumpled body at the end of the trail. Her lace dress trashed and pink hair saturated with blood, Raven's hand is clamped over her stomach.

"Oh, God! Raven! What are you doing here?"

She's unresponsive to my shouts of her name. With Pascal covering the door, I kneel beside her to add extra pressure to what looks like a bullet wound.

"Talk to me, Raven. What the hell happened?"

Grasping her chin, I roll her head from side to side. She sucks in a breath, and her eyes flutter, widening when she spots me looming over her.

"Lexi," she groans.

"I think you've been shot."

"I d-didn't know… it was all a l-lie…"

Ice slices through me. "Know what? Raven?"

More tears slip from her screwed-shut eyes. "The b-bombs… He didn't tell me about the bombs."

Training his aim on Raven, Pascal eyes her. "She's one of them."

"No! She wouldn't do that."

"I just wanted a fresh start," Raven sobs listlessly. "He promised me f-freedom… no more rules…"

"Who did?" I demand.

Her eyes reopen for a brief, heartbreaking second. "Caine."

My stomach bottoms out. "You helped him?"

When she falls silent again, I grab her shoulder and shake. She wouldn't betray us… Right? Raven is my friend. The first I've ever had. She wouldn't do this. Not for some unhinged psychopath hell bent on world domination.

But all the signs were there. Her disappearances. Arguments. Bag-lined eyes and shifty behaviour. The Raven I first met changed when the facility's newest arrival showed up.

"The b-bombs… I s-swear, I didn't know… I came to stop them, but it was too l-late. They sh-shot me."

"Dammit, Raven! Why did you do this?"

Staring up at me with unseeing eyes, a trail of blood leaks from her mouth. "For him. It's all f-for him."

"Who, Raven?"

She gurgles blood. "I'm so s-sorry."

"You're the mole?"

"No… Not me…"

I force myself not to shake her again, no matter how much I want to scream and lash out. She's barely clinging on, the puddle of blood surrounding her gradually expanding.

"Where is Michael?" I stare down at her.

"They t-took him… loading b-bay."

"What do they want with him?"

Head lolling to the side, she doesn't respond. Her face is ashen and waxy from blood loss.

"Shit." Standing up, I retake my sword. "We have to stop them. Caine's abducting gifted Redeemed. He has Michael."

"Caine's here looking for you," Pascal snaps. "Don't you see this is a trap? The kid's the bait."

"I don't care! Michael is in danger. Move aside, or I'll send you up in flames for slowing me down."

Casting Raven one last look, I see she's slipped into unconsciousness again. I don't know if she'll survive, but I won't stick around to find out. She's brought this on herself.

"You're going to get me fired." Pascal jerks his head towards the corridor. "Let's find your damn friend."

Ignoring the blood on my hands, I search the corridor for clues. I've never been to the loading bay, but it must be located at the back of the building, behind the wards.

We move fast, coordinating our steps to clear each corridor. After getting lost several times, Pascal notices the whistle of a wind current coming from the lower level.

Descending the stairs, we emerge on a service floor, surrounded by boxed medical supplies and clean linens. It's freezing cold as snowy air leaks in from the open bay doors.

"Lexi," Pascal says crisply. "If shit goes south, you ram that sword in anything that moves then run."

"I'm not leaving without Michael."

Dragging a palm down his face, he motions for me to move. We creep between packed boxes, inching closer to the bay doors.

There's no sign of movement outside, but a black van with tinted windows is parked by the exit, the doors thrown open.

"Cover me? I'll check it out."

"Not a chance," he declines. "Stay here."

"You're the one with the gun," I point out. "I'm faster. Watch my six. Shoot anything that moves."

After shaking his head in frustration, Pascal nods tersely. "Be quick."

Leaping down the raised platform, I land in the snow. A quick glance around reveals no assailants waiting for the opportunity to strike.

I set my sights on the van then move fast. Inside the shadowy interior, two figures are slumped over, bound and cloaked in hoods. No sign of their captors.

"Michael?" I hiss.

One of the hooded figures lifts their head. "Lexi?"

"It's me. I'm here."

"No! You have to run."

The other hooded figure remains silent. I don't have time to worry about them though. Clambering up into the van, I reach for Michael's bound wrists.

"Not without you."

"Get out of here," he urges desperately. "It's you they really want. We're just the bait."

The rope that binds him is tied into a series of knots, securing him to the van's metal framing. I try to trace the first knot before giving up and using the sword to start slicing him free.

"Lexi, please," he begs. "Go."

"Shut up! I am not abandoning you!"

With the first knot sliced through, I move to the second, my heart pounding harder with each second. Whoever did this can't be far away. We need to get out of here.

"Lexi?" a grating voice asks.

I pause for a beat, my sword hovering heavily. Glancing over my shoulder at the second hooded figure, I'm frozen by a hot burst of recognition.

I know that voice.

My chest contracts as breathing becomes a distant

memory, shock and confusion taking over. That broken whisper is all it takes to halt my movements and destroy my plan.

It's the voice of a ghost—a sick, broken boy, long lost to me now. A voice I never thought I'd hear again. Not in this lifetime.

"A-Alex? Is... Is that you?"

I'm dreaming. Any second now, I'll wake up in Daniel's arms, and this will all have been a twisted nightmare. The bombs. The gunfire. Raven's blood. None of it is real.

"Alex?" I repeat.

His hooded head doesn't lift.

"Took you long enough to show up," a hard voice replies from outside the van.

I whip around to face the loading bay. Pascal's vanished from the doorway. He's now kneeling in the snow, a muzzle pressed into the back of his head.

Holding him at gunpoint is Ravius's sour-faced head of security. Brunt offers me a grin, a single eyebrow raised. He's accompanied by a masked figure in a black balaclava.

"These guys bothering you?" Brunt laughs.

"Let them both go."

"Drop your weapon, then I'll be happy to let Valentine's lapdog go. The other two are coming with me, I'm afraid."

"Want me to handcuff myself too? Make your job even easier?"

"That would be swell," he drawls.

Teeth grinding together, I slowly rise to my feet and drop down from the van. Brunt curses, pushing the gun deeper into the base of Pascal's skull, causing him to hiss in pain.

"What did Caine promise you? Some wonderful, sparkling future in his new world?"

Brunt shrugs. "I wouldn't expect you to understand."

"That you betrayed your own Elder for the promise of some grass is always greener bullshit? I understand perfectly."

"We've lived long enough in the shadows," he utters. "It's time for us to take our rightful place in the world."

"How long have you been working for Caine?"

Brunt narrows his eyes. "You've made my job very challenging these past few months."

"And you've chosen the wrong side of this war."

"Don't worry about me. I'm going to be just fine." He lifts his chin to gesture towards the van. "Get back in."

"I'm not going anywhere."

"Then Pedro here gets to paint the snow with his brains."

"Pascal," I correct, letting the revulsion I feel for Brunt show on my face. "How are you even planning to get out of here? The facility is surrounded by guards."

"They're a bit preoccupied with our diversion." He flashes a toothy grin. "You're alone, little bitch."

Shit. Help isn't coming. Daniel and Valentine think I'm safe with Pascal. I'm the only thing standing between Brunt and his easy exit.

Pascal meets my eyes with resignation, giving the faintest nod of his head. I may not like the man, but that doesn't mean I want him to die for me. Even with his permission.

"My patience is wearing thin," Brunt warns. "The boss doesn't like to be kept waiting."

Shoving all my fear and doubt aside, I focus on the ever-present hum in my chest. It's been biding its time since the first bomb dropped. Gathering. Preparing. Poised for attack.

"He'll have to wait a little longer."

Pushing the wave of red-hot energy outward, I take a risk and direct it into the weapon clutched in my hands. Brunt falters as the blade catches alight, flames coating the sharp steel.

Whipping it through the air, I deftly wield my new weapon. I've been wanting to try this ever since Daniel suggested I could set inanimate objects on fire.

Brunt shoves Pascal aside then raises his gun to fire at me.

I duck, skidding across the snow to avoid being hit. He curses as my sword whips closer and catches his left leg.

"Fucking bitch!"

His blood spurts across the white-covered ground. Brunt reacts fast, blindly popping off a shot. A fiery laser burns through my thigh as the bullet makes contact.

I shove the blistering pain aside, refusing to let it distract me. I'll slice Brunt to ribbons and burn his remains before letting him escape this facility with my friend.

Swinging high, the burning sword slashes across his chest, leaving a charred wound in its wake. Brunt screams, batting out the flames clinging to his shirt.

"That's how you want to play? So be it." He turns to look at his friend. "Show the little bitch we mean business."

The man tears off his balaclava to unveil a deformed, scarred mess where his face should be, warped and terrifyingly disfigured. Shock momentarily halts my attack.

No.

He's dead.

Arrow presses a gun to Pascal's temple. "Nice to see you again, Lexi."

He fires off a shot at point-blank range. Pascal's skull shatters, coating the earth in blood and splattered brains.

"No!" I scream.

Crumpling, Pascal lands in a crimson halo. Those cold eyes remain locked open in an eternal state of emptiness. One hand on his bleeding chest, Brunt points his own gun at me.

"Final warning, Lexi."

"Fuck you!"

He chuckles in amusement. "There's plenty we can do before I have to turn you over. I've heard you like it rough."

The flames wrapped around my sword twist and writhe, reacting to my rage. I want to gut this motherfucker then watch his insides spill out.

"You haven't figured that part out yet?" Brunt studies me. "I know all about your dirty little secret, *sugar*."

That revolting pet name once had the power to inspire my obedience. But not anymore. I've seen the worst this world has to offer and still survived.

No more running.

With a cry, I drop my sword in the snow and charge at him. He fires off two shots, one sinking deep into my shoulder while another penetrates my left side. Not even the overwhelming pain can stop me.

We collide and roll through the snow, locked in a deadly dance. Screaming at Arrow to back off, Brunt pummels every inch of me with powerful punches, crunching bone and bruising organs.

Managing to wind my legs around his waist, I gain the upper hand and straddle him. He can't buck me off in time to escape my burning hands pressing into his cheeks.

"How's this for liking it rough?"

I fry him alive, taking the last flickers of energy I have left and directing it into my palms. The Vitae burns through me, draining every resource until my vision blurs.

His blows decelerate as the skin sloughs from his bones. Melting. Popping. Crackling. The smell of his cooking flesh is everywhere—in my nose, down my throat, coating my skin.

"Go!" Brunt wails.

Arrow starts to backtrack. "But, sir—"

"Secure... the... hostages!"

He takes one look at the meaty scramble I'm creating from Brunt's face then bolts. Van doors slam shut and tyres squeal in the snow. My brain is foggy, but I know I need to move.

Removing my hands from Brunt's smouldering remains, I try to stand yet fail. The world is a blurry kaleidoscope of pain. Letting my vision settle for a second, I attempt to stand again.

My knees buckle and carry me down. I land in a barely conscious tangle between the two dead bodies left behind.

"M-Michael," I whimper.

He can't hear me.

The van is already gone.

THE SUN

CHAPTER 29

DARK BLOOM – AMBER RUN

"*L*exi, wake up! Look, I got a gold star!"

Small, insistent hands shake my shoulders, rousing me. I know that voice and the girl it belongs to. She's woken me up screaming enough times over the years, and I always have to shake her awake.

Now I'm the one trapped in a nightmare I can't escape from. The roles have reversed as I find her crystal-clear blue eyes staring down at me instead.

"I got all my spellings right!"

"Eve? Is that you?"

"Can we go and get milkshakes now? You promised me we could get whipped cream on them, and sprinkles!"

Her rounded, angelic features and tightly braided blonde hair hover over me. A gold star is proudly displayed on her scruffy, second-hand pinafore.

"What's going on? How are you here?"

I wasn't supposed to see her ever again. The Redeemed are my family now. Ravius told me to let her go. But he doesn't know that I never gave up hope of seeing my girl again.

"Don't you want to see me? I missed you."

Sparkling tears fill her blue eyes as the joy leaves her face. She sits back on her haunches, revealing our shared bedroom, cluttered and unorganised like usual.

"Don't cry, Evie. Of course, I want to see you."

I wrap her in my arms then bury my nose in her hair. The familiar scent of strawberry shampoo transports me back to the past. She loves the cheap supermarket stuff, especially when I wash her hair for her.

The bottle has sparkly pink fairies on it. She always says that she wants to be just like them when she grows up. If she's a fairy, she can grant wishes, and we can run away to Neverland.

"You've been gone for so long. Daddy said you didn't love me, and that's why you left me."

Her warm tears soak into my skin. She's sobbing now, tiny hiccups shaking her small frame. I rub her back and try to soothe her.

"I will always love you, Evie."

"Come and get me, then," *she whispers.*

"I'm right here."

Lifting her head, she looks into my eyes. "This isn't real. You're dreaming."

I stroke my thumb over her cheek, feeling my own tears escape. "Then I don't want to wake up."

"But you have to. He's going to come for me now. I need my big sister to protect me."

"Who's coming for you?"

"The bad men. They want you, but you're too strong. Please don't let them take me, Lexi."

"No one is ever going to hurt you. I won't let them."

Eve pulls away from me, slipping from my grasp. I try to hold on, but my hand passes through her, like I'm parting shadows. She's fading away into nothing.

"Evie, don't go! Please don't leave me."

Watching her blonde hair turn to shadowy grey, she takes on a spectral form. My sister disappears before my eyes, her skin turning translucent as she slowly vanishes.

"Come get me," *she begs.*

Gracing me with a final smile, she's washed away like sand on a beach, dissolving into thin air. I'm alone again. Always alone. Always facing the darkness by myself.

"You aren't alone, sugar. I'll always be with you. You won't ever scrub me from your skin."

"No," I gasp.

Searching the dark bedroom, I find nothing but shadows. He isn't here. But I can still feel him breathing down my neck, the ghost of his hands touching every part of me he stole.

"I'm woven into your mind," the sick voice croons. "I won't ever let you forget about me."

"I was never yours. And I'm not a frightened girl anymore. You don't scare me. You're just a ghost."

"You keep telling yourself that, Lexi girl. We'll see soon enough."

Fingers dance over my shoulder, sending a shudder through my body. I rip myself away, a scream quickly building in my throat. I've lost the ability to remain silent and obedient.

"Scream all you want. They'll never hear you."

* * *

PAIN TEARS AT MY THROAT, dragging me back to the surface, kicking and screaming. It feels like my lungs are scraped raw as I try to clutch my chest, only to find myself held captive by wires.

"She's awake."

Eyes streaming, I tear at the IV lines crisscrossed over me, leading back to a port in the crook of my elbow. My vision is too blurry to register the room around me.

"Michael," I keen. "Fuck... Michael!"

"Lexi. Stop! You're going to hurt yourself."

"Does she need sedating?" another voice asks.

"Back off, Ruth. I can calm her down. Go fetch those two idiots."

Ripping the medical tape from my elbow, I grip the IV

needle and yank hard, tearing it from my skin. Blood drips down my arm as I fight to untangle the rest of the wires.

Feeling the springs of a thin mattress beneath me, the firm surface dips as someone sits down. Warm hands wrap around my wrists and pin them at my sides.

"Babe, stop and take a breath. You're in rough shape."

"F-Felix?"

"Yeah, it's me."

Peering through my tears, I suck in ragged breaths as my vision settles. Felix is perched on the edge of the bed, but he doesn't look like the blonde-haired golden retriever I know.

Instead, his face is a technicolour disaster, mottled and bruised into a battered caricature. His legs hang off the side of the bed, one of them strapped in a brace.

"Oh my God." The fight drains out of me.

"I'm looking that good, huh?" He forces a smile. "Leg's broken in two places. Hurts like a bitch."

I recognise the white, clinical room around me all too well. At this rate, I may as well pack up my apartment and permanently move in.

I blow out a breath. "You look like shit."

"I could say the same about you. How are you feeling?"

"Like I'm getting really sick of waking up in this place."

"We should look into getting you some kind of loyalty card. Ruth could stamp it every time you're dragged in here."

Wincing, I look down at myself. I'm wrapped in stiff linens and the usual gross hospital gown. Testing my heavy limbs, I feel numb and woozy, like the world is wrapped in cotton wool.

"Ruth's got you on some heavy stuff for the pain." Felix nods towards the IV line I ripped out. "You gonna put that back in?"

"No. How long was I out?"

"About sixteen hours."

Clamping down on my arm, I staunch the flow of blood. "Where are Daniel and Valentine?"

"They're safe. Ruth's gone to fetch them."

I'm dizzy with relief. "Thank God. What about Michael?"

Felix surveys me, like he's trying to figure out how to tell a hopeful kid that Santa Claus isn't real. Seeing his visceral pain is a kick in the teeth.

He looks so fucking afraid.

Our friend is in the devil's clutches.

"Babe—"

"He's gone, isn't he?"

Felix bites his lip and nods. "Security footage caught a van leaving while the attack was still ongoing. Ravius has dispatched a team to try to track it down."

"Ravius is alive?"

"Josephine's mate dragged them both out of the rubble." He looks down at his lap. "They're still pulling bodies out."

Gritting my teeth, I struggle to sit upright and take his hand. "Felix, I have to tell you about Ra—"

"We know about Raven. Daniel and Valentine found her before you. She was stabilised and is being detained in the prison."

I hate myself for wishing she'd died in that room. No matter what she's done, Raven is my friend. Or was my friend. Because of her actions, Michael's life is in jeopardy.

His isn't the only life on the line.

Did I imagine that broken voice?

I want to scream. Rant. Rave. Burst into flames and tear this hospital apart. I thought I knew what Caine was capable of, the lines he'd cross to get what he wants.

I can take him threatening my life, sending men with guns after me. But hurting someone I love? Using Michael's life as leverage? That's something I refuse to tolerate.

"Has Caine made contact?"

"Nah," Felix replies. "Not a word."

Looking down at his hands, Felix gnaws on his bottom lip. When he angrily scrubs at his face, I realise he's crying.

"Felix? What aren't you telling me?"

"I tried to save her." His eyes squeeze shut. "My leg was pinned. I couldn't reach her until it was too late."

"M-Martha?"

Felix nods. "She's gone."

As the news sinks in, I can't summon a single tear. Mourning isn't going to bring Martha back. Sweet, sassy Martha, magical maker of coffee and grandma to us all.

Seizing the last wires from around my chest, I shove the sheets back then manoeuvre myself out of bed. Fierce pain smarts in my shoulder, thigh and midsection.

"Hold up, babe. You were shot three times and beaten to hell. Get your ass back in bed."

"I can't just lay here and wait to heal!"

"That's exactly what you're going to do."

"Like fuck I am."

My eyes snap to the door where raised voices and the slap of footsteps are quickly approaching. It slams open, letting Valentine and Daniel into the room before I can move.

Standing shoulder to shoulder, they halt at the sight of me awake and standing. While Valentine wears a relieved smile, Daniel scans me up and down, his brows united.

"You're both okay." I sigh in relief.

Daniel's azure stare is locked on the trail of blood streaming down my arm. He remains frozen in place, his fists clenched tight as Valentine rushes to gather me into his arms.

My face is smooshed into his rumpled black shirt. I'm lifted onto my tiptoes, arms winding around his neck to bring us flush together. He hugs me tight enough to jostle my injuries.

"Ouch."

"I'm sorry, mi amor." He quickly releases me. "I didn't mean to hurt you."

"I'm fine." I chew my lip. "Wish I could say the same for Pascal. I'm so sorry, Valentine."

Gently stroking my cheek, he tilts my head up to stare deep into my eyes. I've never seen Valentine look so much as flustered. He's lived too many lives to let fear rule him.

But right now, the suave, confident man I know has been replaced with a stranger, doing his best to hold it together. The cracks are starting to show in his bag-lined eyes.

"Pascal died fulfilling his duty," he says softly. "Finding you with his body was terrifying. Never scare me like that again."

"I'm sorry."

"Injured or not, I will take you over my knee."

"Can you save it for when I don't feel like I've died all over again?"

"I'll have to check my schedule." He manages a small smile. "You need to rest up and heal."

"No. I need to find Michael and kill your fucking brother."

"Lexi—"

"I said no. I'm done resting."

He huffs out a breath. "If that's the case, can you work your magic on my comrade here? He hasn't said a word since we found you half-dead."

Releasing me, Valentine steps aside so I have a direct view of Daniel. He still hasn't moved an inch, systematically clenching and unclenching his hands with each inhale.

If Valentine seems less than his usual perfect self, Daniel looks downright exhausted. His chocolate-brown hair hangs haphazardly over the shaved sides of his skull, sticking up in all directions like he's been tugging at the roots.

But as our gazes collide, the reality of what we've survived is clear in his cold, empty eyes. It's the same heartless stare that once challenged me over the dinner table, refusing to let me close enough to cause any lasting damage.

"Daniel?" I say hesitantly.

His hands open and close.

Clench. Unclench.

"I'm alright. Come here."

Clench. Unclench.

"Please say something."

Clench. Unclench.

I should know by now... He will never cross the bridge between us. Not unless I'm drowning on the other side, and he has no choice but to put his heart on the line once more.

But in this moment, I do feel like I'm drowning. Those damned blue eyes tell the same harrowing tale. We're both sinking to the bottom of our grief and need the other to make it out alive.

Crossing what feels like an endless space between us, I halt beneath his towering height, peering up into the face of a man who gave me the one thing I never thought I needed.

A home.

Not in the physical sense. Bricks and mortar mean nothing to me. But Daniel took the broken woman who arrived in this facility and showed her the possibility of something beyond her pain.

"I'm alive." I cup his cheek.

His throat bobs with imprisoned emotion. Licking his bottom lip, he drags in a sharp, uneven breath.

"Look." Taking his hand, I raise it to my chest and press it to the erratic thump of my heart. "Feel that?"

Daniel nods, still silent.

"You didn't lose me. I'm here."

"I thought you were dead," he bites out. "You were so still. So cold. Blood everywhere."

"Like you could get rid of me that easily."

He shakes his head. "Don't you dare joke about that. I've lost too fucking much to lose you too."

"I know."

"You should've run, Lex. Hid. Anything but chased that goddamn van and put yourself in harm's way."

"I couldn't leave Michael."

"Caine captured him to lure you in! Him and…"

Trailing off, Daniel tries yet fails to hide the truth I can see written all over his face. It's the final confirmation I've been dreading. I didn't imagine that voice.

"Did you know?"

When he doesn't immediately respond, my short-lived calm shatters spectacularly. I shove his hand away from my chest, unable to cope with the comfort his touch brings.

"Did you know he was here?"

"No." Daniel shakes his head. "Not until a few hours ago. Looks like Ravius has been keeping secrets from us all."

"How is this possible?"

Looking between them, a mask of anger warps Felix's features into something unrecognisable. Several pieces of a sickening puzzle snap into place.

"The mystery patient."

Felix stares at the floor. "Raven's been taking care of Alex since his arrival."

I move to rest at the foot of the bed, feeling dizzy again yet for a whole other reason. I trusted her. Let her in. Gave her a twisted, broken piece of my heart because I thought she was my friend.

She knew all along.

Alex was her dirty secret.

"It was all for him." The reality hits me. "That's what she told me. Raven betrayed us all to start a new life… with *him*."

Valentine clears his throat. "It appears they were engaged in some kind of relationship."

"He was her patient!" My hands move to cover my mouth. "Oh, God. You called him… The jumper? He killed himself?"

The flat line of Daniel's mouth confirms my fears. Alex might've been an asshole on his good days and a violent sociopath the rest of the time, but to hear he did that to himself still hurts.

"I need to speak to Ravius. Right now."

"That isn't a good idea," Daniel reasons.

"He owes me the truth. I intend to get it, whether he's willing to answer my questions or not. No more lies."

"We need to know what we're dealing with," Valentine agrees. "This boy turning up cannot be a coincidence. I've had quite enough of that word."

Scrubbing a hand down his weary face, Daniel looks between us, realising he isn't going to win this fight.

"Ruth brought some clothes over for you to wear." He gestures towards the pile next to the bed. "Get dressed, then I'll take you to Ravius."

Nodding, I shove them all outside so I can change in private. Peeling off the hospital gown reveals the patchwork quilt of stitched and bandaged bullet wounds that litter my body.

Brunt did a real number on me—I'm black and blue. My ribs are a tender, purple-stained mess, but the bullet wound in my abdomen is the most painful. Despite being a Redeemed, it'll take time to heal without Michael here.

After easing myself into the loose sweatpants and t-shirt as carefully as possible, I shove my blonde hair up into a ponytail and declare myself human again. Enough to beat the hell out of a lying Elder.

When I step outside the hospital room, Felix has vanished, leaving Valentine and Daniel leaning against the wall. I study them for a moment, checking for any signs of injury.

"You good?" Daniel asks.

"How do neither of you have a single scratch or bruise?"

Valentine scoffs. "Those gunmen were a distraction. Caine sent them in to keep us occupied while Brunt made off with his hostages."

Taking the hand that Valentine offers, I let him wind an

arm around my waist to support me. Everything is stiff and achy as Ruth's painkillers begin to wear off.

Following Daniel through the hospital, it's far from the deserted building I crept through with Pascal. Every room is occupied. There are even people camped out in the corridors.

Tears burn my eyes at the dirty, ash-streaked faces that stare back at me as we pass. People are being bandaged and stitched. Pumped full of drugs and consoled through their tears.

"How many died?" I whisper to Valentine.

"Hard to say. A team has been out there recovering survivors and more bodies all night. Several dozen, at least."

Including Martha.

This isn't fucking fair.

For a tight-knit facility of one hundred and thirty people, the attack has extracted a terrible toll. This wasn't just about getting to me. Caine wanted to teach his brothers a lesson.

There will be no peace.

Not while he's still breathing.

"Here." Valentine removes his suit jacket then wraps it around my shoulders. "It's still snowing outside."

"Thanks."

With a small smile, he guides me into the swirling snow. If it wasn't for the heavy, acrid scent of smoke in the air and the flames still burning nearby, the facility would look like a winter wonderland.

My heart aches when I see the rubble where the dining hall once stood. It's gone. Reduced to still-smoking ash and piles of debris being methodically checked for survivors.

Scanning the snow, I feel my stomach lurch at the zipped black bags being lined up far from the flames. Bodies that haven't been bagged yet are neatly lined up, offering them a scrap of dignity.

The administration building is eerily quiet when we enter. None of Ravius's staff are manning the desk or milling about. We don't see a single soul on the short walk to his office.

Rapping on the door, Daniel strides in then holds it open for us to follow. I let Valentine take the lead before gingerly stepping into the stuffy space.

"I don't wish to be disturbed," Ravius drones.

I find him seated by the fireplace, rolling a half-empty glass of liquor in his hands. When he spots me, his swirling, iridescent eyes widen.

"Too bad," I rebuff. "We don't have time for you to sit and wallow right now."

"Lexi. You're up."

Heading for the armchair opposite him, I sit down before my trembling legs decide to give out. Daniel and Valentine take up sentry positions on either side of me.

"Drink?" Ravius offers.

"You knew. All this time."

He takes a slow slip. "Knew what, exactly?"

"People are dead. Michael is gone. I almost died fighting off your deranged head of security. So cut the shit."

Ravius stares down at the amber liquid in his glass. "Alex."

"Why didn't you tell me?"

"I did not wish to jeopardise your training or progress. You've had a lot thrown at you these past few months."

"He's been living here for God knows how long!" I screech angrily. "Don't pretend you did this for me."

"I did, Lexi. Alex was delivered to us in a very fragile state. Even with Michael's ability, his physical recovery took time. But he still wasn't safe to be introduced to the general population."

"Not safe, how?"

Ravius sighs. "His behaviour has been challenging. The circumstances around his death were traumatic."

"Explain."

"Do you recall our conversation when you first arrived? I informed you there was a suspect in your murder investigation who was later eliminated. It seems Alex fell under suspicion."

My stomach revolts. Of course, the police went straight to him. I hadn't stopped to consider that the impact of my death could also pull him into the line of fire.

"Alex... He didn't do this to me," I force out.

"Evidently." Ravius smiles tightly. "It seems the authorities came to the same conclusion, but I fear the damage was done."

"Damage?"

"He required constant supervision upon his arrival to ensure he didn't harm himself further. That was Raven's role."

At the mention of her deception, my hands screw into fists. All the odd looks and strange encounters with her are cast in a new light. She knew Alex was here and still lied about it.

"I killed Brunt before he could escape." I make myself refocus on the purpose of this discussion. "Arrow took Michael and Alex as we fought."

Everyone gapes at me.

"Arrow's dead," Daniel remarks flatly.

I glance up at him. "Trust me, he's alive and kicking. You didn't see who was driving the van away?"

"Our cameras only caught it slipping away in all the chaos." Daniel looks uneasy. "I saw Arrow die with my own eyes."

"It was him."

"Impossible," Ravius argues.

"Who dealt with his body?"

The pair exchange a silent conversation.

"Brunt," Daniel finally answers.

I can tell Ravius wants to delve into the sheer impossibility of how a man who was burned alive could

427

possibly still be breathing, but we don't have time to tackle that mess.

"Caine will go after Eve next. She's in danger, and I won't leave her unprotected."

Ravius considers me. "I doubt Caine would involve an innocent child."

"The man who just bombed your facility and killed countless innocent people?"

"She's right." Valentine's voice is hard as nails. "Caine will do whatever it takes. Including exploiting the people Lexi loves."

"Perhaps I can contact the RID and arrange for someone to check on her," Ravius concedes.

Summoning the little strength I have left, I move to stand. "No, I will retrieve Eve myself."

"I hardly think so," Ravius baulks snootily.

"I wasn't asking for permission. My sister needs me. Try to stop me from going to her, and Caine will be the least of your concerns."

To hammer home my point, I lift a hand and let him watch the crackle of flames that offer a deadly warning.

"Or would you like to take a peek at your head of security to see what happened to the last person who got in my way?"

Ravius's eyes dart around the room. "You can't just leave. It isn't safe."

"She won't be alone." Daniel rests a hand on my shoulder. "We will get Eve then return here to plan our next moves."

"You cannot bring a human child here!"

"Unless you'd rather we return to Spain with the child?" Valentine supplies. "Fight your war alone, brother."

Ravius looks more disturbed by the notion of being left in this mess alone than the threat of me burning him to death. He's more afraid than he's letting on.

When he remains silent with no further defence to offer, I turn to face the two men standing guard over me. Gratitude warms me at seeing them side by side, their resentments cast aside as we face a far greater evil.

"That flight offer still available?"

Valentine nods. "Of course."

Reaching out to take Daniel's hand, I steal whatever strength he has to offer me. I'm going to need it for what comes next.

"Then let's go home."

THE DEVIL

EPILOGUE

TERRORFORMING – THE HOWL & THE HUM

I used to think fear was my friend.

My constant.

My saviour.

That deeply ingrained survival instinct kept me alive through so much pain. All the evil I endured. Years spent running from the truth that I was too terrified to face alone.

But I'm not alone anymore. That registers as I sit on Valentine's swanky private jet, high above the clouds. I'm not running from my past. This jet is taking me back to where it all began.

Home.

His eyes are closed, but I know Daniel's awake. He's been silent and contemplative since we drove to the small private airstrip and boarded Valentine's jet under the cloak of night.

I hate the visible terror that's infected him. More than ever before. Finding me in that state, bloody and unconscious, has reignited some trauma deep within him that I can't fix.

Nudging his foot, I resolve to try. "You sleeping?"

"No."

"What's going on in that head of yours?"

Eyes opening, he focuses on the dark skies enveloping the jet. "Leave it alone, Lex."

"She didn't deserve to die like that." I feel my throat tighten. "Martha was innocent."

His brows furrow as he battles whatever he's holding inside. Part of me wishes he would just let it all out.

"You knew her for a long time?"

Daniel purses his lips and nods. "Martha and Pen were best friends. She introduced us when I was visiting on business with Caine in the 1920s."

"I had no idea."

"Martha was there for me when… after… everything." He flicks imaginary lint from his cargo trousers. "She never blamed me for what happened to Pen, even when I told her the truth."

"She cared about you. That's why."

"And now she's dead like everyone else. They all wind up dead in the end—the people I care about."

Finally granting me his attention, Daniel lets me see the anguish that's eating him up inside. It's plain as day. I don't know how I ever thought he was an unfeeling bastard.

The truth is, beneath his gruff exterior and obvious mistrust, Daniel cares far too much. Enough to raise his shields sky-high to save himself from further heartbreak.

"I thought I lost you too," he croaks.

"If you want to scream at me for going after Michael, go ahead. But I won't apologise for trying to save my friend."

"I understand why you did it."

"But?"

"But you still put yourself in danger!" he explodes, silencing the hum of conversation around us. "I almost lost you too, and I can't fucking stand it."

Unclipping my belt, I don't hesitate before going to him this time. The jet's carpet is rough beneath my knees as I kneel in front of his chair and take his hands into mine.

"I want to protect you from feeling this way, but the world doesn't work that way." I smile in resignation. "It will try every single day to tear us apart."

He searches my face, seeing my own apprehension. There's no point hiding it from him. Not anymore.

"A better person would give you the option to walk away now and spare yourself from further pain. But I'm selfish. I want you to stay, even if that means you'll get hurt."

"You do?" Daniel asks.

My thumbs skate over his knuckles, scarred from years of fighting tooth and nail for the mere luxury of survival.

"The soul bond brought us together, but I chose to let you in. I chose to be vulnerable. I chose to let myself feel for you what I swore I'd never feel for another soul."

The thinnest smile graces his lips.

"And what's that?"

"We promised not to say it until it was safe."

Daniel turns his hands over to grip mine instead, his thumbs drawing circles against my skin, mottled with scars of my own.

"It will never be safe, Lex. Not for us." He contemplates the healed burns on my palm. "We can never have a normal life together."

"Perhaps not." I roll my lips, searching for the right words. "But we'll have a life. Isn't that worth fighting for?"

"Yeah." He pauses, bending to place a tender kiss on my hand. "I think that love is worth fighting for."

"Love, huh?"

Daniel gently tugs me up and into his lap. I land with a wince, but the pain doesn't stop me from sealing our lips together.

"Love," he whispers into my mouth.

We share a long, languid kiss. The threat hanging over our heads can't keep us apart. Nothing can. Not even our own insecurities.

Breaking apart, our foreheads rest together as we breathe each other in. Daniel strokes a hand over my hair, his eyes screwed shut as he savours a final second of peace.

"Sure I can't kill the Spaniard?"

I laugh weakly. "I'm pretty sure you've had plenty of opportunities to do so."

"You're probably right."

"So why haven't you?"

His defeated sigh brushes over me. "Maybe I'm going soft in my old age."

"I won't tell anyone."

"Especially not him."

Returning from the cockpit, Valentine takes one look at us and grins. He winks at me as he passes to find his seat with Alejandro on the other side of the aisle.

"We're landing in fifteen minutes," he announces. "Newquay airport has been cleared for our arrival."

Daniel releases me. "Strap in, princess."

"Watch it. I'm still not your princess."

Buckled back in, I grip the arm rests tight as we glide back down to land. True to his word, the airport has been locked down and appears deserted as we step off the jet.

We split up into three rental cars. Alejandro refuses to leave our side, directing his additional armed men into the two back-up vehicles to tail us.

Leaving the airport, we ride in tense silence. Sandwiched between Daniel and Valentine, I'm a jittery wreck as road signs appear, directing us to the small, seaside town of Porth.

I never thought I'd be back here, no matter how many sleepless nights I stayed up, plotting my escape. Part of me still believed I'd never see my sister again.

My hands grow wet with anxious sweat the closer we get to home. We drive along the coastal road, past familiar rugged cliffs, surf shops and closed-down ice cream stands.

Dawn is breaking on the horizon, illuminating the

434

ominous waves swelling against the shore. There's no snow here—we're too far south for that—but it's still bitterly cold.

"Take the next left," I direct.

Alejandro surveys our surroundings before turning the wheel to take us into the council estate. It's far from the tourist-friendly town centre with its souvenir shops and up-market eateries.

"Last house on the right."

Parking up the rental car, he flicks off the engine. We're bathed in silence as we all stare at my childhood home. It's a dreary, two-story house, isolated at the end of the street.

The faded curtains in the living room are drawn, but my heart convulses when I see a light on in mine and Eve's shared bedroom on the top floor. It spills through the closed drapes.

"She's here," I say excitedly.

"Lexi, wait." Daniel opens the duffel bag he brought with him. "Anyone could be waiting for us."

Taking out several guns, he hands one to me. I wrinkle my nose but accept. If Caine catches up to us out here in the open, we need to be able to defend ourselves.

All armed, we step out of the car. Alejandro barks at his subordinates in rapid Spanish. They disperse to circle the house and secure the perimeter.

When one returns and nods, he turns to Valentine. "All clear, sir. We'll keep watch."

Valentine gestures for Daniel to go ahead. "After you, comrade."

Gun raised, Daniel takes the lead. I grasp Valentine's hand as we follow close behind. For each unanswered knock on the front door, my anxiety grows until it's choking me.

"My father's probably passed out. Not even the devil could wake him after one of his drinking sessions."

"Stand back," Daniel orders. "We don't have time to waste."

Holstering his gun, he kicks back a muscled leg then rams

it into the door. It gives way, slamming open with an audible crack that feels like a gunshot going off in the silent night.

Stepping into the quiet house, Daniel clears the living room first. It's empty apart from two sagging beige sofas, a scuffed coffee table and countless empty beer cans scattered across the cheap carpet.

With the kitchen declared empty and Valentine's men holding their position out back, we're left to scale the staircase. It creaks beneath our combined weight.

"Eve!" I shout.

"Lex," Daniel admonishes.

"Move. She's here alone. Dad must be passed out at the bar."

Dropping Valentine's hand, I shove past them to approach our shared bedroom. The bedside lamp is on, illuminating the room that entered my dreams last night. It looks exactly the same as it did then.

Cluttered.

Messy.

Empty.

"Eve! Evie!"

Throwing open the wardrobe doors, I search through piles of clothing. When she was younger, Eve would sometimes hide in here to escape the sound of our father smashing shit in a drunken rage.

When that turns up nothing, I check beneath the two twin beds, finding nothing but dust and discarded toys. The tangle of blankets on Eve's bed are empty. More dread pools in my gut.

"He isn't here."

"Who?" Valentine keeps his expression schooled as he studies the room.

"Oliver. Her stuffed elephant. She never sleeps without him."

Checking underneath the pillow, there's no sign of the

stupid, ratty animal that I could never prise from her long enough to wash it.

"Did CPS take her?" I whirl on them.

Daniel shakes his head. "We checked. Your father is still her registered caregiver. It doesn't appear that changed after your death."

"Who the hell was taking care of her all this time? He wouldn't have done it."

"She have any friends? Someone she could be staying with?" he presses.

"No one. I wouldn't let her make friends in case someone got suspicious and brought the authorities knocking on our door. I couldn't risk losing her."

"Maybe they skipped town?" Valentine suggests.

"Then we have to find them! My father won't protect Eve if Caine hunts them down!"

Brushing past them again, I race towards my father's bedroom at the end of the hallway. My footsteps slow, but not because the guys are yelling for me to stop. Something else causes my scalp to prickle.

Daniel halts next to me. "Shit."

"Smell that?"

Valentine takes a deep inhale as he follows us. "Blood. Smells like a battlefield."

Both of them hold their guns cocked. Daniel traps me behind him as he enters the room first, pausing to flick the overhead light on.

I watch his shoulders drop and gun lower. He kicks out a foot to nudge something then mutters a curse. Patience expiring, I step into the room before he can stop me.

You know those moments in life when the entire world ceases to turn? When you're trapped in an alternate dimension, unable to escape the horror? Instead, you're just a hopeless bystander to the defining traumas of your life, barrelling towards you on an irreversible collision course.

I've had a lot of that in my past—times when I was a ghost in my own body, watching from afar while others pillaged and exploited me. I knew how to switch off, how to separate myself for my own self-preservation.

It was easier to step out of my body, promising to return when the pain died down again to a manageable level. And in this moment, I want to step out and never fucking return.

The sight of my good-for-nothing father, slaughtered like cattle and left on display for my benefit, will never be scrubbed from my mind. His throat is a gaping smiley face.

Blood soaks into the queen-sized bed and surrounding carpet. Coagulating. Infesting the air with a copper-tinged fragrance that tells us he hasn't been here long. I'd bet his body is still warm.

On the papered wall above the bed, a message has been crudely spelled out in dripping, crimson letters, ensuring we know exactly who beat us here to move the next chess piece.

Memento mori, sugar.
Little Evie is mine.

I don't stop running until I'm outside the house, retching into the unpruned bushes. Over and over. Vomit rises up from my stomach, forcing its way out of me while Valentine rubs my back.

"Caine..." I sob. "He... Eve... He has her!"

"Breathe, mi amor. We will get her back. He couldn't have gotten far."

"Caine fucking took her!"

"Lexi." Daniel crouches down next to me so we're eye-level. "I swear to you, we won't stop looking until we find her. She's going to be okay."

Memento mori, sugar.

Violently throwing up again, those words echo in my

head. Over and over. But instead of Caine's clipped voice, *he* whispers the words to me. My nightmare. The nameless monster who gave me that nickname.

"He did this." I wipe my mouth with the back of my hand. "I don't know how… but Caine… he's working with him."

"Who, Lexi?" Daniel urges.

The fear of breaking my promise has been replaced by a far larger terror. That sick creature's threats mean nothing if my sister is in the clutches of a maniac. The worst has already happened.

"The man who killed me."

Ignoring their matching concerned expressions, I rise to my full height. Nothing can penetrate the ice solidifying around my heart.

"Are your men out?"

Valentine eyes me. "Yes."

Stepping away from them, I consider the bare bones of my father's final resting place. A house but not a home. This place was our own battleground, where we fought every day to make it out alive.

My hands rise at my sides, a gathering storm trapped in each palm. The image in my head is clear. I swiftly detach my mental chains, the facsimile of control I hold over the volatile power in my chest.

I've spent countless hours cultivating that control, quashing my gift into a heavily guarded prison. But now, I'm letting it go. I need every drop of power. Every scrap of Vitae is poured into my open hands.

I let my eyes close, embracing the darkness. I know it well. The darkness is my friend, my confidante, my protector. The comforting shadow of my childhood. All secrets are best kept in the dark, and in that absence of light, I bided my time.

No more.

I'm ready to fight back now.

The sickness of another may have put me in the darkness, but my mind embraced it. And the individual shadows each had their name. I need it all now to fuel my furious flames.

Every single moment of pain, every agonising second of my plagued existence boils down to this. Rage overtakes me like a towering tsunami, slamming home with cataclysmic ferocity.

Flames build and spread, pouring from my hands in a race to meet their target. A cycle of images speed through my mind, each fresh scene spinning me higher and higher into despair.

Eve's tear-stained face the day she was screamed at by the neighbour for picking their roses. All she wanted was to give me something for my birthday. Instead, she gave me a crumpled handful of petals, the remnants of her efforts, her small hands stained red from clutching the thorny stems.

Alex slumped on top of me, breathing alcohol fumes into my tangled hair, his body sweaty and shaky from the rush of drugs in his veins. The look of self-hatred in his eyes when he sobered up again.

My father averting his gaze and draining his glass whenever he caught a glimpse of what he didn't want to see. The abuse his own friend was inflicting, day in and day out, for years.

And the ultimate face of all my demons, the shadow casting darkness over every single memory. Twisting all the goodness, all the light, all the hope... and ruining it with his filthy hands.

He tainted and poisoned everything around him, convincing me that I had brought it on myself and that something was wrong with me. The family friend who coveted what wasn't his.

My nameless abuser.

Nameless no more.

Ted, the man who stole my fucking future.

Brilliant light and searing heat follow the violent expulsion from my hands. Fire latches onto every surface and lights it up in greedy flames. The house doesn't burn slowly.

It bursts into ungodly fire with the disregard of an erupting volcano. We're all blown backwards as my childhood home crumbles in ash and embers, taking my father's corpse with it.

The Vitae is the giver of life, but under my control, it's the bringer of goddamn hellfire.

Valentine and Daniel stare at me when I stand, looking up into their matching wide eyes. I have no explanation. No comfort or apology.

Only five words.

"Let's go start a war."

To be continued in...
When You Fall (The Redeemed #2)

PLAYLIST

Control – Halsey
Thousand Eyes – Of Monsters and Men
Faith – Bellevue Days
Bury Me Face Down – grandson
Wolf – Highly Suspect
Bad As Hell – Friday Pilots Club
The Day I Die – ISLAND
Dance With My Demons – Blame My Youth
We Are Who We Are – MISSIO
Superblues – little hurricane
Guest Room – Echos
Black and Red – Reignwolf
Gods – Nothing But Thieves
Afterlife – THE HARA
Don't Trust That Woman – James Quick
Kool-Aid – Bring Me The Horizon
Kamikazee – MISSIO
Where We Come Alive – Ruelle

Bells – The Unlikely Candidates
Neon Ocean – New Dialogue
Horns – Bryce Fox
I'm Not Made By Design – Nothing But Thieves
Natural Villain – The Man Who
Maybe, I – Des Rocs
Be My Queen – Seafret
I Was Just A Kid – Nothing But Thieves
Died in My Twenties – THE HARA
I Want You – Reignwolf
Need To Know – Tropic Gold
Dark Bloom – Amber Run
Terrorforming – The Howl & The Hum

ACKNOWLEDGMENTS

I first released If You Break mid-pandemic. It was my debut novel as a dark romance author, spun from an old short story I wrote as a lonely, fantasy-obsessed teenager during a particularly hot summer holiday.

At the time, I had no idea that Lexi's story would begin a whirlwind adventure into the crazy depths of the romance community. Years later, it felt only right to go back and give this tale the love and attention it deserves with a thorough re-write.

I'm so excited to see The Redeemed back out in the world after all this time, and I can't thank my patient readers enough for sticking with me on this wild ride!

Writing contemporary romance as J Rose is the most incredible job, but my inner fantasy geek isn't satisfied with the real world, thus Jessalyn Thorn was born. I can't wait to dive into a whole new genre with this second pen name and bring you more dark stories laced with all the magic and angst!

I couldn't have written this book without my incredible team supporting me. Especially my editor, Kim, who beat this script into shape and refused to give up on it. I am obsessed with you.

As ever, thank you to my best girls – Clem, Lilith and Kristen. I never would've survived the past few years of authoring without your constant love and support.

I want to say a huge thank you to my street team, ARC team and loyal readers for joining me on this detour into the world of urban fantasy. Thanks for trusting me and giving me the inspiration to take this risk.

Finally, I want to thank every single person that's supported me since I first released If You Break. Several years and countless books later, I will forever cherish Lexi's character as my first ever FMC. I'm so ready wait to share the rest of her journey with you.

Love always,
Jessalyn Thorn xxx

ABOUT THE AUTHOR

Jessalyn Thorn is the alter ego of bestselling dark romance author, J Rose. A lover of all things twisted and depraved, Jessalyn writes complex, fantastical worlds set in the grittiness of reality.

Combining darkness, magic and sin, her strong heroines and swoonworthy alphamales will have you hooked from start to finish.

Feel free to reach out on social media, Jessalyn loves talking to her readers!

For exclusive insights, updates and general mayhem, join J Rose's Bleeding Thorns on Facebook.

Business enquiries: j@jessalynthorn.com

Come join the chaos. Stalk Jessalyn Thorn here…

www.jessalynthorn.com/socials

NEWSLETTER

Want more madness? Sign up to Jessalyn Thorn's newsletter for monthly announcements, exclusive content, sneak peeks, giveaways and more!

Sign up:
www.jessalynthorn.com/newsletter

ALSO BY JESSALYN THORN

The Redeemed

If You Break

Standalones

Departed Whispers

Writing as J Rose

Buy here: www.jroseauthor.com/books

Recommended reading order:

www.jroseauthor.com/readingorder

Blackwood Institute

Twisted Heathens

Sacrificial Sinners

Desecrated Saints

Sabre Security

Corpse Roads

Skeletal Hearts

Hollow Veins

Briar Valley

Where Broken Wings Fly

Where Wild Things Grow

Standalones

Forever Ago

Drown in You

A Crimson Carol

Printed in Great Britain
by Amazon